GUILTY AS SIN KISS

Under the spill of light from the bedroom, he felt keenly conscious of everything at once . . . the sudden silence emanating from the corridor, Sydney's shallow breathing, the tempting scent of her perfume and, most disconcerting, his masculine rising.

"I think whoever it was is gone," she whispered after a while.

Perry swallowed hard. He nodded, not trusting himself to speak just yet. "Yeah," he said briefly, "I think you're right."

He relaxed his grip on her shoulders, but his hands seemed stuck to the soft flesh beneath the padded jacket she wore. Instead of retreating, he shifted closer into her enticing warmth.

She was his client, for god's sake; the woman who'd come to him for his legal expertise. He comprehended the rationale of deterrence as surely as he recognized the hunger gnawing at his senses.

Objections overturned, he knew he was guilty as sin when he lowered his gaze. As if the emotions were contagious, her face had a look that clearly matched his own. She'd never seemed more beautiful, more irresistible, more in need.

Perry lowered his head a fraction; Sydney lifted hers. He touched her lips with his, and the sin was committed.

ROMANCES ABOUT AFRICAN-AMERICANS!
YOU'LL FALL IN LOVE
WITH ARABESQUE BOOKS FROM PINNACLE

SERENADE   (0024, $4.99)
by Sandra Kitt

Alexandra Morrow was too young and naive when she first fell in love with musician, Parker Harrison—and vowed never to be so vulnerable again. Now Parker is back and although she tries to resist him, he strolls back into her life as smoothly as the jazz rhapsodies for which he is known. Though not the dreamy innocent she was before, Alexandra finds her defenses quickly crumbling and her mind, body and soul slowly opening up to her one and only love, who shows her that dreams do come true.

FOREVER YOURS   (0025, $4.50)
by Francis Ray

Victoria Chandler must find a husband quickly or her grandparents will call in the loans that support her chain of lingerie boutiques. She arranges a mock marriage to tall, dark and handsome ranch owner Kane Taggart. The marriage will only last one year, and her business will be secure, and Kane will be able to walk away with no strings attached. The only problem is that Kane has other plans for Victoria. He'll cast a spell that will make her his forever after.

A SWEET REFRAIN   (0041, $4.99)
by Margie Walker

Fifteen years before, jazz musician Nathaniel Padell walked out on Jenine to seek fame and fortune in New York City. But now the handsome widower is back with a baby girl in tow. Jenine is still irresistibly attracted to Nat and enchanted by his daughter. Yet even as love is rekindled, an unexpected danger threatens Nat's child. Now, Jenine must fight for Nat before someone stops the music forever!

Available wherever paperbacks are sold, or order direct from the Publisher. Send cover price plus 50¢ per copy for mailing and handling to Penguin USA, P.O. Box 999, c/o Dept. 17109, Bergenfield, NJ 07621. Residents of New York and Tennessee must include sales tax. DO NOT SEND CASH.

Indiscretions

Margie Walker

PINNACLE BOOKS
KENSINGTON PUBLISHING CORP.

PINNACLE BOOKS are published by

Kensington Publishing Corp.
850 Third Avenue
New York, NY 10022

First Printing: July, 1996

Printed in the United States of America
10 9 8 7 6 5 4 3 2

This book is dedicated to the men in my life, Sherman, Sherman and Shomari, for their deeds of support.

To Joy, for pushing me on when I faltered.

To Janice, for helping to clear the forest.

To Denise, for being there from the beginning.

To Monica, my editor, for seeing me through.

Asante Sana

One

Business was good, the market ripe for milking. Sydney knew if she had more time to devote to the larger accounts in her portfolio, she could make considerably more money. She didn't mind working with the boss's girlfriend, though she suspected that setup could turn into her worst nightmare.

No, that wasn't possible, she realized with a start. Her worst nightmare was already staring her in the face. She remembered why she was holding a sit-in in Mr. MacDonald's tastefully furnished waiting room.

"Ms. Webster, it's like I told you before, Mr. MacDonald has a deposition scheduled for two, and it's one-thirty now. I don't expect him to return before five."

Sydney looked across the room to smile appreciatively at the secretary whose name she had learned was Ramona Clay. "Thank you, Ms. Clay," she replied, "but I'll wait a little longer." What was a few more hours compared to life behind bars?

For seven days, she'd expected a knock on the door, a mob scene on the elevator. She'd even felt shaky in the restroom of WDST Radio where she worked. But surely they wouldn't arrest her with her panties down.

The last thought made her wonder if Mr. MacDonald's looks came anywhere near his reputation as a relentless defense attorney who rarely lost a case. The anticipation of meeting him eased a bit as she thought of him in terms that didn't have anything to do with the purpose of her visit.

How could she think of anything but remaining free right now? Uncrossing her right leg from her left knee, she reversed its position and nervously fanned the air with her purple-heeled foot.

All she intended to do was pay back an old debt and lick her wounds. Mostly the latter when she moved from Houston to Dalston a little over eight months ago.

As a child, Sydney Lauren Webster was motherless by the age of four. Her sister Jessica, ten years her senior, had been called upon routinely to make sacrifices on her behalf. Both Jessica's social life and academic pursuits had been secondary to Sydney's needs.

After waiting so long for Mr. Right to come into her life—Sydney was never more sure that Mr. Right would have come sooner had it not been for her—Jessica was nearing the altar. Fearing their father would try to dissuade Jessica, Sydney was determined to ensure that her sister get this opportunity to achieve happiness. She needn't have concerned herself over their domineering father this time, however. He was as enamored with the man her sister had decided to marry as Jessica was.

But she would have stayed anyway, Sydney mused inexorably, in spite of her resolve to forget. She pushed her own bitter memory aside and redirected her thoughts to Jessica's Mr. Right, who wasn't.

Sydney hadn't liked him the first time they'd met, but only recently had she witnessed something that supported her distrust of him. She debated telling Jessica, but compassion had silenced her. She had not been so benignly inclined toward Larry. Consequently, during the week since his death, she had lived in dread and anticipation, awaiting the repercussion of her impulsive act.

The consequence arrived this morning while she was conferring with Mark Frederickson, her sales manager. They were in his office, one of the more lavish rooms at the station. She was sitting across the massive desk from him on the edge of her seat.

"I'm willing to give up any other accounts except those three," she said, schooling herself to sound calm. Even as she voiced the alternative, she had a sinking feeling he wouldn't buy it. "How about the one I'm bringing in today, the two I brought in last month? That's two-thousand dollars worth of advertising combined."

Mark was taking away some of her accounts to disperse between the two new hires. Sydney didn't mind training his girlfriend, but the temporary loss of clients might affect her ability to make payments on her newly purchased home, into which she had yet to move.

"This one," she continued, pointing to the contract on the desk, "is fifty-five hundred. And since it's brand new, I can take her through the ropes, almost starting from scratch."

"These are the ones I—"

"We're looking for Ms. Sydney Webster. Ms. Sydney Lauren Webster."

Both Sydney and Mark glanced to the doorway, where the interruption originated, and saw two men crowding through.

"Uh," Mark tsked disgustedly, waving them away. "We're busy. Will you please go back to the lobby and wait? How did you get back here anyway?"

"I'm Detective Melloncamp," the taller of the two said, flashing a gold shield, "and this is my partner Detective Tomkins." Stepping forward, he asked pointedly, "Are you Ms. Webster?"

The consequence, Sydney thought apprehensively, her heart pounding wildly in her bosom. Swallowing the lump in her throat, she replied, "Yes."

"Please," Mark said, rising, "use my office. Make yourselves comfortable; I've got some other business to take care of."

Coward, Sydney silently commented as she watched Mark piddle nervously with the files on his desk. She noticed he didn't forget to take the check and contract as he all but ran from the room, pulling the door closed behind him.

Both plainclothes officers walked into the room. Sydney rose slowly from her seat, studying them as surely as they studied her. She noted the fairer of the two, introduced as Detective Tomkins, was of a wiry muscular build, wore loafers and had a boyish smile. The good cop, she thought. Detective Melloncamp looked like a big, hairy teddy bear. He was mopping his forehead with a crumpled handkerchief he had pulled from his off-the-rack summer sports coat.

"Ms. Webster, are you familiar with Larry Daniels?" Detective Melloncamp—the bad cop—had spoken.

"State Representative Larry Daniels," Detective Tomkins repeated needlessly.

Familiar implied an intimacy that was not appropriate, Sydney quibbled silently, but she understood full well what they meant. Larry Daniels was engaged to her sister, which she was certain they knew. Their presence indicated they knew even more . . . that she had gone to Larry's apartment the day he was killed.

"Yes," she replied in as even a voice as she could muster. "I knew him."

"We'd like you to come down to the station to answer some questions," Detective Melloncamp said evasively. "You'll probably be more comfortable there."

"I hardly think so," Sydney quipped before she could catch herself. But she would swear on a stack of Bibles that when she left Larry's apartment he was very much alive and laughing at her, she told herself defensively as she tried to keep her composure. Nervous flutterings in her chest, she asked, "Do I need an attorney?"

"Not unless you have something to hide," Tomkins replied innocently.

"Do you think I killed him?" Dismayed, she was grateful

for the chair at the backs of her legs, which nearly gave out on her.

"That's why we want you to come with us to answer some questions."

"Are you arresting me?"

"No ma'am, we just want to ask you some questions," Tomkins replied. "If you have nothing to hide, I'm sure this is something we can straighten out in a matter of minutes," he said with the casualness of inviting her to lunch.

Sydney flicked a brow at him in disbelief. She was scared, not stupid.

The main door of the office opened, pulling her from her reflections and someone entered like a whirlwind—a tall, lean and darkly powerful man. He was moving with the swiftness of a great mammal: Ramona Clay had to call him twice before he stopped. Sydney's tongue slipped from her mouth to glide across her bottom lip as she stared at the back of his head.

Perry strode with hurried purpose into the waiting room of his office suite. He carried a nondescript black leather briefcase in one hand, while the other was unloosening his tie. He was running behind schedule.

Ramona looked up from her typing and swiveled her chair away from the computer screen to face forward. "Mr. MacDonald," she exclaimed, her Jamaican speech accenting his name in an offbeat sproog.

He didn't stop as he cut her off. "You don't have to tell me I'm late. It's not my fault this time. Old Merriweather went off into an hour-long tirade about courtroom decorum when somebody's beeper went off. I know I've got that deposition in about half an hour, but I had to change shirts first," he rattled on, his fingers on the collar button of his white shirt. "It's hot as hell out there," he added, continuing on to his inner office.

"Perry!" Ramona said more forcefully.

He came to an abrupt stop at the door of his office to look sidelong into gray-green eyes in a vanilla-complected oval face as he stared at his first and only secretary, office manager, et al.

"Yes, Ramona?" he replied, patient and obedient.

Ramona tilted her head to the right.

Perry frowned curiously, then slowly turned his head in the direction his secretary indicated. His attention was seized by a pair of iridescent, kohl-lined eyes peering up at him, and a sliver of titillation tingled along his spine.

She was young, probably in her mid-twenties, the age of most of his clients lately. But that was where the similarities ended. He would guess she was educated, definitely a professional; and by the genial mouth and sparkling eyes that set off her arresting warm brown face, smooth and creamy like warm caramel, a sensual minx if he ever saw one, he thought with uncharacteristic impetuosity. Glistening dark hair in a stylishly short cut framed her heart-shaped face, gentle raven ringlets curling across her forehead. Feeling an inexpiable sense of arousal, Perry was intrigued.

"Mr. Mason—I mean Mr. MacDonald, my name is Sydney Lauren Webster. I'm in a heap of trouble and need an attorney."

Perry stared captivated. For a man whose living depended as much on rhetorical as written presentations, he was at a loss for words. It seemed they were in custody of sensations—powerful, pleasurable ones—that had no place in his law practice.

"You are Perry Mason MacDonald, the criminal attorney, aren't you?" Sydney Webster asked, rising to her feet.

"Why, yes; yes I am," Perry replied, achieving a smooth, even tone of voice. "How do you do, Ms. Webster?"

Walking into her wake, his hand outstretched, he caught the scent of her. A gilded-lily sweetness that heightened his senses. She accepted his hand in a shake that was firm, gentle and too brief; yet warmth lingered in his palm long after his hand returned to his side.

"Mr. MacDonald, I've been waiting for over two hours; I'm not sure how much time I have left."

Though Ms. Webster spoke in a rush and finished succinctly, almost breathless, Perry felt sure she had no idea how sensuous her voice sounded. She wasn't as tall as he'd first believed; she simply carried herself with a queenly posture. Take an inch off the low-heeled purple pumps on tiny feet, and he would put her at about five-feet-four-inches. But he was drawn back to her small round eyes. Dark and deep, he felt their power to hypnotize was a fait accompli.

Exquisite or not, he thought with a flex of memory, twice a woman had put him in a precarious position. He had no intention of yielding to temptation a third time.

"Well, Miss Webster," he said with a smile of regret that was in his voice, "I'm sure my secretary here, Miss Clay, told you I'll be tied up for the rest of the evening. I've got a deposition—one that's already been postponed twice—in less than an hour. Why don't you schedule an appointment, and I'll—?"

"The police came to the station where I work this morning and asked me to come in for questioning," she interrupted. "I have a feeling the next time they come, they won't be making a request. It involves the murder of State Representative Larry Daniels."

Whoa! Perry thought, stunned. Dalston was still reeling from shock a week after the news of the murder of the Texas legislator. Unsubstantiated gossip was spreading that an arrest was pending. To thwart charges of being less than thorough, the authorities had kept Daniels's body longer than usual for an autopsy, releasing it to his mother only last evening. Even so, the police were being peculiarly closemouthed, leaving him to envy the fortuitous lawyer who would inherit the high-profile case. It had been a long dry spell since he handled a case of notoriety. Now, he considered that maybe his luck was changing.

"You mean uniformed patrolmen?" he asked, warning himself not to get overly excited. She could be a quack—a lovely one, but definitely not the first person to confess to a killing just to satisfy a loose screw in her brain.

"Detectives Melloncamp and Tomkins," she replied.

Perry bobbed his head up and down slowly. He was familiar with the pair of good-ole-boys—who were not. "What makes you think they're going to come back for you?"

"The rock the police were quoted as saying was used in his death," she admitted with abashed reluctance, "I touched it."

"Oh," Perry replied, his highly piqued interest clashing with the desire to keep his previous commitment. He looked at Ms. Webster, then his watch.

A man who earned his living by making quick estimates, he wouldn't go so far as to declare himself an expert at judging people's innocence or guilt based on a first impression. He was good, but he wasn't God. This time, however, he'd bet the store that Ms. Sydney Lauren Webster was no murderess. Unless she was a damned good actress, caution reminded him.

"Did you kill Larry Daniels?" he asked.

"No, Mr. MacDonald, I did not."

Perry pondered the ardent sincerity of her reply for only a second, but found himself leaning toward acceptance. He reasoned it was the thrill of the challenge in such a case. But unable to deny that he liked what he saw in the haughty tilt of her delicate chin and the unwavering gleam in her alluring eyes, he charged himself with a misdemeanor emotion abetting his decision. Still, that was hardly of any consequence.

"Oh, Ramona," he said, "let me have ten minutes with Ms. Webster."

"I'm counting your time starting now," Ramona replied. "By the way, whose beeper was it?"

"No one spoke up; hence, the whole lot of us suffered the punishment," he replied laughingly. "Come this way, Miss Webster."

The passage of time calmed Sydney's nerves considerably after the police visit. But having laid eyes on Perry Mason MacDonald, another sensation had taken fear's place.

She had known intellectually he would look nothing like the character created by Erle Stanley Gardner. But while she found him passably handsome, she was not prepared for the virile creature that finally arrived. On the tall side of six feet, with a powerful, slim physique, complete with bow legs. Fascinated just below her cool facade, she preceded him into the spacious room.

His inner sanctum was tasteful, the furnishings of ash, the white and green floor tiles cheerful, yet sophisticated. The decor invited trust and optimism, as well as revealed a man who enjoyed a certain level of success in his profession.

She hesitated to put a more definitive value on his accomplishments—beyond what she'd learned from Ginna, the station's news director who'd given her MacDonald's name—for the kind of courtroom victories he had amassed didn't come from being a nice guy. Maybe she was imposing her own analysis on him, she thought. One day she felt intrepid and invincible, like a Sydney; and the next she was Lauren, a lady as defined by her father, obsequious and obedient. Her insides were rife with the opposing parts of her.

She heard the door close, felt him coming to her side and unconsciously held her breath. She glimpsed his chiseled profile as he strolled past, not particularly graceful, but rather with precision and an undercurrent of vigor in his rangy strides.

"Make yourself comfortable," he said cordially, indicat-

ing one of the round-back armchairs on the Peruvian floor
rug in front of his desk. "Give me a second to get situated."

He had a mild-timbred, demulcent voice that resonated
with a bass rumble, she decided, breath escaping her in a
tremor as she accepted his offer. Its tone was impressive,
and soothing to the ear. An unconscious smile crawled into
her lips as naughty pleasure sat alight in her eyes while she
watched him "get situated."

Confident he was too busy to notice, she gazed the length
and breadth of him furtively. Energy radiated from him. On
his head close cropped black hair lay in wavy rows. His
chestnut brown face was clear cut and forceful, with high
forehead and cheekbones, traditional, yet flattering companions to his strong chin and firm mouth. Heavy eyebrows
arched over his direct, piercing gaze, his eyes powder brown
studs that hinted at a trace of compassion in him.

His clothes, stylish, although conservative, obeyed the
commands of his strong body in a supple coordination that
attested to regular exercise. Yet, beneath the veneer of polite,
professional civility lurked a jaguar quality that both un-
nerved and excited her.

Without her conscious consent, she became entranced by
a visceral sight and sound video of Perry MacDonald exert-
ing his power over iron, the dance of sweat-glistening muscles as they rippled across his dark, wide chest. The enticing
picture caused a savory sensation to scurry across her bosom.
She remembered she hadn't had a date since her father tor-
mented the man calling on her at his house so badly that she
refused subsequent requests. That had been in January, and
she couldn't remember her date's name. Then she hadn't been
looking for anything more than a nice evening. That hadn't
changed, she reminded herself. Lately, her energies had been
consumed with securing her freedom and Jessica's. Now,
hers was even more of a priority.

Standing behind the desk, his coat hanging over the back
of the chair, Perry extracted a legal pad from a desk drawer

to take notes. He tested a fountain pen, then laid it atop the pad.

"Would you like a cigarette?" he asked, reaching for a small bronze box on the far corner of the desk.

Sydney shook her head. "I don't smoke. It's bad for your health you know."

"So is murder," he replied quietly.

Sydney winced. Being reminded of why she was in an attorney's office caused butterflies to flurry in her stomach. She repeated silently what she knew was true: Larry was alive when she last saw him, entertaining himself at her expense. Her wits returning to the matter at hand, she saw the inquiring arch of Perry's eyebrows, then noticed the cigarette pinched between his fingers.

"Mind if I do?"

The question sounded like a repeat. "Go right ahead," she replied, averting her head.

As he lit the cigarette with a lighter, she scanned the room, her eyes sliding from the assortment of law books filling the shelves of a built-in wall cabinet to a wood carving on the off-white wall above the computer behind his desk. It was centered and slightly elevated above his degrees and certificates. She squinted, trying to decipher the cursive lettering. He must have noticed her effort, for he recited, "Justice is founded upon evidence, and evidence is founded upon fact."

Before she could comment, he continued, smashing out the cigarette in an ashtray on the computer console, "The ground rules are simple; you tell me the truth, I prove it. And, as I'm sure you're already aware, everything you say to me is protected by attorney-client privilege. Okay, Ms. Webster, you now have *my* undivided attention."

"I was at Larry's apartment around the time he was killed," Sydney blurted out, not knowing where to begin and suddenly too flustered to think to ask. Having all that attention he promised affected her thinking. She shivered inwardly.

"Okay." Serious, he prodded her with a nod.

Perry had been leaning hip cocked on the corner of the desk; now he came around it. He perched on another corner, folding his arms across his wide chest, his black loafers almost touching her feet. The position emphasized the force of his thighs and the slimness of his hips. Whether a whiff of manly fragrance or the mere nearness of his beautifully proportioned body—Sydney didn't know which—arrested her pulse. His look said there had to be more, so she decided to start over at the beginning. Awkwardly, she cleared her throat.

"I'm an account exec for WDST," she said, her heart settling back into its natural rhythm. With ladylike primness, she folded her hands in her lap and pulled her feet together. "I started working there last October." Starting with November, she counted silently the months to the present—June. "About eight months," she added. "I get invited to lots of functions, get to meet a lot of influential people. Sometimes friendships are—"

"Ms. Webster," he interrupted, patience dripping from his deep voice, "you were going to explain to me why you believe you're in trouble."

He was a stingy smiler, Sydney thought, staring at his mouth and seeing one imperfection, a chipped tooth, showing in his scant grin. She drew a tremulous breath, then began slowly, choosing her words with care.

"Yes. I went to see Representative Larry Daniels on Thursday of last week after I got off from work. It was about five-thirty. He was obviously expecting someone, but it wasn't me. His campaign had bought advertising to push casino gambling in Texas, and if I couldn't collect payment within ninety days, I would forfeit my commission."

She remembered once reading that a good lie held a measure of truth. She had already collected the check. The part about the station's policy for account execs was true, if somewhat odd, though it wasn't the reason she'd gone to see Larry.

"Anyway," she continued, her insides shimmering with performance anxiety, "we got into an argument. Well, mostly I argued and he laughed, finding me quite amusing." It was a factual account, she mused. "I got so frustrated at my inability to get through to him, I guess I wanted to see him show some remorse . . . I don't know."

"And?"

Though she sensed motion in him, Attorney MacDonald didn't move a muscle. Except his firm mouth, with the sensual underlip. And those softly colored eyes with the depths of intelligence she so admired were looking at her with a hawkish stare.

"The rock," she replied, as if that explained it all. But his cocked brow prompted elaboration. "The police said the rock was the murder weapon."

"How big is this rock?" he asked, frowning. At her ambiguous look, he rephrased the question. "Can you hold it in your hand easily?"

Cocking her head at an angle, Sydney called on her memories of that afternoon. Gazing absently, she lifted her right hand, palm up. The rock she envisioned was egg-round and beady colored with a smooth texture. It had been awkward, but stretching her fingers around it had firmed her grip before she threw it across the room at Larry.

"Yes, I guess so," she admitted in a barely perceptible voice. She dropped her hands back into her lap. "I threw it at him. Missed him and hit the mirror over the fireplace."

"Okay, go on."

"Then I left," she replied summarily, in her mind her fingers crossed.

A pregnant pause settled between them. Perry MacDonald remained silent, and believing she'd convinced him, Sydney took a breath—the first normal one since she'd sat down—then stared up at him. His long-fingered hands were clasped together in a praying position and propped under his chin. He just stood there, shrewdly still, exuding virility.

Two

The line between them was clearly drawn. Curiously, it seemed to shift off center, Perry thought, watching Sydney's hands fidget in her lap. Guilt or nerves? he wondered.

Suddenly, as if she became aware of the telling display, she arrested their movement. Stretched across the outline of her slender thighs, they were slim, pampered and fine-boned, with a light peachy polish on the nails. She wore an opal stone on her left pinkie, but no band indicating her romantic predicament. Though she was the perfect size he liked in a woman, and probably about a hundred-twenty pounds, he was at this point her attorney; she was his client, and off limits to him as a man.

Nothing except the truth mattered. And Sydney Webster knew more than she was saying. Something that returned the prim stiffness to her posture, he thought, plucking apart the story that came from her lovely mouth. There could be no justice when truth was distorted by lies.

Yet, he couldn't get angry with her as he'd been known to do when a client knowingly lied to him. Maybe it was because he liked the sound of her voice, he mused, a hidden smile of remembered pleasure expanding his chest. But her bell-sweet tone notwithstanding, extracting truth was his purpose, he reminded himself, harnessing his wayward thoughts.

She would learn it was not easy to withhold the whole truth from him. Despite his expensive suit and casual mannerisms—practiced to perfection to minimize the perceived threat of his size—he was born a street kid whose rough edges had been sharpened while prowling the courtroom jungles.

He wasn't practicing criminal law in Dalston because he couldn't go anywhere else. Rather, he stayed to make good on his promise to his late great-grandmother, along with repaying his debt to the community which had nurtured him into manhood when society would have thrown him away. Though the probability of trying media-enticing criminal cases was not high, his legal services were needed now more than ever—more even than when he'd needed a criminal attorney years ago.

He took his work and the law seriously. And he expected those who walked into his office seeking his help to do so, but he was curious about her reasons for lying.

The possibility that she was trying to protect someone dawned on him, prompting a barely perceptible flick of his brow. Meaning she was loyal, if somewhat naive. If he was right, at least that offset the audacious risk she took by lying to him. It told him something else about her: She might be down now, but she was no quitter, he surmised with admiration.

He had even sensed it from the very beginning in the bold, rich colors she wore comfortably, and now felt, as then, a surprising jolt of desire. She looked daring in the sveltely fitted electric blue pantsuit. Cool purple earrings picked up the colors in the loosely draped scarf around her shoulders and accented the radiance of her flesh.

Unbidden, he heard the melody of her voice as his entire name rolled off her tongue. He never liked his birth mother's choice more in his thirty-one years. And her capricious eyes . . . notwithstanding, vulnerability tempered her gaze as she attempted to look coolly composed. He smiled inwardly.

It wasn't mandatory, but it helped to like his clients, he

rationalized to quell the lickerish feelings on the periphery of his thoughts. But he'd had enough of her lies. Either, she was going to tell him the truth, or . . .

"Ms. Webster," he said, taking a step from the desk, his head angled to look at her sidelong, "when I make a decision whether to sign on a client, it's with the understanding that person will be absolutely honest with me. I don't care how distressing the truth may seem." He reversed his pace, then stood still. "Prison is a far more painful experience," he concluded, flashing a closed-lip smile at her. "Now, go back, fill in the holes, and empty the trash."

Her mouth gaping open and her eyes wide with distress, Sydney stared at him. "I . . . I don't know what you mean," she stammered in reply.

Two sentences were crammed into one as he promptly clarified his words. "Representative Daniels had a campaign manager, I'm sure. It would seem more appropriate to take such matters up with the manager, not the representative himself."

"But I told you—" Sydney wasn't allowed to finish.

"Apparently you didn't understand me the first time, Ms. Webster," he said, his voice a whisper of thunder. "You can either tell me the truth," he punctuated the sentence with a slight pause, "or you can leave."

Her heart pounding fiercely in her bosom, Sydney felt he was burrowing his way under her skin, into her head; that he was on the verge of uncovering her lie. She trembled under his intent stare. Never in her twenty-eight years had she been much of a liar. Why she had thought she could tell one to someone adeptly skilled at spotting falsehoods, she didn't know.

"A good starting place would be describing your relationship to Daniels."

Accepting that she had no other choice, Sydney said with

soft resignation, "Larry was engaged to my sister. They were going to announce their engagement the day he was found murdered. That was last Thursday, as you know. I was springing for the party for them at the Four Seasons."

"From that, I take it you had a pretty good relationship with him?"

Snorting, she replied, "I disliked Larry; he made me sick." With disgust in her voice, she added, "But I kept my feelings about him to myself."

"I see," Perry said pensively, his hand rubbing his chin. "Then why did you go to his apartment?"

The quick question needed a careful answer, but Sydney didn't have a response ready that would protect Jessica. She gazed up at Perry openmouthed, a plea for understanding in her eyes. He showed no signs of relenting, and mindful of his promise to kick her out, she took a deep breath, feeling utterly defeated.

"I found out Larry was having an affair with another woman." Her words came out in a rush as if to ease the pain she knew they would cause Jessica. "And I went to . . . I went to . . ." Her look pleaded for pity. "In hindsight, I don't know why I went." Irritation rising anew, she admitted, "I was just so mad that he was cheating on Jessica, the woman he was about to announce to the world he would marry. It was a stupid thing to do," she concluded contritely, though residual outrage colored her tone.

"At least now we're getting somewhere," Perry replied, satisfied.

He rubbed his hands together with relish, as if he'd won a major victory. Sydney was amazed by the vibrancy of the smile that brightened his face, the arresting look in his brandy brown eyes, oblique in shape and enthralling in their intensity. Perry MacDonald was not only legally adroit, he was masculine-gorgeous, and sparks of unwanted excitement shot through her in response to his dual dynamism.

"Why do you believe that your sister . . . ? What's her name?"

With a barely perceptible shake of her head, Sydney returned from her wayward mental meanderings. "Jessica. Dr. Jessica Webster," she replied.

"Why do you need to run interference for Jessica?"

Sydney opened her mouth, but wavered—he had already caught her in one lie—then stilled. Wetting her lips with her tongue, she was forced to admit that neither Jessica nor her father needed her for much of anything. Rather, it was she who missed a sense of familial belonging. She had dared to hope that being close to her family would assuage the bouts of emptiness that stole upon her, seemingly without reason, since her grandmother's death in the past year. Uncomfortable with what that revealed—her own needful nature—she glared at him.

"What does that have to do with the fact that I went to Larry's on Jessica's behalf?" she asked bitingly.

"It speaks to state of mind."

Though he spoke with a margin of sensitivity despite his authoritative tone, she sensed he would not let the matter rest. Still, she didn't like having her weakness exposed so ingenuously by a stranger.

"So, you got into a verbal fight with Larry Daniels because he was cheating on your sister who was to become his fiancée. Is that correct?"

"Yes."

"How do you know he was having an affair?"

"I saw him with another woman at the hotel when I went there to finalize arrangements for the party two days earlier," she replied.

"Who was the woman?"

"I don't know, but I got the impression she was young enough to be his daughter." She began strongly, but her conviction waned. "I didn't see her face. Just her profile," she mumbled, embarrassed, realizing for the first time how weak her evidence seemed now that she was forced to put it into words.

"So, you presumed guilt, then stewed about this information before you decided to take action." She nodded in agreement with his summation. "You're mighty presumptuous, Ms. Webster," he said matter-of-factly.

"You don't understand; I introduced them," she protested, in distress.

"I see. You felt responsible, and maybe a little guilty, too."

It wasn't a question, but a damned good guess. Sydney nodded her head in reply.

"Maybe over nothing," he added. "It could have been a perfectly innocent situation."

"There was nothing innocent about the embrace I saw," she shot back in a flash of temper. "He didn't deny it . . . bragged that he couldn't help it if women found him attractive, and suggested that maybe I would benefit from a night in bed with him."

From a sidelong glance, Perry looked her over rakishly. "Did you take him up on the offer?"

Sydney's heart hammered foolishly in her bosom. More disconcerted by her reaction to his look than the insulting meaning of his words, she snapped in an offended tone, "Of course not. How dare you suggest—?"

Undaunted by her resentment, he cut her off facilely. "The police undoubtedly will, too. Did you tell your sister?"

"No." Her soft response was full of sorrow. "I couldn't bring myself to tell her."

"How do you know she didn't already know about his philandering?"

"My sister would never consider marrying someone who'd demonstrated that he couldn't be faithful," she said resolutely glaring up at him.

"Then maybe you need to have your sister come see me,"

he said, "because you've just given her a motive for murder."

Sydney tried, but failed to hold his look, to be unaffected by the predacious sparkle in his eyes. She might be guilty of a lot of things, impulsiveness topping the list, but she was certain he would find no evidence to link either her or Jessica to Larry's murder.

The buzzer on his phone sounded; then Ramona's voice filled the silence. "Ten minutes, Perry."

He walked behind the desk, pressed a button, then leaned slightly forward to speak. "Thank you, Della," he said sweetly, flashing Sydney a playful wink.

The chipped tooth in the crooked grin invoked provocative sensations in her. Staring at him with startled retrospection, Sydney wondered whether she had made another impetuous mistake.

"In the interests of justice, my client is willing to make a statement, but that's all she's going to do," he said.

Three hours after offering his client to the police for questioning, both Perry and Sydney were free to go, though he was mindful that the deposition had been postponed again, and he'd never gotten the chance to change his shirt.

He was leaning against the wall in the lobby of the police station. His legs were crossed at the ankles, arms folded over his chest. The adrenaline pumping through his bloodstream was running on all eight cylinders now. He was excited, but not jubilant. Rather, he was scared. Really scared for only the second time in his life.

Within seconds, he was oblivious to the in-and-out traffic of police officers and reluctant visitors with business. Wearing a blank stare, he let his mind drift to the past, to his very first run-in with the legal system.

In the seventeen-year-old memory, he saw himself as though in a still photograph. Sitting in a musty old courtroom, he struggled to be a lot to be of things he was and wasn't. He struggled not to show the fear or the anger of the fourteen-year-old inside him, while facing a stern judge and a hostile jury. He struggled to *act right* before a world that would condemn him on sight—his guilt or innocence of the crime inconsequential.

Neither a friendly face nor a peer was before him. He had to look behind—at G.G., born Wilhemenia Berry—and alongside—at his attorney Clark Bishop—for affirmation of his humanity.

Perry's thoughts returned to the present, but a frown was etched on his face. Though he'd never forgotten his past, he wondered why the memory had come to him now. His shoulders heaving, he inhaled deeply, then released the breath.

There had been a lot of pressure then, he recalled. Now it returned, striking him with full force as he contemplated the undertaking before him.

He was anxious to see the crime scene. Without explaining, Melloncamp vetoed his request. But there were other ways, he decided, a knowing glint in his eyes.

Hearing the click of feminine heels on the glass-tiled flooring, Perry shifted his eyes to the right. Ms. Webster had emerged from the ladies' room and was walking his way. He noticed the smile on her mouth, soft, well formed and wide. He smiled back because . . . because it was impossible to resist her bright mood. This was the most animated he'd seen her since they left his office. With desire rippling along the edges of his flesh, he let himself think of her in ways he knew he shouldn't.

A couple of uniformed officers escorting a man in handcuffs crossed into Perry's view. That broke the monotony of his basking mood. He remembered the place was totally unsuitable for wayward thoughts—which were equally unsuitable to this situation no matter the locale. He pushed

away from the wall and picked up the briefcase on the floor
next to his feet.

"I'm glad that's over."

In hindsight, Perry realized he never should have told
Ms. Webster that her sister had more motive than she did
to kill Daniels. With that in mind, he decided not to tell
her this was just the beginning.

"Let's get out of here," he said, more gruffly than he'd
intended, leading them toward the exit. "We've got work
to do."

The police were anxious to catch their perp and wrap up
the case. It was going to be tough on all charged with the
mantle of delivering justice. Especially the attorney for the
accused. That was the second thing that scared him. Justice
didn't stand on firm ground when the police were in such
haste to deliver it, he knew. The murder victim—Daniels—
was adored by the public: both blacks and whites admired
him because he had risen above his humble beginnings. His
killer would be hunted to the ends of the earth.

The evidence the police had against Perry's client was
circumstantial at best. However, he knew it was one of the
most exact methods of proof, if it existed at all. And *if* it
was interpreted correctly. The interpretation could make his
defense even tougher, should they actually bring a murder
charge against her.

"Where to now?"

"I'd like to meet your family," he replied tactfully. Without waiting for her assent, he pushed open the door and
they walked out of the police station into the oppressive
early evening air.

Outside, the charm of Dalston was evident despite the
most modern of its downtown buildings. The six-story police station housed the latest equipment for crime detection
and the school for cadets. Compared to the stately Dalston
County Courthouse across the street, it was an eyesore of
smooth red brick and black glass. Though Dalston lagged

far behind her sister cities in the way of crime, the citizens had bitten the mayor's bait that a modern police department was the answer to heading crime off at the pass before it reached their quaint but rapidly growing city.

Perry tugged his tie loose, missing the cool air conditioner they had left behind, and looked up and down the street. It was shortly after five; people were scurrying home. Soon downtown would shut down and roll up for the night.

"What about my car?"

They'd come to the police station together, leaving her car in the parking garage of his office building. In an effort to preserve some of the countrified charm of the area, the citizens of Dalston refused to allow more parking outlets downtown.

"It's as safe as it would be anywhere."

"Why do you want to meet my family?"

Perry gave her a look discouraging conversation as a group of people walked past. But he didn't want to stand around in front of the police station, either. Taking her by the elbow, he started them out for his car, parked in a lot two blocks away.

As they walked, Perry mentally reviewed the police evidence against Sydney Lauren Webster. They had her prints on the murder weapon—a rock measuring three-inches in diameter, weighing 3.2 pounds. They had three witnesses who could place her in the building near the time of death, which the coroner put at 5:45 P.M.. There was the attendant who'd parked and then retrieved her car, the guard stationed at the security booth in the lobby, and the cleaning lady who claimed to have overheard Ms. Webster verbally attack Daniels as soon as he opened the door to her.

He planned to talk to all of them. Especially the cleaning lady with such keen hearing.

"Perry.' "

Sydney's balmy voice gliding into his thoughts, Perry stopped walking to look down at her.

"Are we going to a fire or something?"

He'd have bet she had no idea how enticing she looked, staring up into his face, a provocative smile in her black-pebble eyes. He nearly grunted from the effort it took to pull his wayward emotions back under control.

"Sorry," he said, forcing a look of chagrin. After he adjusted his strides to hers, they walked at a leisurely pace along the long block. He was constantly conscious of her nearness.

Where was he? Oh, yeah, the police interpretation, he reminded himself, his brow bunching into a staunch frown. They believed Daniels wanted to break off with Ms. Webster on the eve of announcing his engagement to her sister. She didn't want to, *so said the police*. Hence, she and Daniels argued; then she lost her cool and picked up the handy rock and smashed him on the back of the head. Stunned, Daniels stumbled, giving her the opportunity to hit him again and again and again, until he stopped moving. She left the rock on the floor beside his bloody head and calmly walked out of his apartment. Both the guard and parking attendant said that she was her usual friendly self and showed no signs of agitation.

By the time they reached his car, Perry felt stiff from fighting the unprofessional thoughts teasing his subconscious. They clashed with the police's image of Sydney Webster, as well as with the ethical code of conduct he swore to uphold.

He opened the passenger door and helped her inside. Closing it, he walked around to the driver's side. He had several problems with the police interpretation.

But because they were such outstanding Samaritans for justice, he recalled, sarcastically amused, his hand on the driver's side door handle, they offered him a *mens rea* defense—insanity. Second-degree murder. He opened the door, slid in under the wheel and brought the car to life, thinking that for Sydney it would be a death sentence.

"You didn't answer my question," she said.

"Which was?"

"Why do you want to meet my family?"

He was not accustomed to answering every whimsical inquiry from clients, and he wasn't about to start. Generally, they were so petrified with fear of going to jail they did exactly as they were told.

"What's the address?" he quibbled.

"Do you always intend to answer a question with a question?" she demanded irritably.

Perry angled sideways in his seat to look at her, his right arm stretched to reach the passenger seat. The inside of his roomy Beemer suddenly seemed hot, the space confining as he stared into her petulant gaze. Wisps of fine hair curled from the heat and peachy-colored soft cheeks were within temptation's reach. He gulped and turned on the air conditioner to full blast before he spoke.

"Am I your attorney?"

"Why yes, I guess so," she replied, puzzled.

"All right," he said, as if having drawn an acceptable conclusion. "There's a small matter of a retainer fee, but aside from that, I run the case from start to finish. If you don't trust my judgment, bail out now. If things heat up the way I expect they will, it wouldn't look favorable if you hire a different attorney."

Sydney opened her purse and pulled out a pen and her checkbook.

"I didn't mean you had to pay me now," he protested, wondering if he should disqualify himself before it was too late.

"It's not a matter of trust," she replied, writing the check. "But since my life's on the line, I insist on being informed of what you're planning." She tore the check out and passed it to him. "This is what your secretary told me the initial cost would be. If it's not enough, say so."

For some inexplicable reason, he didn't want her money.

"This is fine," he said, disgruntled, accepting the check. Without looking at the amount, he folded the check in half, then shoved it in his coat pocket. "Now, you were about to give me that address so I can meet your family."

"And you were about to give me a reason for needing to do that," she retorted.

"Do you really want me to spell it out for you?" he asked with somber regret. "I'm your attorney; I work for your best interests. Your sister and your father, if need be, will have to get attorneys for themselves."

Her lively disposition collapsed. Even the sprightly contrariness vanished, leaving a haunted look on her face. *Don't look at me like that!* He wanted to yell it at her, feeling an instant's remorse. Instead, sanity prevailed in the guise of a reminder about the dangers of becoming too involved with one's client.

"Fifty-two-thirty-six Stonehedge Circle."

"Thank you," he replied. Driving the car off the parking lot, he stole a sidelong glance, noting her forlorn resignation. He would do anything to wipe the sadness from her face. "You obeyed my instructions during the interrogation," he said, forcing a smile. "Answered their questions succinctly and confidently. I hardly had to intervene at all."

"I was too scared not to."

"Good," he declared, more in response to the chuckle in her voice than her words.

"Why is being scared good?" she replied smartly; yet she was smiling. "I didn't feel good about it."

"It didn't show," he replied.

"Well, I was," she said softly as if embarrassed.

Intent on the elegant curve of her lashes as they swept down over her eyes, Perry didn't realize the light had turned green until Sydney lifted a manicured nail and pointed.

"Light's green."

He cautioned himself to pay more attention to the road and less to her as he pulled off into the traffic.

"Those detectives seemed like phonies to me."

"I assure you they are very serious about wrapping this case up in a hurry."

"No, that's not what I mean," she replied. "Their Texas accents seemed put on."

"They are," he replied, mirth in his voice. "Melloncamp is from New York, and Tomkins is from California. They've only been here about seven years, but they're cowboys at heart."

"Hmmm," she snorted. "I didn't detect anything chivalrous about Melloncamp. He kept looking at me like I was a morsel of food, and he was just biding his time before preying on me." She shuddered.

Perry laughed out loud. "He loves his job, and he's damn good at it."

"Tomkins seemed okay," she said with a shrug.

"Don't be fooled. He's good, too."

"You seem to know them quite well. In fact, I got the distinct impression they like you."

She was perceptive, Perry noted, even if she was wrong in her presumption of friendship. "I assure you, we're not drinking buddies."

"Well, respect you, at least," she amended, dissolving into gentle laughter. "Not that I'm the expert, mind you, but it seems all they have is circumstantial evidence."

"The best kind if you can get it," he replied.

"Then why didn't they arrest me?"

"How tall are you?"

Sydney frowned. She looked like a young girl trying to analyze a complex problem, Perry thought. Ironically, he was struck by a surge of protectiveness, something not usually in his nature. What the hell was wrong with him?

"Five-three," she replied at last.

"Off by an inch," he said aloud to himself, questions of an alluring nature hounding his thoughts. "I imagine they're trying to figure out how someone five-three could walk up to a man six-three-and-a-half, which Daniels was, and hit him on the head at the angle indicated by the wounds. If he were sitting with his back to you and not paying attention, then yes, it could be done. I'm guessing the evidence didn't show that," he said absently, his thoughts drifting back to the interrogation. Something about Melloncamp's manner caused an uneasiness in him. He suspected the detectives were withholding pertinent information. "But I can promise they won't give up," he declared, deciding to give Javier a call later on tonight. By way of warning her not to get overly confident, he predicted, "As soon as they figure out the how, an arrest will be made."

Three

As the car moved ahead and downtown receded, Sydney became somewhat excited. It was relief that she'd gotten through an intense police questioning unscathed. Perry MacDonald had been far more probing than Detectives Melloncamp and Tomkins, even though she hadn't appreciated it at the time.

The arrangement was going to work out perfectly, she thought, leaning her head against the rest as she squirmed comfortably in the passenger seat. Recalling her earlier doubts about him, she realized it was the newness of the entanglement that required his services, coupled with his brash personality that caused her to second-guess herself. He was no diplomat, she chuckled to herself, recalling his detracting rejoinders. She had wanted to slap his handsome face. Risking a sidelong glance at him, something warned her that that wouldn't have been wise at all.

She admired his ability to think on his feet, quickly grasping the essentials of a situation. While it posed a serious drawback for her, for he also seemed endowed with the ability to read her private thoughts, she trusted his legal mind. Maybe more than she trusted herself. She was unable to shake the damnable notion that he was capable of performing the miracles of his television namesake. And the more she thought about him, the more unable she seemed to shake the disturbing emotions he created in her.

She had a feeling that her role, albeit distant and indirect, in Larry's death was going to test her mettle more than she could guess. Though positive Perry would unearth nothing duplicitous about her family's relationship with Larry, she wondered how his death would affect the Websters. Of course, Jessica was her principal concern: she had waited so patiently for love.

Sydney averted her gaze to stare out the window as they passed through an African-American section of town. Adults were sitting on the three-step brick porches of row houses painted in pastel colors, watching children play in the streets.

"Why did you move to Dalston?" Perry asked, interrupting her quiet rumination. "I can't imagine a future in radio is as bright here as it is in Houston?"

Sydney swallowed before she spoke, thinking about her reply. "I got a call that my father had been rushed to the hospital. Everybody thought he was having a stroke. It turned out to be only a case of anxiety, but the doctors warned him to take it easy."

"And you decided to stay on afterward?"

Sydney heard another question in his tone and ignored it.

"Yeah," she said, bobbing her head up and down. Her initial intent had been to lighten Jessica's burdens: their father had a way of eliciting a sense of guilt which, under the guise of obligation, eventually led to capitulation to his demands and wishes. Sydney had conveniently put aside the fact that her sister exerted more influence and control over her father than she did, for he considered her too in-experienced to make a sound decision.

Then Perry suddenly asked the one question she couldn't answer outright. It was an extension of the one he'd posed in his office.

"Why?"

Dalston held the promise of home, even though it wasn't, she guessed. Except for her godmother, who had her own family, she had begun to feel deserted in Houston. She had

taken another chance, believing she would find what she
was looking for in Dalston. But it was beginning to appear
that every chance she took turned to chaos.

Aloud, she said, "None of my family was there anymore.
Nearly all of them have died, returned to their roots in other
parts of Texas and Louisiana or started lives elsewhere," she
added wistfully. "Houston was a pit stop for the Websters
and Taylors."

As they rode deeper into the community, a middle-class
neighborhood came into view. Here, families lived inside
air-conditioned brick homes with well-tended yards and
two-car garages. Sydney imagined their lives were patterned
on those of the people in her vaguely remembered childhood, when her mother was alive and her father didn't have
such a high-powered position.

Wouldn't it be nice if . . . ?

Sydney looked up to catch Perry staring at her with those
penetrating eyes of his. A stream of warmth curled through
her, and she promptly abandoned the pleasant supposition
before it was completely realized. It was a dangerous game
she was playing, she told herself, the admonishment opening the door on her memory of Ross Merrell.

Ross was a car salesman, an energetic, fun-loving man
of thirty-nine, with a good head for numbers. Too late, she
realized she would have been better off buying a car, instead
of his seemingly winning ways.

He was nothing like her father, caring and attentive . . .
on the surface. The relationship began with a bang the year
before last. Shortly after they'd consolidated their funds for
the purpose of saving toward marriage, it petered out with
hardly a fizzle.

Her dissatisfaction with the arrangement had surfaced after her grandmother's death last April. Or maybe it was
caused by their living together. Ross had lost all interest in
sharing, talking things out, or soliciting her input on decisions. He wanted to run the show, though they shared the

expense of running the house she'd inherited from her grandmother. Finding herself acquiescing to his every command, she hadn't liked what she saw long before she did anything about it. It was June before she took action, and even then, it was an attempt to save what they had. He soon proved to her that what they had wasn't worth saving. She kicked him out, but that didn't solve her problem.

Feeling despair slipping into her conscious, Sydney broke off the memories. She directed her thoughts to the future when the case would be over and the real killer discovered. But in the interim, she reminded herself, she and Perry would spend a considerable amount of time together. The thought caused a spine tingling thrill to course up her back, and she shivered imperceptibly.

But she needn't fear Perry. He was bound by an ethical code of behavior, and she had self-imposed rules, as well. Having come off one disastrous relationship, she wasn't ready for or interested in anything beyond his privileged counsel.

Believing she'd had a glimpse of his courtroom style, she felt she would never fall victim to his disarming brand of charm again. Smiling confidently to herself, she consigned the pleased look to her face and angled her body toward Perry. "Are you from here?"

"Born a few blocks over at County General," he replied. "Graduated from Dunbar High."

A few short blocks away, the administration building of Texas College rose into view, it's clock face depicting the hour as a little after five.

"Texas College?" she asked. The college was a symbol of progress and pride for some, a way out for others. To her father, it was his life.

"No. Went to Houston for that. Texas Southern. Undergrad and law," he said, a hint of pride in his tone. "Came back in the summer of eighty-nine, and hung out my shingle."

"Missed home, or just to fill a need?"

"I guess you could say Dalston is my 'Tobacco Road,' " he replied without hesitation.

"Huh?"

He chuckled. " 'Tobacco Road,' the song, Lou Rawls."

"Oh, now I remember," she replied, an embarrassed smile on her face.

"How old are you?" he laughed.

"Don't go there," she warned, laughing softly. "I have a hard enough time with my father. He still acts like I'm sixteen."

"Just you and Jessica?"

"Only the two of us," she said on a lengthy sigh. Jessica wasn't like her mother. Or maybe she was, Sydney mused, aware that her memory was faulty, causing her to glorify the few things she did remember about Sonni-Lauren. "Jessica's ten years older, so we weren't exactly close when growing up."

"You said she was a doctor," Perry replied. "What kind, medical or philosophy?"

"If you're trying to build a case against her, you won't find it," she said.

"Humor me," he urged.

"Jessica teaches English at Dalston University. She was granted a full professorship last fall."

"How does your father feel about her teaching at a rival college?"

"It's one of the rules he can't change," she replied with amusement in her voice. "Texas College has a nepotism clause in its bylaws. It forbids her from teaching there because he is—"

"—the president," Perry chimed in.

"Never married? Jessica, I mean."

Sydney shook her head, melancholy touching her face. "I was four when my mother died. My mother was Jessica's stepmother." She added, "Jessica's mother had died long before I was born. Even though my father hired live-in help, Jessica assumed the bulk of responsibility for me."

"So your father never remarried?"

"I'm afraid he's married to Texas College," she said wistfully. "Anyway"—she sighed—"Jessica's been making sacrifices since she was fourteen years old. She didn't get to go off to college until I did. She had to turn down a scholarship to William & Mary. As a matter of fact, she earned her bachelor's degree from Texas Southern. She was twenty-eight then and just starting her master's. I remember," she said, her tone lifting with a fond, humorous memory, "when I reached that all-knowing teenage stage, I thought it was my fault she'd never married."

"Oh, yeah," he said, chuckling, "I remember those years well."

"She assured me otherwise." Sydney laughed at herself.

"Of course, you didn't believe her."

"No." Sydney soberly shook her head. "But I can't say I'm sorry it won't be to Larry Daniels."

"A very popular man," Perry replied, in a similar heavy tone of thought.

It was half past the hour when Perry turned onto Stonehedge, a one-way in-and-out street of grand two-story homes partially hidden by decoratively trimmed hedges and shady oaks. A deep concern was gnawing away at his insides.

He listened carefully to Sydney as she spoke about her family and heard what she didn't say. Melloncamp and Tomkins were wrong about her, he thought. Blinded by secondhand impressions, they couldn't see the protective shield she drew around herself. But he had seen past the learned control of the woman and had had a glimpse of a little girl wanting her mother.

Pretending to read the street numbers painted in black on

the curb, he glanced sidelong at her. A finger stuck between her teeth, she was undeniably a contradiction. Lissome. He wondered what thoughts were in her head at that moment.

Her idolization of Jessica troubled him. While commendable, he hoped it wasn't some misplaced sense of guilt she harbored. The word sacrifice hadn't been used an inordinate number of times, but its use was heartfelt.

He turned into the circular driveway. This home was like the others in the wide cul-de-sac. The absence of burglar bars on doors and windows indicated hidden security. Perry braked behind a black stretch limousine parked in front of the palatial Victorian home in the center of the block.

He hadn't realized black folks lived as well as this until he'd reached his teens and ventured farther than the four-block radius of his impoverished world, he recalled wryly. Every black person he had known then was as poor as he and G.G.

No, not poor, Perry amended; before Stephanie, he didn't know he was poor. G.G. made sure he got everything he needed. *She* showed him there was more to be had and whetted his appetite for it.

Her name was Stephanie Austin. Her father was a doctor; her mother, a nurse. They lived in a house like the Websters, a symbol of progress and prominence, on a dead-end street. He had thought it a mansion. And in this neighborhood, dead end was a misnomer, he thought, chuckling at the irony.

"Sydney?" he called her name softly so as not to startle her. She looked up at him, her eyes wide with disorientation. "We're here."

"Oh." She looked out the window. A frown flicked across her face as she noticed the car parked ahead of them; then a caustic sigh escaped her.

"What's the matter?"

"I forgot all about the memorial service tonight. I never wanted to go, but . . . I said I would," she replied as if amending her previous decisions, a note of reluctance in her voice.

"Then I won't stay long," he said, getting out of the car. He walked around to open the passenger door. As he helped her out, the incidental touch rekindled the spark that had been flickering just below the surface.

Perry released Sydney's hand, allowing her to lead the way. Catching his eyes stray to the sway of her hips as she traipsed up the brick path, he struggled to divert his mind to lawyerly thoughts. But he didn't like those either, he thought, telling himself that meeting her family now was not the most efficient use of time. Javier could provide all the information he would ever need about Jessica or Walter Webster.

He was here because of his reluctance to part company with Sydney Webster. He had to resolve this attraction before the day ended, he reasoned. After satisfying his curiosity, he'd be sure to discover that lust motivated him; then he could begin to build a case that would acquit her of suspicion of murder.

Reaching the door, Sydney proceeded him into the large foyer where classical music played softly from an unseen source. Perry recalled his teenage awe as his gaze scanned the particulars. A crystal chandelier hung from the high ceiling, a circular staircase snaked around the upper level, and a decorator's touch was evident in the placement of every piece of expensive furniture, each painting and plant. The place was a showpiece befitting the president of any college.

"I wonder where everybody is," Sydney said. "Let me run upstairs a minute."

"Sydney . . . ? Sydney is that you?"

At the stentorian voice coming from his right, Perry turned slightly to see Dr. Walter Webster in the flesh. Out of the corner of his eye, he noticed Sydney stop dead in her tracks, one foot on the bottom step. Though it was hardly noticeable, her shoulders stiffened, and her hands twitched at her sides before she faced her father. There was a look of forced patience in her expression, a smile on her lips that didn't reach her eyes. Sensing a decided chill in the atmosphere, he wondered if he'd stepped into the middle of a family feud.

Walter Webster emerged into the foyer, shouldering his way between the sliding doors. Of average height and a build that was spreading in the middle, he was dark skinned with strong features. Strands of gray lined his short, woolly dark hair. Dressed in a gray suit with a flower pinned to his lapel, he looked the part of a high-powered academician.

"Where have you been young lady? We've been waiting for you. Do you realize what time it is?"

Perry instantly disliked the man. He knew it was because of the melancholy he detected in Sydney's voice when she'd alluded to her father on the drive over.

"Father, I'm—" though apologetic in tone, Sydney didn't get to finish her explanation.

"Where is your sense of obligation?" Walter Webster demanded, staring contentiously at Perry.

Perry shifted ever so slightly, the perception of a smile on his mouth, and looked down his nose at the shorter Walter Webster. He simply stared, transmitting a code recognized only by men. He could tell when the older man got the message, and the smile on his lips then matched that of the man smiling up at him, albeit with grudging respect.

"I'm afraid Sydney Lauren has other plans for this evening, M. . . . ?" Walter Webster said in a civil tone.

"Perry MacDonald, sir." Perry extended a hand.

The handshake was brief, firm.

"Well, Mr. MacDonald . . ." Walter Webster's features suddenly bunched into a frown. "MacDonald?" he echoed thoughtfully. "Perry Mason MacDonald, the attorney who got that police officer off—the one accused of killing a kid, oh what, three, four years ago?"

"Four," Perry replied. Crucify him! the African American community had cried, he recalled. He'd been labeled a traitor to his race for defending Melloncamp. He remembered telling the detective that if he ever found out he had actually killed that kid, he would hold a press conference announcing his withdrawal as Melloncamp's attorney and join the prosecution team. Of course, such behavior would have invited disbarment, and in all likelihood, he wouldn't have done it, but the thought expressed the value he placed on truth.

Walter Webster's attitude changed slightly, this time to grudging admiration, then wariness. He turned on Sydney, his eyes so narrowed the corners almost met over the bridge of his nose. "Sydney Lauren Webster—"

"I'm on my way to get dressed now," she replied, spinning into a quick about-face to race up the stairs.

"Not so fast young lady," he said, his jaws tight. "I want to talk to you *and* Mr. MacDonald—in my study right now."

Even though he'd never had a father, Perry recognized that parental tone. It demanded immediate compliance, brooked no argument. Confident in obedience to his command, Walter Webster ducked back into the side room. Sydney's shoulders slumped with resignation, as she descended the steps with frustration lining her expression. Perry flashed her a look of encouragement and followed her into the room.

It was a man's room, done in a dark brown color scheme. A massive desk of ebony fronted the wall-to-wall bookshelf at the back of it. Under a side window between gold-base standing lamps resided a portable bar, all glass and gold. A chunky, but expensive, leather couch with matching chairs and an ebony and glass coffee table occupied the rest of the space. Evenly dividing the front wall was a red brick fireplace. It was there that Perry noticed her, standing at the far corner. Dressed in black, she had a drink in her hand and a look of wretched solitude on her brown face. Sydney announced her without introduction.

"Jessica . . ." she said, ignoring her father's impatient demand for answers.

Jessica Webster, doctor of letters, did not fit the schoolmarm spinster image he had imagined, Perry thought. The grief she wore did not distract from her comely looks. Though they shared the same dainty, feminine aura, only a thread of similarity was visible between the two sisters. Sydney was slightly smaller in build and taller by an inch. The gentleness of her expression and the caring in her tone as she headed straight for Jessica denoted a closeness between the sisters. Aware that he did not know Jessica, he still felt Sydney was the more precious of the two.

"We've been trying to reach you all day," Walter Webster said accusingly. "I asked you to stay with your sister this morning, and you insisted you had to go to work." Warming up in his tirade, he babbled on, "I never wanted you working at that station in the first place. I could have gotten you a decent-paying, respectable job somewhere else if you hadn't been in such a hurry to claim your independence."

Watching the exchange, Perry noticed Sydney seemed to ignore her father, intent on reaching Jessica. All of a sudden, her steps faltered and a curious frown settled between her brows as she gazed at her sister. "Something unexpected happened," she said, her thoughts engaged elsewhere, "and I—"

"Something unexpected?" Walter Webster harrumphed in disbelief. "Something unexpected like what?"

Over her shoulder, Sydney stared at Perry, bewildered. He sensed there was something that wasn't being said, and from the look in Sydney's eyes, the quiet intensity of her demeanor, so did she. But he could only return her nonplussed look with one of his own.

* * *

What was going on? Sydney wondered, puzzled. Jessica wouldn't even look at her.

"Sydney Lauren, I'm talking to you."

"I'm sorry, Daddy," she replied, dragging her gaze from Jessica, "what did you say?" She was standing an arm's length in front of Perry, who had assumed a tentative position next to the first handy chair. Offered no seat, however, he hadn't claimed one, and Sydney had ventured no farther, as if knowing instinctively she was safe near Perry.

Dr. Webster stood near the massive dark wood desk, his command post. "Your sister and I both tried reaching you at the station, and that woman answering the phones kept saying you weren't in," he said. "You told us both you were going to work, but clearly you weren't there."

One. Two. "Gee, did I miss something important?" Sydney replied. *Three. Four.*

"Save the sarcasm, Sydney. This is important," Webster said wearily. "We got a visit from the police."

So did I, Sydney silently commented. "And?"

"They asked us to answer some questions. I suspect I shouldn't have to tell you what it was about. I believe the presence of Mr. MacDonald confirms that."

A devilish look in her eyes, Sydney replied, "Well, Daddy, if you've guessed where I was, what's so important about your seeing me now?" But that was the only mischief she allowed herself before again looking to Jessica for answers.

"Lawson Douglas accompanied Jessica and I when we gave our statements," he replied. "The police told us you refused to talk to them."

Sydney gazed quizzically at Perry. Looking like a big contented cat, he had not uttered a word. But of course, he hadn't been given an opportunity to speak, she smiled to herself. Perry hunched his broad shoulders in a quick shrug.

"Well?" Dr. Webster prodded. "Is it true? Why would you do something so stupid if you didn't have anything to hide?"

Asked, answered, and convicted, Sydney thought angrily. Now, where did she leave off? *Five. Six.*

"Young lady, are you going to give us any answers?"

"You seem to have everything under control," Sydney replied. "What else can I say?"

"I see it's no use trying to talk to you, as usual. Mr. MacDonald, I trust you're a reasonable man."

Seven.

"I try to be," Perry replied lazily.

"I don't want you to take this personally," Dr. Webster said, unabashed, "but I believe it's best that Lawson represents the entire family in this matter until the police complete their investigation."

Sydney's mouth fell open. "Lawson Douglas is the legal counsel for Texas College," she declared astonished. "I hardly think he's qualified to represent any of us in this situation."

"I'd have you know that Lawson earned his law degree from Harvard University."

"Eight," Sydney ground out, her hands clenched into fists at her sides, with her head back, and eyes closed tightly as if praying for restraint.

"Again, Mr. MacDonald, this is not a reflection on your qualifications or competence," Dr. Webster continued, ignoring Sydney. "It's just—"

"Niiinnneee," Sydney interrupted, her voice rising toward a screech.

"As you can see"—Dr. Webster directed his words to Perry—"my youngest daughter has yet to grow up."

The "t" of "ten" was on the tip of Sydney's tongue. Before she could utter it, Jessica spoke.

"Why did you go to Larry's?"

Sydney's eyes widened, her fists opened limply as she

swung her stunned gaze on Jessica. The expression on her sister's face was not clear. Pain protruded from the depths of her eyes, to be sure, but there was something else, as well. A look she couldn't decipher.

"Yes, why did you?" Dr. Webster echoed. "And don't try to deny it. The police told us you did."

"I've been to Larry's before," Sydney directed her answer to Jessica, "and you never asked me why." She realized she was trembling. Not out of guilt, but because of that other look clouding Jessica's expression.

"He never died after your visits before, either," Jessica snapped, a tearful gulp escaping her.

An eerie stillness settled over the room. Sydney's ears were ringing. One of her fears had come true. Five . . . ten . . . fifteen . . . twenty-four years rolled back in her mind. What she couldn't remember was supplanted by assumptions, and she was four years old again.

It was a spring morning, the time of year when teachers were as anxious as students for the end of school. She was dressed and ready to go; her kindergarten class was going on a field trip to the zoo. She had given her mother the permission slip to sign the night before. At the last minute, of course, her father had grumbled.

Sonni-Lauren was sitting at the dining-room table, preoccupied with her paper house. Strips of fabrics, miniature furniture, notepads and other paraphernalia of her interior design trade littered the wood surface.

"Let's go, Sydney," her father yelled from the front door. He was to drop her off at Lockhart Elementary School on his way to TSU where he taught business courses.

"Okay," she called back. "Mama, where's my permission slip?"

"It's here on this table somewhere," Sonni-Lauren replied, lifting her work in search of the single sheet of paper.

Sydney helped her look. Despite the chaos, she knew her mother would not let her down.

"Here it is," Sonni-Lauren replied, plucking it out from under a swatch of blue velvet wallpaper. "Gimme a kiss."

Taking the note with one hand, Sydney lifted her cheek for her mother's big noisy kiss that tickled her to no end. " 'Bye. See you later," she said, giggling as she tore away to scamper from the room.

School had been fun, as it would be until the summer. Mama was going to pick her up, take her home and get her situated, then return to her work, if she had more to do that day. But she didn't. Instead, Mrs. Grant, their neighbor came. It was not unusual. Whenever Sonni-Lauren got in a bind, Mrs. Grant would pinch-hit.

Sydney didn't know to be suspicious, rather, she was curious when they pulled into the crowded driveway. She didn't know fear until she walked into the living room and found her father being comforted by friends of the family and neighbors.

Her mother was not there. She was never going to be there again. An aneurysm had burst in her brain, killing her instantly.

A faint moan escaped Sydney's lips as the past receded. Aware again of her present surroundings, she sought and focused on Jessica's face, on her eyes. She couldn't help thinking that the sister she had left this morning was not with her now. Another person—a stranger—had taken her place. The look she couldn't define heretofore came to her. Jessica was looking at her with revulsion.

Quickly, Jessica averted her gaze. "I'm sorry," she said softly. "I didn't mean to yell."

"Oh, it's all right to accuse me of killing Larry as long as you don't yell?" Sydney retorted, her voice rising hysterically.

"I'm not accusing you of killing Larry," Jessica said in a barely audible voice.

"Then what are you accusing me of?"

Four

Sydney felt as if a large chunk of her heart had been cut out as she watched Jessica who said nothing, nor returned her look. Finally Jessica lowered her gaze to stare into her glass. The silence spoke volumes.

She shivered as if cold, then sensed the protective shield of Perry as he sidled alongside her. She risked a sidelong glance up at him, and her insides began to thaw despite the awful chill that had settled on the room. He was looking at her, not with the inimical gaze she had seen in Detective Melloncamp's eyes. His eyes did not hold presumptions supporting a motive for murder, or worse, as Jessica's did. No, they shone with another look, a kind of wonder . . . one that deepened the stream of warmth in her. Slowly the lids fell shut over her eyes. She couldn't bare it if it were just her imagination, vicariously filling one of the empty slots in her life.

"Your sister is just trying to get some straight answers from you, which you are refusing to give," Dr. Webster said in an attempt at conciliation.

"Sydney . . ." Jessica's voice was soft, her chin was trembling, her eyes were strangely veiled.

Sydney's head snapped towards Jessica, her insides teeming with the need for an explanation. But none seemed forthcoming. Jessica swallowed hard, then pressed her lips together tightly. She was as silent as the tear that rolled down Sydney's cheek.

Sydney swiped the embarrassing blemish from her face. She was anxious to escape. "Will you wait while I throw a few things together?" she asked around the lump lodged in her throat. She couldn't even look Perry in the face. Her hurting, her humiliation too great.

"No problem," he replied.

"Sydney? Sydney Lauren, where are you going?"

As they walked side by side on the long driveway from the garage apartment behind the Webster's house, Perry could feel Sydney's anguish. They were returning to his car, each weighted by luggage. The requested few minutes equaled fifteen before a large suitcase and dress bag were entrusted to him. She carried a shoe bag, makeup case, and tote.

Conversation between them had become stilted. Emotionally spent, she was reticent to talk about anything. Least of all about what had happened. Perry wasn't sure he understood what he had seen and heard, either.

He'd never consciously let himself wonder what his life would have been like had he been part of a family, with parents and siblings. The offspring of uneducated teenagers whose parents had been teenagers themselves, he knew only he held the power to end the vicious cycle he had been born into and to redefine the family he would one day partner.

Getting a peek at Sydney's, he realized more than ever the gift G.G. had bestowed on him. He represented another chance at parenting for her, and he didn't intend to let her down. She may have paddled his butt a couple of times— and he deserved every spanking he got—but she never belittled his humanity or cursed his spirit.

With a slanted gaze, he looked at Sydney. She walked determined, her chin up; but she was expressionless, as if the look of forced dignity on her face was carved in wood.

Unable to erase the picture of discord he'd seen in the Webster household, Perry could happily have committed double homicide on her behalf. Though he didn't believe she was suicidal, she struck him as a woman who took the downward trend in life hard. Maybe, too hard. She would never survive in prison.

"Where are you going to stay?"

Sydney shrugged. "I'll go to my house," she said impassively.

"But what if your house isn't ready?" Perry asked. "A little while ago you said you weren't scheduled to move in for another week."

He believed she was ripe for foolish behavior. It wouldn't surprise him if she decided to do something to prove to her father and sister that she had had nothing to do with Larry Daniels's death. Though in hindsight, murder was not really what they accused her of.

"Sydney, talk to me," he implored her.

"If the house isn't ready, I'll ask my neighbor to let me spend the night with her," she replied at last, though reluctant and void of emotion.

"You know your neighbor already and you haven't moved in?" he asked amazed. "What's her name?"

"Jasmine Moreland," she said dutifully. "She works at Cobblestone Books."

Reaching the car, he set down the heavy suitcase to pop the trunk open, the dress bag still over his shoulder. They both heard the car, then saw the sporty gray Porsche with the license tag A-1 as it pulled up several feet behind them and stopped. Perry set the luggage in the trunk and turned in time to see a man emerge from the driver's side. He recognized him instantly as Lloyd Andrews, the former confidant, campaign manager and close personal friend of Larry Daniels.

"I'm ready to go now," Sydney announced, starting to walk away.

Her steps faltered slightly, and Perry sensed something was happening. He angled his body to look over his shoulder in the direction of her gaze.

Lloyd was holding open the door for a woman who was getting out of the passenger side of the Porsche. Laughing gaily up at Lloyd, she spoke with her hands as much as her mouth and must have said something humorous, for he smiled broadly.

"Do you know her?" Perry asked Sydney.

"You'll get no introduction from me," Sydney replied flippantly, her arms folded across her bosom, her ire evident.

I'm innocent! Perry wanted to protest, though Sydney's reaction tickled as surely as it baffled him. He took a second glance at the woman, wondering who she was and what she meant to Sydney as she and Lloyd neared. She was tall and voluptuous, with long black hair that flowed lustrously with the toss of her head. A simple, elegant navy cotton dress hugged her body flatteringly. She was a stunning-looking woman who aroused nothing in him but curiosity.

"Perry, my man, what's happening?" Lloyd said, as if delighted to greet an old friend.

"Same as usual, and all praises for that," Perry replied in a similar tone as he shook hands with Andrews, who was little more than a passing acquaintance. They didn't move in the same circles.

In his forties, with a café au lait complexion and curly black hair, Lloyd Andrews appeared erudite. His raisin-brown eyes were lively, his strong nose and wide mouth giving him an aura of strength. Like his former boss, he had political talent, natural charm, and the gift of persuasion. But unlike Larry Daniels, he had a family with money and a *sincere* ready smile. Still, Perry wouldn't trust Andrews as far as he could throw him. The man's profession, plus Perry's inherent suspicion made him wary. He was interested in learning where Lloyd had been at the time of Daniels's death.

"Have you met my wife, Ursula?" Lloyd asked, about to introduce the woman clinging to his side. "Ursula, this is Perry MacDonald."

Flashing a bright smile, Andrew's wife extended her hand. "Not *the* Perry Mason MacDonald?" she cooed, her shoulders shifting as she took in his entire personage.

Perry sensed that Sydney was rolling her eyes and wondered if his shins were safe. He filed Ursula Andrews's name in his memory bank. "The one and only," he replied, careful not to grin too broadly.

"Oh, Ursula," Lloyd said, "have you met Dr. Webster's youngest daughter, Sydney?"

"No, I can't say that I have," Ursula replied. "How do you do? It's a pleasure," she said to Sydney.

"Same here," Sydney replied dryly.

At that moment, Walter Webster and Jessica came out of the house. "We were wondering what was taking you so long," Walter said, his scolding tempered with a smile.

"Sorry we're late," Lloyd said. "Perry, I'll catch you later."

Lloyd excused himself to meet Walter midway between the front door and the limousine. Ursula headed toward Jessica, and the two women fell into conversation. Sydney, Perry noticed, stood stiff as a board, her face pinched and her eyes narrowed.

"Lloyd, you know I hate to rush you," Ursula wheedled, "but we really need to go, or we're going to be late."

"You're right," Dr. Webster replied. A man emerged from the limousine and opened the back door.

"Sydney's not riding with us?" Lloyd asked, looking back and forth between Walter and Sydney.

"No," Walter replied succinctly.

"Ready, Jessica?" Ursula asked.

With one final look at Sydney, neither regret nor hostility

in it, Jessica turned and followed Ursula into the back seat of the limousine.

Perry stared at the back of the car as it drove away, with questions in his expression. "Come on, let's go," he said, leading Sydney by the arm to the passenger side of his car.

The return trip to the parking garage seemed short. Too soon, Sydney thought as Perry transferred the last of her luggage from the trunk of his car to her purple Toyota. Within seconds, she would be free to wrestle with her feelings in private; yet she was reluctant to leave.

Her mind susceptible to any stimulus, she recalled that when she first arrived to meet with Perry MacDonald, all the parking spaces were filled. That had forced her to seek one on the sixth floor, though his office was on the fourth. After six in the evening, parking spaces were plentiful, as the building's occupants had vacated them for the day.

But there were plenty of hours left, she thought. She wished it were much later, that the night would be shorter, and morning closer, so she might find release for the awful hurting in her soul.

"Okay, that's it," Perry said, pulling the trunk closed.

"Thank you," she said, forcing a smile.

The smallest of sounds echoed loudly throughout the open area. Patches of light from the open exterior let in the late day sunlight.

Perry tried to smile back at her, but sympathy lurked in the depths of his eyes and his irritation shone through. She appreciated his effort, nonetheless.

"Sydney," he said, passing a restless hand over his head, "I'm afraid I don't know what to say to make you feel better."

"I know," she nodded.

Aware that their voices carried in the hollowed space, they spoke in whispers. The intensity of his lowered voice caressed her. He was almost purring, and it conjured a sense of intimacy in Sydney.

"I don't want to leave you like this," he said, frustration hanging on the edge of his words.

She was surprised by this unpredictable man. One who sought truth with the vengeance of a wounded animal, was now as gentle and helpless as a kitten. But there was nothing disabling about his powerful body, or the way he was looking at her. Her insides softening, she could almost forget. "I'll be all right."

"Let me see a smile first," he said, giving her an example, his mouth quirking with humor, his eyes twinkling. "A real one this time."

There was something warm and enchanting about his playful mood; her defenses were melting away. "I don't feel like smiling," she said, struggling to keep a straight face.

"I know, but give me one anyway. Come on," he cajoled persuasively. "Let me see that look you give clients when you know you've made a sale and there are dollar signs from your commission in your eyes."

Just as a flash of humor crossed Sydney's face, the give-away heat of desire coursed through her. She flushed, embarrassed.

"No," she insisted stubbornly, but a smile wobbled onto her lips anyway. In a desperate attempt to resist his captivating mood, she ducked her face, leaning her head against the wall of his chest. Still, she couldn't suppress the laughter he had teased from her.

And she might have gone on laughing, just for him . . . had it not been for the want she felt as his hands came around her shoulders, spanning her back as he pulled her close to him. She could find nothing funny about the exquisite gentleness of his touch. She closed her eyes, sank closer into his bracing strength and reveled in the sensation of being one who is cherished.

His mouth next to her ear, he said, "Why don't you stay at a hotel tonight?"

His breath was warm, and there was a faint tremor in his voice as though some emotion had touched him. She trembled. "No," she murmured against his chest.

"What about my place? I have an extra bedroom. And you don't have to worry about me sleepwalking. I'll rest better knowing you're all right."

Sydney sank into him, a delicious moan slipping past her lips. Her head nestled against his chest, his heart sang a passionate song in her ear. She declined the offer by shaking her head from side to side, while silently cursing herself.

"Don't worry about me," she said, but didn't mean it. She couldn't help believing that she had been wrong to assume a familial bond was the thing missing from her life. The only thing she really missed was this feeling—a sense of being wanted and a wanting sensation—she got right here in his arms.

She lifted her head, and his face was within inches. She read the unmistakable message in the murky depths of his eyes, the lure of his mouth, the absolute maleness about him. Her heart pounded loudly with affirmation that Perry MacDonald was the most majestic, intelligent, and sexiest man she had ever met. The animal magnetism that radiated from him set a tingling current circulating through her. Erotic fantasies surfaced in her thoughts. If she wasn't careful, she would reveal all of her intimate secrets to him.

"We'd better go," he said softly.

Sydney nodded mutely, but couldn't budge. Fuddled with longing, she merely stared. She took in the line of perspiration across his top lip . . . and on his brow, the tight restraint in his expression. It intensified the feeling inside her.

"Sydney . . ."

She knew unequivocally she didn't want to leave this place where sincere emotions sprouted from within her. But the warning look that came over his face, almost apologetic, ended the moment. He would go no further than to comfort her, would not grant her the kiss that her lips craved. It was *his* law.

As one pair, they separated slowly, neither speaking. He shifted positions with her to open her car door. She got in and started the engine.

"Be careful," he said, stepping back from the car.

The pain of unfulfilled desire simmering in her, wordless, she nodded, backed out, then drove off.

"Come on Melloncamp. I don't know what the big deal is," Tomkins whined, downing a swig of bottled beer.

Friday night, and patrons with appetites for alcohol and informal dining packed The Bandana Bar & Grill. It was one of the few places in Dalston that wasn't dry, and the food wasn't bad at all. Barbecue was a staple on the menu; the smell of mesquite-smoked meat scented the air.

Tomkins and Melloncamp were sitting at the bar, two long necks before each man. A large brown envelope lay between them.

"We're not going to cut any corners on this; I don't care if the governor himself gets involved," Melloncamp said emphatically.

"This package seals it," Tomkins said, tapping the envelope. "Why don't we just pick her up, book her, and let the courts decide."

"This package doesn't do anything but put a burr in my butt," Melloncamp countered, getting in Tomkins's face. "Who sent it? Why now? I'm telling you this smells funny to me." He downed more of his beer.

"The chief wants us to move on this," Tomkins reminded him gravely.

"Yeah, and the chief will help them put a noose around our necks if we act too hastily. We're going to completely check out her story, just as thoroughly as we will everybody else's."

"I think gratitude is shading your objectivity," Tomkins razzed.

"I don't know what you're talking about," Melloncamp replied.

"Bull! Just because MacDonald saved your butt on that bump rap, you better remember that was four years ago and you paid him handsomely for his services."

"You're just in a hurry so you can get away on your vacation," Melloncamp countered. "Otherwise, I'd ask for another partner. Hey, Joe, how about another beer?"

" 'You don't know . . . what love is . . . until, you learn the meaning of the blues. . . .' "

The sultry alto of singer Cassandra Wilson wafted from inside the lakeside home, the melody a bittersweet juxtaposition to the birds merrily singing their early morning song from the trees.

The clear brown waters of the White Lagoon streamed along quietly below. Tubers had already hit the water to beat the heat of the sun, now a white blur roosting in the blue skies overhead. Save for the music, the birds, the sounds of fun muted by distance, it seemed a quiet, peaceful morning.

Wearing the borrowed, short flower-print cotton robe of her neighbor, Sydney was sitting at the table sipping coffee. A tablet opened to a lined page, notes and decorator sketches scribbled on it, lay within her reach.

Under the melancholy strings of the violin solo, she felt abandoned, completely alone in the world. No matter how hard she tried to be grown up about Jessica's distrust, the hurt lingered. In a way, it even intensified in the new day. Betrayed by the woman who had been her maternal surrogate, she saw her personal history as an empty picture in a pretty frame. She wondered how long Jessica had hated her.

Drawing in a deep breath, she lifted the mug with two hands to take a sip of coffee. It was nearly empty, and the remains had grown cold. She turned up her nose, set the mug down, knowing her disgust was not with the drink.

Momentarily suspended in thought, she wished she could remember her mother better. She retained only vague perceptions of a tenacious spirit and a happy booming voice. Though she had many pictures of Sonni-Lauren and could see they shared a much-admired smile and mercuric disposition that sparkled in their eyes, she missed a mother's arms around her, a mother's voice soothing her, a mother's wisdom guiding her.

"More coffee?"

Sydney faced her hostess, her forced smile wavering. Jasmine Moreland was walking toward her carrying a pot of coffee. "Yes, please."

She had known Jasmine two months, and found her the most quietly, self-possessed woman she had ever met. With a smooth, brown toffee complexion, Jasmine was tall and graceful. Her serenity was marred only by the touch of sadness that frequently came across her face when she thought no one was looking.

"Breakfast will be ready in a moment," Jasmine said in her soft, lusty voice as she topped the two mugs with hot coffee. "Can I get you anything else?"

Since she was into wishing this morning, Sydney thought jocosely, she wished Jasmine were her sister. Though nothing in their physical looks showed a blood kinship, she felt they were kindred souls. Like her, she believed Jasmine had secrets.

With a half-smile on her lips and a flippant note of hope in her voice, Sydney replied, "A new family?"

Jasmine laughed out before she replied. "Sorry, fresh out of those." Then the humor faded slowly from her expression. "Sydney, sometimes if you don't tell people what you want, they can't give it to you. Crystal balls and magic lamps are the sole purview of genies," she added, a quiet smile in her dark eyes.

"Is that the wealth of experience talking?" Sydney asked, also serious.

Jasmine first replied by sibilating a sigh of frustration as her shoulders drooped. "I'm afraid it's advice I know intellectually, but can't seem to internalize."

Jasmine took the coffee pot inside, leaving her fresh mug untouched. Sydney noticed the music had stopped. She wondered fleetingly if Jasmine, too, was becoming ensnared in its bluesy discourse.

Left to ponder her own wants, she stared absently out over the mildly rippling waters. The persona of Perry MacDonald permeated her being and erased the frown from her face. As if he were always there, patiently biding his time, she thought, effervescent waves of longing sweeping through her in capacious, dulcet strokes. The sensation teased her with the sense that he was a man who could fulfill all her wants.

Realizing he could have thrown her cocksure defense of her family in her face, she shuddered, embarrassed anew. They had made her look like a fool in front of Perry.

But he'd proved himself more honorable a gentleman than she would have guessed him to be. He had made no comment about that poor first impression. Rather, he'd been more concerned about her reaction than their bad manners.

She smiled warmly in memory of his invitation to put her up in his home. Why hadn't she taken him up on his offer? she asked herself. She could have been having coffee with him. A grin brightened her expression.

Chiding her mind's whimsical journey, absently, she lifted the mug to take a sip of coffee. The steam rising above the rim stopped her. Still too hot. Like Perry, she mused.

She blew at the mist over the mug, took a careful sip, then set the mug on the table. She had needed to be alone, she reminded herself. To think about her life and plan the direction it would take.

What did she want?

If she knew, she wouldn't feel so lost. *That* was not quite true. She sighed. Part of her knew exactly what she wanted; she just didn't know how to ask for it without feeling infantile. *My youngest daughter has yet to grow up.* Her father's words resounded in her head.

But how old did she have to be not to want or need the unconditional love of her family?

"Breakfast is ready," Jasmine announced from the door, balancing two plates and silverware wrapped in orange cloth napkins.

Sydney bounced up to help relieve her of one plate and a setting to place them on the table. "This looks and smells great," she said, adjusting her chair at the table to sit. Pretending mouth-watering hunger for the appetizing meal of melted cheese and scrambled eggs sprinkled with chili peppers and tomatoes, she lifted her fork to her plate.

"But you're not really hungry, and don't deny it," Jasmine said, teasing laughter in her voice. "That doesn't hurt my feelings, but eat anyway. You're going to need strength to move into your place today."

"How can I argue against logic?" Sydney replied laughingly, looking over Jasmine's shoulder. From where they sat on cushioned patio furniture, the raised deck protruding from the back of her similarly designed multilevel home was visible. A rocky vale in which towering cypress grew separated the two lakeside homes. Grateful for the reminder of what must be done, Sydney dug in heartily.

For a while, each woman ate, lost in her own thoughts. Not even the arrival of a picnicking family across the water intruded on the easy silence.

Sydney recalled meeting Jasmine while house-hunting in Westwood, a still-developing suburban area roughly eighteen miles outside the city proper. She'd stumbled onto Lagoon Boulevard, a winding street that curled into a dead end at a hill near the mouth of the White Lagoon, where the restaurant of the same name was situated.

All of the homes—summer retreats for a few of the occupants—were built on the same side of the lagoon. A peek in hers last night had shown her that the painters had finished. With only minor details to be completed, she could move in. Because neither water nor power had been turned on at her place, she had begged a bed for the night from Jasmine, who'd been more than happy to have a guest.

Jasmine, a native of Houston, was a few years older, thirty-three, and she liked to play checkers, which was what they had done until exhaustion had claimed them at three in the morning. Surprisingly, they'd both awakened three hours later for coffee.

Sydney's thoughts strayed to her reason for staying up late; she had been unable to forget her family's conduct. Unconsciously, she began to gnaw at her bottom lip while shoving food around on her plate. She believed she now knew the effect of Larry's death on each close relative.

Considering the results stemming from her ill-considered visit to his apartment, which made her a suspect in the eyes of the police, she was the one with reason to behave irrationally. She couldn't fathom their embarrassing conduct.

Her father had always abhorred airing dirty linen in public. Indeed he'd been so persnickety about proper behavior that he'd insisted she and Jessica call him Father unless they were alone. It had been a struggle to keep from making a joke out of that paternal address.

As for Jessica, she was usually like their father. One never knew what she was thinking unless she voiced her thoughts.

Still, Sydney thought disconsolately, she had never given Jessica cause to suspect her of trying to steal a man. Their ages and the qualities each found attractive in those of the opposite sex were so different that Jessica's conclusion was ludicrous.

"Stop stewing over last night," Jasmine said. "You have something more important to think about."

"Stop reading my mind," Sydney replied, chuckling as she resumed eating. She hadn't told her neighbor the whole humiliating story, and Jasmine hadn't asked, though she'd learned enough to guess the problem involved Sydney's family.

"I can't help it," Jasmine replied, "it's all over your face. Seriously though, there's something important I need to tell you." She set her fork on the side of her plate. "I didn't want to bring it up last night, for obvious reasons"—she paused slightly—"but a detective came by before you got here.

"Don't tell me," Sydney said, nettled. She was chewing her food very slowly, "Melloncamp."

"That's him," Jasmine said. "His partner was with him, but he did most of the talking. After going through the usual routine—whether I knew you—et cetera, et cetera—he asked me where I was the night Larry Daniels was killed. I told him the truth, of course, that you and I went to see *Black Orpheus* at the Esoterica Theater, and afterward had drinks at the Bandana, then I dropped you off at your father's around two and came home." She resumed eating. "Do you have an attorney?" she asked, looking at Sydney, one brow cocked.

"Perry Mason MacDonald."

Jasmine stopped chewing. "What?" she asked, amused bewilderment on her face and in her tone.

Sydney couldn't halt the smile spreading across her face, splitting it into a grin. "Perry Mason MacDonald," she said proudly as if he was her invention. "He accompanied me to the police station to give my statement." Just the mention of him buoyed her mood. She had to force herself to remain still. "I'll tell you, it was one of the scariest moments I've ever had."

"Do you trust him?" Jasmine asked.

A gentle radiance glowing inside her, Sydney returned

Jasmine's equanimous gaze unflinchingly before she replied. "With my life," she replied, wedded to the thought.

Jasmine bobbed her head insightfully, then forked a bite of food into her mouth.

"No doubt he's going to give me headaches," Sydney said. *And aches in other places, as well.* "But he's competent and very skilled. Hell, he grilled me thoroughly in his office. I never believed attorneys cared whether their clients were guilty or not as long as they got paid."

"Some don't," Jasmine quipped.

"Perry's not one of them," Sydney defended. She swallowed her food, then took a sip of coffee before continuing. "After I gave my statement to the police, he told me they have a pretty good case based on circumstantial evidence. When I think back to why I confronted Larry—now that I saw Jessica's reaction last night—I can't believe how incredibly stupid I was," she said, shaking her head, bemused. "I really can't blame the police for thinking I killed him. My own family doesn't believe I'm innocent."

"Come on." Jasmine reached across the table to squeeze Sydney's hand. "They don't believe you killed Daniels."

"No, but they think I was having an affair with him. Which is worse?" she asked, a rueful smile on her face.

"Oh, Sydney, I'm so sorry," Jasmine said.

Five

A weekend of unpacking, moving furniture around and cleaning up had left little time for self-pity. The sun rose early Monday, and Sydney felt on top of things.

She was stuck in a line of morning traffic on Nottingham Street, a pine-lined, two-lane boulevard bordered by rows of small wood-sided houses with high porches. It was a desirable location, connected with the museum and the cultural district. The original homeowners—senior residents—had vacated the area, selling out to the wave of untraditional entrepreneurs whose small operations blended with residential living.

Tapping the steering wheel nervously, she began thinking about the call she had to make before going to work. The car clock showed the time as 6:13. She had seventeen minutes to reach her six-thirty appointment.

She had done some introspection over the weekend. It had forced her to face painful truths and to make aggressive decisions. She refused to let her family's appalling opinion of her get her down. Someone else's opinion of her counted more than theirs . . . the maid who claimed to have overheard her arguing with Larry before his death.

Knowing that, an idea had come to her. She'd decided not to risk laying proof of her innocence solely at her attorney's feet, but to take the lead.

It was not ironic that she had been thinking about Perry at the time, she thought, an unconscious blush stealing

across her face. The man provided ample reason for spark-
ing her curiosity.

Just remembering their serene interlude and her body's
seditious reaction to his compassion, she blushed anew. In a
parking garage of all places! she reproved herself, shaking
her head.

The movement rerouting her thoughts, she reminded herself that it had already been her intention to be present
during Perry's questioning of witnesses. Although he hadn't
seemed displeased by the idea, she wasn't so sure he had
taken her seriously. If he had, she felt he'd have tried to
convince her otherwise. And she would have been tempted
to leave everything in his capable hands.

She knew from experience that one accommodation could
lead to another. Mindful of dominant personalities the likes
of her father and Ross, she feared slipping back into a habit
that stultified her and led to dissatisfaction—distrusting her
instincts.

Traffic advanced, and Sydney took her place before the
red light.

Last night she had placed a call to Ginna, the station's
news director to ascertain the maid's name. Ginna had not
only provided that, but her place of employment as well, a
professional cleaning service called Clean Sweep.

Thumbing through the *Yellow Pages,* she'd learned the
business opened at five-thirty for employees to pick up their
assignments and hurry to jobs, some of which required their
presence at seven-thirty A.M. She'd stayed up putting together several advertising plans, then had called the office
to set up a meeting. The owner was a woman named Kathleen Franks, who could only meet her early as she was a
worker, as well as the owner.

It being her turn to proceed, Sydney drove off, her gaze
split between the traffic ahead and to her left. Clean Sweep
was located on the opposite side of the street.

She spotted its address displayed before a house, but had

to drive another block before finding a parking space at a strip center that featured a restaurant, a bakery, and a printing shop. With less than a minute before her scheduled appointment, she hurried from the car, slipped a long jacket over her ensemble, dropped her keys in her pocket and dragged her briefcase across the front seat.

Jaywalking between traffic, she rushed to the other side and kept going at a brisk pace. An oversized blue broom, its handle stuck in the ground and its wide straw brushes in the air, designated her arrival. She skipped up the three steps at the center of the porch that spanned the front of the single-story house. Business hours and logo were painted on the blue door behind a glass screen.

She pulled open the door and walked in. A hefty, plain-looking woman with alert eyes and wearing a flower-print dress was sitting behind the desk in the converted living room.

"Yes, may I help you?" she asked politely.

Sydney opened her mouth to speak, but faltered as she heard the door open behind her back and another customer walked in. Glancing over her shoulder, she stared directly into Perry MacDonald's face. By the inclement look that came over his expression when he saw her, she knew he was peeved.

Sydney stared insipidly fearless into his gaze, feeling sensations picking up where they'd left off Friday night.

As it turned out, one of the employees had called in sick, and Ms. Franks was covering the job. It made getting out of the scheduled meeting easy, but Perry was not mollified.

She could sense his angry warmth as he wordlessly marched her back to her car, forcing her to keep up with his long-legged strides.

"Can we slow down a little?" she asked, her pace diminishing to an ungraceful canter.

Perry stopped inches in front of her, then treated her to a

glare over his shoulder. "No, we cannot," he replied succinctly.

Before she realized what was happening, he reached back to take her by the arm and pull her along. Sydney gasped in surprise. He swung his face to her, and his eyes softened transitorily with apology. Incorrectly fearing he'd hurt her, he relaxed his firm grip. The electrical sparks that shot up Sydney's arm lessened to a mellow current and bobbled like a float on gentle water within her.

During the somewhat leisurely pace he set, she stole glances at him, as if renewing her weekend-old memory. He smelled as fresh and magnificent as he looked. His rock hard brown body was attired fittingly in a camel-colored, soft suit jacket and trousers set off by a smoky brown shirt and a silk tie with triangular patterns in complementary colors.

But his demeanor didn't repel her. Rather, it elicited a reckless passion. She wondered what kind of lover he was. Slow and methodical? Or fierce and demanding? Did he ever shed the control he exerted so strenuously over his emotions? The questions alone caused tremors of rapture to catch in her throat.

They reached her car, but he still wouldn't look at her.

"I'll talk to you later," Perry said, sternly walking off.

Sydney sighed, less from relief than regret as she watched him walk away. She turned to unlock her car door.

"Have you had breakfast?"

Perry had tossed the almost-invitation at her. Sydney's emotions danced jubilantly as she stared in openmouth disbelief that her luck changed. Without waiting for her response, he guided her to the restaurant.

It was one of a chain with a French name. Like the others, it featured oven-baked breads, rich pastries and a gourmet fare. Perry chose a table for two from those set up outside. From the various coffees sold, he ordered the house brand, black, with a blueberry muffin. Sydney ordered a meatless, traditional breakfast with cappuccino. Perry stared across the table at her during the few moments they waited for their coffees to be served.

With his flinty eyes piercing the scant distance between them, she could tell the predator in him was itching for freedom, but he controlled it with supreme grace.

"Do you ever lose your temper?" she asked.

He tilted his brow, looking at her uncertainly. "Why? Do you want to see it?" he said the latter as if ready to accommodate her.

Sydney shivered inwardly. "No," she mumbled, glad that her cappuccino and his coffee had arrived. "No, I'm sure I don't."

"Is it that you don't trust me to do my job?" he asked quietly.

Sydney stammered as she looked into his uncompromising face. "Of course not," she replied. But she couldn't hold his gaze as she struggled to ignore the sensations churning within her.

"Then what were you doing there?"

"I . . . I just thought I'd . . ."

"Forget it. Let me tell you what you would have done if the situation hadn't turned out the way it did, or had I not gotten there in time to stop you. In addition to taking away the element of surprise," he said with emphasis, his eyes flashing. "Once you identified yourself, you would have gotten nothing but excuses. 'I'm sorry, but Ms. Lockhart is out in the field and can't be reached,' " he contrived a feminine voice of apology.

Sydney's mouth trembled with the threat of laughter, but his stern expression stopped it cold.

"On top of that, she would be notified that you were looking for her, after which, she would *always* be unavailable. She might even call the police and accuse you of harassing her. And with beforehand knowledge, she'd have enough time to embellish what she had already told the police."

The waitress returned with their orders. Sydney was grate-

ful for the brief respite from Perry's lawyerly lashing, which
had no discouraging affects on her emotional reaction to him.

Okay, she reasoned silently, so she'd never met a man
like him before: he was still a man, and she'd been around
plenty. Some she'd met were even more good-looking, more
powerfully built, more sophisticated. But none affected her
as Perry MacDonald. She was like a sycophant, feeding off
his sexual energy. If she planned to tag along during his
defense preparations on her behalf, she'd better learn to con-
quer her involuntary lustful reactions to him.

"Can I get you anything else?" the waitress asked.

"No, thank you," Perry replied, buttering his muffin.

When the woman left, Perry opened his mouth to start
in on her again. Sydney cut him off.

"I wasn't going to give them my real name," she said,
peppering her hash browns. "Well, I was, but my approach
was going to be of a professional nature. I got the owner's
name and called, requesting a meeting to discuss advertising
her business on WDST. While we were talking, I was going
to ease Ms. Lockhart into the conversation, saying a friend
of mine swears by her, then have them assign her to clean
my house." At his look that obviously questioned her intelligence, she said with exasperation, "I had to do something.
Don't you ever take chances?"

"No; I stopped taking chances a long time ago," he replied with a deadpan expression, his tone definite. "I don't
think my clients would appreciate such risky practices when
their lives are at stake."

The reprimand sat between them like a mighty weight.
Sydney adjusted herself in her seat in discomfort, mulling
his words.

"Well," he said in a summary tone of voice, the scowl
lifting from his expression, "I'm glad to see you gave your
interference *some* thought." He wiped his hands on the napkin before continuing. "But there's one little thing wrong
with your plan." He put his briefcase on the table.

"What's that?"

He relaxed his mandible and a furtive look filled his gaze that never left her face as he withdrew something from the briefcase. He was holding a newspaper, which he glanced at and then turned so that she could see the front page right side up.

POLICE ROUND UP SUSPECTS IN DANIELS KILLING blazed across the top fold. Sydney snatched the paper and held it close to her as her gaze flew over the story.

The article below the headline was wrapped around pictures taken of people as they were leaving the police station. Jessica was identified as the late legislator's fiancée. Her father was shaking hands with Detective Melloncamp. Lloyd Andrews looked as if he were holding a press conference, Ursula at his side. There was also a photo of the young parking attendant Roger Simmons, his toothy grin directed at the camera. Mentioned, but not shown, were Beverly Lockhart, the maid, and Hank Evans, the security guard for the Worthington high-rise where Larry lived.

The photographer hadn't missed her, or Perry. But rather than associate her with the Websters, the caption identified her as the leading suspect who'd retained the famous local criminal attorney Perry MacDonald. The camera caught them standing in front of the building, their heads together as if they were conferring.

"You're a celebrity," he said smugly.

Sydney sensed that Perry was enjoying her struggle to recapture her composure. After a long pause, during which she pretended to read the article with great interest, she drew a deep breath, forbade herself from betraying her agitation, then smiled up into his face.

"You don't look so bad yourself, Counselor," she quipped.

"Very funny," he said, but he was smiling.

"I can't believe the police suspect Roger Simmons. He's just a kid," she said, miffed.

"Until the real killer is found, everyone is a suspect," he replied dryly.

"All right, point taken," she quipped, returning the paper to him. "What's next?" she asked, picking up her fork.

"Next? You go to work and let me handle this," he answered with his facile tongue.

"Uh-uh, Counselor," she quipped, forking food on her utensil. "It doesn't work that way."

"I thought we had an understanding."

His voice, though quiet, had an ominous quality.

Sydney looked up into Perry's face. He was studying her with a curious intensity. She opened her mouth to speak, but couldn't seem to find her voice. As the silence stretched, all but their presence escaped her, and she sensed another temperament in him despite his subdued demeanor. She felt her whole being fill with waiting.

"I gotta go," he announced suddenly. "I, uh," he added rising, "I need to do something about that deposition that keeps getting postponed." He threw some bills on the table, then picked up his briefcase. "I'll talk to you later."

Sydney wanted to scream, demand his return. She watched him go, disappointment cascading through her.

The atmosphere of the inner office was relaxed. On the surface. Take-out sandwiches, sodas, and chips cluttered the coffee table.

Perry couldn't stand or sit still. He was pacing the length of the room, from the desk to the door from which he glanced into the reception area. He felt the high energy of anticipation. His heartbeat increased each time he looked into the waiting room as if he were expecting Sydney to arrive.

It had been a chore trying to erase her from his mind since breakfast. Sitting across the table from him, telegraphing insouciant innocence, he wondered what it was about

this woman—this particular client—who made him work
so hard to retain his anger at her.

He liked the curve of her mouth, the diamond-bright
twinkle in her eyes, but most of all, her inner strength. There
was also the way he felt in her presence, enlightened, flattered; a sweet tide of emotions was undulating in him at
just thinking about her.

But he had a social life, he reminded himself sharply.
There were several female attorneys whose company he enjoyed occasionally. None had drawn him toward commitment so far, for like him, they were committed to ensuring
justice. Maybe he needed to give one of them a call. After
all, even Justice had a mate in Truth.

Deciding he'd procrastinated long enough, Perry returned
to his inner office. With his tie looped around his neck, the
top button of his light pink shirt undone, he wore a fierce,
but forced, mask of concentration. His team expected the
look. They'd seen him like this before, nervous as a cat. As
if his own life were on the line. He felt it was, for the case
bore striking similarities to the one in his past. He wondered
if they realized it.

Tall, scrappy and old at twenty-five, Javier Jones was the
private investigator Perry used whenever a case required
more legwork than he was capable of doing alone. Jones was
of mixed Hispanic and African-American ancestry that
showed in the wavy black hair he wore in a ponytail at the
nape of his neck and in his broad features. He had taken up
his usual place during meetings, sitting behind Perry's desk.

Ramona occupied the couch, pad and pencil at the ready.

This was their second meeting of the day. He'd apprised
them earlier of the situation: Javier had already known some
of it as they'd spoken over the weekend. They were reassembled to review the suspects, play devil's advocate to his
theories and develop a strategy. He especially needed their
input, for already he was too involved for complete objectivity. Possessing a deep-seated intuition that Sydney was

innocent of killing Larry Daniels was not a viable defense in a court of law.

"Perry, the fight hasn't started yet," Ramona reminded him. "You'll tire yourself out before the bell rings."

"Yeah man, sit down, you're making me tired just watching you," Javier chimed in.

Obediently, Perry dropped onto the chair adjacent to the matching couch, his hands hanged loosely between his legs. "We've got to get in Daniels's place," he said. He released a long breath as he impatiently passed a hand over his head, a hint of frustration in his expression.

" 'We,' Kemosabe?" Javier chided laughingly.

Javier had been Perry's first client, when he was still green. It was by sheer luck that Javier, then a juvenile, had become a productive member of society instead of a prison inmate rotting in jail. "All right, forget 'we,' " Perry said laughingly. "But you've got to find out what ace Melloncamp and Tomkins are holding."

"I've tried, but nobody's talking," Javier replied.

"Well, you've got to try harder," Perry insisted. He sprang to his feet and resumed pacing. "We don't want them dropping a bombshell on us," he said, recalling that would be equivalent to what Walter and Jessica Webster had done to Sydney. "It's . . ." He suddenly clamped his mouth shut to listen. Sounds hinting at movement in the other room attracted all eyes in that direction. After listening intently, Perry stepped quietly to the door and saw a young man in a brown courier's uniform looking around curiously.

"Yes, may I help you?" he asked.

"I've got a package for Mr. Perry MacDonald," the courier replied, holding up a small padded envelope in one hand, the clipboard at his side in the other.

"I'm he," Perry replied.

"Will you sign here, please?"

Perry complied, and the courier released the envelope to his care.

"Have a good day, sir," the courier said on his way out.

Shaking the package next to his ear, Perry returned to his office.

Pretending to take cover, Javier looked amused. "If it's a bomb, we're all dead."

"Who's it from?" Ramona asked:

Glancing at the envelope, Perry shrugged. "I have no idea." He opened the envelope carefully, prying loose the glued ends before dumping the contents onto his desk. Crisp one-hundred-dollar bills spilled out. With Ramona at his side, he counted twenty of them. Javier whistled.

"Is there a note?" Ramona asked, staring down at the money.

Perry looked inside the envelope, then withdrew a half sheet of paper. "A contribution for the Sydney Webster Defense Fund," he read aloud.

"The hen that cackles lays the egg," Ramona pontificated.

"Yeah," Perry concurred pensively, "but who's the hen?"

"Jessica maybe? Out of guilt," Ramona offered, looking up at Perry from under arched brows.

"Maybe."

"Whoever sent it must have wanted you to be able to identify them," Javier said, "or they wouldn't have used a traceable courier. Unless, they think we're a bunch of *estúpidos.*"

Perry chuckled to himself, recalling Walter Webster's supreme confidence in his Harvard-educated school attorney. He returned the note and money to the envelope, then handed it to Ramona. "Put it away," he instructed. "Okay, where were we?"

"Naming the players," Ramona answered, returning to her seat on the couch.

"Add Ursula Andrews," Perry said as he resumed pacing.

"Who's Ursula Andrews?"

"Is she a player in this game?" Javier inquired, taking his own set of notes on a small pad.

Perry was sandwiched between the questions, queries directed at him from opposite sides of the room.

"Maybe a bench warmer," Perry replied absently, recalling the attractive woman who had turned out to be Lloyd Andrews's wife. He'd had ample opportunity to question Sydney about that this morning, but he hadn't been thinking like a lawyer then. Finding himself falling deeper under her spell, he made up a weak excuse and left before finishing his coffee.

"Hello, in there."

Pulled back to the present by Ramona's voice, Perry said, "She's Lloyd Andrews's wife. She's a flight attendant. Our client had an unusual reaction to her. And now I'm not so sure jealousy fully explains it," he speculated aloud.

"Lloyd Andrews was Larry Daniels's campaign manager," Javier said.

"She's a looker, too," Perry continued, taking a swig of soda.

Ramona cut a dubious glance at him. "Is this personal or business?" she asked.

"You know me better than that," Perry chided, then doubts boomeranged inside him, but not about his feelings about Ursula. "Okay, give me the list again."

"At the top is Jessica Webster, our client's sister," Ramona said. "It's sad."

"Naw, not sad, it's sick." Javier clucked disgustedly.

"Put yourself in her shoes," Ramona protested. "Imagine having the police haul you in to make a statement as you're about to bury the person you were going to marry, and they tell you someone close to you, a person you practically raised, was at his house before he was killed. Knowing the police, they made it sound as ugly as they could. His death was bad enough, but to learn that maybe your sister was involved with him . . . It had to be devastating."

"All that might get sympathy from a jury, if it turns out that Jessica killed Daniels," Javier countered. "But it means she would have had to know he was cheating on her in the first place."

Perry listened quietly, intently; taking in their responses. They were expressing the reactions of jurors sequestered in protected rooms.

"Maybe she didn't know who the other woman was until after he was dead," Ramona suggested.

"If that's the case," Javier said, "once she found out the police suspected her sister, the right thing for her to do was speak the truth." Looking to Perry, he asked, "You don't think she'd frame her own sister, do you?"

Arching a brow, Perry shot him a significant look. Seven years ago, Javier had been wrongfully accused of sexually assaulting a woman who was a distant cousin to him. The real perpetrator, her abusive husband, had forced her to claim she'd been raped when someone had unexpectedly called the police and equally unexpected, they'd shown up. "It wouldn't be the first time," Perry reminded him in a soft yet critical tone.

Lips pressed together in piqued memory, Javier said, "I got it covered. I can get her statement from my contact at DPD, check it out, then do a background check on the dear old sister."

Perry looked to Ramona, who replied, "Walter Webster."

"What motive would he possibly have for killing Daniels?" Javier said. "It's widely known that Daniels was on the Education Committee, and because of that, Texas College had a natural protector. Webster wouldn't dare harm the school's savior."

"But what if Daniels changed his mind?" Perry shot back. "It's no secret that the Governor wants the State Co-ordinating Board to recommend some pretty harsh changes that would negatively affect every small college and university in the state. With an enrollment of less than five-thousand students, and that dwindling, Texas College's head is on the chopping block."

"But is that a reason to kill a man?" Ramona asked. "What if Daniels couldn't get the support needed to keep the school alive? He couldn't be blamed for that. He only had one vote."

"Let's see if we can find out what moves Daniels had up his sleeve," Perry replied undeterred by her argument.

"Your good friend . . . what's her name . . . the congressman's daughter," Javier said, snapping his fingers.

"Deidre Holloway," Ramona supplied. "She was appointed to the board of Texas College this past term."

"Make a note," Perry said, "I'll give her a call."

"Okay, that just leaves the witnesses," Ramona said, reading from her notes. "The security guard, the parking attendant and the cleaning lady."

"There's one more," Perry said. Just as he was about to speak, he heard the door to the outer office open again and fell silent. He shared a look of frustration over the intrusion with Ramona, then gestured for her to remain seated as he checked it out. Reaching the doorway, Perry came to an abrupt halt. Sighting the unexpected visitor, he blinked in astonishment. "To what do I owe the honor of this visit?"

Mechanically, Sydney shoved a rate card inside the pocket of the station's colorful brochure, inserted it into an envelope, folded the clasp, then tossed the package onto a growing stack. She was efficient and at-ease with her work, yet strain showed on her face. A gamut of perplexing emotions warred inside her, bit by bit eroding the confidence and cheer which had launched her that morning.

She was in her cubicle, assembling advertising packages to mail to prospective clients. Beyond her opened door, the sales area bustled with activity, and inside her space, the station's programmed music aired. She'd spent the morning hours making calls, training Mark's girlfriend Cindy, and conferring with Bob, the production manager who also wrote advertising copy. Though no one at the station had said anything about the article in the morning newspaper, she was keeping a low profile.

She was not particularly disturbed by the article. She understood the reason behind it, she thought, examining her feelings. Even though she'd been thwarted in helping to work on her own defense, she believed she had made the right decision. While there had been no verbal agreement, she knew Perry had exacted a promise from her not to go behind his back again. Still, it was lunch time, and she could have spent the hour talking to Roger and Hank, the attendant and the security guard. She pouted.

As much as Sydney hated to admit it, she knew the real source of her dissatisfaction was not the concession. Her mind was still full of breakfast with Perry. She seriously doubted that her legal troubles consumed as much of his practice as the attention she was awarding him.

But she couldn't help but think about him, she told herself with a shrug. He played a pivotal role in her life. Not one that had to send her insides on an incipient rampage, the cynic in her protested.

Sydney stopped her rote activity to ponder whether she was transferring her need for emotional support, which one normally expected from one's family, onto Perry's shoulders. Wide and brawny, they seemed strong enough to carry the weight of the world, she thought.

Groaning under her breath, she shook her head with dismay. Proving she had killed no one, clearing her name—these were important, she reminded herself firmly. She had only to trust in his word, not fill her head with cozy allusions supplied by her imagination.

Jessica had called Jasmine yesterday to ask whether she had seen Sydney. Jessica knew about her sister's house, but

not the address. When Jasmine had lied on her friend's behalf, Jessica hadn't bothered to inquire about the location.

Sydney sighed, resigned, telling herself it didn't matter
as she resumed her task. She'd come to realize she spent
too much of her life trying to win the approval of her family—her father in particular, for she had believed she already had Jessica's support.

It seemed to her now that all she had created with her
efforts was trouble. Remembering one of her escapades, she
could laugh now, but it hadn't been funny once. With a
chuckle, she envisioned her botched attempt to surprise Jessica and her father by preparing dinner.

It was a feast to a twelve-year-old, and a challenge for
one who'd never cooked a day in her life. The pork chops
were half done, the gravy lumpy; and the rice burned, leaving a foul odor in the house. Her father was furious. He
sent her to bed and made Jessica clean up the mess. Re-
flecting on that incident, she could understand why Jessica
might resent her. Her laughter faded into a melancholy sigh.

A knock on the metal frame around the door of the cor-
rugated partition interrupted her musing and Sydney looked
up to see Debbie's big, round, fair-skinned face peek
through the opening.

"May I come in?" Debbie asked.

"Sure," Sydney replied. Of German descent as were a lot
of Dalston natives, Debbie was the general manager's secretary. She had a good working relationship with him.
"What's up?" Noticing a frown ribbed Debbie's forehead
and her blue eyes were narrowed, Sydney said, "Oh-oh, I
know that look."

Debbie stuck the folder she carried under her arm, tugged
the door closed, then faced Sydney before she spoke. "Richard called a little while ago and told me to get the last
quarter report together," she replied, laying the folder, open,
on the desk. "When I saw this, I thought I'd better double-
check with you."

Sydney stood alongside Debbie to read the top sheet. It was WDST's standard billing form, this one applied to the Daniels account. "What's wrong with it?"

"It's marked off that payment has been made, but accounting doesn't show any payment," Debbie replied. "When I asked Mark if his report was complete, he swore I had everything he did."

Sydney's face contorted into a frown of disgust. This kind of situation made her remember that the owner and general manager, Richard Frederickson, had implied that she would become sales manager because she had the best sales record of all the account execs for the short time she'd worked at WDST. Instead, Richard had made the position a graduation gift to his son Mark, who just last month had received his MBA.

She pulled her briefcase from under the desk to open it. Withdrawing a collapsible file folder and thumbing through it to the month of May, she tilted the folder so a white-tabbed manila folder tagged DANIELS slid out. She opened it so that both she and Debbie could read from it.

"Here's a xeroxed copy of the draft and my personal copy of the transaction," she explained, her finger guiding Debbie's gaze down the page. "I don't know what game Mark is playing, but as you can see, I did my job."

The door rattled as someone began to open it. Debbie and Sydney assumed innocent positions.

Mark appeared in the opening. "Oh?" he said. "I thought you were alone." He directed the comment to Sydney, his gaze taking in Debbie.

With wavy black hair, gray eyes and gangly build, Mark looked years younger than twenty-four. *And he acts like a kid,* Sydney mused, peeved by his uninvited intrusion as she returned her files to her briefcase.

"What are you two up to?" Mark asked gaily.

"My son's track team is going to California for the nationals," Debbie lied smoothly, "and we poor parents are out scuffling to pay for it. I'll be coming to you as soon as I get a pledge from our number-one salesperson."

While she admired Debbie's adroit comeback, Sydney didn't feel like being tactful. She wanted to know what had happened to that money. For an account exec, being suspected of theft was worse than being thought a murderer.

"How much can I put you down for, Sydney?"

"Fifty is about all I can spare, Debbie," she replied. "I'll give it to you this Friday—payday."

"Thanks," Debbie replied. "Mark, you want to ante up now, or shall I catch you later?"

"Later," he replied. "I promise," he added when she gave him a pointed look.

"What can I do for you?" Sydney asked casually as Debbie took her leave. Wondering what had happened to the money and how Mark was going to proceed after clouding her reputation, she was far from calm; in fact, her heart was tapping disturbingly against her ribs. Waiting for him to make the first move, she got a handful of envelopes from her drawer and set them on the desk next to the briefcase.

"I, uh, I wanted to thank you for taking care of Cindy," Mark replied as if embarrassed. "She says you're a great teacher." He chuckled, "As I knew you would be."

"Thank you, Mark," Sydney replied politely. Unfazed by his compliment, she returned her briefcase to its spot under her desk. "Is there anything else?" she asked, resuming her previous task.

"I see you're getting some packages together," he observed. "Got some clients lined up?"

"Just hawking our wares," she replied airily. "Nothing definite." She stacked about a dozen of the colorful brochures on the desk, then retrieved a handful of large white envelopes, the station's embossed red and black lettering on them.

"There is something else, Sydney, and I don't quite know

how to bring it up," he said, combing his hair off his face with his fingers.

"Just say it," she said, stilling in her task to look him squarely in the face.

"The Daniels murder," he said. His glance ricocheted about the room before landing on her face. "I understand you're a suspect."

Sydney struggled to contain the quick flare of her temper. All of Dalston knew she was a suspect, but so what? She gave Mark a puzzled look that cued him to continue.

"Well, I don't know if it's a good idea for you to be making calls on clients," he said hastily. "I mean, you represent the station and all. Not that we believe you're guilty, you understand, but Richard and I sort of talked about it—"

"You did, did you?" Sydney replied evenly. Debbie had spoken with Richard—no doubt he'd called from his golf cart—but she hadn't mentioned a word of this. It made Sydney wonder whether Mark was lying.

"Yeah, and, uh, we decided it would probably be better if you worked inside for a while," Mark replied, fiddling with his hands. "Just until this matter is cleared up. Gosh, we don't like it any more than you do. We need you out there drumming up business; you're our number-one salesperson," he added as if leading a pep rally.

"Okay, Mark, if that's what you decided," she replied. "I understand."

"I knew you would." He bobbed his head excitedly. "Just till this matter with Daniels is cleared up. Dad, I mean Richard, said it wasn't fair to take all of your accounts, and in hindsight, I agree with him, so I'm going to let you have those accounts back."

"That's nice; I appreciate it," she replied wryly, her gaze going to the envelopes on the desk. She was glad she hadn't affixed the labels yet.

"But I still want you to work with Cindy," he added, a mollifying grin on his face.

Sydney looked at him, her air chipper. "Sure, no problem," she said, with a wave of her hand. This was a good excuse to contact Perry, she thought with growing excitement. Mark had just handed her the perfect reason; she almost thanked him. "Well, there's nothing left for me to do today, so I might as well leave a little early. You got a problem with that . . . boss?"

"No, no, that's fine," he replied.

Six

Carrying her briefcase at her side, Sydney adjusted the strap of her handbag on her shoulder as she sauntered into the reception room of the station.

"Oh, Sydney. I was just buzzing your office. You have a call on line three."

Recognizing the voice of Gloria, the regular receptionist, Sydney didn't even stop as she replied, "I'm gone for the day. Take a message." Then she pushed open the door and walked out.

"Hello," Gloria said into the receiver, "I'm sorry, but Ms. Webster is gone for the day. Would you like to leave a message?"

By the time Sydney stepped off the elevator at the first floor, she had changed her mind about running to her attorney to tattle on her boss. She could handle the problem created by Mark on her own, she told herself confidently. Besides, she feared testing the strength of her resolve so soon on the heels of making it.

She would contact Lloyd Andrews, though, she decided upon reaching the lobby of the high-rise office building. She passed the fountain spouting water into a pond in which colorful goldfish swam beneath and between lily pads.

If he wasn't at Daniels's office, she thought, exiting the

building by a side door, she would call Ginna to get his home number.

Stepping out into the blazing heat, Sydney halted. Absently, she looked across the large covered parking lot. Hundreds of cars hid from the sun under several rows of long sheds.

What about her promise to Perry?

Her lips twisting into a pout, she stood uncomfortable with her quandary. Lloyd Andrews was a suspect, she reminded herself, debating as to whether or not talking to him was a breach of her word to Perry.

She really wasn't breaking her promise. The matter about which she needed to talk to Lloyd Andrews didn't have anything to do with Larry's murder. She would be on professional ground, and Lloyd would know about the draft. She was satisfied with the rational.

She would have to be careful in talking with Lloyd, though. She couldn't risk giving him the wrong impression or provide a motive for his calling Mark. Nor did she want him to alert his wife to her suspicions. It was possible she was mistaken and Ursula Andrews was not the woman she'd seen with Larry Daniels at the hotel.

She skipped down the three steps to the paved ground, heading for her car in the first row, not far away. Preoccupied with planning her strategy, she didn't notice the white van pulling off the lot onto the street.

Keys out, she reached the white Cutlass Oldsmobile that was owned by the station. It was one of the perks offered to sweeten her stay at WDST.

Noticing that all the locks inside the car were up, a frown darkened her face. It was not like her to forget to lock the car. Apparently she had, she thought, and knew the cause of her forgetfulness.

She had been in the clouds, following her breakfast with Perry. He had sat across the table from her like a caged animal, yet transmitting a sensuality that had seeped into her senses.

Sydney released an exhaustive sigh, then pulled open the car door.

She heard it with such horrible suddenness that she stopped moving instantly. Head still, eyes darting around nervously, she listened intently. Barely perceptible over the pounding of her heart, the rattling sound reverberated in her ears, as terror coursed through her.

Still, she wondered if her mind was playing tricks on her. In the broad light of day, she was in the throes of a nightmare more terrifying than any she'd ever experienced. Perspiration exuded from her pores as she stood stock-still, pinned to the spot, sandwiched between her car and the one at her back.

"Ms. Webster . . . Ms. Webster, I see we caught you just in time. We want you to come to the station and answer a few more questions."

Sydney heard the voice and recognized it as Detective Tomkins's. But every muscle in her body was rendered immobile; she didn't even dare move her head an inch in order to face him to ask for help.

"Ms. Webster, will you step away from the car, please?"

With a scream clawing to get out of her throat, slowly, Sydney's jaws worked, a hint of words on her mouth. But they wouldn't come. Not even to warn Tomkins not to come any closer.

Suddenly, Detective Melloncamp appeared in her sight over the top of the car on the other side. He frowned at her curiously, his elbow arched. She could tell he was reaching for his gun. But she still couldn't get the words out. Only her expression, which she knew showed pure fright, signaled him that she was in grave trouble. Her eyes . . . She used her eyes to say what her constricted vocal chords couldn't.

She saw Detective Melloncamp follow the descent of her gaze to peer inside the car through the passenger window.

She heard his amazed whistle, but it was still too soon for her to breathe.

"Hey, Tomkins, get the animal control people over here right away," he instructed loudly. "I don't know much about snakes, but it looks like a rattler was planning to take a drive."

"An olive branch."

A curious tension sizzled in the atmosphere. Those present were startled into silence.

Ramona was the first to stir. Rising, she gathered up some of the lunch remains as she spoke. "I'll get this typed up." Perry knew what "this" was.

"I'm going to get started, too," Javier said, heading for the coffee table. He grabbed the remaining soda cans. "I'll call you later if anything turns up," he called from the door.

Alone with his unexpected visitor, Perry noted that she didn't always wear eyeglasses. Her face was perfectly made up, and wisps of baby-soft hair outlined it, escaping the locks swept up and then twisted into a ball atop her head. Her reddish-orange ensemble complemented the earthy brown tone of her skin and caressed the curves of her full, but petite, build. Her perfume was subtle and expensive.

Perry pulled aside the chair fronting his desk. "Won't you have a seat, Dr. Webster?"

The chair was eyed and eschewed. Jessica Webster sauntered to the couch and sat in the middle of it, crossing her legs at the knee. She folded her hands over the leather purse on her lap. "Please," she said kindly, "call me Jessica, or Ms. Webster if you must. The use of the title is not necessary."

There was no disputing that Larry Daniels attracted good-looking women, judging by Jessica Webster. Yet, curiosity aside, Perry couldn't explain his lack of feeling in her presence. He felt sexually abstemious with her. The realization alarmed him fleetingly and his mind scampered to the image of Sydney. He was relieved as an enchanting bustle of sensations coursed through him, bracing his sexual identity.

"Okay, Jessica," Perry said as if her given name were uncomfortable on his tongue. "What can I do for you?" He remained standing, seemingly casual, a hand on the back of the chair.

"My father and I are usually not so rude," Jessica began hesitantly. "I want to apologize . . . for the both of us. It's not every day that we get a visit from the police, or that we're asked to go the station to answer questions. I guess in your business, that doesn't faze you."

"No, it doesn't," he replied, taking the chair across from the couch. Hands clasped loosely between his legs, he asked, "Have you extended this olive branch to Sydney? She needs it; I don't."

A look of dejection appeared on her face. Jessica sighed before she spoke. "Sydney won't return any of my calls."

"Hmmm." Perry nodded.

"Despite my father's insulting comment regarding your qualifications, I'm well aware of your courtroom successes, Mr. MacDonald," she said to cover the embarrassing silence. "I remember the case you handled four years ago involving a policeman accused of shooting a kid. You proved that another man had wrestled the gun away and had shot the kid accidentally. As a matter of fact, it was Detective Melloncamp you defended, the man who interviewed us at the station this past Friday. Actually, his partner, Tomkins," she said with distaste, "did most of the talking. He was a nasty little man filled with insinuations"—she shivered—"but I remembered him."

Perry remained wordless, wondering about the real reason for her visit. Jessica Webster, he knew instinctively, was not impulsive. Though he couldn't accuse her of condescension, she struck him as a woman preconditioned to know her place, one who never stepped out of it. Her presence was out of character.

"Apology accepted," he replied at last. Her powers of deduction were remarkable: she was right on the mark about Tomkins, even though Melloncamp was the dominant partner. But reminded of the work he'd done for the detective, he now had to consider that maybe Melloncamp, in his own way, was trying to protect Sydney. If so, Perry thought, it was not the kind of favor he needed. "What else can I do for you?"

"I know Sydney is strapped for cash," Jessica replied, opening her leather handbag. "She recently bought a house, and since we haven't seen her since Friday night, I guess she's moved in." Withdrawing a thick mauve leather billfold from her purse, she said, "But the bottom line is I want to pay her legal expenses."

Another attempt to assuage a guilty conscience? Perry wondered. "It's already been taken care of," he told her.

"Oh?" she replied, surprised.

Perry jumped on her stunned silence. "I'll bet Sydney was a handful as a child," he said casually. *You got to give a little, to get a little.*

"Handful isn't the word," Jessica replied, humored by the notion. "Sydney was downright arduous. We could hardly keep up with her, especially Father."

"That bad, huh?"

"Oh, she wasn't a bad child," Jessica said hastily, traces of laughter in her voice. "Don't let me give you that impression. She was just active. Nearly scared Father to death many times."

"I would think a parent would be grateful for a healthy, energetic kid," he commented, lounging comfortably in his seat.

"That's just it," Jessica quipped enthusiastically. "Sydney had asthma. She didn't develop it until her mother died. It was the foundation of Father's fear. The doctor said she would grow out of it, but Father's fear never diminished."

"How did her mother die?"

"A blood vessel burst in her brain," Jessica replied, her enthusiasm waning. "She was a young woman, not even thirty. It was horrible for all of us, but particularly so for Sydney. She was just four at the time and had a hard time grasping the concept of death. She just wanted her Mama, which was understandable. When the absence got the best of her, she'd suffer an attack of asthma so severe we had to rush her to the hospital."

Perry grew uncomfortable with the somber quiet and with Jessica's dispirited air. He didn't want to include her in his empathy for Sydney. "Dr. Webster," he began, then smiled at her, "I mean, Jessica, where were you the Thursday that Representative Daniels was murdered?"

Jessica stiffened, and the frown that came to her face gave her a pained look. She stalled on replying, returning her billfold to her purse, her movements jerky and clumsy.

Perry waited patiently. Because she claimed to want only to make amends, he mused, didn't mean he would miss a fortuitous opportunity to satisfy his curiosity. Later he would compare her story to what Javier uncovered, to draw a more complete picture; because right now he couldn't tell whether she was lying or not.

"I didn't come here to answer any questions about Larry's death," Jessica replied haughtily. "I did that for the police, and I don't intend to indulge in any more responses."

"You can do it now," Perry replied lazily, "or, if worse worsens, you can answer my questions on the witness stand." She didn't need to know that he had every intention of keeping that from happening.

"What do you mean?"

Leaning forward in his chair, Perry said, "Your sister, Dr. Webster, is the leading suspect in Larry Daniels's death." His tone was soft, serious, lowered to inspire fear. "This is not a class project. The possibility of the police charging Sydney with his murder is very real, I assure you."

"Sydney didn't kill Larry," she replied vehemently, her mouth taking on an unpleasant twist. "She didn't even like him. Of course, she doesn't know I knew that. Bless her heart, she tried real hard to make him feel comfortable whenever we were together."

"How do you know she didn't like him?"

"I know Sydney." She sounded confident, matter-of-fact, not smug. "I practically raised her. That's why"——she faltered, her voice lowering—"that's why I haven't been able to live with myself since Friday. I can't believe I said something so incredibly stupid to her. The only excuse I have," she said, looking at him with pleading in her big brown eyes, her hands splayed before her helplessly, "is the shock of everything happening so fast, and finally"—she clapped her hands together tightly—"coming to grips with what was not going to happen just made me crazy."

Sitting back in the chair, crossing his legs and propping his elbows on the armrests, Perry struck a nonconfrontational pose. "Where were you when Daniels was killed?"

"I was in my office at the university," she said, her tone daring him to challenge her. "I had a four-thirty appointment with a graduate student."

"What's the student's name?"

"Joanna Albritton," Jessica replied, wetting her lips with her tongue. "She didn't show up."

"Did anybody see you?"

"Dr. Gravlee, the head of the English department," she said.

"What time was that?"

"It was around five," she said confidently. "He dropped by my office to tell me to lock my door because he was leaving and everyone else had already left, so I'd be alone."

"How long did you stay after he left?"

"I waited an hour for her; it was five-thirty when I left.

I went home to rest before the party. Larry was supposed to pick me up at seven; we were going to have a light dinner first, but . . . he never came," she finished on a soft vibrato, then she fiddled with the strap of her handbag. "Lloyd called and told me what happened."

Reserving judgment, Perry hunched over, his arms resting on his thighs. "Tell me, Jessica, what was your relationship with Larry Daniels?"

Jessica looked at him, vaguely puzzled. "Larry and I were engaged," she replied in a clipped tone. "Certainly, you know that if nothing else."

The answer was not what he was trying to get at, and she knew it. Perry stared at her, on his lips a smile. Sydney may have been fooled into believing her sister needed her protection, but Dr. Jessica Walter was no hot-house flower. It was Sydney who was the innocent, believing the halls of academia were sacred and walked by honorable men and women. She either didn't know or had forgotten the bloody fights over advancement in those hallowed halls.

"What else is there to know?" he asked guilelessly.

"We set the wedding for October," she said softly. Sadness enshrouded her now, and she swallowed hard before continuing. "October twenty-fifth. My birthday."

"Did the representative have any enemies?"

"He was a politician; what do you think?" she retorted.

Perry smiled to himself. "The usual procedure for getting rid of a politician is to vote him out of office, not take his life. Otherwise, we would have too few representatives at any level of government."

A frown distorted Jessica's expression as she bit down on her bottom lip. The nervous gesture must be a family trait, Perry thought, recalling Sydney had done the same thing many times. Jessica, however, didn't look nearly as cute as Sydney when she did it.

"Point well taken," Jessica conceded. "If he did"—she

sighed, gathering her composure—"have personal enemies, he didn't say anything to me about it."

"No troubles either here or in his Austin office?"

Jessica replied with a negative shake of her head.

"Were you aware that he was having an affair with another woman?"

Questioning some witnesses had brought him a tinge of regret, but not this time. Perry didn't care about Jessica Webster's feelings. Despite denying she believed Sydney was having an affair with her fiancé, she had given someone else that impression. And that someone else also doubted her explanation of shock.

"That's rubbish," she denied hotly, her eyes flashing with outrage. "All of that talk is nothing but an ugly rumor created by jealous people who were out to tarnish his good name and to belittle all the wonderful things he did as a man, as well as a politician."

"Then why did you accuse your sister of being that other woman?"

Jessica stared at him, speechless, her brown eyes glittering with profound remorse and her mouth gaping open.

The intercom buzzed. "Excuse me," Perry said, rising to walk behind his desk. He lifted the receiver rather than speak over an open line. "Yes, Ramona?"

"I thought you'd want to know that we just got an anonymous call," Ramona replied. "Our client Ms. Sydney Webster is being transported by ambulance to Memorial Hospital."

Perry felt a tight place of anxiety congeal in his stomach. "Is she all right? What happened?" he whispered uneasily as he looked across the room to see Jessica watching him.

"It seems she suffered a heart attack," Ramona replied, puzzled.

His heart beating like a kettle drum in his chest, Perry turned from Jessica to conceal his fear as he gripped the receiver with both hands. "What?" he asked in disbelief.

"The caller gave no details, but he sounded suspiciously like Detective Melloncamp."

"I'm on my way."

The downtown park was nearly deserted. Except for a few city workers in orange coveralls picking up trash with pointed sticks, Jessica was alone with her thoughts, though none shone on her face. She was sitting on a cement bench under twin oaks whose branches intertwined overhead, blocking the rays of the sun.

Still, it was hot. A sheen of perspiration covered her upper lip, as well as her neck and shoulders, which were bare since she'd shed the waist-length jacket of her ensemble. A damp, crumpled handkerchief in her hand, she swabbed her forehead.

"Must be some heavy thinking you're doing to be sitting out here in this heat."

Jessica looked up, startled; then a smile softened her face as she gazed at the hefty, brown-skinned woman who appeared to be aged more by hard times and alcohol than the passage of sixty-something years. Wrinkles branched out from her slightly protruding dark eyes that had a jaundiced cast in their depths even when she smiled. Her name was Beverly Lockhart.

"Are you off for the day?"

Beverly looked the part of a professional domestic, a patch with Clean Sweep etched in dark blue lettering on the breast pocket of her light blue uniform. "No, just taking a break," she replied. "How have you been doing?" Her manner of speech—the cultured tone and clear enunciation—hinted at the ironies of life which had lead to her present employment.

"I've been doing okay," Jessica replied, adding, "Better. I'm getting used to it now."

"What are you doing sitting out here in this hot weather? You've got to start taking better care of yourself now."

"I just left a meeting with Sydney's lawyer," Jessica replied. "He said she's in real danger, and—"

Irascibly, Beverly cut her off. "I don't want to hear about her troubles. That girl needs a keeper, but that's not your job," she added hastily. "You've been that long enough— too long, in fact," she said emphatically. "Maybe a little adversity will teach both her and Walter a lesson."

Gently tossing back her head, Jessica chortled, amused. "They're too much alike," she said. "They would take issue with each other on the moral of a story."

"I still say you should let Walter worry about Miss Sydney."

"I wish that were possible," Jessica said, her lips twisted wryly. "But I doubt seriously that he's powerful enough to keep her from getting arrested and going to jail."

"That's not your problem. Like the old folks say, what's gon' happen, gon' happen anyway," she said, deliberately slipping into Black English. "You just keep your mouth shut. You've got more important things to think about now. If she would have minded her own business, she wouldn't be in this mess."

"You know I don't like you talking that way," Jessica said softly. "I've had to grow up fast." Quickly she added, "I'm not saying that to cause you any guilt, and my experiences have served me well in the career I've chosen. You know what it's like. I haven't survived this long without learning how to take care of myself."

Beverly stared at Jessica's profile longingly, the look decreasing the hue of harshness in her face. "I know, sugar. It's just that I know what you had to go through living with Walter Webster all these years, being his slave and taking care of his child."

"I get my rewards," Jessica replied.

"Crumbs," Beverly spat out.

"Please," Jessica exclaimed.

"I'm sorry," Beverly said contritely. "I'm sorry. It's just that I get so mad at her sometimes." She pounded the air with balled fists. "I feel it's like she just couldn't bear to see you have a little happiness in your life."

"That's not true." Jessica said wearily. "I admit thinking that myself, but"—she paused, pondering—"but I'm not sure I ever truly believed it. I closed my eyes to—"

With sudden urgency, Beverly grabbed Jessica's arm, pleading, "Leave them, Jessica, and come stay with me. Let me take care of you."

"You mean make amends?" Jessica replied softly, affectionately rubbing the hand on her arm. "That's not necessary, you know."

Beverly exhaled a morose sigh. " 'The humble pay for the mistakes of the betters,' " she quoted ruefully.

"I inherited a strong constitution." Jessica smiled proudly, squeezing Beverly's hand with gentle affection. "Everybody is not so fortunate." Wiping away the ringlet of perspiration at her neck, she added, "Before you came, I was sitting here thinking I should leave town. The idea is becoming a fixation with me. It's like I've always known it's what I had to do."

"Why should you be the one to go?"

"You know why," Jessica replied. "It's a little late, but I think I can talk Dr. Gravlee into letting me take a sabbatical." As she spoke, the plan formed in her mind. "There's some research I've been wanting to do for quite some time."

"You never said anything to me about doing research. Where will you go?"

"I'm not sure yet," Jessica replied, staring off into a private space. "But I've always wanted to study ancient Egyptian customs."

"I'll end up loosing you again."

"That's not true," Jessica said, attempting to cajole her by injecting a bright note of hope in her voice.

"I knew it was going to happen," Beverly said softly, fatalistically.

"I'll just be gone a year, and when I return—"

Beverly shot up from her seat. "I've got to go," she announced a split second before she was up and walking off.

"Mother," Jessica called after her, "when will I see you again?"

Seven

Sydney tried not to think about it, but every time she closed her eyes, she could see the snake she hadn't even gotten a full look at curled near the steering wheel in the car. Her imagination embellished the reality of her frightful ordeal.

But there was another part to her experience, as well, that she wished she could forget. She began to shiver all over again.

"You can go ahead and dress now," the nurse said, unwrapping the blood pressure cuff around Sydney's arm.

"How high is it?" Sydney asked, rising on her haunches on the narrow hospital bed. Though she was breathing easier, the wheezing had decreased and the tightness in her chest was not as gripping, she felt lethargic.

"The doctor will tell you," the nurse replied, making a note on the chart. "I'm sure she'll be here in a few minutes. It's been a light day so far," she added, tucking the chart under her arm as she replaced the blood pressure kit in the cabinet. "Don't run off now," she teased, slipping through the door.

Sydney chortled sarcastically as the nurse vanished into the hallway, where the din of hospital efficiency was more pronounced. Glimpsing white-uniformed figures passing by, she grumbled, "She could have closed the door all the way."

Slowly, she pushed herself upright, then sat sideways on

the bed, her feet perched on the bottom rail. Her top half was bare except for the lilac silk bra.

She scanned the white walled, utilitarian room for the rest of her clothes. The smell of antiseptic and medication was nauseating. On the bedside table sat the portable respirator with its long, ribbed plastic tube that she had relied upon to help her breathe when she'd first arrived.

She hadn't had an asthma attack in so long, she couldn't recall the last one. She was disgusted with herself. All it had taken to send her into a breathless fit was her phobia about snakes. She shuddered, trying to drive the image from her mind.

The doctor blamed the episode on severe stress and offered some relaxation techniques. Though Sydney doubted they would have helped in the situation she had faced, she hated her weakness.

She spotted her purple blouse and gold blazer folded neatly on the chair across the room, then frowned. Reluctant to move, she would rather lie down and sleep. But her recent trauma made that impossible. She must remember to ask the doctor for sleeping pills, or nightmares would torture her dreams.

With a resigned sigh, she slipped off the bed onto the cold tile floor. The simple act caused her to stop and take a breath before proceeding.

"Hi."

Startled, Sydney jumped. Her sky-rocketing pulse didn't begin to descend until her eyes assured her of the warm-blooded, firm fleshed figure on two bow legs who sidled through the partition opening.

"I'm sorry," Perry said. "I didn't mean to scare you." He pulled the door closed as tightly as he could before facing her again.

Though her pulse returned to normal, a melodic tension pervaded the atmosphere. Sydney felt positively aware of her nakedness, and embarrassingly so, at the swell of her bosom filling the fabric of her 34-inch size, her nipples painfully taut. But she noticed, for her eyes were locked on his—that Perry's gaze never dipped lower than her face, and the expression in his beveled brown eyes spared no gentleness.

"I . . . I spoke with the doctor," he said with uncharacteristic uncertainty.

The look on his face answered a disallowed longing in her. She could feel the tingle of her skin vibrating for want of him. When her pulse ascended again, she found herself repeating breathing instructions to her brain.

"She said you're going to be okay. She's having a prescription filled for you."

The mention of medication jarred Sydney's wits, and she became flustered. She hadn't instructed the hospital personnel to call anyone. Why was he here? She didn't want him to see her like this! She crossed her arms over her chest as if embarrassed, but it wasn't shyness she was feeling. It was confusion. For each time she saw him, a new warmth surged through her, more powerful than the last.

The sensation warred against her reason and her determination to disavow even the intimation of desire was fizzling out. She wanted to run to the comfort of his arms, wanted to curse him at the same time as her gaze took in the picture of perfect health he projected.

She couldn't believe what was happening to her. A syncopated rhythm punctuated the beat of her heart as she took in his lofty physique, the familiar animal assurance he possessed, the manly scent exuded by the pores on his dark skin. She'd just seen him hours ago: how could he have changed?

No, she amended, perplexed, a current of pure prurience flowing. How did she explain the intensification of feelings in so short a time? She knew the answer. It had been a year since she'd been intimate with a man. What she couldn't determine was whether she needed a man as much as her body professed.

Perry snapped her from her provocative pondering. Casually, as if he belonged, he sauntered to the chair holding her clothes, picked up her blouse and returned, holding it out to her. She snatched it from his hand, then glared up at him. He turned his back.

Slipping the blouse on, she said, "What are you doing here?" To achieve the note of ingratitude in her tone, she called upon her disgust with her marred health and her weakened resolve to mask the tumble of conflicting emotions rampaging through her.

"Do you want me to leave?"

"I'm dressed now," she retorted, but she felt no anger toward him. It didn't matter that he knew of her imperfection, she told herself. Their relationship was pure business. Besides—she forced herself to remember a more pressing concern that not even a sleeping pill could obliterate from her mind—someone had tried to kill her. And, she realized with frightening clarity, that someone had to have known her well. "You didn't answer the question," she reminded Perry.

"I got an anonymous call that you'd had a heart attack," he replied, his back still to her.

Looking up at him from under raised brows, she echoed his words amazed, "A heart attack?" His broad shoulders rose and fell in a shrug. "Well, it could have been that," she said lightly, but she was far from cavalier about it as she strode to the chair. "So, I guess you know what happened?" She sat to slip on her heels.

"That's why I'm here," he replied, turning to face her. "To find out. And to make sure you're all right."

With one leg crossed over a knee, a foot poised to be shoed, Sydney gazed across the room at him, subdued but her heart pounding. The tenderness in his expression amazed her. Absolutely, no one—certainly, no man—had ever looked at her like that, as if she truly mattered. Tongue-tied, she wet her lips and stared at him, dumbfounded as feelings assailed her. They were so sweet she could cry.

Instead, she gulped as she slid the shoe on her foot, then stood upright and busied herself with dressing.

"The police made good on their motto today," she said, averting her gaze as she buttoned the double-breasted blazer. "To serve and protect. Melloncamp and Tomkins came to the station to pick me up as I was leaving. I thought I'd never live to say this, but I'm glad they did." Tugging her jacket into place, she said, "Somebody put a snake in my car."

With a flippant smile on her face, she risked a look at Perry to see his entire demeanor metamorphose before her eyes. He shed his veneer of civility to stand with jaguar like rigor. His shoulders bunched into stiff muscles, and his eyes glowered from slits in the fierce frown on his face.

Immensely touched, Sydney was across the room in a flash, standing inches from Perry. With unconscious volition, she reached up to brush away the tightness in his jaw, aware only of an urgent need to alleviate his concern. The light contact altered her conscious intent, making her words gentle euphemisms, delightful as the sensation flowing through her. "Hey, come on," she cajoled, smiling softly. "I'm a survivor."

Abruptly, the door opened. A black-haired, white-coated doctor entered, and Sydney stepped back from Perry. The emergency-ward physician looked back and forth between them, then settled her irked, aqua gaze on Perry. "Excuse me," she said significantly.

Perry looked momentarily undecided. Finally he spoke to Sydney, "I'll wait for you in the lobby."

Outside, in the corridor, Perry pressed his back against the wall. He closed his eyes and drew in a deep, soul-cleansing breath, then let it out. Opening his eyes, he raised his hands before him, disturbed to see them trembling.

Mea culpa! Mea culpa! he railed at himself, annoyance stamped on his face. He knew he should have left Sydney as soon as he'd seen she was not dressed to receive him. Instead, he'd stood like a teenage boy accepting a dare, to prove he was unaffected by her except as a legal counsel to a client.

Temptation without action was not a crime, but he was guilty of lust. His insides had melted upon glimpsing her lightly roasted brown skin, he recalled, sighing raggedly. He saw proof of what he'd only heretofore guessed: her breast would fit perfectly in his hand.

And he'd discovered that a lie couldn't hold up against the truth. The truth yielded only one interpretation of the evidence: his emotions were out of control. If he didn't gather them back in, he warned himself, he could face disbarment for improper behavior. From this moment on, he vowed, he'd imposed a restraining order on his feelings.

"Hello, Counselor."

Trouble don't set up like rain; it just comes. Perry smiled feebly as he recalled one of Ramona's homey aphorisms. "Why, hello, Detective Melloncamp. It's good to see you again." He knew the detective wouldn't believe him, but he meant it—for Sydney's sake.

Despite his years in Texas, Melloncamp was still not used to the heat. He carried his customary handkerchief in one hand, and, Perry noticed with interest, a large brown envelope in the other.

"Ha," Melloncamp chortled. "I just bet you're glad to see me. Have you seen your client yet?"

"She's still in with the doctor," Perry replied, pointing a thumb over his shoulder toward a door. "I understand you were about to pick her up for further questioning."

"Yeah," Melloncamp replied, "let's find a quieter spot."

"That's okay by me," Perry replied, following the detective down the corridor toward the entrance. He tried not to stare at the envelope Melloncamp was clutching like a winning lottery ticket.

They reached the main waiting room of the emergency

section, where only a few patients remained. A couple of adults were slouched on curved back plastic chairs, looking worn out from the waiting.

Perry and Melloncamp took a position off to the side, where an opening veered off into a snack area. Tomkins could be seen beating the soda machine.

"I guess this is as quiet as it's going to get," Melloncamp said, holding up the envelope significantly. "We need to talk to your client about—"

"What's the word on Sydney?"

Interrupted, Detective Melloncamp cast a peeved downward glance at the *GQ*-dressed young man looking up at him with familiarity. Perry sized him up quickly and was unimpressed, though curious.

"Who are you?" he asked.

"I'm Mark Frederickson," the young man said it as if his were a household name. "I'm the sales manager at WDST—Sydney's boss. Who are you?"

"I'm Ms. Webster's attorney, Perry MacDonald."

"Oh." Mark stuck his hands deep into the pockets of his slacks, humbled slightly. "Has she been taken care of yet?"

Assured that Mark Frederickson was nothing more than a pesky interloper, Perry was annoyed, for he was eager to talk to Melloncamp. "Why are you here?" he asked.

"I'm concerned, that's why," Mark retorted, indignant. "From what I understand, that snake was placed in a company car."

"Is that significant?"

"You're the detective," Mark replied, looking at Melloncamp, "you tell me. All I know is we've got the used-to-be-number-one station worried. I wouldn't put it past them to do something like this. Sydney is one of the best account executives in town."

"So you think a competitor is responsible for leaving a rattler in her car?" Melloncamp inquired with a deadpan expression.

"Yes, I do," Mark replied boldly. "I also want to know what you plan to do about it."

"Where were you when the incident happened?" The question came from Perry.

Mark swung a puzzled face up to look at him. "Where was I? What kind of question is that?"

"Seems simple enough to me," Melloncamp replied.

"I don't like what you're implying," Mark said in a huff, looking back and forth between them. "I'm going to see what I can find out," he tossed dismissively over his shoulder as he walked off.

Melloncamp and Perry exchanged smirking grins.

"I'm glad you arrived up when you did," Perry said, staring after Mark. "I'd hate to have to depend on him if my life were on the line." Reverting to business, he added, "You were about to tell me why you'd gone to see my client a second time."

"Have a look for yourself." Melloncamp withdrew the contents of the envelope. "I shouldn't, but I will tell you that these were sent to us last week." Holding the contents away from Perry's waiting hand, he added surly, "I get mighty suspicious when Mr. Anonymous starts giving me things in the interest of justice."

Staring at the contents in his possession, Perry reacted too slow to conceal his shock. After surprise, a cold, congested expression settled on his face as he stared at the eight-by-ten, color photographs. There were four of them, all taken in a nightclub; Sydney's winsome smile appeared in every one. So did the lecherous-looking Larry Daniels. Jessica was in none of them.

Studying the photographs, Perry felt the rise of a character flaw he'd been unable to outgrow. He recognized the feeling as jealousy, and silently ordered himself to think. But he couldn't get past the evidence of a lie.

Sydney was provocatively dressed. The grin splitting Larry Daniels's face looked like a leer, Perry thought, a nervous tick twitching under his left eye. He shook his head slightly and shuffled the pictures for a second look, unable to control his fascination with her dress. It was a short, royal blue-sequined evening gown. Cinched tight at her narrow waist, it exposed creamy cleavage in the front and the delicate expanse of her back.

Each picture—Sydney and Larry Daniels dancing a slow drag; Sydney and Larry Daniels cheek-to-cheek and smiling into the camera's flash; Sydney and Larry Daniels snuggled side by side, his arm curled around her shoulder; Sydney and Larry Daniels toasting, their glasses touching and their gazes sweet—justified the detectives decision to question Sydney further. But none of the photographs gave Perry just cause for his reaction, he told himself.

"As you can see, Counselor," Melloncamp said, "your client lied about her relationship to Larry Daniels. I'm sure you can recall she claimed to have disliked him. But they look pretty cozy in these pictures to me."

"I trust you've had these authenticated."

"Like I told you, I've had them since last week," Melloncamp answered.

"They were delivered anonymously, you said," Perry replied thoughtfully, recalling the money sent to his office for Sydney's defense. He had guessed the sender was her father, but he had no proof of this. "Anonymous is working overtime," he mumbled to himself.

"What was that?" Melloncamp asked.

Perry sighed heartily as he shook his head. "Nothing." He was about to return the photographs to Melloncamp, then changed his mind. "Can I hang on to these for a couple of days?"

"Sure," Melloncamp replied with a shrug. "The originals are back at the station."

"Hey, Melloncamp, you got a quarter?" Tomkins called. "This stupid machine took my money."

"And you're going to feed it again?" Melloncamp replied,

digging into his pocket for change. "Who's stupid?" he quipped, tossing a coin.

Catching the coin out of air, Tomkins asked, "Has she been released yet?"

"I don't think so," Melloncamp replied.

"Can you postpone the questions for today?" Perry requested. "If she was upset enough to have a serious asthma attack, then I don't think she's going to be up to answering any questions."

"I heard that," Tomkins shouted over his shoulder, scooping up the can of soda that rolled through the slot. He popped the top, sauntering toward them. "The sooner we get this done, the better," he said, before quenching his thirst.

"Let me bring her in tomorrow," Perry replied, with deference speaking to Melloncamp. "It's pretty obvious to me that someone is working overtime to frame my client."

"Or frighten her to death," Melloncamp said.

Perry met the detective's significant stare head-on. The case was taking an unexpected turn, he mused, frown lines ribbing his forehead. He liked Mark's suggestion better, but he trusted Melloncamp's instincts. He shrugged exhausted. "Right," he said.

At that moment, Mark Frederickson strode past on his way toward the automated, sliding doors.

"Hey, what did you find out?" Detective Melloncamp called out, his mouth trembling with suppressed laughter.

"They won't give me any information because I'm not a relative," Mark replied, offended. "These are the most incompetent people I've ever seen. I'm her boss, for christsake; her family couldn't be reached! Well, if they think they've heard the last from me, they're mistaken." One more step, the doors slid open and he walked out.

Melloncamp gave in to the laugh, clapping his hands. "That guy's a jerk."

Perry concurred, but he was not concerned about a snooty pup of a boss. He had a client whose life was in jeopardy, yet she continued to welch on the truth. "Like I was saying, Ms. Webster has a phobia about snakes. It's what brought on the asthma attack."

"Yeah, that's what the doctor told us," Tomkins said. "But I'm not convinced she didn't place the snake there herself. We're waiting to hear from the animal-control folks to find out whether or not it was poisonous."

"Aw, come on, Tomkins," Perry rasped.

Tomkins countered, "Who else would know about her phobia?"

Jessica Webster's name instantly popped into Perry's head, but he remained silent, mindful that silence was golden. Maybe the detectives knew something he didn't. He caught the tail end of the shushing look Melloncamp shot at Tomkins, who donned a goofy expression, and they became closedmouthed.

"Don't worry, Counselor;" Melloncamp said, "we're going to do our job thoroughly and by the book."

Damn! Perry thought, concealing his disappointment. "What about my postponement?" he asked.

"Yeah, well I guess," Tomkins said, shifting his position. "All right, MacDonald. Tomorrow morning, bright and early."

"I'm due before Judge Merriweather in the morning," Perry replied. "Can we make it the afternoon, say around two?"

"Ouch."

The gold watch band's links caught in the hairs of his wrist and caused Lloyd's hand to jerk, spilling drops of clear liquid from his drink onto the plush gray carpet. Unconcerned about the spill, he took another swallow of what remained in the glass.

Standing at the floor-to-ceiling picture window, Lloyd Andrews gazed down absently onto the street eleven floors

below. A few pedestrians scampered along, eager to escape
the torrid heat; traffic was light as the lunch crowd had
already returned to their cool offices to watch the clock for
another two hours or so before quitting time.

At hearing the outer door open, Lloyd took a handkerchief from his pocket, wiped the bottom of the glass, then
set his drink on the black baby grand piano. A woman's
heels clicked on the marble tile floor of the foyer as he
brushed his fingers together for want of a towel.

His gaze passed over elegant and expensive furnishings—
the color scheme black, aquamarine and white—to where
Ursula stood, poised in one of her designer pantsuits, the
cranberry one that picked up the reddish hue in her divine
brown skin.

"Where have you been?" he demanded accusingly. "Your
flight came in four hours ago."

"Well, I guess you checked, so there's no use belaboring
the point," she replied.

"Damn it, I asked you a question!"

Ursula sauntered into the living room and dropped onto
the plush green leather couch, setting her airline bag on her
lap before she replied. "Lloyd," she said with forced patience, "if you're going to be suspicious every time I leave
the house, maybe I should leave permanently."

"Don't threaten me again, Ursula." He took a menacing
step toward her. "There's never been a divorce in the entire
history of my family." Shaking a finger at her, he added.
"And there certainly won't be one here."

Ursula feigned a yawn, patting her lips lightly. "Oh, yeah.
I forgot your political aspirations." Projecting utter bore-
dom, she set the bag from her.

"Politics aside," he replied, "a man can only take so
much."

"That works for a woman, as well," she retorted, stretching an arm along the top of the couch as she crossed her

legs. "You think I don't know why you've been acting like an ass for the past six months?"

"How do you expect me to act?" he rasped belligerently. "My wife, the woman who vowed to be mine truly and only, can't keep her drawers on except when around me."

Ursula snorted. "That's your own guilt talking," she said. "Larry's dead now. You're free to go to her."

"What are you talking about?"

"Who?" she corrected, uncrossing her legs to sit on the edge of the couch, hands clasped together. With mocking sweetness and batting her eyelashes, she said, "I'm talking about the illustrious, wonderful, Dr. Jessica Webster, the little black southern belle. As if you didn't know." Disdain etched each word.

He smacked his tongue to the roof of his mouth with disgust. "You don't know what you're talking about," he declared, reaching for his drink.

Ursula rose from the couch. "You've been in love with her from the beginning." She sauntered toward him. "Only Larry moved faster."

"Now I know you're crazy," he said tiredly. He turned his back to her and resumed staring out the window as he sipped his drink.

"Give me a divorce, Lloyd," she pleaded softly. "Let me go, so you can go to her."

"Drop it, Ursula," he ground out quietly.

"She's pregnant, you know."

Lloyd whirled, spilling the remains of his drink on Ursula's clothes. She jumped back, voicing an insult.

"What?" he demanded. "What did you say?"

Seeming to take perverse delight in his shock, Ursula brushed herself off and looked at him, a sugary-sweet smile on her face. "I guess you didn't know," she said smugly, indolently shrugging her shoulders. "Is it your baby?"

Eight

It could have been a cold day in hell for all the warmth she felt, Sydney thought. Perry had grown distant upon her release from the hospital. She didn't know why, but wouldn't inquire.

"I'll get someone to deliver your car later," he said.

"I'm never going to drive that car again," she replied vehemently. "They can burn it for all I care."

Except for that exchange, intermittent instructions on the route to her house had been the extent of the conversation between them during the thirty-minute ride.

Perry was already deeply embedded in her senses, but he was not her top priority at the moment. For once—a miracle—she could ignore him. Her mind was congested with doubts and fears, and it seemed a construction crew hammered inside her head.

"My place is the last one on the left," Sydney said. She pointed to the cantilevered house of weathered wood, limestone and glass situated between Jasmine's similarly constructed home and a sloping hill covered with new grass, weeds and baby trees.

"Looks like you have company," Perry observed as he turned onto the circular, descending driveway.

Sydney had already seen the patrol car. Gray with blue lettering, it was parked on the street blocking the address post at the edge of her yard. The instant she saw him, a tiny mewl of relief escaped her. In a gray uniform, with a gun holstered at his waist, he swaggered from the tree-lined sidewalk leading to the front of the house like he owned the place.

"Stop!"

Perry brought the car to an abrupt halt, and Sydney jumped out the car and strode across the yard to meet the security guard halfway. In his mid to late twenties, with big biceps and a chest that made his tight-fitting uniform strain, he looked like a bronzed warrior.

"Good evening, Ms. Webster," he said politely, removing the shades shielding his dark eyes from the sun.

He wasn't particularly good-looking, but he had a competent manner about him. "Hi, Nick," she replied. "Are you just getting here?"

"No ma'am, just leaving," he replied. "I checked out the place as you requested, and everything looks fine."

"Thank you so much," she said with a grateful sigh, offering her hand.

"Oh, you don't have to do this," he said, noticing the two Lincolns she'd placed in his hand.

"Please," she said, walking off, "have something cool on me." She hurried back to Perry's car still idling, and got in. "Okay, keep going," she said.

"What was that about?" he asked, driving on.

"I called the security company from the hospital and requested they send someone to check out my place," she replied. "I wanted to make sure there were no creatures crawling around."

Perry brought the car to a slow stop under a brick portico in front of a short porch and a wooden door. Getting out, Sydney strode toward the door, key in her hand. Despite her growing headache, her heart danced with excitement. Aside from Jasmine, Perry would be the first guest in her home.

She unlocked the door and beckoned him to follow. They entered a darkened area, and a four-step stair took them up to a hardwood landing that branched off into several corridors surrounding the stairway that curled up from the center of the house.

Holding her breath, Sydney crossed the landing and stepped into the sunken living room where the light coming through the sheer curtains over the picture window revealed a homey elegance.

Shades of blue abounded. Powder blue in the living room, a rich royal blue for formal dining and electric blue in the kitchen area. The artifacts, paintings, rugs, and photographs had been chosen with care and their ancestral value was evident, as was the dramatic appeal of the wood furnishings.

Perry was a cool shadow in her wake. He moved constantly, never pausing to compliment her skillful decorating. She deemed him a meat-and-potatoes man like her father.

Two steps down into the sapphire blue den, she pulled open the adire-clothed curtain to reveal an ensemble of African head masks in the bay window at the center of the back wall. Peeking between those one could get a splendid view of the rock-pebbled earth edging the lake roughly forty feet away. To the right and nestled in the far corner a buckish Bambara-head decoration sat atop a glass cabinet filled with more African art.

At the opposite side of the rectangular-shaped room, a wine rack rose behind a bar spanning three-fourths of the wall. An elaborate entertainment system was at its right, aligned with a wood table that had a pedestal base and octagonal top. Around it were four swivel armchairs upholstered in a beige velvet accented by a white diamond pattern.

Still no reaction from Perry. When he did speak, the words were not what she had expected to hear.

"It appears your family underestimates your capabilities."

Sydney frowned. "What do you mean by that?"

"I won't make that mistake," he said before setting himself on one of the three matching wood-framed sofas placed about a large, low coffee table with a glass top. It held at least a dozen small pictures in variously styled and colored frames.

Sydney thought she heard him tag "again" on to his cryptic comment, but she said nothing. Turning her head, she glimpsed him as he shrugged out of his suit coat, folded it neatly and laid it across the back of a sofa. His shirt showed wrinkles from his day long labors, but it didn't take away from his masculine appeal.

Now that one threat had been resolved, another seeped into her thoughts, making itself at home with her headache. Despite Perry's closed expression, she felt a certain tiny glow of cheer.

"Can I get you a drink?"

He looked at her as though she'd offered him a joint, and Sydney emitted a disgusted tsk. She considered his indifference to her well-being a contributing factor to her discomfort. She wanted to be held and coddled, to hear promises of happiness, even if they were lies, she thought disappointed, recalling his solicitousness at the hospital.

"No." Unlocking the briefcase on his lap, he said, "We need to talk."

"About what?" she asked, rubbing the back of her neck.

"Make that, I need to ask questions and you need to answer them," he said looking up at her with a sidelong, emotionless gaze.

"Oh, it's like that, huh?" she replied, rolling her eyes skyward.

Perry didn't reply, except to "get situated," she noticed with amusement as she unbuttoned her jacket. She knew he would get around to explaining the thorn in his paw when he got good and ready, though right now he was behaving like a totally unpredictable bear. She just hoped she could hold out that long.

She tossed her jacket onto the adjacent sofa, then sauntered about the room, rolling her head around on her neck.

"Where is Jessica's mother?"

Sydney froze, then slowly sauntered to the window and leaned against its sill before returning his look. "Jessica's mother?" she asked warily, wondering if he was trying to throw her off guard with this inquiry.

"Yes," he replied, a legal pad on his crossed leg and a silver fountain pen in his right hand. "Is she alive?"

"Jessica's mother died before I was born. I've only seen pictures of her, wedding pictures that Daddy let Jessica keep. I haven't even seen them in years."

"Do you know anything about her death?"

"Just what I remember overhearing when I was little," she replied. "I think Jessica's mother was an alcoholic."

"What about your mother?"

The frown on Sydney's face deepened. "What about her?" she asked defensively. "Why are you asking these questions?"

"How did she die?"

"She had an aneurysm."

He seemed to notice the gaggle of photos on the table for the first time. He scanned them critically, then selected two for closer scrutiny. "Is this her?" he asked, looking back and forth at the pictures in his hands.

"Yes," she replied hesitantly, still puzzled over his motive.

After a moment, he said softly, "She was a beautiful woman."

"Thank you," Sydney thawed a bit. She relaxed against the sill.

Replacing the pictures, he asked, "Have you heard from your sister since Friday?"

"No."

"A lie, a truth," Perry said pensively.

"Are we done with the Q and A?" she asked, running her fingers through her hair.

"What do you know about Ursula Andrews?" he shot back in reply.

Sydney shifted uneasily, remembering he'd once pointed

out how she could have misinterpreted the evidence supporting Larry's philandering: she wasn't sure Ursula was the other woman. And she wasn't up to Perry's backdoor approach to interviewing. She was already sensing a crack in her fragile shell of composure.

"Sydney . . ." Perry coaxed.

She wet her lips with her tongue before she spoke. "She's Lloyd Andrews's wife," in a matter-of-fact tone of voice.

"What do you know about Ursula Andrews?" he repeated in a quiet, stubborn tone as if undaunted by her evasiveness.

"Perry, can't we put this off for a little while? I really don't feel up to talking about any of this," she implored, her shoulders drooping as she let her hands drop limply to her sides.

She tried to assess his reaction, but she couldn't focus under the intensity of the pain in her head. She sensed that his control was deteriorating, but ignored the warning sign of utter silence due to the fierce need to massage her temples.

Under-the-breath curses came from him, then, "Doggone it, I've had enough of this!"

The shout captured her full attention. Her hands stilled at the sides of her head, her mouth fell open in puzzlement as her gaze locked on him. In one lightning quick motion, Perry was on his feet, a blur of yellow heading for the table. The pad missed, slipping over the side to become a mat as he stepped on it, then kicked it out of his way.

In stunned trepidation, Sydney probed his face, candid bewilderment in her wide-open eyes, her pulse pounding. She had seen him upset before, but not like he was at this minute, his anger a scalding fury. As before, she wasn't afraid of the promise of violence he projected, and she wondered why.

He was across the room in a flash, pinning her to the windowframe at her back. He just stood there, tall and enraged. Fractious, in a temper, he let his oblique brown eyes maul her like claws. She licked her lower lip, struggling to remain calm before the storm.

"For someone who claims to want to aid in her defense," he snarled down at her contemptuously, "you've got a helluva way of showing it. I've felt like a damned dentist with pliers, trying to extract the truth from you."

"Perry, I swear I haven't lied to you." She swallowed hard, wringing her hands together, nervous and confused. "Not since that first time," she amended weakly. "I don't know what you're talking about."

Perry helplessly flung his hands in the air. There was something finite about the action, and it made her feel suddenly weak and vulnerable.

"Forget it. I don't know why I bother. Get yourself another attorney, Ms. Webster. I quit."

As if incapable of moving, Sydney stared after him, watching as he gathered his things together to leave. Her heart was hammering, her breathing was ragged, her thoughts were racing dangerously. Though contrite about her uncooperativeness, what with the headache, the events of the day, the horrible suspicion growing inside her and the threat of his abandonment, Sydney felt herself sinking into a deep pit of purgatory.

"I don't get it," he said bitterly fed up. Tossing things back into his briefcase indiscriminately, he added, "Detective Tomkins is ready to lock you up and throw away the key, and you're helping him do it. I don't know who you think you're protecting. Or if you're thinking at all," he added, snapping the briefcase shut.

Alarm rushing along her spine, Sydney dashed across the room to him. "Perry," she exclaimed anxiously. "Wait a minute, will you?" she beseeched.

Their hands met at the handle of the briefcase. They were inches apart, their gazes locked as if they were suspended in a tableau.

The animal in him locked up, Perry stared down at her,

his wrath under control. Though residual anger shone in the depths of his gaze, it came from an emotion born of hurt. She couldn't bear it if he just walked out, not just on the case but her life. She was ashamed of having taken advantage of his trust when he was the only one who believed in her. Her family didn't. Hell, she wasn't even sure they liked her.

"You think I haven't realized that the person who knows of my reaction to snakes has to be somebody I know well?" Her voice trembled, her eyes were liquid bright. "There are only two people in this city who qualify," she said, despite the threat of tears that clogged her throat. "And how"—she paused, her voice catching—"how do you think it makes me feel to suspect a member of my family of trying to kill me?"

A beat of silence, then the doorbell rang. Neither moved. Anxious with waiting, Sydney saw a spark of indefinable emotions flash across his eyes before he lowered his gaze to where her hand was still clutching the briefcase handle alongside his.

"Aren't you going to answer that?" he said tightly.

Slowly, she released the handle, her eyes never wavering from Perry's face.

"Go on," he said gently. "We still have things to talk about."

Sydney exhaled deeply, relieved; then she turned and walked from the room. Heading for the front door, she accepted that she needed Perry MacDonald. Not only because of the case, nor was she simply drawn to the raw sexuality he exuded. It was the sensitivity he hid so well that attracted her. He made her be honest with herself, more than she had been willing to do on her own.

On looking through the peephole, her pulse leaped and she shuddered when she saw who it was. Larry Daniels's death was tearing her family apart, she thought sorrowfully. She had never been more ashamed in her life, for even thinking, not to mention voicing to Perry the horrid admission. He must think her family completely dysfunctional.

Silently, she begged God's forgiveness and opened the door. "How did you find out where I live?"

"Sydney Lauren, there's very little you do that I don't know about or can't find out," Walter Webster replied matter-of-factly. "You look terrible; your eyes are bloodshot." He peered into her face. "Why didn't you call me or Jessica?"

"Call you for what?" She secured the door.

"From the hospital," he replied gruffly. She turned, surprised and looked at him. "I called the station, and some woman told me what happened. I happen to know Dr. Celia McCracken who attended you."

"What did she tell you?"

"Only that you had been rushed to the hospital in an ambulance for an asthma attack," he replied. "I'm sure there was a lot more, but she wouldn't say, so I came to see for myself. Have you taken your medication?"

So, he didn't know, she thought absently, wondering whether she should feel guilty for the sense of relief she felt. "Daddy, I'm fine," she replied as she walked off, leaving him to follow her at will.

"I'll bet you haven't been taking care of yourself," he said to her back. "You know you need to eat when you take that medicine, or you'll only make yourself feel worse. And you need to stay out of this heat."

Reaching the family room, Walter Webster stopped in the doorway. His expression hardened with disapproval as he spotted Perry casually sitting on the couch. "I see why you didn't call any of us," he said, his mouth set in an unpleasant twist. "I guess I shouldn't be surprised."

Neither man spoke to the other. With an air of arrogance, as if he rightly belonged, Perry returned her father's hot stare. Sydney was glad for his presence, but she wanted to strangle him for exacerbating the already tense situation.

"Father," she said, ignoring his mood, "can I get you a drink? I have your favorite brand in the cabinet."

"No, thanks, Sydney Lauren," he replied, exasperated. "I want you to come back home where we can take care of you. This place is too far. If anything happens to you—"

"I told you I'm fine." Sydney flashed him a steely look. "I can take care of myself."

"There are some things about Mr. MacDonald you should know. I'm sure he didn't tell you," Walter Webster said, directing a snide look at Perry.

"Would you like to take a seat, Father?"

Irritation deepened the frown on Walter Webster's face. "Sydney, I absolutely insist you find someone else to represent you. Mr. MacDonald just won't do."

"And why is that?" she asked placatingly.

"He has a record," Walter Webster replied. "A police record."

Her father was a pro at making her second-guess herself, Sydney thought, but she suppressed her incipient surprise. Despite his often infuriating habits, her trust in Perry was unwavering. In her crazily shifting world where emotions swung back and forth like a pendulum, that was the only thing she was sure of. A sidelong glance at Perry told her he hadn't moved. He offered no defense, and she expected none. The fact that he was a licensed attorney settled the matter.

"Nobody's perfect."

"You would entrust your life to a man who is no better than the hoodlums he represents?" Walter Webster argued. "Did he tell you about his forays with the law? Did he tell you he went to jail as a juvenile for murdering an old man? Hummph, I'll bet he didn't."

Sydney shook her head, amazed. "Father, I think you'd better go," she said, tiring of the intrusion. "Perry and I have a lot of things to discuss."

"I didn't think I raised you to be a fool, girl," Walter Webster shouted angrily.

"Come on, I'll walk you to the door." She smiled with forced patience, taking him by the arm to usher him out.

Walter Webster grumbled, argued every step of the way. She blocked out the sound of his voice, wondering why she hadn't done it before rather than let him chip away at her self-confidence.

They reached the front of the house and she opened the door. He stared at her stubbornly, as if about to refuse to leave. She leaned into him and kissed his cheek. His look of surprise made her realize that her Father, in his own way, did indeed love her.

"Thanks for stopping by to check on me, Daddy," she said with heartfelt sincerity.

"You're going to regret this, Sydney."

Maybe so, but not for the reasons you think I will, Sydney thought, closing the door as he walked off. On returning to the den, she found Perry was not where he had been sitting. Noticing the opened door, she sauntered out onto the wood landing and looked up on the raised deck, a half level above.

She spotted Perry fiddling with something on the patio table. His profile filling her gaze, she let herself wish for a second, or two. Though it was hot out, it was a different heat that warmed her as she stared at him with longing.

He finished whatever he was doing, then stood by the rail, looking out over the lagoon, a long neck in his hand. He had rolled up the sleeves of his shirt, revealing the well-toned muscles in his arms. She didn't even have to guess now, she mused, the rest of the thought speaking to her the awakened feminine sensibilities.

He must have sensed her presence, for he looked down to where she stood. The expression on his face told her everything she could hope to know.

"It's completely up to you," he said.

Those weren't exactly the words she'd wanted to hear, but he was again the man whose presence she relished. Walking up the stairs, she said, "What's up to me?"

"To retain me as your lawyer."

Standing but inches from him, Sydney could barely find her voice, so strong was the undertow of desire coursing through her. Nor could she tear her eyes from the wiry black hair revealed on his chest1 now that his shirt was unbuttoned.

"I'll understand if you don't want to."

Perry spoke into the quiet, his voice sizzling with suggestion. His gaze never left her face as if trying to gauge her truth, and looked even deeper into her.

"I thought I'd already retained you."

Irrelevant now, words ceased to be passed between Perry and Sydney. Neither seemed aware of the playful sounds made by the gaggle of youths skipping along the bank below the patio. Or the carefree hilarity of tubers floating on the lake beyond. The tension between them was almost reverent, and each attended it silently.

In Perry, emotions warred. The pleasant ones—almost lascivious in nature—threatened to override the not-so-pleasant, though sensible, ones. Finally, he broke the quiet.

"Your father was only half right," he said, somehow getting the words out. Memory of the grief he'd caused G.G. could still nauseate him; Walter Webster's vindictiveness hadn't. He swallowed before continuing. "But I suspect he knew what he was doing."

Despite her bold assertion, Perry thought, looking at her kindly, he couldn't help but believe it had been a purely rebellious gesture against her father. If she dropped him tomorrow, he deserved it. But not because her father had dredged up his shameful history.

Walter Webster had come in and seen right away what he himself had failed to notice, Perry railed silently. Staring into her face, he saw the strain visible in the dullish hue of her eyes, the pinched set about her mouth. She simply had not been up to the grilling he'd put her through. He had even used her health to persuade Melloncamp and Tomkins to postpone *their* questions.

Reaching out, he grazed the side of her cheek with his knuckles; her skin was soft as velvet against his touch. He saw the pulse beating in her throat, the sensual descent of her lashes as her lids closed. Raptly attuned to the nuances of the bliss in her expression, he, too, closed his eyes and reveled in the moment of shared glory, feeling a great accomplishment in bringing her delight.

When he opened his eyes, she was staring with longing at him, and he felt an eruption inside him, as if hot lava spewed through his blood. Looking, wanting, yet knowing he dare not touch was cruel punishment.

"Come eat," he said, his hand slipping down to capture hers. "Your father was completely right about that. You need rest, not my badgering." He escorted her to the table.

As if short-winded, she asked, "Oh, what have we here?"

Perry pulled back a chair. "I raided your refrigerator," he chuckled. "You don't keep it stocked, but I did find a brown bag with some goodies in it."

"Last night's leftovers. They were to be today's lunch," she said, looking over the platter of cold chicken, carrot sticks, and bite-size squares of wheat bread. "Only I was in such a hurry, I forgot to take it to work." She went straight for the tall glass of iced tea.

"Well, eat up now," he said.

"I can't manage all of this by myself. Aren't you going to have some?"

"Eat what you can, then I'll leave so you can rest."

"What about the questions you had?"

None of them seemed so important right then. He chuckled ironically. "I've decided to save them for another time."

"Wait a minute," she rasped warningly, her brows lifting in ire. "You get all riled up, make a big deal about my lying to you, and now you say it's not that important that it will keep? Is that what you're telling me?"

His hands rose as if to ward off further attack, but he laughed, exclaiming, "All right, all right. Just in case you felt that way," he said, walking to the other side of the table, "I brought the pictures out." He lifted an envelope from the seat of an adjacent chair tucked under the table. "You're not eating," he said, opening the clasp.

"I am." She took a bite from a chicken leg.

Perry spread the pictures out on the table. "These are why Detectives Melloncamp and Tomkins wanted to talk to you today. By the way, we're scheduled to meet with them tomorrow afternoon at two."

Frowning up at him, she asked, "This is what had you so upset? I've got the whole roll of pictures. I can put my hands on them right now." She pushed up from her seat.

Staring after her with egg on his face, Perry slapped his forehead. "Aw, man," he said repeatedly. He snatched up his beer and took one swallow, then set the bottle on the rail, his conscience lashing out at him.

Seconds later, Sydney raced back up the stairs carrying a red leather-bound photo album. Catching her breath, she opened it on the table. "Be my guest," she said, then she resumed eating.

Perry eased into the opposite chair and began looking through the photo album. It looked as if more than one roll of film had been shot on that occasion. Unlike the photos he'd gotten from Detective Melloncamp, Sydney's album contained plenty of Jessica, including shots that captured her and Larry, as well as the three of them together. Jessica looked absolutely stunning in a colorful African ensemble, complete with headwrap and matching shoes. Larry looked the same regardless of his companion in a photo. But if he hadn't seen it for himself, Perry would never have believed Jessica was capable of exuding such joy and love.

With a niggling suspicion at the back of his mind, he gathered the photos he'd gotten from Melloncamp and placed them alongside Sydney's. He frowned, recalling what

Jessica had said about Sydney trying real hard to hide her dislike of Larry. Looking at both sets of pictures, he knew that Jessica had spoken the truth.

Perry looked up at Sydney who was pretending to enjoy her cold meal. With an apologetic look on his face, he said plaintively, "I am deeply sorry."

Pointing a drumstick at him, the expression on her face playful, she replied, "Okay, but don't let it happen again."

Perry joined her in laughter, but his faded as humiliation taunted him. It hadn't been just the thought of Sydney's lie that had kept the fire of his anger alive, it had also been jealousy. The photographs of her and Daniels together had been engraved in his mind, and he'd been unable to overcome the feeling that he'd been betrayed.

Compelled to confess his guilt, he realized he had stopped acting like a lawyer and had behaved instead like an injured lover. His vow of emotional detachment was meaningless as he stared at Sydney, trying to gird himself against the customary turn of his heart as it flip-flopped in his chest. There was but one option left him.

Closing the album, he said, "Maybe your father was right. Maybe you would be better served by another attorney."

Nine

Sydney felt an instant's squeezing hurt. She dropped her lashes quickly to hide it from Perry. "Maybe you're right," she said softly, "but I never took you for a coward."

She rose quietly from the patio table and sprinted down the stairs and into the house. The threat of tears stinging her eyes, she wiped their corners and sniffed. With a tired sigh, she took a step and then another traipsing aimlessly from the family room to the living room.

Her insides were roiling in the way they had on occasions when she was trying to win the approval of her family. In the aftermath, whether she won or lost, she was fatigued, then disgruntled. And she swore never to do it again.

If all it took was her father to dissuade Perry, she thought bitterly, then he wasn't worth the bother. She was tired of fighting to get what should have rightfully been hers. Or, as in Perry's case, what she'd paid for.

"Sydney? Sydney, where are you?"

She didn't answer. She waited for him near the landing between the front door and the living room, blaming herself for her disappointment in him. She had disregarded the danger signs posted over her heart. In her head whimsical notions of a perfect man lingered, then settled in. She knew that was not possible, the perception not plausible. There were no perfect men in real life, and lasting emotions took a long time to build, she reminded herself solemnly.

"Sydney?"

She looked across the distance to where Perry appeared in the hallway, and her heart reacted immediately to his presence. He stood hip-cocked, his left arm bent and the hand extended palm up, a studied look on his lean, dark-skinned face. In spite of the rueful set of his mouth and the pain befriending his gaze, there was an inherent strength to his face. She remembered her first impression of him and smiled inwardly, deciding her second one had been far more accurate. Long broad nose, lips moderately thick, his was certainly an appealing face, she thought, a softness invading her senses.

She felt a pluck of longing to see him smile, then shook her head chidingly. Their inevitable separation at hand, she lowered her gaze and retreated, one step down into the living room. "Since we have nothing further to discuss," she said, her back to him, "you might as well leave."

"I realize that," he replied, sounding resigned, "but I don't want to go without your hearing the truth from me."

Sydney turned, her gaze roving the length of him. Despite his hooded expression, she sensed a vulnerability in him. "You don't have to tell me if you don't want to," she said softly.

"I know. I've already rationalized it to myself. After all, I'm a licensed attorney, board certified in criminal law. That should speak for itself." His mocking smile held no amusement. "But I'd rather you hear it from me; then you can make a more informed decision. You may find I'm not the ma—the attorney you need," he said.

Sydney wet her lips with her tongue. "All right, Perry," she told him, taking a seat on the long velvet couch.

Perry stepped down into the room, his hands in his pockets, and stood in front of the picture window. Withdrawing his hands, he placed them, clasped together, under his chin in a pensive pose. He opened his mouth to speak, but no words came, and he dropped his hands to his sides, then sighed.

"I was fourteen and full of myself," he said at last, a hint of self-derision in his tone, the accompanying chuckle mirthless. He stuck his hands in his pockets and schooled his body to remain still.

"I was raised by my great-grandmother from the time I was eight," he added as an aside, thinking that at fifty-two she was already too old to care for an energetic boy. "I called her G.G. She kept house for an attorney named Clark Bishop, so I had a lot of unsupervised time. I was a handful, but we got along fabulously, except during the summers when she dragged me to Bible School. But I put my foot down that summer; I wanted to hang out with my buddies, Gary and Lewis. They weren't bad, but when we got together, well . . . suffice it to say, we were true to our youth," he said, a half smile on his lips at remembering mischief.

He put the window squarely at his back, gazed into a private space over her head as if in splendid repose. His magnetic appeal tugged at her senses before she drew her wandering attention back from distractions. She fixed a neutral look on her face.

"I needed money for something and we didn't have it. Options were few. There were no summer-job programs for youths."

"What did you need the money for?" she asked.

Perry grinned sheepishly before he spoke. "New clothes to wear to a dance." They both laughed. "Not just any old dance, mind you, but a Jack and Jill social."

"And of course, your Sunday best just wouldn't do," she said, tickled.

"No, they wouldn't. So, I went out to find a way to earn some money."

Sydney raised an interfering finger. "I forgot to ask . . . what was her name?"

"Stephanie. Stephanie Austin," he admitted with a chuckle.

Sydney merely bobbed her head amused, then squirreled

deeper into the couch. She had intended to remain dispassionate while hearing his story, but lulled into relaxing, she was soon mesmerized by the myriad of emotions he revealed in his voice, his expressions.

"I went to old man Isaac." He pinched his bottom lip between his teeth, a nostalgic look in his eyes. He grinned then, adding, "He was an eccentric old buzzard. I asked him if there was anything I could do for him to earn some money."

She could tell he was slipping back into the past, his expression changing from fond to flippant to fierce.

"Joe Isaac was an eighty-one-year old widower, who lived in a shack of a house with a rickety fence around it, along with a mutt named Daisy. He had hardly any grass around his yard because of the junk he collected, and he was always talking about the good old days. I had to endure a lecture on the sad state of young black men," Perry said tiredly, quoting: " 'no jobs and no potential; they should all join the Army.'

"Finally, he agreed to pay me for straightening up his yard. Man, I was so proud of myself." He seemed to be cherishing the memory. "I started early one morning and worked like a dog all day until I finished."

"And? Did he pay you as promised?"

"Oh yeah, he paid me all right," Perry chortled, cynicism in his tone and expression. "It was a financial lesson I'd never forget—set your fees up front." Then as if laughing at himself, he said, "He paid me five dollars, and threw in a lecture on the value of money."

Sydney whistled.

"I was so mad." Perry shook his head. "My buddies ribbed me good. How was I going to buy a suit and dress shoes with five dollars?"

"So what did you do?"

"Besides get madder and madder?" He smiled. "I let this

guy named Horace talk me into loaning him some money to buy a bottle of Boonesfarm."

"Oh, no," Sydney exclaimed laughingly.

Perry sighed. "I was stupid, I admit it. Horace was twenty, a big man on the block." He said this mockingly. "I didn't notice at the time, but he fit Mr. Joe's summation on the condition of young black men to a tee. He lived at home with his mama and five brothers and sisters, had dropped out of school, had no job and held court on the corner. So, here we are, Gary, Lewis, and me, drinking wine with Horace and listening to him tell us how unfair the world was to black people. As a prime example of how the white man prohibited us from helping each other, he talked about Mr. Joe. Said he was a wealthy old man, even though he lived like a bum. Horace seemed to know quite a bit about Mr. Joe . . . including, where he hid his money in his house."

Sydney's eyes widened, apprehensive with fear for Perry. "Horace talked you into confronting Mr. Joe about your money?"

Perry nodded, obviously ashamed as he shook his head. "Yeah," he whispered. "Horace had called me a sucker for letting Mr. Joe treat me worse than a slave. And the guys were still teasing me about my meager earnings. That cheap liquor made sense of what Horace had said. I knew I should have gone home. Damn"—he shook his head—"I had the worst headache. But I couldn't let it go." Scowling, he shook his head determinedly. "I went back to get the money I'd rightfully earned," he declared, defiance in his tone. "Gary tried to talk me out of it. He went home, so that left me and Lewis, who was supposed to stand watch while I went inside. I later learned that a car had driven by and scared Lewis off."

"So you were alone and didn't know it," Sydney surmised, her tone full of foreboding.

Perry nodded. "I should have realized something was not right when Daisy didn't bark. After Mr. Joe didn't answer,

I went around to the back door. It was open, so I went in. I heard the TV coming from his bedroom and figured he was watching it. When I got to his room, he was lying across the bed, his head hanging over one side, his feet hanging over the other. I didn't think anything of it."

"That Boonesfarm was in your head," Sydney interjected, but she could tell he didn't hear her. He was back in Mr. Joe's house. Beads of perspiration lined his forehead, and the tempo of his breathing picked up. So did hers.

"I called out to him, but he didn't answer. I kept going until I got to the room. I stumbled on the lamp that was turned over on the floor. I just picked it up and kept walking to the bed. That's when I saw what the disarray meant. Blood was oozing from a big gash in Mr. Joe's head. I touched him, you know, shaking his shoulder to wake him up. I guess my mind refused to believe my eyes," Perry murmured absently, his eyes dazed. "When I pulled my hand back"—unconsciously he looked at his raised right hand—"it had blood on it. I took off, running, and didn't stop until I was home.

"That was the worst night of my life." He whistled tensely. "G.G. heard me come in, but I headed straight for the bathroom to wash the blood off. I took a shower and a bath"—he snorted—"then went to bed and lay in the dark, reliving everything over and over. I don't remember when sleep came, but the police were knocking on the door the next morning. They took me away in handcuffs. They grilled me all day and finally let me sleep that night. They wouldn't even allow me to talk to G.G.; I just knew if I could explain it to her, she would make them understand I was innocent. The next morning, Mr. Clark Bishop came. By then, I had been booked and damned near convicted of killing Mr. Joe."

Perry inhaled as if emerging from deep cold water, then shivered, shaking his head as if to remove the memory.

Sydney sighed with relief as if she herself had suffered the experience. "You must have been scared out of your wits."

"The courtroom was worse," Perry said. Wholly returned to the present, he now spoke matter-of-factly. "They brought in countless witnesses who put me at the scene of the crime. Even my own friends Lewis and Gary had to testify against me, reciting what they believed was the truth about my intent in going to Mr. Joe's. To the jurors, the judge, to almost everyone, the conclusion was obvious. They were ready to put me away for good.

"It was on their faces. They felt sorry for G.G., a decent, hardworking black woman struggling to raise her great-grandchild because his own parents didn't know how to be parents. She had done the best she could. Since she'd failed, the law was going to step in and take over. . . ."

"What happened?" she inquired when he became silent.

"Clark Bishop hit the prosecution so hard they didn't know what had happened to them." A broad smile came to his face. "He used what he had in the way of evidence and offered a different interpretation of the crime to make up for what he didn't have. The man was a genius."

"And when you grew up, you wanted to be just like him," she said, smiling proudly because he was.

"Yes, but I'm not there yet," he added as if cautioning her. "So now you have it." There was entreaty in the arch of his left brow.

If he thought his past would make her want him less, he was grossly mistaken. The story of what had shaped the man heightened her admiration of him. A burning sweetness seemed to come alive in her.

"I think Ursula Andrews was the woman I saw with Larry at the hotel that day," she said. "I'm not positive, mind you, but the height and the hairstyle were familiar."

Instead of going home after leaving Sydney, Perry was returning to his office. The pressure of his vow weighing on him, he needed a moment of quiet to get his thoughts into perspective.

He drove up the ramp in the parking garage of his office building and parked in his reserved space near the elevator. Proximity was necessary for quick departures and returns when he was in court.

Heading for the elevator, he recalled having given Sydney the abridged version of his exoneration. What he hadn't told her, he recalled on the ride up, was that every night of the time he'd been arrested—in late June and on through August—he'd feared his lonesome cell would become his permanent home: At the time, Dalston didn't have a separate building for juveniles.

Nevertheless, the disclosure, the remembering had served a purpose. It had restored his focus on what was important. An added plus was that she'd gotten a real sense of what could happen if she didn't cooperate. And he didn't mean just by answering his seemingly off-the-wall questions.

He hoped he never lived to regret rescinding his decision. Only a fool proceeded with defeat in his path.

Perry opened the door to the reception area and pulled up, surprised, when Ramona hurried into the room from his private office.

"I know it's late, and I wasn't even sure you'd come back today." She spoke quickly and in a whisper. "I figured we'd just hang around until after I finished typing a couple of letters." Before he could ask, she added, "That's Carl Glover sitting in your office." She pointed a thumb over her shoulder.

Frowning, he followed its direction to see the back of the man slumped in a chair before his desk. "Glover? Glover?" he repeated absently. Taking the cue as a sly smile spread across her face, he said, "Your boyfriend," and chuckled softly.

"Remember, I told you a little about his troubles with his daughter," she prompted.

Nodding, he replied, "Yeah, I remember."

"Well, it all hit the fan." Ramona elaborated. "She got picked up for shoplifting. Do you feel up to talking to him, or should I reschedule?"

"Where's the daughter now?"

"They're holding her in juvenile detention," She looked toward the other room, then added, "He's at his wits end."

Perry could have kissed her for delivering a surefire elixir for what ailed him. Work was his weapon against the enemy of emotion, he thought, thinking he'd use it to take his mind off Sydney. "I'll talk to him now and see what we can do." He took one step forward, then angled to look back at Ramona. It was just a hunch, but he hadn't yet reached a stage in Sydney's case where he could afford to overlook any possible clues. "What astrological sign falls in October?"

Without a second thought about the strange request, she replied, "What date?"

"The twenty-fifth." It was to have been Jessica's wedding day, he recalled.

"Scorpio," she answered. "What's your sudden interest in astrology?"

Proceeding to his office, he replied thoughtfully, "A snake."

The room was compact, with a cluttered look that was enriched by the cultural identity of the owner, Roscette Merrill. A woman with a warm brown complexion, lightly dotted with reddish freckles, was bedecked in a gold African-print caftan, tiny gold earrings piercing her ears.

"Can I get you another glass of lemonade, Mr. Jones?"

"Yes, please," Javier replied, handing her his empty glass. "I'll be right back."

Javier stared after his hostess, a short, round woman full of vitality, blond highlights winking in the sandy brown hair she wore in a short natural cut. He was sitting on the

couch in the living room of her southwest Houston home,
Samsonite luggage resting on the white carpeted floor in
front of the brick fireplace at the center of the side wall.
The growing shade of late evening was visible through the
picture window at his back.

As she returned to the room, he asked, "When are you
leaving?" He nodded toward the luggage.

"Tomorrow afternoon. My husband and I have been planning this trip for a long time. I can hardly believe we're
going."

"Thank you." Javier accepted the glass of lemonade and
took a long swallow, then set the glass in the coaster on
the coffee table.

Mrs. Merrill settled herself in the comfy armchair adjacent to him. "Tell me, just how bad is the trouble Sydney
is in?" she asked, drawing up her legs into the chair.

"Falling under suspicion for any crime is pretty bad in
my book, Mrs. Merrill," he replied. "I assure you, however,
that she has retained one of the most successful criminal
attorneys in Dalston. Mr. MacDonald is very thorough,
which, as I explained to you over the phone, is why I'm in
Houston."

"Okay, what information do you need from me?" She
seemed eager to cooperate.

"Background information. I'd like to start with Walter
Webster. How well do you know him?"

"Huh," she snorted, as she rolled her eyes. "Let me count
the ways."

A dewdrop fell. It landed on the tip of Sydney's nose.
She chuckled. It seemed the closest she'd come to laughing
this past week, she mused, pedaling upward.

With the mist of morning on her face, she had the newly
paved, winding street to herself. It was shortly after seven.
The sun was barely awake, the temperature a pleasant

eighty-nine degrees. From the forest of trees on her left came fragrant air that lifted her mood.

The ten-speed was a remnant from her time with Ross. They used to ride the bayou trail that wound through the southwest Houston neighborhood where they'd lived in the house left her by her grandmother. But a sentimental journey was not on her mind this morning. She was following doctor's orders. Or trying to.

Sleep had been impossible. Each time she'd closed her eyes, Perry and a snake had appeared in her dreams.

For sleepless hours she had tried to assign significance to the nightmare in which Perry fought the snake that struck at her viciously. One interpretation of it led directly to her bed—with Perry in it.

But she knew that he, for all his many moods, would not cross that line. It was as comforting as it was frustrating. She was tempted to rescind her choice of him as her attorney, to be able to pursue a more satisfying relationship, for she was sure he felt some attraction for her.

As proof of that, she recalled the fierce tightening of his face when he'd thought she had lied to him. And even more telling was his profound look of relief when she'd initiated the renewal of the discussion he had begun. The way he'd jumped in told her he was as reluctant to quit as she had been.

Just thinking about these telling instances brought her joy, the sensation spreading out from within to fill her. It tempted her to contemplate letting him go just to get him.

The road twisted sharply upward before her. Leaning forward and gripping the handlebars, Sydney pedaled harder; the steep climb demanded it. She would have sworn she heard *Take a chance!* singing in the breeze as she sped forward.

The street curved, and rounding the bend, she wondered whether she was deluding herself.

* * *

Perry hurried into his office, looking haggard and tired. He carried his suit in a garment bag, the hand holding it resting on his shoulder; the gray workout tee shirt he wore was damp from his haphazard rush from the gym.

Ramona was sitting behind her desk, talking on the phone.

"Yes, I'll tell him," she said. "Thanks for calling." Hanging up, she looked at Perry skeptically. "Must have been some night."

"I don't even want to talk about it," he said, passing a tired hand across his face. Nothing had worked—reasoning; a long, cold shower; several beers gulped at the ice-house where he'd spent most of last night shooting pool; not even the strenuous workout at the gym, which had left his muscles achy and sore. Nothing seemed to dissolve that other ache, or the astonishing realization he'd come to.

"There's an envelope from Javier on your desk."

Ramona's voice drew Perry from his distraction. A perplexed frown came onto his face. Javier was to have gone to Houston to do a background check on the Websters, since Sydney was born in that city and had lived there half of her life. "I thought he was supposed to be in Houston."

"He is," she replied. "Apparently, he had someone drop it in the overnight chute."

Perry relaxed his guard. "Okay," he said, passing a hand across his mouth. "You got that brief typed up yet?"

"You won't need it. That was Merriweather's office on the phone when you walked in. There's been a switch; your hearing has been moved to two this afternoon."

Perry bit off a curse, and the phone rang.

"Hold that thought," Ramona quipped laughingly as she answered. "Good morning, Perry MacDonald's law office. . . . Oh, morning, Ms. Webster, how are you?"

Perry's eyes widened. He got right in Ramona's face, shaking his head. "Tell her I'm not in," he whispered vehemently.

He was down to his last resort—out of sight, out of mind. He was hoping it would provide the sanctuary he sought from thoughts of Sydney Lauren Webster. He was in turmoil over the questions she had him asking himself, and found his answers even more unsettling.

"I'm sorry," Ramona replied into the receiver, staring at Perry, puzzled, "he had an early court appearance. Is there anything I can help you with . . . ? All right, I'll be sure to tell him you called." Replacing the receiver, she asked, "What's wrong with you?"

"Nothing." He exhaled in relief. "I've got something else to do."

"Are you sure nothing's wrong?" she directed at his back.

"I'm sure," he said, continuing on into his office.

"Is Sydney Webster still our client?"

Perry growled her name under his breath, imitating the irascible tone her father had used. In reply to Ramona, he slammed the door shut behind him.

"Good morning, sir; gonna be here long?"

"Are you Roger Simmons?" Perry asked as the parking attendant in white shirt, navy bow tie and dark slacks opened his car door.

"Why, yes, sir," the gangly youth replied.

Perry had known exactly what to do with this moment of free time. He'd been tempted to call Sydney—only because of Ramona's incessant prodding—but had held off. After meeting with his recalcitrant new client Lindsay Glover, he'd come to the Worthington, a twenty-story high-rise apartment building that looked like an ostentatious hotel.

"Hello, Roger Simmons; my name is Perry MacDonald." He placed his card in the young man's hand. "I'm the attorney representing Ms. Sydney Webster in the Larry

Daniels murder. I'd like to talk to you if you have time to answer a few questions for me."

"Sure thing, Mr. MacDonald," Roger replied excitedly. "I've never talked to a lawyer before. And I thought this job was going to be boring."

"Is there some place where we can talk?" Perry asked, looking around.

"Well, I'm on duty now," Roger replied. "But if I park your car, you can ride with me and ask your questions then."

Roger Simmons was a funny-looking kid. He had buck teeth, a wide smile and big ears that seemed even bigger due to his short hairstyle. Though small in size, he had to be at least sixteen, and Perry would guess that he possessed a hardship-case drivers license. He seemed a pleasant young man.

"You're pretty fast on your feet," Perry said, being complimentary as he walked around the car to reenter from the passenger side.

"I try to be." Roger slid under the wheel. "This car sure is a nice ride. I've always wondered how fast it would go. Most folks here drive Lincolns, Towne Cars, and Cadillacs." He looked at Perry with a hopeful sparkle in his blue eyes.

Perry buckled his seat belt. "Okay; be my guest," he said, one hand on the dashboard.

Roger gunned the engine, then spun off, burning rubber on the short drive into the underground parking garage.

It didn't take Perry long to discern that Roger Simmons didn't have anything to add to the story he had given the police. He was hoping his luck would improve with the security guard, Hank Evans. As he walked inside the cool lobby, he noted the large chandelier that lit the open area with green marble walls and flat gray carpet. Antique-looking furniture was set up between the two elevators.

"Can I help you?"

The question was polite, the tone wasn't. Perry spun to his right to see a man emerge from a side room. He looked around for the hidden camera, counted one over the entrance, was positive there were more. "Yes, I'm looking for Mr. Hank Evans." He already knew he was talking to the security guard by this man's blue suit and guarded demeanor.

"Whose looking for him?"

"Perry MacDonald," he replied, pulling out a card from inside his coat pocket. Hank took the card, studied it an awfully long time, then offered to return it. "Keep it," Perry said. "You never know."

"What can I do for you, MacDonald?" Hank replied, unmoved.

"I'd like to ask you a couple of questions about Larry Daniels."

"He's dead."

"I'm representing the woman who's suspected of having a hand in that," Perry replied. "Sydney Webster, Daniels's would-have-been sister-in-law."

Hank mulled the request, then turning, said, "Come into my office."

Shortly after he began the interview, Perry sensed the guard was holding back information. Hank perched on a corner of his desk, seemed to have an inflated perception of his power. Perry was tired of dancing with him.

"You can face jail for lying to the court," he bluffed.

"But I ain't in court now, am I?" Hank replied belligerently.

He'd tried it the civilized way, Perry thought, recalling the ammunition Javier had provided. Now, he'd go for the jugular. "You like to take pictures, Hank?" he asked disarmingly. "I hear you've got quite a collection."

Hank uncoiled like a snake about to strike. "Hey, I don't take them pictures no more," he said hotly.

"Hmmm," Perry replied, rubbing his chin thoughtfully. "I wonder if your employer, a very staid and proper company, I hear, knows about the kinds of pictures you enjoy taking."

Eyes narrowing and face puffing up, Hank said grudgingly, "What do you want to know?"

"Whatever you can tell me about Larry Daniels."

His lips twisting into a sour expression, Hank said, "All right, you want to know about the great black hope. I'll tell you. Daniels was a gambler." Following a snide chuckle, he added, "Among other things."

"Oh?"

"When people thought he was in Austin, chances are he was either upstairs with some broad or playing poker."

"Who were some of his buddies?"

Hank hesitated for a second, staring ponderously at Perry before he finally spoke. "Mr. Montcrief, for one. You know, the corner banker."

Perry's brow flew up. "You mean the drug dealer?" he asked, amazed. Montcrief, as he was simply called, was the local community banker who had branched off to provide the African-American community with other services they either couldn't afford or couldn't attain legally. Unfortunately, these services usually led to their detriment, and his.

"He was that, too," Hank replied sarcastically. "He and Daniels were high-school chums."

"Did Daniels owe him any money?"

"I wouldn't know that; I was never invited to play, just sneak 'em in and out of here, every once in a while," the guard replied.

"Who else did Daniels play with? Poker I mean."

"Some little snot-nosed white guy; I didn't get his name." Snidely, he added, "Looks like his mama still wipes his nose."

"Can you describe him?"

"Long face, black curly hair, big-shot attitude. Dresses like he just stepped out of that fancy men's magazine."

"GQ?"

"Yea, that's him—*GQ*." Hank chortled unimpressed.

The description fit Sydney's boss, Mark Frederickson. "Did Lloyd Andrews play with them?"

"I don't know. I never saw him there. Mr. Andrews lives two floors up, so there's no way to tell."

"The Andrewes's live in this building?" Perry asked himself aloud.

"Yea. He and his wife are on the eleventh floor."

Either of them, Lloyd or Ursula could have gone to Daniel's place unseen, Perry mulled. "How often did Jessica Webster visit Daniels? You are able to distinguish Jessica Webster from Sydney Webster?" he asked pointedly.

"Anybody who ever seen both of them could do that," Hank replied with a snort. "The one he was going to marry, Jessica, was a snob. Now her baby sister," he said, his tone lifting in approval, "she was something else. Nothing like the other one. She was friendly, always spoke. It's like listening to an angel." Lifting his hands in a gesture of holding something between them, "And she has the cutest little . . ."

Yes, he was well aware of Sydney's estimable anatomy, the dynamic attributes of her personality, and the effects the mere thought of her had on him, Perry thought. He felt the familiar sensual prelude creep upon his flesh, into his bones. Struggling against the growing hardness of his body, an unconscious frown crept into his expression.

Hank cleared his throat and dropped his hands. "I can tell the difference."

"How often did Sydney Webster visit?"

"Hmmm," Hank muttered as he thought about his reply. "About three or four times, I guess. I remember at the close of the legislative session Daniels threw a small dinner party. She came for that. But there were about seven or eight other people. Then, a couple of weeks before he was killed, and of course, like I told the police, she was here that day, too."

"Except on the day he was killed, did she ever visit him alone?"

Hank shook his head. "Not to my knowledge."

"Did Daniels have any other visitors that day?"

"None that I saw, but that's not to say he didn't," Hank replied.

The walkie-talkie on the desk buzzed, and a woman's voice came through the static. "Hank, can you get up to Mrs. Woodrow's room, please?"

The guard picked up the instrument and pressed a button. "What's up this time, Sally?"

"She swears someone has been in her apartment; her lingerie drawer is mussed," Sally replied laughingly.

"All right, I'm on my way." To Perry he said, "I gotta go. The woman is a pain, but she's a paying customer who tips well."

"One more question, Hank," Perry said. "How did you sneak people in and out for Daniels?"

"Parking garage, service elevator."

Leaving the Worthington, Perry headed for Clean Sweep, hoping to catch Beverly Lockhart. He wanted to get what he believed were minor players out of the way, so he could concentrate on the major ones. Unsuccessful in ascertaining the places she had been assigned to clean, he'd worked his way up the list.

"I stopped by the university and your secretary told me you weren't in. Since I was in the neighborhood, I figured I might as well stop by."

"And what . . . catch me by surprise?" Walter Webster replied, flicking up an inquiring brow.

"No. Simply to catch you, Dr. Webster."

"Quite frankly, Mr. MacDonald, I'm wondering what took you so long. Come in."

Said the spider to the fly. Perry followed Walter Webster into the study of his home.

"You don't like me, do you, Mr. MacDonald?" Walter Webster asked. "You think I'm too hard on my girls."

You no longer have girls, Perry thought, but he remained diplomatic. "I'm not inclined to judge parents when I myself have no children."

Walter Webster angled his body to look sidelong at Perry, amusement in his expression. "Maybe I should be more careful where I put my foot, eh, Mr. MacDonald?"

"It's your foot," Perry said.

"Please," Walter Webster said graciously, gesturing toward the couch, "have a seat."

Perry accepted the offer, but took the comfortable chair he remembered from his first visit. Walter Webster was at the portable bar across the room. He returned to sit on the couch, drink in hand.

"Tell me, Mr. MacDonald," he said casually, "was it your juvenile escapade that influenced you to go into law?"

Perry smiled politely, thinking Walter Webster had a very low opinion of him. He knew instinctively the high-powered administrator hadn't gotten to his position without cunning—and that his personal life was not at issue. Control was. "Where were you the evening Larry Daniels was killed, Dr. Webster?"

"Awww," Walter Webster exclaimed, pretending disappointment, "still not old enough to recognize the importance of repartee. I see I forgot my manners." He pushed himself up. "Can I get you a drink before you leave, Mr. MacDonald?"

Ten

"Thanks, Ramona. Just tell him I called." Sydney was unable to keep the disappointment from slipping into her voice.

She closed the portable phone and set it on the patio table beside her, folding her arms. It was Thursday morning. She hadn't seen nor heard from Perry since Monday, despite repeated attempts.

She and his secretary were becoming quite the phone buddies, she reflected, irritated and unhappy. She really had nothing significant to pass on to him, but that didn't lessen her sense of abandonment.

She had believed that something wonderful and unique had happened between them when he'd shared his past with her. That he trusted and respected her as much as she admired and trusted him.

With insight, she now realized that trust was what had been missing from her relationship with Ross and her family. Whatever their reasons, they couldn't or wouldn't entrust her with their love. She wondered whether some flaw in her explained their emotional miserliness.

She didn't want to believe she was wrong about Perry. If she didn't know any better, she decided, flustered, she would think he was avoiding her on purpose.

She shook the myopic muse from her head as if to clear it, deciding to get dressed. The lethargy from the medication had worn off, and she was raring to go. She refused to just sit around the house all day doing nothing, the second one off with pay Mark had so generously given her. Jasmine had gone to work, and the domicile Sydney had created with such care seemed lonely and cold.

It had never felt more like a home than when Perry was present, she thought, her eyes misty and a rivulet of desire streaming through her. Although his time here had been short and rife with tension, he had belonged.

He'd call when he had something to report, she chastised herself. Though her pessimism continued to grow, she hoisted herself up from the chair. The best she could do was go on with her life and just put him out of her mind.

Right! declared her skeptic self.

She could no more block him from her thoughts than she could erase the memories of their times together. Just thinking about him fed her craving for him and kindled the flame spreading through her like liquid heat.

Maybe she should drive to his office and wait to catch him in the parking garage.

"Coward," Ramona exclaimed, rolling her eyes at Perry.

"Prudent," he snapped back. "Besides, she doesn't want anything, and I don't have time to sit and chitchat."

"You may have the stamina of a sprinter, but you can't run forever," Ramona predicted.

"Says who?" he retorted over his shoulder.

Laughing, Ramona asked, "Where can I reach you?"

"Going to talk to Lloyd Andrews at Daniels's old office," he replied, as he sauntered out the door.

Perry looked across the small cramped room at Lloyd Andrews, who was standing by the air conditioner, one arm resting atop the now quiet window unit. This was the last room in the suite of offices Larry Daniels had maintained in Dalston.

"Lloyd," Perry said hesitantly, as if embarrassed, "I hate to ask you this, man, but I have to." He was actually experiencing no discomfort. Just the opposite, his insides were on the alert for reactions that could help distinguish a lie from the truth. He was sitting at an angle, with his legs crossed, on a hard wooden chair in front of the scarred desk.

"Sure, Perry," Lloyd replied. "I know you've got a job to do."

"Was your wife having an affair with Larry Daniels?" He had no evidence to support the question, just a gut instinct based on Sydney's suspicion.

Lloyd's eyes flickered wide in surprise, then dulled as if he were painfully offended. "Aw, not you, too," he rasped, disappointed. "Come on, Perry man."

Perry watched him emotionlessly. If such a rumor had been going around, then Lloyd had had ample time to perfect his response. Though not an elected official, the man was nonetheless a politician.

"If I have to ask it in court," Perry replied, his expression firm, "I will."

"I still resent the question." Lloyd glared at him sidewise, his hands on his hips. "Larry Daniels was my best friend. We go back to college."

"That would make his betrayal all the more painful, wouldn't it?" Perry replied solemnly.

Sydney would have sworn she saw Perry's car driving off as she had turned onto the street facing the African-American Professional Building. Entering the cool lobby, she decided it was her imagination playing tricks on her, and she saw no reason not to proceed with the plan she'd conceived the day she'd stumbled upon the detestable passenger in her car.

It was an old, red brick building that had had a facelift. Immediately visible were an art gallery, pictures and sculptures visible in its glass window, and a bookstore featuring a display of volumes on the right.

She looked around for the listing of tenants and found it on a side wall. It was alphabetical. She searched for *D*. Larry Daniels's Dalston office was on the third floor.

Sauntering toward the elevator, Sydney was struck suddenly by a bout of nerves, a twinge of conscience telling her that she was committing a breach of her promise. If Perry had returned her call, she could have apprised him of what she planned; but he'd kept her wholly in the dark as to what he had done or was planning to do. Which could be construed as an infraction, as well.

Annoyed, she punched the button, and the rickety old elevator jumped into action, the car stuttering down to the first floor to receive her. It arrived noisily, and she stepped on, directing her thoughts to how she was going to broach the subject with Lloyd.

Still dealing with residual frustration over Perry's behavior, she whispered, feigning utter innocence, "Was your wife having an affair with Larry?"

No, seriously, she chided herself. Squaring her shoulders and pasting a professional-looking expression on her face, she decided to start by requesting a copy of the record of the money paid to WDST. She would explain that she usually kept one for her own protection, but had forgotten this time to get it. Then, while he was searching his files, she would subtly shift the conversation to Larry.

The elevator delivered her to the third floor safely, and she stepped off onto what appeared to be a new deep red carpet. Most of the doors along the poorly lit corridor were closed, each marked by stenciled letters identifying a company. She read them off, passing the Main Street Travel Agency, Good Times Entertainment and TechTronics Computer Repair before reaching the end of the corridor where the official seal of Texas was emblazoned on a door with an opaque window.

Sydney turned the knob and entered the anteroom. It was ultra quiet. Behind the counterlike desk on the wall hung a stately, oil portrait of Larry Daniels. She knew he'd been tall, several inches over six feet, and of medium brown complexion. With his lithe physique and rust-brown bedroom eyes, there was no denying his rakish good looks.

She almost felt sorry for him, then remembered what a miserable lowlife he was. Still, thinking about what he'd meant to Jessica, her hostility waned.

She took a restorative breath and rerouted her thoughts to her purpose. She knew someone had to be in the office somewhere because the front door had been unlocked.

"Hello," she called out, heading toward the opening that led to the back of the suite. In the rooms on both sides of the narrow hallway the only inhabitants were packing boxes. Midway along, she heard voices. The words were indistinguishable, but their tones were unmistakably intimate.

She debated whether to call out or go back and then return, making lots of noise. As she turned, she heard a woebegone cry, "Oh, Lloyd!" and recognized the voice instantly. Startled, she wondered what Jessica was doing here.

She involuntarily advanced another step, and soon was close enough to peek into the last room on the left. A man's back was visible to her, his hands in front of him. She readjusted her position for a different view, and a woman— she knew it was Jessica—came partly into view. It looked as though Lloyd was holding her hands to his chest, his chin lowered so that it touched the top of her head.

"I've spoken to him, too. But it doesn't mean anything. Please don't make a hasty decision. We can work it out," he said.

"I've given it a lot of thought. There is no other way, Lloyd," Jessica replied.

Their voices were so soft she had to strain to hear more. Startled by the rustle of movement in the room, Sydney hurriedly tiptoed from the hallway, back to the reception area. Her heart was pounding as she struggled to figure out what she'd just witnessed. Curiosity wouldn't let her leave as her mind instructed.

Instead, she opened the door as if newly entering, then loudly, rapped on the wooden counter. "Anybody here?" she called out. "Hello? Anybody home?" She repeated her summons, directing her voice down the narrow hallway.

Shortly, Lloyd appeared in the doorway between the anteroom and inner offices. "Sydney, what a welcome surprise. How are you?"

"Did I catch you at a bad time?" she asked.

"No, I was just going through some old papers, getting the office ready to close up. Come on back." Leading the way, he asked over his shoulder, "What can I do for you?"

The front door rattled open, and Lloyd stopped, then turned about. "Uh, go on back to my office. It's the last room on the left. Let me see who this is."

Following his instructions, Sydney walked into his office. The room was bland, off-white in color. It contained several black, metal cabinets, an empty waist-high bookcase, and his desk. Boxes were stacked high near the window that held a portable humidifier. There was another door at the back of the room.

"Guess who's here?" Lloyd said, walking into the room.

Sydney turned to see Jessica at his side.

"I was in the neighborhood," her sister said, smiling feebly. "Down the hall at the travel agency as a matter of fact," she added, holding up several brochures.

"Oh? You're planning on taking a trip?" Sydney couldn't think of anything else to say. Unable to erase the loverlike conversation she had overheard, she was profoundly bewildered. One thing was certain, she couldn't say anything to Lloyd now.

WE HAVE 3 FREE BOOKS FOR YOU!

FREE BOOK CERTIFICATE

Yes! Please send me 3 *Arabesque* Contemporary Romances without cost or obligation, billing me just $1 to help cover postage and handling. I understand that each month, I will be able to preview 3 brand-new *Arabesque* Contemporary Romances FREE for 10 days. Then, if I decide to keep them, I will pay the money-saving preferred subscriber's price of just $12.00 for all 3...that's a savings of almost $3 off the publisher's price with no additional charge for shipping and handling. I may return any shipment within 10 days and owe nothing, and I may cancel this subscription at any time. My 3 FREE books will be mine to keep in any case.

Name _____

Address _____ Apt. _____

City _____ State _____ Zip _____

Telephone ( ) _____

Signature _____
(If under 18, parent or guardian must sign.)   AR0896

GET 3 FREE ARABESQUE ROMANCES TODAY!

3 FREE
ARABESQUE
Contemporary
Romances
are reserved
for you!

(worth almost
$15.00)

see details
inside...

ZEBRA HOME SUBSCRIPTION SERVICE, INC.

120 BRIGHTON ROAD

P.O. BOX 5214

CLIFTON, NEW JERSEY 07015-5214

AFFIX
STAMP
HERE

"I'm thinking about it," Jessica replied. "What are you doing here?"

"Oh," Sydney replied lightly, "I was in the neighborhood, too. The gallery downstairs . . . I was thinking about getting something for the house."

A masculine form leaned against the door frame at the edge of the room, a slither of light behind him in the hallway, darkness before him.

It was late, he was tired, but he had to do this. The police left him no alternative. For fifty bucks, he was in for fifteen minutes.

He reached behind him along the side of the wall. His fingers, right on the mark, flicked the switch, filling the room with light. Perry whistled.

Tastefully furnished didn't begin to describe Daniels's ninth floor residence in the expensive, high-rise apartment building. Perry felt he'd stepped onto the pages of *House Beautiful*.

The black marble fireplace with matching wet bar was complemented by a burgundy and white marble tiled floor. On plush white leather couches even plusher pillows had been placed. Moroccan rugs adorned the walls, Persian the floor. Originals works of famous artists hung on the rose-colored walls.

Awed, Perry whispered to himself, "Maybe I do need to go into politics."

Only one thing tarnished the luxurious environment, the white chalk outline of Daniels's body as it had lain when the police arrived. Approaching the area, he noticed a section of carpet had been cut out, revealing the concrete flooring underneath.

He frowned, bewildered, as he knelt near that spot, then glanced back and forth from it to the chalky outline that showed the fetal position of Daniels's body as it had lain

in death, his head toward the fireplace, his feet between the
couch and coffee table.

Perry pulled at his chin, trying to figure out what he was
looking at. Guessing the police had cut the carpet, he pondered as to why. Then he withdrew a small camera from
the kit strapped to his waist.

He did realize it meant the police had even more of a
case than they had let on. It must be something the killer
had overlooked or didn't know the police would recognize
as evidence. Snapping pictures from different angles, he
suspected it was the latter. That shored up his belief that
Daniels's death had been a crime of passion, not premedi-
tated.

He wondered whether the passion was a byproduct of
sex. He knew firsthand the hot temper love caused. He had
wanted to wring Sydney's pretty neck when he'd seen those
photos and had concluded she'd lied to him.

But the evidence didn't say that, he recalled, absently lowering the camera.

Love wasn't the only reason for murder. Passions ran the
gamut, from love of money to love of an ideology.

"Did you die for a cause, Larry, or for love?" Perry asked
the silence.

He pushed himself upright and began to amble about, but
never went far from the site of death. His gaze catalogued
the items on the gold-lined, glass coffee table. A dozen pictures of Daniels at different stages in his life, either alone
or posing with family, were arranged to capture attention.
A turtle-shaped bronze ashtray bore no signs of use.

At the far end of the table was a portable phone propped
upright in its base, looking like a dog begging for a bone.
The image was comical to Perry, and he choked off the
laughter deep in his throat.

He headed for the phone, a strange anticipation guiding
his steps. He nearly picked it up before snatching back his

hand. Shaking his head from side-to-side in dismay, he exhaled a weary breath.

He stared at the instrument and got an impression of Sydney through his entrancement. He thought he had passed her car as he'd left the interview with Lloyd Andrews. But she wouldn't go behind his back again, he reminded himself. No doubt his guilt over not returning her calls was playing havoc with him. He could assuage his curiosity by simply calling her.

However, the sound of her sirenic voice would have him finding excuses to see her, though he had nothing positive to report. The only thing he had managed to accomplish so far he recalled, was stalling Melloncamp and Tomkins by giving them a duplicate of the entire roll of pictures Sydney had. But his lack of progress on the case was the real cause of his frustration.

That was due to the feeling growing inside him. Refusing to put a name to it and unable to explain it, he'd tried to deny it. Chalk it up as an undisputed fact, he told himself, his gaze going to the last item on the table.

It was a black porcelain vase with a single white lily engraved on its curving surface. Another decorative piece, he thought, raising the camera to his face. He shot several more pictures before remembering the rock Sydney had thrown at Daniels.

The rock was in police custody. The newspapers had printed Daniels's entire history, including his attachment to the rock. It was the one he'd thrown through the window of a wealthy white homeowner who'd turned out to be none other than US Congressman Samuel Dean Holloway. Daniels had been seventeen at the time, angry at the world, and probably Dalston's first black revolutionary. The congressman was then a Texas representative, but Daniels hadn't known whose home he'd vandalized until after he'd been picked up by the police patrolling the neighborhood. Rather than prosecute, the congressman took Daniels in and became a mentor to him. *Local bad boy makes good.* That theme had followed Daniels throughout his political career.

Perry ventured farther into the apartment, searching for clues.

Sydney welcomed the opportunity she simply couldn't pass up. "Hi, Hank."

"Oh, hi, Ms. Webster. How have you been doing?"

"Pretty good, all things considered," Sydney replied, forcing a smile. Ever since her happenstance meeting with her sister, she couldn't quell the image of Jessica and Lloyd locked in familiarity. She abhorred the feeling of distrust inside her. "Uh, look, Hank, Jessica thinks she left a locket Larry gave her up in his apartment, but she didn't want to come and check for herself, which is understandable. She asked me to do it. Is that okay?"

"Well, I don't know," Hank replied, scratching his head, a look of indecision marring his expression. "The police still have their tag across the door. They really don't want anybody in there."

Sydney's face collapsed into a woebegone expression. "Oh, wow!" she exclaimed softly. "I don't know what to do. She's really been out of it, you know. I was hoping I could find that stupid locket and lift her spirits a little."

"Mmm," Hank muttered, looking at his watch. He mumbled something Sydney didn't catch, then smiled at her. "I guess it's all right, but don't be long, okay."

"Not to worry," Sydney replied, thinking she had to hurry in order to beat Jessica back to her house. "Thanks a lot," she added brightly as she skipped toward the elevator. When the car arrived, she stepped on and pressed the button for her floor.

Since running into Jessica, she had been stuck with her sister for most of the day, she recalled. From Larry's office, they'd gone to the gallery: she'd had no choice. Jessica had insisted on buying something. "For your house," she had said. Afterward, they'd lunched, window-shopped and finally had dined together. As they'd left the restaurant, Jessica had deftly wangled an invitation to spend the night at her home, then had shocked her by expressing a desire to drive her sporty Toyota. That left her with Jessica's Lexus, as well as a ring of keys. One fit the lock to Larry's apartment, where she was hoping to learn something substantial that she could offer Perry.

Smiling proudly over her ingenuity, Sydney lifted her left arm to check her watch. Jessica had claimed she'd needed to run home first, but she was to be back at Sydney's house by nine. It was eight now.

Silently, Sydney hurried the elevator to her floor. As if on cue, it arrived, and she stepped off.

Daniels's expensive tastes reigned throughout his home. The bedroom bordered on decadence, done in black leather, red velvet and chrome.

Perry fully expected to find a video camera hidden among the expensive entertainment system against the wall near the walk-in closet. Checking, he didn't. Instead, he found something that he could only define as the carryover of youthful innocence, a starter fish bowl with a single fat goldfish swimming through the miniature tunnel buried in the small colored rocks.

"Who's been feeding you, little fellow?" he asked, peering through the bowl.

A piece of silver slightly protruding from the rocks caught his attention. Perry pulled back his sleeve and stuck his hand in the bowl to retrieve a key. Turning it over in his hand, he wondered what it opened.

Hearing a faint sound come from the front of the apartment, he tiptoed quickly into the hallway and waited, his breath suspended in his throat. The door opened, and someone walked lightly into the tiled foyer and into his view.

He noticed a woman's form, and instinctively identified her, a shock running through him. He deliberately frowned and quietly headed in her direction. He saw Sydney tiptoeing to the couch and cleared his throat with a loud harrumph. She jumped, startled, and spun to face him. Cheeks flushed, her face held an "Oh-oh" look.

"What are you doing here?" he grated in a whisper. His mind told him to resist the compelling thought produced by his involuntary response to her presence. Blood coursing through his veins like an awakened river, it seemed his body had a will of its own.

She held up a set of keys; her expression still revealing fear and surprise. He was almost embarrassed by his deliberate attempt to frighten her. Almost.

"I got Jessica's keys," she said weakly.

He feasted his eyes on her, pleased by his precise memory. It was a struggle to maintain the stern expression on his face. "I thought we had an understanding," he said harshly.

"But this was a chance I couldn't pass up."

In disgust, Perry shook his head. "What am I going to do with you?" With weary patience, he said, "I thought I had your word that you wouldn't go behind my back and try to do my job."

"I thought maybe if I looked at things again, I'd remember something you could use," she explained hastily. "Since Jessica and I switched cars, and I ended up with her keys as well, this was the perfect opportunity. I would have told you."

Conversation from the corridor drifted into the apartment. Perry put a finger to his lips, warning Sydney to silence. As the voices neared, he reached out to grab her and pulled her into the hallway.

Instantly assailed by a rush of warm feelings, Perry realized his mistake. His heart now had a ferocious beat; he knew Sydney heard it. Pressed against him, she was resting her head on his chest. But he was helpless to control it.

Under the spill of light from the bedroom, he was keenly conscious of everything . . . the sudden silence emanating from the corridor, Sydney's shallow breathing, her silky hair under his chin, the tempting scent of her perfume, his urgent inner warning to push her away and, most disconcerting, his masculine rising.

"I think whoever it was is gone," she whispered after a while.

Perry swallowed hard, nodding, not trusting himself to speak just yet. "Yeah," he said briefly, "I think you're right."

He relaxed his grip on her shoulders, but his hands seemed stuck to the soft flesh beneath the padded jacket she wore. Instead of retreating, he shifted into her enticing warmth.

She was his client, for god's sake; the woman who'd come to him for his legal expertise. He comprehended the rationale for deterrence as surely as he recognized the hunger gnawing away at this senses.

Objections overturned, he knew he was guilty as sin when he lowered his gaze. Concurrently, Sydney looked up at him. As if emotions were contagious, her face expressed a sensuous desire that matched his own. She had never looked more beautiful, more irresistible, nor more in need than he.

Perry lowered his head a fraction; Sydney lifted hers. Her mouth welcomed him when he touched her lips with his, and the sin was committed.

Eleven

The crowd at The Bandana Bar & Grill was light, though nonetheless rowdy. Customers had their choice of seats and were spread out all over the place, chatting above the taped C&W music playing in the background. Mark was sitting hunched over the table at a back booth, staring contemplatively into his mug of beer.

"Not playing tonight?"

Mark looked up as if awakened from sleep. He pulled his arms back to sit up straight before he spoke. "Naw man, I'm broke."

"But you're the boss's son," Lloyd said, sliding into the booth across from Mark.

"That ain't never cut no quarters with my old man," Mark said snidely. "He's a strictly work-for-pay kind of guy." He turned up his iced mug of beer for a swallow, then set the glass down hard on the wood table, still holding the handle. "Where's your lovely wife this evening?"

"Can I get you something, Mr. Andrews?" asked the black-and-white uniformed waitress who'd sidled up to the table, eager to earn a tip.

"Uh, just bring me a glass of Riesling-Spätlese, Molly," Lloyd replied.

The waitress placed a cocktail napkin before him, then left. Lloyd relaxed, resting a crooked leg on the booth's seat. He watched with a hint of amusement tinging his nonchalant expression as Mark fingered the ring of water left on the table by his mug. "Guess who came to see me today?" he asked casually.

"Who?" Mark asked, disinterested.

"Sydney Webster."

Mark stiffened in his seat. "For what?" he demanded.

"She was in the neighborhood," Lloyd replied, smiling complacently.

"Bull," Mark retorted.

"She bought a picture from the gallery," Lloyd said. "Nice picture. A John Biggers, as a matter of fact. You must be paying her pretty well."

"Quit the chitchat and get to the point," Mark said.

Lloyd did. "I got the canceled draft. It was payable to WDST, but it was endorsed back to Larry. I found it when I was going through his papers." Directing a taunting glance at Mark, he added, "I wonder how that happened."

Mark emitted an expletive and collapsed with a jolt against the back of the booth.

"Now, the way I figure it," Lloyd conjectured, placing his elbows on the table as he leaned inward, "somebody at your station must have asked Sydney about that money. I'm just guessing now, but I also imagine it didn't show up on the books like it should have."

"You've got to give it back," Mark said urgently, a look of pleading in his eyes.

Lloyd chuckled sarcastically as he sat back, fiddling with the bar napkin. "Why should I?"

"Because Larry promised me a chance to win it back," Mark replied, his jaws tight in anger, "then he ups and gets killed." He cursed again, shaking his head in a combination of bitterness and regret.

"How do I know he didn't change his mind and you killed him because of it?" Lloyd countered.

Mark sprang from his seat like a praying mantis and grabbed the collar of Lloyd's shirt, teeth bared, his beer breath fanning Lloyd's face, his own now a thunderous mask.

Stoically unexpressive, save for the warning smile on his lips, Lloyd wagged a finger under Mark's nose. "Now, now. Calm yourself. I'm the man in possession of something you want very badly."

Swallowing his defeat, Mark released Lloyd, slipping back onto his seat. His face was red with anger as he stared across the table, malevolence blazing in his eyes. "What do you want from me, Lloyd?"

Sydney's lips tingled. Her heart was still racing as her mind wrestled with the aftermath of words that didn't match the deed.

To the accompaniment of African-American Classical music—jazz—with the distinctive full-bodied flute of Hubert Laws bringing a new intrepretation to a traditional Latin composition, Sydney relived her amorous experience. Points of light from free-standing lamps cast her in a silhouette. Dressed in a long, orange-and-white-ringed nightshirt, she was sitting at the eight-sided table in her den, her feet stretched out under it, her head resting along the top of the chair and her eyes closed. Though she'd poured herself a glass of wine, she'd yet to bring the glass to her lips as if fearing it would somehow sully her memory of Perry's kiss.

He had been furious at her appearance. But she couldn't forget what happened afterward. Unconsciously, she smiled in the dark, recalling the smoldering passion that had thrilled her.

Then, before ushering her out of the apartment, he had ruined it all with an apology, she recalled, sobering. Rationally and calmly, he'd explained the kiss as an incident, a biological occurrence, a mental lapse on his part for which he was truly sorry. He went on to warn her against attributing anything significant to it. But she wouldn't believe him, nor would she forget the feel of his mouth on hers.

She opened her eyes and conjured his image in the dark.

His warmth, his stress from battling for restraint. She could sense his arousal, saw when he gave in, and a ripple of sensation that became a flood settled in her loins. His lips were firm, exact and demanding on hers. Wanting more, she shifted closer to the fire. Then he put it out, she recalled, still feeling the sting of his rebuff.

In parting, he'd claimed he was on his way to a late date. Though her mind swirled in bewilderment, she consoled herself with the reminder of his momentary loss of control.

She took a deep, deep breath. Seconds passed before the trembling inside her subsided: the insatiable ache didn't.

The overhead lights popped on, and Sydney sat up with a start. Jessica, dressed in one of her short nylon gowns, was standing at the doorway, steam rising from the mug in her hand. She looked refreshed and wide awake.

"I made tea," Jessica announced, holding up the heavy cup, "want some?"

Sydney lifted the glass of wine sitting on the table in reply. She watched curiously as Jessica crossed the room to the table and sat in an adjacent chair. There was something different about her, Sydney thought, masking her examination of her sister by taking a swallow of wine. Jessica looked . . . prettier, as if she was aglow from an inner sense of well-being.

"Say it," Jessica commanded. "I'm ready."

"What?" Sydney asked, a curious frown on her face.

"Everything you've always wanted to ask or say, but were afraid to," Jessica replied, her smile broadening into a grin.

Sydney was wary of the invitation and debated accepting. She realized how shortsighted she'd been made by her life-long love and admiration for her sister, to the point of refusing to believe what her eyes had seen.

"How do you like what I've done to the house?"

"I love the place, though I haven't a clue as to where you're going to hang that picture you let me buy and then left in the car." Jessica chided her, but she was smiling.

Sydney had the good sense to laugh at being caught in the act. "It's still a great picture, and I appreciate the gift." She sipped her wine, then set the glass on the table and folded her hands over her flat stomach.

"You know, we haven't had a day like this in many, many years," Jessica said. "Not since you were a teenager, endowed with honesty and no tact whatsoever." They both chuckled, but the moment of levity was brief and faded into the music. "I missed that," Jessica said with melancholy, the mug at her lips as she took a small sip.

"Me, too," Sydney mused aloud.

Jessica set her mug on the table and looked at Sydney pensively before she spoke. "I'm sorry. Really sorry."

Frown lines deepened across Sydney's forehead. She was trying hard to keep up with the game Jessica had initiated. "About what?"

"For accusing you," Jessica replied. "There's no valid reason for my behavior, as I told your Mr. MacDonald."

Sydney sat up straight in her chair. Her heart renewed its galloping beat, and her bosom swelled with remembering. "You talked to Perry?" she asked, tempering the excitement in her voice.

"Yes. I went to his office last Friday. He's a very, uh . . ."—Jessica paused, searching for the right word—"dynamic man, shall we say? He allows no quarter," she added, picking up her tea. "Anyway," she continued, "I hope you can forgive me."

Sydney squirmed uncomfortably, embarrassed, before shyly admitting, "It hurt." But no more than the pang of Perry's leaving, she decided. "I wondered whether you'd always hated me for ruining your life."

"Oh, Sydney!" Jessica exclaimed, remorse on her face as her hand reached out to her sister. "How can I ever make it up to you? Just tell me."

At least one feeling out in the open, Sydney thought. "An apology is enough," she replied.

"I hope you mean that," Jessica said seriously. "I know you; at least, I used to. Lately I haven't been able to figure out whether I still credit what I thought I knew." She seemed sullen.

Sydney wondered what she meant. "Did you love Larry?"

Jessica gave her a sidelong look, her interest piqued. "That's a strange question. I didn't expect it."

Lashes lowering over her eyes as she looked down into the wine glass, Sydney asked, "Is it still too painful for you to talk about him?" Noting the distress that shadowed Jessica's expression, she added hastily, "Forget I asked. I'm sorry."

"No," Jessica said softly, a hand reaching out to squeeze one of Sydney's affectionately. "I invited the question, and I'll answer it."

"Jessica, you don't have to be brave for me. I'm not a little girl anymore." In one respect, she felt like a neophyte, for she'd never experienced such a gamut of perplexing emotions because of a man. Perry put her in a perpetual state of flux—and desire.

"But you're still my little sister. Yes, it's painful, but I want to talk about it." She got up to pace the room aimlessly. "I know you didn't like Larry," she said, looking at Sydney from under slightly uptilted brows.

A sheepish look coming to her face, Sydney said, "Don't worry. I won't deny it. I was sorry I introduced you to him."

"Oh, Sydney, you're so naive," Jessica chortled chidingly, a bittersweet look on her face. "And sweet," she tacked on, her expression now kind and sincere. "Stay that way."

She took a sip of tea and then stood at the windows, staring absently at the lights blinking in the distance, across the water. "I'm not sorry," she said in a faraway voice. "Larry was the best thing that ever happened to me. I knew what I was letting myself in for." She seemed to be speaking to herself. She sighed at length, adding with a note of envy,

"But I don't have to tell you about it. You've never been afraid to take chances."

Flabbergasted by this admission, Sydney's head jerked up and she stared hard at her sister. She wondered whether Jessica was sincere or was patronizing her. But Jessica was in her own world now, and it was too late to warn her against the pitfalls of gambling.

"I'm quite familiar with the rumors about his so-called womanizing. He even warned me about them."

"He did?" Sydney asked, confounded. She still hadn't gotten over her surprise at Jessica's previous revelation.

Jessica angled her body to look at Sydney over her shoulder, a sad smile on her face. "Yes," she said, then again faced the windows. "He did. I think you'll agree that Larry was a handsome man."

Sydney shrugged indecisively. Good looks and muscles in all the right places weren't everything, she mused.

"You dare deny it?" Jessica asked incredulously, mirth in her tone.

"Okay, I'll admit Larry was a fine-looking man," Sydney conceded grudgingly. But he couldn't have held a candle to Perry MacDonald, she thought smugly.

With a sly look, Jessica said, "But I suspect not as handsome as your Mr. MacDonald."

Sydney sputtered, bristling with contrived ignorance. "What do you mean, *my* MacDonald?" The heat stealing into her face negated her rebuke. Falling back against the chair, she clamped her mouth shut, abashed that she was so easy to see through.

"Never mind." Jessica laughed lightly. "To each her own," she added, flashing a wink at Sydney before she turned her attention to the outside as if her secret thoughts drew her there. "Larry was also—undeniably—a big flirt." At some memory she let out a fond chuckle. "And politics made him even more attractive to groupies who foolishly believed his power would somehow rub off on them. But they would never have what we had together. Yes, I loved him very much."

Sydney wasn't sure she believed Jessica, but she did understand the law of nature, and the attraction between opposites, which defied reason. "What were you doing at the office?" she asked, knowing Jessica understood.

Jessica faced her fully, holding the mug with both hands, her expression bland. "It was as I told you, Sydney; I'd gone to the travel agency. I'm leaving town next month. I'll be gone for at least a year. Maybe longer," she added thoughtfully as she turned her back on her sister.

"Jessica?" Sydney was up and across the room. Standing before her sister, frowning, she asked, "What's going on?"

Jessica stroked the side of her face, smoothed a wayward strand of her hair before she replied. "Sydney, I'm pregnant."

The CD changed and a straight-ahead composition featuring John Coltrane's saxophone blew in on Sydney's stunned silence.

The next morning at WDST, Debbie was standing next to the door of her boss's office, eavesdropping. The mirthful expressions that crossed her face were revealing.

"Damn it, Mark! How could you be so careless? Do you realize I almost called her in here to chew her out about stealing my damned money? And here you come waltzing in here like some dog with his tail tucked between his legs, talking about you're sorry. Goddamn right you're sorry. You better . . . !"

Snickering softly, she tiptoed away from the door to saunter jauntily down the narrow hallway to Sydney's office.

Everything inside Perry seemed to have changed with that kiss. There was no denying his lust—his body grew rock hard at just thinking about Sydney. But a feeling alien to him partnered his desire, a poignantly emotional response that permeated his senses.

It exposed him to a different kind of fear because it was an unknown entity. He didn't know if he could control or destroy it. But the thought passed fleetingly, for as childish as it sounded, he knew he wanted to do neither.

For the first time in his adult life, he wished he were as all-knowing as his TV namesake, because he damn sure didn't know what to do.

Disgusted, he entered his office by a side door. Indiscriminately, he flung down his briefcase, and it clacked against the desk before landing with a thud on the floor.

What a way to start the day, he thought bitterly, unloosening the knot of his tie.

Undoubtedly drawn by the noise, Ramona looked into the room warily, first poking her head through the door, wavering between offering commiseration or a morning greeting.

Perry eschewed both with his ferocious frown. "I gather you've heard about my defeat," he said, as he dragged the tie from around his neck. It wasn't the only courtroom defeat that accounted for his foul mood. He couldn't let go of what had happened last night or of his complete disobedience to common sense.

"Don't take it so hard." Ramona entered the room. "It's probably best for Lindsay to stay at a girls' home for a month. I know Carl thinks so."

"Well, I don't," Perry said heatedly, poking his chest with a stiff finger. He knew he was being unreasonably hard on himself, but he couldn't help it. Though aware that he was being victimized by his own apprehension, it bothered him that this failure could avalanche into another. One with dire consequences that didn't have anything to do with his ego.

"This was her first offense," he disputed, repeating his argument to the judge. He'd have to come up with a more potent defense in a murder case, he chided himself. "I hate going before Hartong in the first place. If he had his way, every kid in the city would spend the summer in boot camp," he added his voice heavy with sarcasm.

"Javier called," Ramona interrupted. "He got back from Houston this morning. He should be here any minute now. He said you're going to be pleased."

"I damned well better be," Perry growled to himself. "Nothing's going right. Nothing." He rammed the drawer shut loudly.

"Can I get you something?" Ramona asked, though the look on her face revealed she found that doubtful.

"I'll take some answers," he said at last. "And preferably with some truth in them," he added, bending to right his briefcase. He retrieved a collapsible file and spread its contents—several manila folders—across the top of his desk.

"Okay, I'll see what I can manage." She smiled sweetly before ducking from the room.

Perry didn't hear Ramona leave. A dazed look on his face, he was recalling Lindsay Glover's eyes when Judge Hartong had announced his decision. They had glittered with fear and a smidgeon of disbelief. Then tears had flooded them as she'd collapsed against him, blubbering and pleading for him to make the judge change his mind.

Perry shook his head, then pinched the inner corners of his eyes, sighing wearily. He didn't want to, but he imagined Sydney's reaction, should he fail her, and a wave of panic assailed him, so strong that it gnawed at his confidence.

An inkling of failure and a tangible sense of desire clamored inside him as if they were savage opponents. Though in reality, he knew they were related.

Telling himself his fears were premature, he determined he couldn't fail. He wouldn't let that happen.

His gaze riveted on the folders, he unbuttoned the top of his shirt, rolled up each sleeve to the elbow, then pulled up the chair behind him to sit at the desk.

His eyes narrowed in heavy concentration as he reviewed

the typed notes in the folders labeled, ROGER SIMMONS, HANK EVANS and WALTER WEBSTER. One at a time, he replayed the interviews and went over conclusions he'd drawn from each in his mind.

Larry Daniels had dazzled the attendant Roger Simmons, and had bribed the guard, Hank Evans. Neither of which had been hard to do, considering the teenager was impressionable and the guard cynical and money hungry. Still, each had an opinion of this man, a different one.

Walter Webster . . . Perry chuckled. The college president had been as slippery as a banana peel when he'd tried to pin him down before he'd been kicked out. He recalled their brief meeting yesterday. Unlike Hank, Dr. Webster hadn't been intimidated by his cross-examination and had yielded only what he'd wanted known, which was nothing useful.

The college president had been right about one thing, Perry told himself. He was going to have to change his tactics, at least in dealing with him.

Perry slapped the WALTER WEBSTER folder down atop the other two, then stacked them on the far corner of the desk.

He opened a separate folder; it was the thickest of all and bore the name LARRY DANIELS on its label. The answer rested with Daniels, he thought with certainty. He leaned back in his chair, the opened folder resting on his knees as he reread the materials on the late politician.

On top was a newspaper article dated last year. A photo captured Daniels with rage on his face and his fist in the air. In quotation marks, the caption quoted Daniels as declaring, "They'll close Texas College over my dead body!"

Perry wondered if the politician had predicted his future, then turned to the next piece of information. Reading through the stapled pages, he noted it was a listing of Daniels legislative bills. The number passed was impressive, and while Perry didn't agree with all of the measures Daniels had introduced, he saluted his accomplishments.

"I heard you were looking for some truth," Javier said jovially as he strolled into the room. He was dressed in a loud print shirt, pressed white walking shorts and navy deck shoes.

"You look like you've just come off a boat," Perry commented with a grunt.

"Ramona told me you were in a foul mood," Javier replied, pushing the door closed. He crossed the room to the couch, sat and stretched his legs across the coffee table.

"This better be good," Perry declared, closing the folder and laying it on the desk as he rose. Striding to the sitting area, he sat in an armchair. "Speak."

"Where should I start?" Javier asked rhetorically, flipping open his notepad.

"At the beginning—and don't leave anything out."

"Can I get a drink first?"

"No."

Javier sighed, emitting a tsk as he shook his head. "All right. For every person I found who admired Dr. Walter Webster, I found two who hated his guts. Mostly women.

"Since most of them dislike him for the same reason, I'll give you a summary based on the interview with Mrs. Roscette Merrill from Houston. She was the most interesting, and she knew our client's mother," he explained. Perry nodded his assent, and Javier continued, "She was Sonni-Lauren's friend all through college and afterward. Sonni was working for an interior design company while taking business classes part-time. Walter was one of her graduate professors. Since she was over twenty-one, there was nothing to prevent them from dating. Anyway, Mrs. Merrill claims to have believed the good doctor lied about being married, and Sonni fell in love with him; so you can figure the rest. By the time Sonni discovered the truth, she was pregnant. At least according to Mrs. Merrill."

Perry whistled. "So he was still married to Jessica's mother," he said.

"Yes," Javier confirmed. "The marriage was already shaky; he was living with his mother. The first wife, it seems, was an alcoholic. A couple of the women who didn't even know her *blamed him for her condition.* They all said he was too controlling."

"I can believe that," Perry said to himself, recalling Walter Webster's overbearing attitude toward his daughters. "What was the first wife's name?"

"Corinda Webster. Maiden name, Pigott," Javier replied, shuffling through pages of notes. He found the page he was looking for, and added, "She was committed to a private mental institution in 1967, and Walter moved back into their house, with sole custody of Jessica."

"Wait, hold up," Perry interrupted bewildered. "Where was Sonni-Lauren during these happenings?"

"She had her own place. She and Walter married three months before Sydney was born."

"Okay," Perry said, shaking his head as if confounded. "When did the first Mrs. Webster die?"

"Die?" Javier replied. "Who said she died?" At Perry's surprised look, he explained. "The last known address for her was the Berryhill Home in Temple, Texas, 1988, roughly eight years ago. I tried reaching this place, but it burned down shortly thereafter. A couple of people were killed in that fire, supposedly one of the worst in the history of the town. But there's no record of her death."

Perry sat on the edge of the chair, leaning forward, his hands dangling before him. "So, Corinda Pigott Webster could still be alive."

"It's possible. She would only be in her sixties."

"Okay. We veered off the subject; go back to the good doctor," Perry instructed.

"Like I was saying," Javier resumed, crossing his legs at the ankles, "according to Mrs. Merrill, he was a control freak. He tried to determine everything, from where Sonni-Lauren went—and when—to what she wore and who she saw. Only that didn't work with her." He seemed amused. "The woman definitely had a mind of her own. And she was a looker, you could say, an asset to his career; so he suppressed his macho bullying. She was well liked, talented, outgoing. The police never found her murderer. . . ."

Twelve

"I'll have the sautéed lobster with ginger and vinaigrette on my salad."

Her selection made, Sydney closed the red leather-bound menu that was as tastefully designed as the room. A nod and a smile commended her choice. Then with an obsequious bow, the waiter took the menu, diverting his attention across the table. Sydney's thoughts returned to sibling camaraderie and the good feelings the memory wrought.

Jessica pregnant.

Sydney smiled at picturing her sister's tummy swelling with new life. She didn't know if she was more excited over Jessica's pending motherhood or the prospect of becoming an aunt.

Jessica had clammed up after dropping the news about her pregnancy, claiming a sudden need for rest. Consequently, Sydney's questions remained, and she didn't know whether she had the nerve to ask Jessica if Larry was the father of her unborn child. Maybe by this evening she'd have thought of an approach. Jessica had promised to be waiting with her favorite meal cooked. Just like old times.

"You picked the most expensive meal on the menu."

Though tempered by a chuckle, the mildly scolding tone cut into Sydney's thoughts.

"Why not? You're paying," she replied, smiling cheekily. "Who knows when another treat from the boss will come my way? For all I know, this could be my last." She reached for the crystal glass filled with a bubbly liquid.

Regardless of her words, Sydney was confident this was not her last meal on the boss. Mark didn't know she knew, but she did; she smiled secretly into her glass as she took a sip of champagne. The reprimand from his father had undoubtedly included instructions to take her to lunch. And who would turn down such an invitation? Particularly from a boss as parsimonious as Mark.

Low lighting from yellow-bulbed chandeliers hung from the high vaulted ceiling made for hard reading, but created a relaxed environment for dining. In the middle of the day, Sils, the most expensive and elegant restaurant in Dalston, was crowded with power brokers conducting business in muted voices. Waiters in starched white tops, well-defined pleats in their black slacks unobtrusively promenaded from the dining room to the kitchen. The maître d', in a black tuxedo, stood ready at the head of the room.

It seemed an abomination to waste the intimate atmosphere on Mark, Sydney thought. They were sitting across from each other at a table for four, a bottle of champagne chilling in a silver ice bucket near him.

"It's not," Mark announced. "In fact, it's a form of celebration." He raised his glass toward her for a toast. She complied, and he announced, "To continued great sales and the account exec that made them so."

"What?" she asked, amazed.

"I thought you knew by now," Mark said, studying her intently. "It was in yesterday's newspaper in the radio section."

Sydney stared, frowning, wondering what he was talking about. She hadn't read the paper, and as far as radio was concerned, what occupied her mind was the missing payment on Daniels's account, which he'd denied receiving.

Smiling with disbelief that she didn't know, Mark said, "You're number one in the city in radio sales."

"Oh," Sydney exclaimed with pleased surprise. "Well, that is cause for celebration then," she concurred happily, touching her glass to his to complete the toast.

"We have to stop meeting like this."

Startled, Sydney did a double-take at identifying the voice, and then recognizing Lloyd Andrews. "Hi," she said, her gaze taking in his wife, who had sidled up to the table with him, their arms linked.

"Hi, Sydney." Ursula wiggled her fingers in a wave.

Sydney had forced a warmth into her voice she was far from feeling. Sils was a public restaurant; anyone could eat here, she told herself, despite her suspicious curiosity about their presence. Remembering her manners, she turned to introduce her companion. "Do you know Mark Frederickson? Mark, Lloyd and Ursula Andrews."

Mark half rose from his seat, extending a hand to Lloyd, "Yes, I remember the name. Daniels's right hand man. Ursula . . ." He shook her hand. "Why don't you join us?"

A frown came to Sydney's face; then she caught herself and pasted on a smile. "I'm sure Lloyd chose to enjoy lunch in this lovely atmosphere with his wife. Ursula's a busy airline stewardess who's hardly ever in town."

"We'd love to join you," Lloyd said. He looked around for a waiter, and the one assigned to the table arrived in a flash. "We're going to join Ms. Webster and Mr. Frederickson."

"Yes, sir," the waiter replied. He seated Ursula next to Mark and Lloyd next to Sydney. He then gave each newcomer a menu. When Lloyd and Ursula did not wish to order cocktails, the waiter brought two more champagne glasses.

As if by tacit agreement, no one spoke until the waiter had poured champagne, filling all four glasses. During the process, Sydney stole stealthy looks at Ursula Andrews. The woman was truly a classical beauty, she decided, immaculate and with an elegant aura about her. Berry-brown skin stretched smooth and unblemished across her perfectly symmetrical features. She had the dark eyes of a doe, which gave her an innocent look at odds with her slender, though voluptuous body.

"What are you going to do now, Lloyd?" Mark asked after the waiter had taken their orders. "It's all right if I call you Lloyd, isn't it?"

"Sure," Andrews replied. "And I don't know. Councilman Grenias requested a meeting. I'm going to listen to what he has to say."

Ursula's age was hard to determine, but Sydney thought her to be younger than Lloyd, who had to be in his midforties. He was good-looking, debonair in dress and demeanor. Together, they seemed like the perfect couple. Though Sydney wondered if they were; she wasn't sure why.

"Didn't he hold Larry's seat?" Mark asked.

"Yeah," Lloyd said, pride in his smile. "We took it from him."

"Think he wants it back?" Mark asked.

Watching Lloyd shrug his broad shoulders, noting the cocky smirk on his lips, Sydney found that he, like Larry Daniels, did nothing for her. While physically appealing to look at and endowed with a healthy dose of confidence, Andrews lacked something. Perry was a far better man, better than any other she'd ever met. And he teased her senses whenever she was near him, or just in thinking of him.

"I thought there was something shady about his past," Ursula said.

Sydney was hoping Perry would make a surprise appearance, when she caught the look Lloyd shot Ursula. Was he flirting with his wife, or warning her to say no more, she wondered.

"People forget," Lloyd said. "Ah," he exclaimed, opening his napkin on his lap, "here comes lunch." Turning to Sydney, he inquired in pleasant tone, "How is Jessica today?"

* * *

Perry felt a headache coming on. He stared into space, plagued by the ramifications of the likelihood that Walter Webster was capable of murder. As anyone would be, given the right situation. Sydney would be devastated. Even if he could convince her it was possible Webster had done it, which he doubted.

"I thought you told me Jessica Webster lives with her father?" Javier asked, breaking into his thoughts.

"She does as far as I know. Why?" Perry asked.

"She's been paying twelve hundred a month to the Landow Reality Company for the past six months," Javier replied. "I haven't gotten around to checking the address, but I thought you'd want to know."

"I do, and let me know as soon as you get that address," Perry replied, jotting down notes on his legal pad. "How did you get that information, by the way?"

"It's best you don't know everything about my job," Javier replied.

Perry looked up from his writing to stare at him. He knew the investigator was not being flippant but correct. Sometimes during investigations, an attorney needed deniability. He nodded.

"Well, that's all I have so far," Javier said. "Did you get around to interviewing the cleaning lady? What's her name . . . ?" he asked, flipping pages of his notepad.

"Beverly . . ." Perry squinted as he struggled to remember the last name.

"Lockhart," Javier supplied from his notes.

"That's it. No, I haven't gotten to her yet. I did meet with the parking attendant, Roger Simmons, and Hank Evans, the security guard. He's such a nice guy he let me into Daniels' place—for fifty bucks." Digging in his briefcase, he added, "And speaking of that, I found something interesting." He pulled out a black kit and unzipped it on the desk. "Here's the roll I shot of the place," he said, passing the undeveloped film to Javier. "I won't tell you what I think until after you've developed it and had a look for yourself. I found another interesting item in the fish bowl, of all places," he said, passing his investigator a small block of clay.

Examining the imprint in the clay, Javier frowned, "What's this the key to?"

"That's for you to find out and tell me."

Nodding, Javier said, "Fair enough. Later." He headed for the door. "Oh, and another thing." He spun about to face Perry. "According to one of my sources, our client is still footloose and fancy free because her old man has connections."

"Connections. What connections?"

"Walter Webster is a hunting buddy of the major who's the cousin-in-law of the district attorney," Javier explained.

Perry drew his bottom lip into his mouth. "That means they've got something else."

"Yeah," Javier echoed.

Javier left Perry pondering, elbows on the desk and chin resting on his hand. There was only one way to deal with the information he'd been given, he decided, pressing the intercom button on the phone. Sooner or later had arrived, he thought with mounting excitement and trepidation.

"Yes, Perry?" Ramona answered.

"Ramona, see if Ms. Webster can meet me for a late lunch or something?"

"Excuse me," Sydney said, rising from the table. Both men stood, Lloyd helping her from her chair.

The presence of Lloyd and Ursula dampened the celebration, she thought, heading for the ladies' room. The meal she'd been famished for had tasted like rubber in her mouth, and she wished there was a way to get out of dessert.

Reaching her destination, she proceeded to the wash area. A tsk of disgust escaped her as she headed for the sink where she opened her purse and pulled out a tube of lipstick.

Examining her face in the mirror, she wondered why

Lloyd had accepted Mark's invitation to join them. Though strangers, the two men seemed to have struck it off, carrying the bulk of the conversation. For the most part, she and Ursula had contributed little. She found it a bit like being in her father's company. "Seen, but not heard," she said to herself, applying lipstick. Seconds later, Ursula walked in.

"Are you as bored as I am?" she asked, sauntering to the next sink.

"Not really," Sydney lied. "I'm just not as familiar with the people and issues they're talking about."

Opening her handbag, Ursula replied, "That's right; you haven't been here that long, have you?" She retrieved her lipstick and began applying it, using her index finger to dab on an errant line of color.

"No, I haven't," Sydney replied, recapping her tube of lipstick and dropping it in her purse.

"You don't like me, do you?" Ursula said.

"What makes you think that?" Sydney asked

"I can tell," Ursula told her. "Well, you can take this anyway you want, but you'd better be careful."

"The streets of Dalston are no more dangerous than any other place," Sydney retorted. "Why would you say that?"

"I'm not referring to dangers on the streets," Ursula replied, washing her hands. "Haven't you wondered why we happen to be here at the same time as you and Mark?"

"You mean it's not a coincidence?" Sydney replied, feigning naiveté. Though Ursula's intimation hadn't struck her, she had felt that lunch was somewhat strange . . . or strained.

"You'd just better be careful. Lloyd collects people," Ursula said. Then she dropped the balled hand towel in the trash and walked from the room.

The pure, sensuous soprano of diva Kathleen Battle delivering Gershwin's bittersweet "Summertime" only increased the impatience of the room's lone occupant.

With a drink in hand and a scowl on his face, Walter Webster paced the floor of the president's office at the university. He never trod far from the massive desk, nor did he loose sight of the telephone. Finally it rang, and he snatched it up before the end of the first bell. "Hello."

A swallow of the clear liquid burned his throat as he grunted in reply to the caller. He listened keenly, then grunted a response. A mocking smile teased his lips as he began to meander around the desk, still on the phone.

"That's nothing," he said, one hand resting on the leather chair behind the desk. "He won't find anything." He gave an arrogant snort and sipped his drink.

His eyes squinting, he mouthed thoughtfully, "Javier Jones." Then astonishment widened his gaze. The realization brought wrinkles across his forehead. The high back of the leather chair squeaked as he grabbed it viciously.

Then he stiffened, panic on his face. "No! No!" he exclaimed, clutching the glass so hard it cracked. "Yes, yes, thank you."

He ended the call quickly and began to dial immediately.

"I saw you last night."

"Where?"

Standing behind the mahogany chair in Sydney's dining room, Beverly absently fingered the olive-leaf pattern in the design. She was in her Clean Sweep uniform. Jessica stood in the doorway of the kitchen.

"Driving in front of Sydney's house," Jessica replied. She crossed into the dining area to stand inches from her mother. "What are you up to, Beverly?"

"Oh, it's Beverly when you're angry with me, huh?" the older woman replied.

Jessica held back a curse. "Don't change the subject. You knew about Sydney's phobia."

Beverly frowned innocently. "What are you talking about?"

"You know very well what," Jessica retorted with impatience, censure in her voice. "Are you the one who put that snake in Sydney's car?"

"Do you actually believe I'm capable of doing something like that?" Beverly asked, hurt.

"I only know that people are capable of doing strange things when they don't get what they want," Jessica replied, rubbing the bridge of her nose as if a pain had settled there. "But," she added contritely, a feeble smile on her lips as she looked at Beverly, "to answer your question, no."

"Let's not fight anymore." Beverly's expression was pleading. "I just thought maybe we could spend a little time together since I was in the neighborhood, that's all."

"We do need to spend some time together, but not here at Sydney's."

"Why don't you come by for dinner tonight?" Beverly suggested hopefully. "We'll have a little celebration. I'll cook your . . ."

The phone began to ring, its extensions echoing throughout the house.

"Let me get that," Jessica said.

A message awaited Sydney at the station upon her return from lunch. She called back to accept Perry's seven-thirty dinner invitation, speaking with Ramona. Then she drove home on a cloud, eagerly looking forward to being with him.

What if he merely wanted to discuss business? she wondered, her elation diminishing. But he had invited her to dinner, and Ramona confirmed it.

Putting the matter out of her mind, she began thinking about what she would wear. A dozen outfits had been discarded before she arrived home.

Jessica had been all but forgotten until Sydney walked into the house to sniff the delicious aromas of a soul-food dinner. Snapping off a curse, she wavered, debating her choice of dinner companions. In her heart, it was easy, but not without consequences. Her sister would understand, she thought, swallowing her guilt.

"Jessica," she called out, heading for the kitchen.

The room was sparkling clean, a cooked meal waiting on the stove, but there was no Jessica. She peeked into a pot of rice, a skillet of gravy loaded with mushrooms and onions, baked chicken in a roasting pan, and cornbread in the oven. She sighed ruefully because her sister had gone to so much trouble.

Then a fondness in her heart, she ran through the house, upstairs and down, looking for Jessica.

Returning to the kitchen, curious now, she looked around the room, wondering as to Jessica's whereabouts. Snapping her fingers, she checked the refrigerator door. She recalled that years ago Jessica had posted messages for her on the fridge when she'd had to leave unexpectedly. But there was no note among the miniature magnets promoting businesses she patronized.

She suddenly felt jubilant, and her guilt vanished. She was going to dine with Perry. Joy sparkled in her eyes, and a ditty came from her throat. The way her day had gone so far, it could only get better. Maybe there was something to the adage that good things came to those who waited.

She cut off a small slice of the cornbread, popped it in her mouth, then covered the pan with foil before racing upstairs, determined to dress to dazzle Perry Mason MacDonald.

Under the sprays of a lingering, lukewarm shower, she settled on her attire. It would be certain to arouse his masculine interest. At least to put him in a quandary about his strictly professional stance toward her.

She lathered her every tingling pore with an ambrosial

scent that augmented her choice. The act teased her flesh to sensuality. Perry had big, confident hands, she recalled, her imagination intensifying her expectations for the evening.

After she dried off, her skin wanted for no attention she could give it. She lotioned and powdered it until it glowed, primed for another's touch. A liberal brushing of her hair, some conservative strokes of makeup, and she was ready, assured.

Scented and dressed in rose from head to toe, she made the return drive to the city, flushed with glorious anticipation.

Thirteen

RJ's was not as fancy a restaurant as Sils, but it was homey, comfortable, and clean if not stylish. It had a reputation for serving Creole and Southern fare that was unsurpassable. Perry had commandeered a small meeting room, which let Sydney know immediately that business rather than sweets would be served for dessert. Her appetite deteriorated, as did her hopeful frame of mind.

"I'll just have a salad," she said to the waitress, not even bothering to look at the menu.

Sitting across the table from her, scanning the carte, Perry looked every bit the brilliant strategist preparing for battle. A flicker of optimism ran through her at seeing his stalwart presence. His broad shoulders and wide chest were set off by his smoke gray suit, powder blue shirt and power tie of silk. Even with the uncanny poise he possessed, and with his thoughts obviously elsewhere, she was painfully aware of the sexual magnetism that made him so self-confident.

Perry lowered his menu to look across the table at her. "Just a salad?"

"I'm not very hungry," she replied, flashing him a half smile to conceal her disappointment.

"You don't have to impress me by not eating," he replied.

With his dark eyebrows arched in amused conjecture and a smile twitching his firm mouth, Sydney fought back her wayward attraction to him. "I'm not trying to impress you," she said saucily. "I'm just not hungry."

"You know you need to eat," he said in a take-charge tone of voice that brooked no argument. Examining the laminated, single-page menu, he instructed the waitress, "Ms. Webster will have the grilled snapper with broccoli and wild rice, and a glass of iced tea."

Slowly, Sydney lowered her head. Her left brow rose above the narrowing gaze she directed at Perry, ire bubbling in her like a hot spring.

Oblivious to her austere disposition, Perry completed ordering. "Make mine the blackened red fish, with the same vegetables," he said, returning the menu to the waitress.

"Iced tea, as well, Mr. MacDonald?" the waitress replied, scribbling on her order pad.

"No, make mine a beer," he replied.

"I'll be right back with your beer . . . in the bottle," the woman tacked on familiarly before walking off.

Sydney wouldn't have minded Perry's selecting for her had she been hungry. But the fact that he completely ignored her wishes was intolerable. "Why did you do that?" she asked, truculence in her voice.

"Do what?"

The strong features of his coffee brown face collapsed into a look of such boyish guile, Sydney was momentarily daunted and wondered whether she was in the wrong. She shook the idiotic notion from her head, wondering why she was so cross. Tapping on the table with her fingers, she admitted the truth in the primitive sensations growing inside her. But Perry didn't take chances, she realized with a pang.

"Determine that I'm not old enough or intelligent enough to know whether or not I'm hungry and need to eat. Why did you do that?" she demanded. But before Perry could reply, she added in an ingratiating tone that mocked her anger, "You think I don't have enough sense to know when I need to eat and how much? I don't need anybody to tell me what's best for me."

"Had a bad day at work, huh?" He unfolded his napkin, spread it across his lap.

"What the hell kind of day I had has nothing to do with your dictatorial decision," she riposted. Muttering in disgust, she tossed her balled napkin as she pushed her seat back from the table to rise.

"Where are you going?" he asked, a puzzled look on his face.

"I don't need this," Sydney said sharply, as she got to her feet, slipping the strap of her purse over her shoulder. Spinning about, she walked out as coolly as her anger allowed, mumbling about the "damn good" day she'd had at work.

Reaching the parking lot, she looked around for her car. Among the dozen or so cars parked on the gravel, she couldn't find it. Assailed for a second by fright that it had been stolen, she then remembered she wasn't driving it. Switching directions, she headed for the black Lexus at the back of the lot as Perry came running out the front door of the restaurant.

"Sydney, please come back," he said, reaching for her arm.

"No," she said obstinately, snatching her arm from his grip. She was pleased that he'd come after her, and she really didn't want to leave, but she didn't want to stay under the circumstances. Recalling her situation, she realized that as long as the suspicion of murder hung over her, she had absolutely no chance for anything more than a client-attorney relationship with Perry. Now, embarrassed by her behavior, she was eager to escape. "Leave me alone."

Walking alongside her, he said, "But there are some things I need to discuss with you."

She pulled a set of keys from her purse. "Then have your secretary call me, and we'll agree on a mutually convenient time to meet at your office," she said brusquely.

Why she had ever lusted for him she would never know. She seethed. He was uncompromising, overbearing, and insufferable—just like her father. And she didn't need another man like that!

As she was about to insert the key in the car's lock, Perry got in the way. He draped his hands across her slender shoulders, bare except for the straps of the sundress. The pressure of his hands, the clean shaven manly smell of him, his all-pervasive virility assaulted her senses. Sydney had a wild urge to throw herself into his arms, so desirous was she for the feel of his firm body pressed to hers. She added shame to longing as a breathy whimper of sheer need escaped her lips.

"Sydney, I'm truly, truly sorry." He looked down into her face, his apologetic. "I *promise*," he said, with parenthesis, "it will never happen again."

For a moment she waited, silent, staring. A sensual revolution raged inside her; she was not trying to determine the sincerity of his words, but whether she wanted to return to what Perry had in store for her. She knew it was not compliance to the desire burning inside her.

"Please."

Distinctly undecided, she looked up into his face, feeling hot and flushed simultaneously. Maybe she was coming down with something. That could account for her sudden fit of temper. Ha! the taunting cynic in her chided, you've already got it.

"Are there any criminal-law attorneys in town you would recommend? Besides yourself, of course." She peered up at him.

Perry stared at her, looking very leery. Sydney almost laughed, but managed to contain herself.

"Ah . . . yes, of course." He lightly brushed his hands together. "One or two," he said with a begrudging shrug. "Want me to call one for you?"

"I'll do my own calling, thank you."

Under an eclipse of tension and tentative truce, Perry and Sydney returned to the restaurant. The waitress met them at the table, a glass of tea in one hand and a bottle of beer in the other.

Seating Sydney, Perry said to her, "Ms. Webster would like to change her order."

"Sure," the waitress replied, setting their drinks on the table. "What would you like?" she asked, flipping open the order pad attached to her belt.

"Never mind," Sydney said, shaking her napkin open. "I'm sure the fish will be fine."

"Fish is cooked to order. Yours will take a few more minutes."

In the long, brittle silence, the *cluck-cluck* of wood rotating in the overhead ceiling fan seemed especially loud. Eschewing small talk, Perry grew cagey. He hadn't intended to have dinner with Sydney. That had been Ramona's doing. Having had an inkling of what could transpire between them, he had been suffering from anxiety, had feared he would somehow incriminate himself.

He was aware that her eyes followed his movements, and he sensed her guarded anticipation. He knew the onus was on him, but he stalled, checking the cleanliness of his silverware and fiddling with his napkin.

Desire undulating through him, he didn't want to look at Sydney. Every time his gaze met hers, his heart beat harder. Though his observations confirmed his unerring memory of her, he could have described in minute detail what she wore, how she smelled, and even how the briefest touch of her brownish-pink skin felt. The delicate, doll-like face, the mercuric eyes so vivid they radiated vitality, the baby-fine hair and skin smooth as velvet. His hands warmed from thinking of it.

Ultimately, the quiet began to grate on his nerves. He chided himself for wasting time, but mindful that he'd almost run her off once, decided to take a different tack to ensure her stay. A few social pleasantries wouldn't hurt, he told himself.

"You look very nice."

Perry flinched inwardly as the trite words left his tongue, for he found her a daring beauty in the dusty rose sundress that exposed her elegant neck and slender shoulders. The fitted bodice outlined firm, jutting breasts; and her wide shirt flaring at mid-calf. High-heeled slippers in a cloth fabric and a tiny shoulder bag studded with beads that matched the color of her dress completed her dazzling ensemble. Though his gaze lazily appraised her, his innards were riotous with want. He could be jailed for his thoughts, he decided.

"Thank you," she replied woodenly.

He'd gotten a glimpse of a temper she had successfully contained till now; he was sure she was capable of a full-blown tantrum when she didn't get what she wanted. But what did she want? he wondered, his resolve to maintain a strictly professional relationship weakening. He wanted to ask, but feared the answer.

"So," he said. "how's work?"

"Fine."

"Talked to your father lately?"

"No."

"What about Jessica?"

"She spent the night at my house," Sydney replied. Then, with sudden animation, "You didn't tell me she went to see you."

Perry grinned at her, abashed. "It slipped my mind. She offered to pay your legal fees."

"That's just like her," Sydney replied, a fond look softening her expression.

Perry noted that her look matched her sweet tone of voice, and she smiled. It was unlike anything he'd ever seen before. He took a large swallow of water before he spoke. "In fact, someone else sent an envelope containing money to your 'defense fund.' "

"Who?"

"There was no name attached, but it came shortly after I met your family. I invite you to take a stab at the donor."

"My father," she said with a snort.

"Sydney . . ." He hesitated, then fell silent, pondering. He was still undecided about informing her of what he had learned about her mother's death. He knew it was not going to endear him to her.

"What?" Sydney prodded, her liquor-bright eyes lively with curiosity.

"Here we are."

Saved, Perry thought, as the waitress returned, placing their orders before them. "This looks great," he said with forced enthusiasm, eyeing his fish.

Eating was a chore for Sydney. She had to pretend to enjoy herself and keep vigil over her emotions from showing. While safe conversation accompanied the meal, her thwarted desire for him was a burden.

"The weatherman predicted record-breaking temperatures this summer," she said.

Tacitly, she followed Perry's lead, indulging in talk suitable for dining. She sensed he wasn't entirely comfortable with the social amenities, but at least he tried.

"I can believe it," he replied. "I seem to go through more shirts a day than ever."

Her imagination capturing him shirtless, she shuddered inwardly. A knot rose in her throat, and it took all her willpower to permit her to chew and swallow the food in her mouth. She set her fork on her plate and sat back in her chair, resting her hands in her lap.

She was entirely caught up in her own emotions. Knowing she must do something to rid herself of the overwhelming attraction for her attorney, she tried distorting his fine physique in her mind, but a hunchback just would not fit his powerful, leveled shoulders.

"Had enough already?"

Sydney looked right at him, and his compelling gaze held her. There was concern in his eyes, but also a gentleness that was uncanny in the way it affected her. She swallowed, but the pulse beat strongly at the base of her throat, as though her heart had risen from its usual place and was lodged there. Unable to speak, she smiled weakly at him and picked up her fork to resume eating.

Sydney toyed with more than ate her meal, Perry noticed, but at least she got some food down.

"I failed to attend a meeting at Our Park Community Center and was volunteered to head up the fund-raising committee for the swim team," he said. "I don't know where to start."

Sydney paused in the middle of chewing to look at him, serendipity in her eyes, a smile-to-be on her wide, kissable lips. Unconsciously, Perry wet his own lips with his tongue and reached for the bottle of beer as if thirsting for a drink.

"Are you asking for my help?" she said lightly.

Leaning slightly inward, a nearly bare shoulder tilted toward him suggestively, she ended what little control he had over his libido. His body felt heavy and warm, weightier in his loins, as if they were the depository for his cravings. He drank a careful sip of beer before he spoke.

"Would you be willing to?" he asked, still gripping the bottle.

"Sure," she replied, flipping that tempting shoulder nonchalantly. "Professional fund-raising is my sideline career. I did well in Houston. I put together a brochure and laid out the plan Daddy used for Texas College's twentieth anniversary year before last."

"I'm impressed," he replied in a tone that mirrored his words.

"I'll get started on it right away," she said, as she resumed eating. "You'll have something before the week is out. And I won't even charge you the normal ten percent."

The mention of Texas College and her father destroyed his appetite. Consuming him was Sydney's reaction to what he had discovered.

He had paid a visit to Deidre Holloway, a board member of the university, who had shed some light on the relationship between Daniels and Walter Webster. She'd also passed on a disturbing rumor that would alter his friendship with Sydney, if proved true. It could move Walter Webster to the top of the list of murder suspects. Again, he considered the effect of this information on Sydney's mental state. Maybe he should hold off on telling her, wait and see what happened. It was possible Webster had a good explanation for lying to Sydney about her mother's death.

In empathy with Sydney, he glanced stealthily at her. Excluding his promise to G.G. to make good on his life, he wondered why he'd never made a commitment to a woman. Or even why he contemplated doing it now. Though his childhood lacked a loving couple for him to emulate, he didn't subscribe to pop psychology. He was a mature, responsible adult with a finely honed sense of what was right and wrong for him. He felt Sydney was both.

He looked up to catch her observing him, not merely in passing, but with such scorching intent, her eyes had darkened to a dusky shade. Perry drew a quick, deep breath and tried to ignore the sudden ache in his loins. He returned her look, expecting her to back down. In the end, he did, and to his growing embarrassment, noticed that his hands were trembling.

"What do you think about Philip Morgan?" she asked coyly. "I heard he's a pretty good attorney."

"Not bad," Perry replied. He wasn't worried about that

kind of competition; he was fighting his own battle here. If Sydney wasn't careful, she could very well wind up replacing the food on his plate. "But I can find you someone better."

"Better than even you?"

"Everything all right here?" The waitress popped out of nowhere to ask.

Javier watched helplessly from a safe distance. He could imagine what the driver of the sporty car ahead of him was going through. Concern, then anxiety. Finally, panic. He swallowed calmly, waiting for an opportunity to be of use.

The foot pumped and pressed, but rather than slowing, the car sped up.

At the upcoming winding curve, the driver reacted quickly, grabbing for the emergency brake. Again, an undesirable effect. The car careened faster.

The driver was steering with both hands now. Perspiration rolled down the driver's neck despite the cool temperature in the sporty car.

Lights flicked on in the dark. A big car seemed to appear out of nowhere. Mashing the horn incessantly, the brakeless driver swerved in an attempt to miss the oncoming vehicle. The wheel jerked uncontrollably; a collision was inevitable. Bracing for it, the driver watched horrified as the car spun off the road, and slammed into an oak that had long claimed this spot along the highway.

He'd gotten through the chitchat, and Sydney seemed okay. Perry was now eager to wrap up their business and escape from her disturbing presence. With her open-sesame personality, she was the password to his senses and sensibilities. And he was fast running out of diversions. Fortunately, the waitress returned to clear the table.

"No dessert?"

"You hardly touched your dinner," Perry reminded her. He opened the briefcase next to his chair and pulled out a manila folder.

"I guess my body's not used to three squares a day," she replied.

"Hmmm?" he replied, distracted, and deliberately buried his head in his notes.

"Jessica spent the night and got up this morning and fixed breakfast. Then my boss got a case of the guilts and treated me to lunch at Sils. You called with a dinner invitation, and there's another meal waiting for me at home. Jessica prepared it. I guess it will be tomorrow's leftovers."

His interest piqued, he looked up at her. "Why did your boss have the guilts?"

"One, he misplaced a check I had given him. Two"—she bent back her index finger—"and most important, the station doesn't want me to make calls on clients. In other words, I've been grounded until I'm cleared as a suspect in Daniels's murder," she added with a hint of disgust.

"Why didn't you tell me about this before?" he demanded. He could deal with that handily, he thought, uncapping a pen to write a note to himself.

"With everything that's happened, it slipped my mind." She flashed him a smart smile.

"What else has slipped your mind?" he asked.

"Lloyd and Ursula joined us for lunch," she replied.

"No wonder I couldn't reach him," Perry said, aloud but to himself. "I'm sorry." He directed to Sydney. "You were saying?"

"Ursula said something rather curious. It made me feel that lunch had been a setup."

"What was that?"

"She said I should be wary of Lloyd because he likes to collect people."

"He likes to collect people?" Perry repeated. "Hmm," he added, making another note.

"Any idea what she meant?"

"Absolutely none. But you can be sure I'm going to check it out. What else have you stored away and forgotten to tell me?"

"Well, if I saw you more . . ." She left the rest of the reproach hanging between them.

Not about to touch that, Perry made another note. He scanned the typed pages stapled together that lay on the table before him. He'd found nothing to support Sydney's belief that Daniels was a philanderer who cheated on all his women. But two vices of his had stood out. One was illegal, and the other was only a vice in the eye of a jealous lover. Daniels was a flirt, and he loved to gamble. The African-American community didn't care about those indiscretions, not with the good Daniels had done. Basically, the man was just another politician greedy for power. Nothing unusual about that, Perry thought.

"When you went to Daniels's, how was he dressed?"

"Dressed?" she frowned.

"Yes," he repeated. "You said he was obviously expecting someone, but not you."

"Oh," she said with understanding. "Okay." Wetting her lips, eyes hooded, she explained. "He, uh, had on a rust-colored silk shirt. It was wide, with a rounded hem. Not the kind you tuck in. And he wore a thick, gold chain, so his shirt was unbuttoned. He had on white pants, billowy, like lounging pajamas, and sandals. Open-heeled. Oh, and he was about to shave. He had an electric razor in his hand. Or he'd just finished. I remember smelling . . . uh"—she frowned—"Royal Copenhagen maybe."

"Then what happened?"

"I lit right into him," she replied. "At first he was surprised. Then he said something about 'baby sister' as he was closing the door. I never did make out what he was mumbling about."

"Then what?"

"He walked off, and I started to follow. When I realized he was going back to his bedroom, I stopped and yelled to him from the hallway that I'd be waiting. I went to the living room."

"What was the lighting like?"

"The drapes were closed, but streaks of daylight came in. Mostly, the light came from those standing lamps he had set in a triangle. It was a little dark, kind of . . ."

Recalling the decorator's touch to Daniels's home, Perry envisioned Sydney going there with the most innocent of intentions, and the scene playing out like one in a sinister movie. The results could have been different, and though it was too late to scold her imprudent decision, he'd rather defend her on a murder charge than represent her as a victim.

"Intimate?" Perry supplied.

"Yeah." She nodded her head in assent. "Luther Vandross was playing on the box."

"How long was it before he reappeared?"

"It seemed like forever, but I guess it was a minute or two."

"Was anything different about him? How did he act?"

"Amused," she said, with a mocking twist of her lips.

Either Daniels was expecting a woman as Sydney had guessed, or one was already present, Perry thought. Which was it? "In hindsight," he asked, "do you believe he made a serious play for you?"

"In hindsight?" She considered prudently. "No. I believe he was making fun of me."

"And that's when you picked up the rock and threw it at him."

It wasn't a question, but a statement with an ugly interpretation. Perry observed her closely. He could tell she took it as an insult. She looked absolutely adorable, just the same. He suppressed a smile, then remembered something Jessica had implied, which he had had occasion to see first-hand was true: Sydney did need a keeper.

"I threw it at him because he was mocking me," she reiterated, defending herself against the unspoken accusation. "I did not want, nor did I pursue his attention, for your information."

"But you can see now how the police could reach their conclusion," he replied. "Could you tell whether anyone else was in the apartment, in the back maybe?"

Shaking her head from side to side, she told him, "I wouldn't know for sure. A bottle of wine was chilling on the bar, and two glasses had been set out. Why? Do you think someone else was there?"

"Yes, I do. A nosy neighbor said there was a parade of traffic in and out of Daniels's apartment that day since he returned from Austin, around four that afternoon. She saw at least two different women, neither of which was you or the cleaning lady who was there earlier. I was just trying to get the time element down." Holding pages down on the table, he asked, "What do you know about the state coordinating board?"

"That's a helluva jump," she said. "My father hates them, for one thing. If it weren't for Larry, he'd be out of a job."

"He still could be," Perry retorted. His gaze widened as the waitress approached their table, carrying a portable telephone.

"Mr. MacDonald, there's a call for you."

Perry exchanged a curious look with Sydney, as he accepted the call. "This is Perry MacDonald," he said with his customary professionalism into the mouthpiece. A smile of recognition brightened his face. "Javier, what's up?" He stiffened instantly, his lips thinning and frown lines ribbing his forehead as he stared at Sydney. "Okay," he said. "We're on the way." He hung up the phone, then passed it to the waitress. "Thank you," he said, withdrawing a slender wallet from inside his coat. "We've got to go," he said to Sydney, tossing several bills onto the table as he got to his feet.

"Go where?" she asked.

"The hospital," he replied, walking around to help her from her chair. "There's been an accident."

Fourteen

The last meal of the day progressed into the best, Sydney recalled, her face animating slowly into wistfulness. Caught in the memory of it, she was compelled to play it out.

With that familiar tingle working its way up her spine, joy came over her, and she envisioned Perry stealing glances at her—a series of revealing looks that built up her hopes before he replaced them with deep-in-thought expressions. His lawyer look, she mused, giddy with mirth and longing to croon a dulcet melody. Yet she had been ready to fire him as her attorney.

Her vision of a blissful duet faded into a bittersweet sigh. She wished she could get back to one of those precious moments . . . before the waitress arrived with the phone . . . before Perry took the bad-news call about Jessica's accident that brought them to Dalston Memorial Hospital.

But was it a fair exchange?

Three floors above ground level in an ordinary hospital room, Sydney stared out the window into the black night. The one person she could always count on, and she'd ended up ruining her life. First, Jessica's fiancé Larry Daniels, had died after contact with her, and now Jessica herself was in surgery due to multiple injuries.

Sydney moaned as guilt wrapped her in its disquieting embrace. Knotting her hands together under her chin, a silent prayer on her still lips, she felt responsible for Jessica's fate.

It was speculated that Jessica had been returning to Sydney's house, but where had she gone? Had she been called away by something as unexpected as the dinner invitation from Perry that had put their plans for the evening on hold?

They'd never finished their talk, Sydney recalled with frightening regret. She didn't want to believe there would not be another chance.

Chances. What had started so fortuitously had now become a verdict. It just hovered in her mind like Perry. She felt a tangible, resonating connection to him, as if he were a part of her.

How could she even think about him at a time like this?

If hindsight was indeed twenty-twenty, then she shouldn't have moved to Dalston. In which case she wouldn't have met Perry MacDonald. She clung to that thought as if it were a life preserver, something intimately solid.

Sydney pushed away from the window to walk around the bed, her hand grazing the stiffly tucked spread. It seemed everything she touched withered. She snatched her hand from the bed to rub anxiously at her neck. She prayed Jessica wouldn't die.

Ambling about the private room—she had requested it for Jessica's convalescence—brought her to the door. On the other side of it, her father and Perry stood in the corridor. She didn't know what was going on between them, and at that moment she didn't care.

Her father had met them at the door upon their arrival at the hospital. The first words out of his mouth had been an accusation in the form of a reprimand. *If you had gotten a sensible car, none of this would have happened.*

Perry had come to her rescue. Not for the first time, she recalled somberly, had he warded off her father's wrath.

She backed away from the door and returned to stand at the foot of the bed. Bending, she slouched over the rail, her head lowered. Coming full circle with her remorse, she wished she had remained in Houston. Again, it struck her that she wouldn't then have met Perry.

But he was only hers in wishes made in her bed, late in the night. In the final analysis, the only exchange of emotion between them was in her mind and her mendicant heart.

The door burst open, and Sydney spun about startled to see an unfamiliar woman standing in the opening.

"You," the stranger rasped bitterly. "You always turn up where you shouldn't be, like the proverbial bad penny!"

"You're just out to destroy my relationship with Sydney!"

A predatory glint in his narrowed eyes, Perry returned the contentious glower. You don't know how close to the truth you are, he wanted to shout back at Walter Webster. "You're the one who lied. Give me a reason to keep the lie secret, Dr. Webster," he added pretentiously, as if willing to listen to reason. He wondered fleetingly how Webster had found out about Javier's investigation of his family.

"It's for Sydney that I did so," Walter Webster retorted defiantly.

Perry's brow shot up. Walter Webster had warped expectations for his daughters, he decided, recalling the information he'd gotten from Javier. They had to be perfect as he defined it, and to him, perfection meant blind obedience to his wishes. Sydney had run away from him because of his unrealistic demands. But each time she'd returned, hoping for approval and a hint of affection, that never came. Though exacting revenge against her father would be sweet, Perry couldn't do it at her expense. He wished the truth never had to come out, knew she must learn of it yet hoped he didn't have to be the one to tell her.

"You may not believe me," Walter Webster continued, staunch in his own defense, "but everything I've done, I did for the good of my girls,"

"The good of your girls—or yourself?" Perry retorted sarcastically.

"If you had seen how sick Sydney became after learning

about her mother's death, you would understand why I be-haved as I did."

His jaws clenched and his eyes locked hard on Walter Webster, Perry pressed the man further. "For twenty-five years," he rasped, his voice almost a whisper, "you let her believe her mother died from an exotic illness. And when she became ill, you used protectiveness to control her."

"That's not true, not true at all," Webster stammered bel-ligerently. "You don't know what you're talking about."

"If it weren't for Jessica's sneaking Sydney to a psy-chologist when she was a teenager, where she learned to control her asthma," Perry shot back acerbically, "you'd have a pathetic shell of a daughter."

Javier's fact-finding jaunt to Houston had provided many revealing tidbits about the Websters. The investigator had done a thorough job, and Perry commended him silently. Walter Webster had faked an illness, then had reveled in the attention he'd gotten when Sydney had rushed to his bedside last October. Perry suspected that was not the first time Walter had manipulated Sydney, playing on her fears of losing him as she had lost her mother.

"That's the only reason Sydney is not your puppet," he continued, glaring at her father, "and now, you're afraid of losing the little influence you still hold over her."

"You're a liar, Mr. MacDonald! You're no better than——" Walter Webster suddenly clammed up.

"Than who?" Perry replied with a saccharine smile and a taunting arch of one brow. "Larry Daniels?"

"I did what was best for Sydney, I tell you!" Webster insisted intently, but his shoulders drooped and his head low-ered as he turned to walk off. Then, changing his mind, he faced Perry, his desperation visible. "What is it going to take to make you understand?" he demanded, a pleading look in his eyes.

Seeing Webster lose his cool helped Perry regain full com-posure. "Did you kill Larry Daniels?" he replied unmoved.

"You don't want the truth." The older man bit off the words contentiously, shaking a finger in Perry's face. "You want dirt. You were born in it, and you wallow in it."

"You'd better pray to your God that I never have to put you on the witness stand. I'll bury you in that mud," Perry whispered, menace in his tone and expression.

"Who are you?" Sydney asked, staring bewilderedly at the stranger who had walked into Jessica's room as if she had a right to do so.

"I'm Jessica's mother, that's who I am."

Sydney's head snapped back. "Jessica's mother?" she echoed in disbelief. She inventoried the woman's features, noting the similarity in the shape and color of the eyes; though hers were marred by the hatred in them. And the woman's build was similar, except a fattening diet and lack of exercise showed in her girth. Despite the resemblance, Sydney said what she knew to be true. "Jessica's mother is dead."

"I assure you I'm not, Ms. Hotsy-totsy Know-it-all," Beverly replied.

Sydney was aware that her heart began to beat irregularly as she struggled to cope with the woman's assertion. "But I thought—"

"You never think! You're just like your mother was, a destructive little bitch."

Sydney was taken aback, more by the venom than the biting insult. She bristled at the woman's audacity, but respect for her elders ingrained in her, she kept her mouth shut.

"It must be in your genes to destroy other people's lives. The irony is that you only see fit to involve yourself in my daughter's life." She snorted full of disdain. "Everywhere she goes, you follow like a puppy, nipping at her heels, chewing on everything she has until it's all gone."

"That's not true," Sydney protested weakly. Hadn't she just had almost the same thought a few minutes ago?

"Oh, yes, it's true," Beverly retorted. "First, you couldn't stand it that she was here, finding peace—even with Walter. You were jealous of her relationship with him. She knew how to control him; you didn't. So here you came, trotting into her life again. But he'd always loved her more than you. She was his firstborn. You refused to accept that, couldn't stand it, in fact," she concluded, her voice hardened by ridicule.

"I don't know who you are," Sydney replied tartly, "but you're not Jessica's mother."

"So sure about that, are you?" Beverly taunted. "It's taken time, but that's changing," she added as if speaking to herself. "Jessica and I are friends," she stated solemnly, a hint of pride in her voice. "Our relationship has been progressing as it should have a long time ago—before your mother ruined it, taking not just my husband but my daughter away from me. Oh, I was winning her back. Until you showed up and started coming between us," she added with renewed rage, the hands balled into fists at her sides trembling. "Again, seeking Daddy's pat-on-the-head for every meager achievement in your life and causing trouble in the process."

Unable to take any more of the painful taunting that mirrored her suspicions, Sydney bolted for the door.

Perry walked off, heading for the room where Sydney awaited Jessica's return. Javier cut him off at an intersecting corridor.

"Hey, I was wondering where you were," Perry said, meeting him half way. Javier's jaw was puffy, and a dark circle ringed his right eye. "What happened to you? I know you didn't get those playing golf."

"More like a run in with a nine-iron," Javier replied, holding a cold compress against his jaw.

"Explain that quickly. How did you happen to be so close to the accident?"

"It's all part of the same story," Javier chuckled. "I went over to Rampart, where one of the regular gambling houses Montcrief runs is located. I wanted to find out if Daniels participated in any of those games."

"According to Hank Evans," Perry interjected, "Montcrief was a regular at Daniels's gambling parties."

"Well, asking the question got me hit," Javier continued, "but guess who I saw driving up as I was being kicked out? Mark Frederickson. Sydney's boss at WDST."

"Oh, really?"

"They stopped him at the door. Seems the young radio heir has a poor credit rating. But he produced the mandatory five g's, so they let him in."

"That's interesting," Perry replied. "And Daniels?"

Javier shook his head in a sign of defeat. "I'll have to go another route. Anyway, I left there heading for the White Lagoon Restaurant."

"What was there?"

"A sweet little honey who promised me a home-cooked meal," Javier grinned, wiggling his eyebrows suggestively. "Anyway, that's how I came to be behind Jessica. When I first saw the car, I thought it was Sydney at the wheel. Tinted windows, you know. But when I was pulling her from the car, I realized it was Jessica Webster. Any word from the doctors?"

"Nothing yet," Perry replied. "She was still in surgery the last I heard—before the old man pulled me off to the side. He met us at the door when we arrived and started right in on Sydney about buying a sports car."

"He blamed her for the accident?" Gently, Javier shook his head in disbelief while maintaining the compress on his jaw. "It could have been Sydney; then who would he have blamed? I got a chance to sneak a peek before the police hustled me out of the way. The brake lines were cut. A hasty job, rather amateurish but nonetheless effective," he added.

His brows knitting together anxiously, Perry demanded, "Are you sure about that?"

"Positive," Javier replied.

Perry bit off a curse.

"I put in a call to Melloncamp. I figured you'd want him to know."

"Good thinking," Perry replied pensively. In light of Javier's disclosure, he should have given the incident involving the snake more consideration, he chided himself. "Did Jessica say anything when you pulled her out?"

"Nothing intelligible. Something about a baby, maybe." Javier shrugged, a speculative frown on his face.

"Baby . . ." Perry echoed puzzled. "Sydney didn't say anything about a baby at dinner," he said to himself, then to Javier, "Hers or someone else's?"

"I don't know," Javier replied. "But I developed that roll of film and saw what you saw. I agree that the police must have something else, something they're holding on to as if it's the key to the secrets of the universe."

"Speaking of keys"—Perry looked pointedly at Javier—"what have you been able to accomplish?"

"So far, I've only had a chance to have one made from the imprint. Sorry. But I did notice something about the pictures you got from our client. Not so much who's in them, but who is not."

"And?" Perry prompted.

"Neither of the Andrewses." With hindsight, he said, "Maybe not so much Ursula, as Lloyd."

Perry arched an inquiring brow. "I'm not getting the point."

"Did you say Sydney first met Ursula Andrews when she and Lloyd picked up her father and Jessica for the memorial service?"

"Yes . . . so?"

"Think about it," Javier sighed heavily. "If Sydney had met Ursula before then, wouldn't she have been able to identify her as the woman she suspected of being with Daniels at the hotel? As you said, Ursula Andrews is not a forgettable-looking woman."

Perry pondered momentarily. A sour-taste frown spreading across his face, he said, "That could mean we're missing another player. Javier . . . ?"

"I'm on it."

Beverly blocked her exit. "Oh, no, you're going to hear this," she said. "You're the one who wanted to be included, to feel like a part of the family, so stay to hear the truth." She poked Sydney in the breastbone. "One would think you'd show her a little more gratitude after all Jessica has done for you. But no, not you. . . ."

Despite the woman's liquored breath blowing in her face, Sydney couldn't leave, for too much of what this woman said was true. Jessica had been her primary caregiver. If it were not for the sacrifices her sister had made, her father would have turned her into a helpless shell of a woman, incapable of independence. Perversely, Sydney felt she deserved this punishment.

"If it weren't for you, Larry would still be alive and my baby would be the wife of a very powerful politician. You wanted it all for yourself. Well, life ain't like that, missy. The world does not exist solely for Ms. Sydney Webster."

Abruptly, the door swung open, and both women spun to face a tall, blond doctor dressed in green scrubs. He entered hesitantly, looking back and forth between Sydney and Beverly.

"Are you relatives of Ms. Webster?" he asked, taking both of them in with his inquiring gaze.

"I'm her sister," Sydney replied, stepping forward. "How is she?"

"Well, first off, you should know we couldn't save the baby," he said somewhat sadly.

Sydney's hand flew to her mouth, but not before a whimper of regret escaped her.

Beverly released a keening moan. "Oh, no, my grandbaby." Tears flooded her eyes.

"I'm truly sorry," the doctor continued. "As for Ms. Webster . . ."

"It shoulda been you!" Beverly shrieked, her tear-stained face a monstrous mask as she turned viciously on Sydney. "It shoulda been you." With unexpected swiftness, her hands went to Sydney's neck. "Not my baby. It shoulda been you in that car!"

"Hey, wait a minute. Stop this!" the stunned doctor commanded.

Perry sighed deeply, running a weary hand down his face. Having to find an unknown woman who might provide a clue as to who had killed Daniels was a major setback. "But that's not the worst of it," he said, about to voice his gravest concern. "Javier, I think you better hire a couple of men. I want Sydney watched around the clock."

"Somebody get security!"

Perry turned, curious about the frantic activity involving a room down the hall. Several nurses were hurrying into it, and he realized it was the room the hospital had assigned to Jessica once she was released from recovery. His eyes widening with concern, he remembered that Sydney was in that room.

With Javier on his heels, Perry raced to it to see a pileup of people on the floor. Walter Webster was standing off to the side, watching and barking commands such as, "Stop this, Corinda Fay!" Otherwise he did nothing.

"What the hell's going on?" Perry said before spotting Sydney in the middle of the melee on the floor. Her neck was in the grip of a heavyset woman. He helped the two security guards who were trying to disengage the woman's hands from Sydney.

"You're making a complete fool of yourself, Corinda!" Walter Webster exclaimed only adding to the din. "Stop it right this minute!"

Sydney tried to block it from her mind, but the question wouldn't go away. How could they have lied to her? she again wondered. She shut her eyes real tight and snuggled deeper into the couch, crossing her ankles which rested on the coffee table in her den. She just wanted to put this day out of her head.

It was around midnight. Not long since she and Perry had left the hospital after the doctor declared Jessica would need minor plastic surgery, but would probably live to a ripe old age. Her father had stayed because learning Jessica had been pregnant had been a shock, the second one that day, for he hadn't known Jessica's mother had reappeared in their lives. He would have been foolish to disregard the doctor's warning about his heart.

"Here, see if this helps."

Sydney opened her eyes and sat up, swinging her feet to the floor. Perry handed her a glass of sizzling liquid. She had come down with a case of indigestion. She knew her nerves were tying her stomach in knots. And Perry by his presence, aggravated her condition, causing an incurable ache in her loins.

"Thank you." She drank the brew and set the empty glass on the coffee table.

"It's been a long day," he said. "You need some rest."

He stood practically over her, legs apart, hands on his narrow hips. Resting was the last thing his nearness inspired in her.

"Fat chance." She chuckled sarcastically as she stood. "I'm too wired to sleep." She sauntered to one of the bay windows to stare out unseeingly. "All this time I believed Jessica's mother was dead."

"That's what you were told. You had no reason to think otherwise."

"Still," she said, uncomprehending, "that doesn't explain her animosity toward me."

"No, it doesn't," Perry concurred, massaging his forehead. "But she's had many years to feed her bruised ego. Your father left her to marry your mother. You're still a child in her eyes, and children are easy victims."

"But why didn't Jessica tell me her mother was alive?"

"I think the woman's behavior is the answer to that. She was drunk. Didn't you smell the liquor on her breath? Even if you discount her occupation, I'd venture to guess that her drinking habits would make her an embarrassment."

"What do you mean her occupation?"

Perry slapped the side of his head with the ball of his palm. "I'm sorry; I didn't realize you didn't know the woman at the hospital. Corinda Webster also goes under the name Beverly Lockhart."

Sydney's brows rose, revealing her astonishment. "The maid the police spoke to? Perry, do you realize what that means?"

"Sorry," he replied, shaking his head, a smile on his lips. "It's possible, but I can't see a woman like that ruining her daughter's chance to marry a powerful politician, can you?"

"I guess not," Sydney responded with grudging acceptance. "Larry would be her revenge against me." She sighed wearily and turned her back on Perry to stare out into the night. "I can't help but wonder, though, what else I've been lied to about," she said in a barely audible voice.

Perry mumbled a bitter curse, then regretted it when Sydney spun about to note the stern look on his face, the worry evident in his dark, usually unfathomable eyes. Just the idea of his concern excited her.

"It's getting to you, too," she said softly, mentally caressing him.

In one fluid surprising motion, Perry crossed the distance between them to pull her into his arms. Sydney drew in a quick sharp breath, then sank into his cushiony embrace, burying her face against the corded muscles of his chest. There was nothing foreign about the yearning tugging at her innards as she wound her arms around him. She breathed in his warmth, the faint smell of his skin.

"I want you to be extra careful," he said, his voice a gentle purr over her head. "Call in sick tomorrow, and possibly the next day, too. When I leave, don't open the door for anyone."

Lifting her head to gaze anxiously up at him, she asked, "Are you leaving now?"

"No, not now, but *when* I do." His large hands took her face and held it gently. "I don't want you to worry."

His eyes held her as if in a tender vise, and she felt cocooned in a greater warmth. Her brain however seemed scrambled; she knew there was something vitally important almost on the tip of her tongue, to ask, but couldn't pinpoint it.

"Since I know you're going to insist on dragging it out of me one way or the other, I might as well tell you," he said reluctantly.

He dropped his hands from her face, and a tiny mewl of displeasure came from her, only to be silenced when he wrapped his arms around her waist to hold her close to him.

"Javier is positive the brake lines in your car were cut," he continued, his chin resting on top of her head. "We don't know whether you were expected to be driving, or Jessica was the target."

"In other words, somebody tried to kill me," Sydney whispered. But fear couldn't penetrate her wanting of him. Even the chaos of her life seemed a distant thing.

"We don't know for sure," he emphasized in a tone designed to comfort her, "but I swear to you, we will—and soon."

The phone rang. It was a bitter reminder, and Sydney sighed.

"That has to be Javier," Perry said. "Where's the phone?"

Reluctantly, she backed from his embrace to retrieve the portable one from the counter of the bar. She picked it up amid the second ring. "Hello . . . He's right here, Javier."

Perry met her halfway across the room to take the phone. "Talk to me," he commanded with a sense of urgency.

In need of fresh air, Sydney headed for the back door. She glanced over her shoulder to see Perry deeply embroiled in conversation, then walked out. Only a half-moon shone in the purplish-black sky. Lampposts from her deck created a crisscross pattern of light. Porch lights were on at Jasmine's, as well.

After a moment of indecision, she skipped down the stairs to the sandy ground and sauntered to the water's edge. The color and temperature of the night matched her black thoughts and hot feelings. She was in the dark about her family, yet her senses tingled with the bright promise of what was almost in her grasp. Perry's presence lessened the ominousness of the present, she thought, a smile touching her face. She was certain the hateful Corinda Webster would not attack her here.

"Sydney?"

She turned to look up to where he stood by the rail gazing down at her. She pulled off her shoes and held them up poised to throw them toward him. "Here, catch."

"What are you doing?"

"I'm going for a walk," she replied.

"I'll come with you."

"But you'll get your trousers wet."

Disregarding the warning, Perry hurried down from the deck. Removing his shoes and socks, he set them on the bottom step, then rolled up his pant legs to his knees. Sydney whistled.

"Nice legs," she said, staring at them shamelessly.

He approached her, a grin splitting his face as he turned his shirtsleeves up. "That's what I like about you."

She cocked her head, a smile more blithe than curious brightening her face. "What?"

"Your ability to spring back from adversity."

His eyes never left her face as he took the shoes from her hands. She saw only him and what could be . . . a chance to find out. It sent a tremor through her.

"I trust you, you know," she said softly, her eyes skimming his handsome face.

"I'm glad. I'll never let you down."

"That's what I'm counting on."

Easing the shoes to one hand, he took one of hers in the other. A flash of heat shot up her arm, and she shivered visibly. Neither embarrassed nor distressed by her reaction, she wondered what he would do if she acted on the simmering desire to taste his lips. She was gravitating toward him, aware that her heart hammered against her ribs.

Perry stepped back. "Let's walk," he said abruptly, but with gentle command.

Aware of the sudden tenseness in him, the pulse beating at his throat, Sydney smiled coyly from under her long lashes, but she obeyed, basking in the knowledge of her power to arouse him.

Perry was not going to be easy to seduce, she thought, glancing sidelong at his military saunter. His eyes were trained straight ahead, his lips were clamped together and his hand gripped hers as if he expected her to bolt at any moment.

He was not a man to let emotions into the courtroom, she mused. Unless they were pertinent to the case. A strategy different from an all-out chase, something that would appeal to his lawyer's mind was called for. The game Perry liked best, she knew, was camouflage.

"Perry . . .

Fifteen

". . . tell me a bedtime story," Sydney said, her velvety voice a whisper in the windless sky.

"Huh?" Perry replied.

Knowing he must have a bovine look, he was grateful for the dark. He had been trying to think: the snake, the accident, the lies represented substantial leads. But he couldn't use them as evidence of his client's innocence. Instead, they dangled like loose ends at the fringes of the desire dominating his senses. With Sydney's soft hand in his, he could barely remember to breathe. And even when he did, she filled his nostrils with her woman's scent.

"Who was she, Perry?" Sydney asked blithely. "The woman who makes you keep your distance."

The serendipitous look on Sydney's face caused an instant's wariness in him. Don't look in her eyes, the voice of reason warned. In the play of light and shadow in their path, her eyes glimmered irresistibly. It seemed he was slowly being sucked into her essence. He blinked, as if to break the lure she held over him, and wondered what game she was playing.

"There's no woman of influence in my life," he said with macho pride. "The law is a jealous mistress," he added dramatically.

"Cliché's from you, Counselor?" she quipped, casting an amused glance at him.

The night was hot; the sand gritty underfoot. Not exactly

a setting for amour, Perry mused. But it was easy to fall victim to Sydney's coy charm. His feeling for her was heavily weighted with want, which gave her unfair advantage. He smiled to himself, believing she was coming on to him.

"It's as though I'm meeting you for the first time," he replied. The reply was a form of procrastination, but the words held a note of truth. "You're quite aggressive, aren't you?"

"Assertive," she corrected, chuckling.

"I didn't know there was much of a difference," he quibbled, still stalling. "Who are you?"

Sydney tossed back her head and laughed with unadulterated delight. "Cut the evasions and answer the question," she commanded with an infectious grin.

Perry's lips expanded into an indulgent smile, but he sighed as if bored, aware of the game. What could it hurt? he wondered fleetingly, his love of competition affecting his sense of caution. With an inkling of the rules, he was confident in his ability to control and win—in spite of his bewitching opponent.

"Her name was Sheila Pinkney," he said matter-of-factly. "We were in law school together."

"Did you love her?"

A "yes" was on the tip of his tongue, but a quick flash of memory stifled it. He recalled the devastation he had known over Sheila's betrayal, and then the ease with which all caring for her vanished.

"Love her?" he echoed ponderously, staring intently at Sydney. What he now believed about emotions—that honest ones grew—had changed his mind. "I don't know. I was loyal to her," he said. "I listened to her first-year law student war stories, and she listened to mine. We shared living expenses. Then she stole a brief I had written for a research class and turned it in with her name on it. It nearly got me kicked out of law school until I produced all my notes. But even before that," he added, the emotions of that time now

dead, "I believe comfort and convenience defined our relationship more than anything else."

"Perry, may I tell you something?"

His mouth dropped open and bewilderment tinged his
expression. He wanted to assure Sydney that she could tell
him anything she wanted, but . . .

"Be very careful how you answer," she admonished,
peeking up at him from under her long lashes.

When she put it like that, Perry paused to ponder this
yet-to-be disclosed revelation. He stared at her lovely profile, thinking if she admitted to killing Larry Daniels, then
he would certainly want to know it.

"I made the mistake once of believing in fairy tales," she
replied softly, as if feeling her way around the words, their
intent. "Daddy and Jessica used to get after me all the time
about allowing myself to be deceived. 'Face reality and stop
dreaming,' " she said quoting one or the other of them. "For
the most part, I listened and obeyed, but it wasn't any fun."
She chuckled, tweaking her nose. "I realize they were trying
to protect me. But it's not good when a person is afraid to
take chances because of all the bad things that could happen. It deprives you of the opportunity to experience something good." She had the zeal of "eureka" in her tone.

Sydney just needed to talk, Perry realized. He was somewhat disappointed in the direction the conversation was taking, having expected something a little more intimate. He
had forgotten that she had laid the ground rules. His sensuality ebbed . . . a little.

"So, I took a chance," she said. "Needless to say, my
timing—and everything else—was badly off."

"You took a chance with the wrong person and he hurt
you," Perry told her.

"Yep. But it was my own fault. I made assumptions I
shouldn't have. I believed he could provide something I
needed at the time, and looked solely to him rather than to
myself as well."

"Have you found it?"

"Yes," she replied promptly. "At least, I think so," she added in a gentle, secretive tone.

That tone caused a mild disruption in Perry. He glanced at her profile and promptly stumbled. Serves you right! he chided himself, squelching his emotions.

"And I know for certain that one has to take chances, regardless of the risks. Even Jessica must have come to accept that."

"You're talking about her engagement to Daniels."

"Yes. She knew he was a flirt, but she decided to risk marrying him anyway."

"Sometimes it doesn't work out the way you want." He sounded resigned.

"No. But that doesn't mean you stop trying."

"It makes you vulnerable to harm," he countered.

"But you can also miss out on good things if you don't try." She smiled up at him. "May I tell you something else? And again, I caution you."

A complaisant grin on his face, Perry replied confidently, "Sydney, you can tell me anything you want."

"I'm attracted to you," she said without hesitation, without missing a step as they walked along the water's edge.

Perry stopped in the sand. The step she had taken placing her an arm's length away, their hands still clasped, Sydney angled to face him head-on. Her eyes sparkled in the dark. A response wavered on his lips as the wanton sensation imprisoned in his loins demanded release. It seemed too much time had passed in hesitation. Though it was only a second or two, he feared it was still too long to successfully pull off a lie.

"Let's go back," he said firmly.

Setting a maestoso pace, he marched back to Sydney's home, chiding himself under his breath for walking right into her trap. Caught by his own damn game! he railed silently, shaking his head. Get the witness on the stand, make him comfortable with seemingly innocuous chatter, then pounce!

There was a very good reason why he felt nothing for Sheila now, he argued silently. It had happened a long time ago. Besides, he was not one to wallow in bitter memories.

It also stood to reason that he had no idea what love was, having never experienced it before. His forced march slowed to a saunter. It could very well be that what he felt for Sydney was . . . what?

He turned to see Sydney meandering along. He couldn't make out the expression on her face, but he wondered if he'd hurt her. It mattered to him, and that made him angrier.

"Sydney," he called out, his voice softened by a hint of remorse. He started back for her, then changed his mind. He could no longer deny what he felt for his client, even though it was wrong. He turned to climb the steps leading to her porch.

"I have another question," she announced in that same slow, hypnotic tone that left him susceptible to its narcotic effect.

Perry turned to her. When she sashayed into the light, he saw her face. Her eyes gleamed voraciously, the look of a huntress in them. His craving for her inflamed, he was rendered tongue-tied.

"Are you attracted to me?"

Perry's tongue came out of his mouth to glide over his top lip where beads of perspiration formed a damp mustache. G.G. told him that sweat on his top lip meant he was mean, but it wasn't meanness he was feeling.

"Sydney, you know there can be nothing between us but a professional relationship," he said irritably, but his tone lacked conviction.

She looked up at him girlishly, her head cocked. "Why?" she asked benignly.

"There's a code of ethics I'm sworn to uphold."

"For whom?"

"For my clients."

"So you can't be a lawyer and a man at the same time?"

"Sydney Lauren," he grated out.

"Well?" she said lightly.

Stampeded like a witness on the stand caught in his own lie, Perry thought.

"Is it that you haven't forgiven yourself, Perry?"

"I don't understand the question," he replied, much too quickly.

"Then I'll rephrase it," she said promptly. "After setting me straight about your arrest, you wanted to back out as my attorney. You seemed to have decided—without my input, I might add—that you were unfit to represent me because of it. That's a very bad habit you have," she scolded.

"What bad habit?"

"Deciding on your own what's best for me," she replied. "Did you understand the question this time?"

"I'm not sure; you've thrown several things at me at once." She was wearing him down.

"Quit stalling, Counselor." She pressed on undeterred, a mitigating smile on her lips, sauntering right up to him, to inches away, and placing her hands on his chest. A gleam of impertinence in the depths of her eyes, utter confidence in her clear voice, she announced, "When I decide to take a lover, it's with the understanding that there will be no secrets between us."

Perry's heart almost jumped out of his chest. "Oh." He swallowed hard. "And have you decided to take a lover?"

"Oh, most definitely," she said softly, lightly touching his lips with hers. "And in case you're curious, he's a dashing, intelligent attorney. He hates small talk, and he's a little bossy," she went on, "but those are minor idiosyncrasies. I can deal with them." Her lips found the center of his mouth.

Their sampling of his lips all but dismissed the last of his resistance. His body responded to the vibrancy of her shivery kisses, long suppressed instincts coming to the fore. Shocking, yet it was not. He was conscious of nothing but her and the pungent feel of the desire sweeping through him. He held her loosely in the circle of his arms, as if to allow her a last-minute escape. "Sydney, you don't know everything about me. I'm possessive, I don't like to share, and sometimes I take myself too seriously."

"You forgot one thing." She grinned.

"What's that?"

"You like to tease."

"I've been known to do that, too. But this is no game. You'd better be damned sure this is what you want, that I'm what you want." He tugged her to him with rough affection.

"Oh, I'm sure," she professed cozily before her lips captured his.

Her mouth was persuasive, demanding in an irrepressible way that reminded him of her persistence and impetuosity. Ethical obstacles had no chance as he yielded to the searing need which had been building for weeks.

"The defense rests," he ground out against her lips, as he held her possessively against the length of him and tasted the inside of her mouth.

Morning shone mildly through the window, but Sydney was seething with residuals of last night's unfulfilled passion. She was standing before the mirror in her bathroom, attempting to trace an even line around her lips.

Dressed, she was almost ready to leave the house. She knew Perry was downstairs, probably on the phone, waiting for her to hurry. Another mishap with the lip pencil found her wiping her mouth clean and starting over.

The previous hours had been torturous ones, she thought, as another reminder of her sexual discomfort knotted her limbs. Momentarily lulled by the erotic sensation, she stared at her reflection, mesmerized by her memory of the near-perfect evening. Perry's face, cloaked in passion, appeared to her, and longing filled her.

Sydney grunted softly, then waited until her quickened pulse quieted before raising the lip pencil to her mouth.

Perry had absolutely refused to assuage the ache when it had become apparent that neither possessed protection. Since he was a child conceived in the heat of the moment, he refused to chance another "accident." She had known that no amount of cajoling or seduction would change his mind.

"Though I wouldn't mind having a child with you," he had said, "now is definitely not a good time."

Sydney cursed his untimely bout of practicality, but took comfort in the fact that he'd suffered as she had. He had showered for hours before going to bed, she recalled laughingly.

Then her mind moved on, correcting the problem. She decided that while visiting Jessica at the hospital, she would stop at the pharmacy and stock up on safe-sex paraphernalia. She exchanged the pencil for a tube of lipstick, and an idea came to her as she colored her mouth. Her hands stilled on her slightly parted lips, her gaze now intent.

She had always known it, hadn't she? she asked silently, staring clearly at her reflection. The chance she had feared to take had been taken from her.

Perry was no substitute, no replacement for the feelings she had missed getting from her family. He was the man of her girlish dreams who'd become her reality. He filled the woman's need in her.

She was in love with Perry Mason MacDonald.

Sydney was vulnerable and much too precious. When she came to him, he wanted nothing to be clouding her judgment.

That had been the rationale that had gotten him through

the night. The showering had helped, but not even cold water could entirely wash away his sexual wants. Or the truth that had became painfully clear as he'd lain alone in the guest bed across the hall . . . mere feet from Sydney's room.

Holding a portable phone in his hand, he was standing in the doorway of the rectangular room, staring into her suite. It was a room with a dual purpose, communal entertaining and bedroom privacy. Pictures and symbols of life and energy abounded on the lavender and white walls and even on the bright hardwood floor. He noted the clues to her personality, her childhood, her woman's wishes.

Directly across from where he stood hung a large ankh carved of smooth mahogany and measuring approximately eighteen-inches in length and fifteen across. Beneath it was a glass case that contained three rows of trophies, plaques, and ribbons. Between the case and the picture window at the front of the room was a two-story dollhouse occupied and surrounded by a family of international dolls.

He advanced into the room. It was as elegant and feminine as he'd expected. The sitting area was cozy, the navy blue velvet couch and oversized chairs deliberately cluttered with pillows and throws. On the floor between them, decorating magazines and broadcasting journals had slid from their stacks.

Her bedroom furnishings were near the back of the room, most notably a wooden four-poster queen-size bed with an off-white, silk comforter. He shivered with the threat of renewed arousal, then dragged his gaze away, back to the dolls.

He'd known Sydney longed for her family's approval, but he hadn't realized just how lonely she was until that moment. His thoughts becoming more intimate, he felt on the precipice of a new beginning.

He couldn't pinpoint exactly when it had happened, though several telling incidents filtered through his mind.

Sydney had done that to him; he smiled unconsciously: she'd made his senses reel so he didn't know what had hit him. He only knew he could no longer deny his feelings. He was in love with his client. No. He shook his head, correcting himself. He loved Sydney Lauren Webster.

As if she'd heard him thinking of her, Sydney appeared from a blocked-off area at the opposite end of the room. A bright flare of desire sprang into his eyes, and his heart thudded in his chest.

Sydney halted, sucked in a dulcet breath, which eased its way to her bosom and then, within, burst into sun-rays. She stared at Perry, points of light beaming inside her. Like electrical currents, they whizzed across the room to him from her gaze.

She shivered imperceptibly, aware of the meeting of their minds. A part of her seemed suddenly shy, while another wanted to blurt out her feelings for him. Finally, and she wasn't sure why, prudence won.

"Good morning. You about ready?" he asked.

She noticed his eyes darken with approval. The tempo of her pulse increased, and she reveled in his open admiration. "About," she replied.

"Well, let's get going," he said. "After I drop you off at the restaurant to get Jessica's car, I'm going to run home and change before heading to the office. I'll meet you at the hospital around noon. I want to talk to Jessica about the accident."

His tone was all business, and he was wearing his lawyer look. But amid the seriousness and intensity, she saw desire and need in the depths of his eyes. Everything she felt. She wanted to believe he was still suffering from last night.

Her secret fluttered in her bosom, as she picked up her purse from the dresser. Never once loosing Perry in her sight, she sauntered across the room to meet him. She stopped close enough to feel the heat of his body, which set off a major disturbance in hers. "Did you rest well?" she asked demurely, batting her lashes at him.

Humor flitted across his face before he stepped forward and clasped her to him with one arm. Her cry of pleasant surprise was sucked into his mouth as his lips covered hers hungrily. His kiss singing through her veins, her knees weakened and she wrapped her arms around his waist. Then his lips left hers to nibble at her earlobe and brush her cheek. She sighed winsomely, wanting more.

Twin peals echoed in the room and shocked them apart. They laughed like guilty teenagers caught necking, the joyful sounds of their voices joining simultaneous ringing of doorbell and telephone.

"It must be Ramona calling to remind me of something I forgot." He looked at her, pursing his mouth in regret. "Why don't you run down and get the door?" He guided her out of the bedroom. "I'll be right behind you." He pressed the speaking button on his phone. "No, Ramona, I didn't forget," he said. "I'm on my way now. Has Javier checked in with you this morning?"

With a sunny cheerfulness in her step, Sydney skipped down the stairs. Her lips were still warm and moist from his kiss. She had an aching need for another, though she knew just one more wouldn't do.

Reaching the bottom of the staircase, she sauntered to the door and opened it with a flourish. "What are you doing here?" she asked in a nervous whisper.

Detective Tomkins walked in, uninvited. "Ms. Sydney Lauren Webster, you're under arrest for the murder of State Representative Larry Daniels."

Her eyes widening in terror, Sydney would have sworn her blood had turned to ice. "Perry?" she exclaimed weakly.

"Ramona, let me get back to you," Perry said into the mouthpiece as he descended the steps anxiously, closing off the phone.

"Counselor, it's good to see you."

Sydney hadn't even noticed Detective Melloncamp walk in, and she barely heard the Miranda speech, delivered by Tomkins with relish as he snapped the handcuffs around her wrists.

"If you cannot afford one, one will be appointed . . ."

Stunned, guarded, Perry looked back and forth between the two detectives. "What's going on, Melloncamp?" he demanded.

"We have a warrant to search the place," the detective told him, holding out a folded sheet of paper for Perry's review. "Let's get busy," Melloncamp said over his shoulder, and a team of four men entered the house and dispersed in different directions.

Sydney stared at the activity around her as if viewing it from a distance. Subjected to the terror running rampant through her, she watched Perry and Melloncamp as they walked off to stand in the living room. Though they remained visible, she couldn't make out their words because of their lowered voices. Perry's features were distorted by outrage. His teeth bared in a snarl, he shook the warrant in the detective's face, then stomped and waved his hands in the air with disgust.

"I got 'em."

Sydney spun about to look to where one of the policemen was descending the stairs, carrying a pair of her shoes in one hand. Frowning, confused, she recognized them as the most expensive pair she owned. She wondered what was so significant about those shoes. They were covered in a decorative cloth with a zigzag pattern in red, black, blue, and gold.

The plainclothes policeman delivered the shoes to Detective Melloncamp. He took them, then sauntered to where she was standing. Perry followed, and stood alongside her, transmitting his heat to her chilled body.

His brow furrowed, Perry whispered loudly in disbelief, "A pair of shoes?"

"Not just any pair—Ozani's."

"What the hell is an Ozani?" Perry asked contentiously.

"Not what, who," Detective Tomkins replied. "He's some big-shot African artist from Nigeria who's become an overnight sensation in New York."

"Yeah, you see these shoes, they're made from narrow strips of cotton woven by a horizontal treadle loom, "Detective Melloncamp piped up knowledgeably. "Only a thousand pair were made. They're very expensive, sold exclusively at Neiman Marcus in Texas." Holding up the shoes, he asked, "Are these yours, Ms. Webster?"

Sydney couldn't speak. Fear had lodged in her throat. She nodded her head affirmatively.

"These are not necessary," Perry said, looking at the primary detectives, his hand holding the chain between the handcuffs.

"Sorry, Counselor," Tomkins replied.

Sydney's knees almost gave in as Tomkins pushed her toward the door. Stumbling, she cried out, and both Tomkins and Perry helped right her before she fell.

"One bruise, Tomkins," Perry warned hotly, sticking a stiff finger in the detective's face, his eyes narrowed, "one tiny bruise on her skin, and I swear I'll own you."

"Then, I'll be very careful, Counselor," Tomkins quipped, a smug smile on his face.

"Okay, boys, let's go," Melloncamp said to his team.

Perry looked at her encouragingly. His back to the police, he winked confidently. But in her fright, Sydney could only manage a pallid smile as she nodded to indicate her trust in him.

"Don't worry," he said softly. "You'll be home by dinner. I promise."

Sixteen

Her world had come crashing down with such sudden horror, Sydney didn't want to think. Her usually lively eyes glittered with mental fatigue, yet her thoughts raced on. The frightful ordeal of being fingerprinted, thoroughly searched, then tossed in a cell kept recurring to her.

She was sitting on the couch in her bedroom suite, absently fingering Jessica's ring of keys, just beginning to consider herself fortunate. At least for the time being she was free. She sighed as she gazed toward the picture window. Night glimmered through the sheer curtains, the light from the standing lamps brightening until it was clear as day.

True to his word, Perry had orchestrated her bail and she had been released the day of her arrest: the Tasmanian Devil clock on the wall put the time at ten. She couldn't imagine how he'd accomplished the feat, recalling that her cellmates had warned her against getting her hopes up too high. She had been incarcerated roughly ten hours. Some of them had been in jail for weeks, she recalled with a shudder.

She had never believed it would go this far, she admitted to herself, realizing how naive she had been. She had always assumed the police would find Larry's murderer among his political associates or the groupies who chased him relentlessly.

"The bath seems to have served you well."

At hearing his soothing voice, Sydney looked up, a smile animating her face. Desire nudged despair aside, her heart thudding and warmth suffusing through her. Perry appraised her lazily with his arresting gaze, and a familiar shiver shimmied down Sydney's spine.

He walked into the room, carrying a lap tray laden with small cartons of take-out dinner. He set the tray on the chest that served as a coffee table, then dropped down next to her. "Feeling better?"

"Much," she replied, glad for the sight of him.

He took the keys from her. About to toss them aside, he turned them over in his hand, examining them intently. "Are these yours?" he asked, cutting her a sidelong look.

"No, Jessica's," she replied. "Remember, I was supposed to get her car from RJ's today?" Noticing the ridges suddenly lining his forehead, she asked, "Why? Is something wrong?"

"No," he replied, setting the keyring aside. "We'll get it tomorrow; don't worry about it." He snatched a white cloth napkin from the tray, shook it open, then spread it on her lap. "Eat up. After that, I want you to get a good night's rest. We have a big day tomorrow."

Her brow arching and her tone mocking, she replied, "Bigger than today?"

"Yes," he retorted in a slightly amused voice. Passing her a container and a fork, he said, "We're going to review everything—from A to Z—tomorrow, and I want you sharp and ready."

"Tomorrow is Saturday," she reminded him, forking a bite of shrimp fried rice into her mouth.

"Our first appearance is Monday."

"So soon?"

"The wheels of justice turn swiftly," he said, chewing a mouthful. He swallowed before continuing. "Particularly, when members of the community threaten to publicly accuse the DA of dragging his feet because the victim was an African American."

"Oh, great," she responded with flippant weariness, setting the carton and fork on the table, "I'm not hungry anymore."

Perry likewise put aside his food, then took her hands in his. "Sydney, I'm not going to say don't worry; that's utter nonsense. But I don't want you to let this get you down. Your positive attitude and persevering nature are our greatest weapons, and I need you ready to fight. Trust me?" he asked, his voice lowering to a whisper as he looked directly at her.

"Yes," she replied, returning his riveting gaze with one of her own. "You know I do."

They sat silently for a moment, simply staring, enjoying the other's warm presence. Sydney felt like both voyeur and participant as they were both caught in a sensuous web.

Then Perry touched her again with his eyes and something intense flared through his entrancement. She felt as if she was one of a kind, an invaluable treasure; and she wanted to be the thing reflected in the depths of his gaze. He lifted his hand to caress the side of her face, and the touch was suddenly, almost unbearable in its tenderness. She held his hand there, basking in the feel of his big, cool palm on her warm face.

"Oh, Sydney," he crooned, drawing her into his arms.

She cried out at the sheer relief of the contact. He was strong and warm, the pressure of his embrace firm yet pampering. She could feel him tremble and his heart beat like a thumping thumb on bass strings. His hands began to move over her back in methodical, hypnotic strokes that stoked a fire in her.

An expressive sigh came from her lips. "Perry," she moaned. It was the only word in her head, the want awakening her.

He moved back just a little to look down into her face, tracing her features with passionate eyes. She watched him with equal fascination, her lungs laboring in her chest. Her mouth watered to taste his arousal on her lips. As if reading the hunger in her expression, he lowered his head, and a small sound of wonder came from her throat as his mouth moved over hers in a sensuous exploration.

Her hands gripped his shoulders, kneading the taut muscles and soft flesh beneath the intrusive shirt. Involuntarily, she shifted closer, her hands dropping to caress his chest. They lowered, and a moan of encouragement slipped past his lips, as his kiss became fuller, deeper, longer. His tongue foraged the inner recesses of her mouth, stealing her breath away. His hands wandered everywhere at once, staying nowhere long enough, but her heart seemed to rush to every spot he touched. Finally, he tore his mouth from hers and lifted his head to gaze into her flushed face for a second. His broad shoulders were heaving with his every breath.

Sydney started to tell him right then how she felt. But she could see he already saw it. It must have been on her face, in her eyes, as his feelings were mirrored in his expression.

As he unzipped the front of her caftan, she shivered visibly. Her sensations intensified when he bent his head to lick a taut-tipped nipple. A groan announced affected emotions and then lingered in the air; she couldn't distinguish from whose throat it had escaped as he tasted her bosom. His tongue was wet, hot, fiery and firm, and he treasured each swollen mound. His lips caressed silken flesh, leaving a trail of embers as it then made its way up to her neck. He nibbled there at the base of her throat, where her pulse beat wildly.

Finally she drew his head to hers and fastened her mouth on his. She pressed her tongue against his lips, they parted, and she was in, kissing him greedily and intimately. Flooded by deliquescent sensations, she didn't notice when he removed the only piece of clothing she wore. Slipping his arms under her, he lifted her from the couch, and cradling her against his chest, he carried her to the bed, where he gently set her in the center.

High and hot with anticipation, she looked up at him dreamily, but he remained standing at the side of the bed, his gaze boring into her. His eyes were muddy with yearning and a hint of proud, bold possession.

Propping a knee on the bed, he leaned over to trail a finger down the center of her slender body, eliciting a low moan from her. She reached out to him, a plea to end the sweet torture on her face. He smiled slowly as he stood upright, his mouth widening salaciously, his desire-befuddled eyes tantalizing.

"Last chance," he said meaningfully in an affected voice.

"Fat chance," she quipped in soft reply.

Her eyes locked on his, Sydney rose and walked on her knees to the opposite end of the bed. She noticed the inquiring arch of his brows and the flicker of apprehension that crossed his face as she reached inside the drawer of the bedside lamp table. Gentle laughter wafted from her. Then she crawled back toward him, clutching a small plastic packet between her teeth, a risqué grin on her face.

"You little imp," he growled erotically. "Where did you get that?"

"You'd be surprised at the things they sell in the restrooms of the jailhouse," she retorted delightedly, reaching for the top button of his shirt.

She removed his clothes, dallying reverently over the task, teasing his exposed, firm dark flesh as she stripped him. With each glimpse of his rock-hard body, a delightful shiver zinged through her. Finally the last barrier landed on the floor. Awed, her eyes raked his magnificent, lean chestnut-colored body. His broad shoulders were muscular and level, with hair sprinkled across his wide chest. It tapered to his slim waistline and flat stomach, set off by powerful thighs.

He was more stunningly virile than she had ever imagined. His sweetly intoxicating musk overwhelmed her. Her only impulse was to touch. His flesh felt like satin. She shuddered at the thought of him draped over her as she ran tantalizing fingers up the inside of a muscular thigh, eliciting a tight groan from him.

His ardor was surprisingly, touchingly, bridled. With deliberate slowness, she tore off the top of the packet and removed the prophylactic.

Unraveling it, she poised the opening over the firm, round head of his thick manhood. He gave her a look that said, *If you can dish it, I can take it.* As she rolled the condom into place over him, she heard his sharp intake of breath unfurl over her head as his stomach muscles contracted into knotted ropes. Her smile widened into a naughty grin.

"I'll get you for that," he said, a passionate menace in his tone.

Sydney looked up at him with felicity on her face. She noted the perspiration lining his upper lip as he struggled, but failed to suppress, a medley of sensual whimpers as she slid the protection snugly over him. Her work done, she sat back to observe him leisurely.

"I'm looking forward to it," she replied, a quiver surging through. Then she pulled him back onto the bed and straddled his magnificent body. Her hands skimmed the coarse black hairs on his chest, the muscular planes and hard-muscled ridges of him.

In deep gushes, air was repeatedly expelled from Perry's lungs as she worshipped his body. She rejoiced in her power, alternately kissing and stroking his sweat-glistening skin. She excluded no part of him from the caresses of her hands and lips, each fervent murmur elicited from him heightening her own arousal and drawing her closer to the center of her heat.

A wild gasp escaped her when he reclaimed her lips and crushed her to him. His hands locked against her spine, he ravished her mouth, her body trapped atop sinuous limbs that turned a flame into a wildfire. Her breast tingling against his hair-roughened chest, she wrapped her arms around his neck, sank into his power and kissed him back feverishly.

With unexpected speed and agility, he flipped her over, crushing her under the hardness of him as he settled his mouth over hers. His hands resumed their magic touches, playing havoc with her senses. Teasing caresses roved down her back to her buttocks and up again. He grazed a nipple, achingly attentive, with his palm, and she groaned. He nibbled at the underside of a breast, then bathed the mound with his tongue. His hands explored her stomach, located the sensitive spots behind her knees. She clung to him. Her hands roamed intimately over his back and thighs. Her flesh burning for him, she was frustrated by her inability to touch more of him at once.

He slipped a wayward finger inside her, and whimpers of sheer need punctuated her ragged breaths. Her body writhed in a sensuous dance over his as she arched her hips into his, taunting his tumescent manhood with promise as her tongue dipped in and out of his ear. It was his undoing and her reward. His labored breathing chorused hers as he parted and lifted her thighs to enter her in one hard thrust of possession.

She cried out at the shock of his filling her. Waves of ecstasy throbbed through her as she adjusted to and matched his arduous assault. He was almost untamed as he moved in and out of her in bold, fluid thrusts that took her higher and higher. His raw sensuousness drew her to a height of passion she had never known before. There was no place to go but up. Driven to heaven, she shattered into a million glowing stars. Shortly after he drew back his head and propelled himself into her. With her name on his lips, he joined her in the clouds.

"We got caught with our pants down," Perry railed. "I can't think of anything more undignified."

Though acting embarrassed to the point of anger in front of his staff, inside where no one could see, he was joyous.

Javier slouched behind the desk, nursing a Styrofoam cup containing coffee. Ramona, quiet as a church mouse on Sunday morning, was sitting on the couch. She drank her coffee from a white mug that had SECRETARIES DO IT WITH EFFICIENCY emblazoned on it. Perry was sitting in front of his desk, holding a cup of coffee he really didn't want. In the tepid silence, he lost his sober expression, a memory lighting his mind.

He took a sip of the lukewarm coffee and frowned bitterly. He and Sydney had awakened at sunrise to enjoy each other and then have a leisurely breakfast. After bathing and dressing, they had left the house, reluctant to part. He'd dropped Sydney off at RJ's to get Jessica's car; from there, she was going to visit her sister at the hospital. He missed her already, already experiencing the dull ache of desire at the thought of her.

"Are we going to have this meeting, or are you going to spend the entire time daydreaming?" Ramona said.

"Where is she?" Javier asked impatiently.

Jarred, Perry sighed restoratively. "She'll be here. While you were being nursed back to health, the DA was springing his trap." His voice lacked the energy given by anger. "What happened to Beverly Lockhart? Why wasn't she arrested?"

"The hospital didn't want to press charges," Javier said with a pitiful shrug. "She was a distraught mother in their forgiving eyes."

"Great," Perry muttered snidely. "Well, Melloncamp didn't get your message about the brake lines. If he had, it's possible he could have stalled the DA a little longer."

"What?" Ramona exclaimed hotly. "We're relying on Melloncamp to make our cases for us now? Is the sun in your eyes?" she asked, as she rolled hers.

The gibe struck his gut like a sharp-tipped arrow, bringing to Perry the full impact of his guilt. He blew out his cheeks.

"You're right, I'm sorry," he replied, shame-faced. He stilled as if preparing himself for a performance, actually trying to catch up with the strategies racing through his mind.

"Okay, here's what we're going to do," he said, rifling through his briefcase. He withdrew several long legal pads filled with pages of handwriting. "I want these ready just in case." He crossed to Ramona with an easy gait, placing a pad at a time in her hand and explaining each one. "Motion to dismiss; search and seizure; motion to suppress and motion for discovery. And we're going to conduct a secondary round of interviews. I'll take Mark Frederickson. Javier," he instructed, "see what else you can dig up on Hank Evans, the security guard. Maybe we'll be able to determine whether Daniels was blackmailing him due to his background. I know it sounds farfetched," he added in response to the look of objection that flashed across the investigator's face, "but let's check anyway. Next is Joanna Albritton."

"She was Jessica's alibi," Ramona said. "Why are we going back to her?"

"I didn't get her," Javier replied, looking up. "Did you?"

Perry sighed exhaustively. "Apparently I forgot to put her on the list."

"Maybe you should have disqualified yourself from this case," Ramona said.

"I'm not going to argue with you there," Perry agreed reluctantly, making a small sound at the back of his throat. "Just back me up, okay."

"Then we'd better review our lists to see whether anyone else has been overlooked," Ramona flipped the pages of her pad. "What about Dr. Gravlee, the head of Jessica's department?" She looked from Javier to Perry.

"He's still out of town," Javier replied. "And I got something else. Or rather," he amended, turning the pages in his notebook, "someone else. A Mrs. Woodrow." He looked up at Perry. "Remember, you gave me her name after you interviewed Hank." Perry nodded. "She's an old woman; lonely; plenty of time on her hands. She claims she saw Ursula Andrews going to Daniels's place the day he was killed."

"Put her down," Perry instructed. "I'll do the follow-up." He looked pointedly at Javier. "Any leads on the invisible woman?"

"Nada."

At the hint of a sound, all heads turned in the direction of the outside door. Perry had to force himself to walk, not run, as he strode toward the reception area. The instant his eyes confirmed Sydney's presence, his pulse rocketed. As she gave him a wide, warming smile, a sigh of satisfaction broke from him.

"Hi."

"Hi, back," Sydney replied, her voice soft and eminently intimate.

"We've been waiting for you," he said, his eyes sending a different message.

I missed you, too, her eyes replied. "I came as soon as I could."

"How is Jessica?" he asked, getting his urges under control.

"She's in therapy already."

"Come." He extended a hand to her.

"Is that man going to follow me everywhere I go?" she asked, somewhat exasperated. They had reached the inner office.

"Yes," Javier replied firmly. "His name is Franco, so get used to him."

"Good morning, Mr. Jones," Sydney said glibly, flashing a disgruntled smile at him before turning to Ramona. "Morning, Ramona."

"Morning." Ramona smiled back, a glint of amusement in her eyes. "And how you doing this morning?"

"Fine," Sydney said, the word stretched into multisyllables by the breath she released.

"Good morning," Javier said, his tone friendlier than before.

"Sydney"—Perry rearranged the armchair adjacent to the

couch—"you can make Franco's job a whole lot easier by not leaving home so much." He gestured for her to sit. Their placement allowed each a view of the others.

Perry walked away from her, his back to the center of the group and his hands in his pockets. Even before he asked the question, he was frightened because of the answers he already had. "Sydney, what do you remember about your mother's death?"

He faced her fully. She shifted uneasily, pondering her reply. He had saved the question for her until now, counting on the professional and impersonal atmosphere of the office to lessen its painful effect. Trial or not, if the truth came out, he thought with a shiver of anxiety, it could all blow up in his face.

Sydney took a deep calming breath before she spoke. "I was four years old," she said, melancholy coming into her gaze. "I remember seeing her before I left for school one morning, and she was gone by the time I returned. Other than that, I only remember what other people told me about her. Why is it important now?" she looked at him curiously.

"I only asked because of what we've learned about Jessica's mother," he replied softly, a hesitant, questioning look in his eyes.

"My mother is not still alive," she said defensively. "I'm certain of it. My grandmother wouldn't have let me believe all these years that she was dead if she wasn't."

"Okay, okay, calm down," Perry soothed. "Let's move on." He walked to his desk and ran a finger down the page of a yellow pad filled with notes. "I have a note here about Mark Frederickson. He's a gambler, did you know that?"

Frowning, Sydney shook her head. "No," she muttered thoughtfully. "But it may explain the snafu with that draft."

"What draft?" Perry and Javier chimed.

"Daniels's campaign bought advertising to promote gambling in Texas. Lloyd paid for it with a draft. I turned it in to Mark, along with a copy of the contract. Right before

since then, she felt as if she were seeing him for the first time.

He was the same, yet not the same, she thought. Handsome as ever. Even more so in her eyes now.

"I love you."

She spoke the words without thought of the consequences, then bit her bottom lip nervously. He hesitated, measuring her for a moment, probing and inscrutable.

"I should have kept that to myself, huh?"

She smiled weakly, but it vanished as he hesitantly stepped toward her. She had gotten him into her bed, but had not gotten into his heart, she decided, floundering in distress.

She didn't realize she was holding her breath until it escaped in a wild rush when Perry cupped her face between his cool hands.

"I've committed so many indiscretions as far as you're concerned," he said in a gentle tone, his breath fanning her face, "what the hell is one more?" Tenderly, he touched his lips to her forehead. "I love you, Sydney Webster," he declared, his voice lowered to a caress as he held her tightly to him.

Sydney stared up at him, her bright black eyes brimming with emotion. She'd never felt more needed in her life. Tears of joy streamed down her face.

Ursula Andrews wasn't on the plane. Perry wondered briefly what to make of that as he bit into the tea cake.

The apartment was spacious, but the living room was rich with a clutter that revealed the history of its owner, Meghan Woodrow. In her late seventies, she was a petite, spry woman with hair tinted a lighter shade of blue than her small round eyes.

"I haven't had tea cakes since my grandmother died," he said, giving his hostess an appreciative smile. He was sitting in a chair near the end of the coffee table on which a silver serving tray held a teapot and dainty crystal cups.

"My own children hate them, but my grandchildren just love them," she said proudly. "They're coming to visit me in a couple of weeks, and I have all kinds of activities planned for them."

Perry wiped his hand on the starched blue cloth napkin. He knew he had to get started or she would ramble on for hours. "Mrs. Woodrow," he said unhurriedly, "why don't you tell me what you saw on the day Representative Daniels was murdered."

"Well, I remember the cleaning lady, Beverly, was on the floor about that time," she replied. "She had already done my place, and I saw her leaving Angela—that's my neighbor down the hall. Her place is across from Representative Daniels's. It's usually her last stop on this floor."

Mentally, Perry snapped his fingers. He'd developed no plan for the cleaning lady, Beverly Lockhart. "Anyone else?" he asked.

"Well, Mrs. Andrews—Ursula. But I haven't seen her lately. I bet she left him. Oops." She covered her mouth, embarrassed. "You didn't ask me that."

Leave who . . . Lloyd? Perry wondered, curbing his eagerness. "That's all right, please tell me what you were about to say," he gently prodded the grandmotherly woman.

"Why she stayed with that husband of hers, I'll never understand," she said, her tone scornfully. "I heard from Mabel, Mrs. Titus—she's on their floor, you know—that they fought all the time and Mr. Andrews used to say horrible things to her."

Objection; hearsay. "Did Mrs. Andrews go to Representative Daniels frequently?" he asked, knowing a judge would likely disallow the question.

"Yes."

"Do you recall the last time you saw them together?"

"The day he was killed," she seemed surprised, as if he

hadn't been paying attention. "I was coming out of my apartment and she was going in to his."

The delectable aroma of burning hickory scented the patio deck. Smoke seeped from the red hibachi. Standing nearby, Sydney quenched her parched throat, taking a swallow of beer from the bottle.

Returning home as instructed, she had tried to occupy herself with busywork. Her house was hardly in a mess, so there was little to do. Developing a fund-raising campaign for Perry's swim team had taken barely an hour at the computer. In the middle of the day, when the sun seemed the hottest, she decided to barbecue.

She set her beer on the table, then lifted the lid of the portable cooking pit. The chicken breasts were ready to be turned. She looked for the fork and realized she had forgotten to bring it out. Hurrying inside to the kitchen, she grabbed it from the counter and was about to return when the doorbell rang.

Sydney paused momentarily. Perry must have finished early, she thought, her eyes gleaming. She nearly flew to the front of the house.

She halted abruptly, then backed up to check her appearance in the mirror on the inside of the hall-closet door. She giggled softly, as she turned one way and then the other preening. The handle of the fork held between her teeth, she fluffed her hair, then adjusted the tee shirt, tightening the knot to just-right snugness under her bosom. The doorbell pealed again.

"Coming," she called out around the obstacle in her mouth, then tugged at her thigh-high white jeans.

Deciding she was presentable, though shoeless, she opened the door, now in a state of controlled excitement.

The smile went from her face. She should have known better, she thought, her thrill bottoming out.

"Hi, Sydney. I'll bet you're surprised to see me."

Schooling her expression to politeness, she replied, "I sure am, Mark, but come in." She stepped aside, allowing him to enter.

"I was just riding around with nothing pressing to do, and thought I'd drop in," he said.

Sydney tried not to show her disbelief. "Well, I'm out back," she said, extending a hand for him to proceed her.

"Nice place you have here," Mark said, impressed.

"Thank you. It's a good thing for you I had to come inside to get something, or I wouldn't have heard the bell."

"Something sure smells good," he declared as they climbed the stairs leading up to the deck.

"Dinner," she replied, heading for the hibachi. "There's a cooler over there full of beer; help yourself," she said, lifting the lid of the grill to turn over the meat.

"I certainly could use a cold one in this heat." He withdrew a bottle of beer.

"What brings you here?" she asked. "You're too far from home to be in the neighborhood."

Twisting off the bottle cap, he chuckled before he replied. "I really wanted to see how you've been holding up under the strain. You know, with your sister and all . . ." His voice trailed off as he took a sip of beer.

"Am I fired yet?"

"Come on, Sydney; you know the Fredericksons are more loyal than that," he stated as if his feelings had been hurt. "Besides, you're innocent until proven guilty."

And you wouldn't dare risk a lawsuit, she thought cynically. She lowered the lid and set the long fork at the side of the hibachi. "The way my life has been going, not much would surprise me."

She picked up her beer, then leaned against the rail, looking down ten feet at the rock bed below. Mark came to stand alongside her.

"Nice drop," he commented, looking down.

Seventeen

A sudden unease trickled through Sydney as she looked sidelong at Mark. He was staring out toward the lagoon. His blue eyes seemed strangely glazed.

"I'm not suicidal," she said with an attempt at humor that didn't quite mask the trembling in her voice.

A sift of laughter came from his tenor voice, then faded into the quiet heat. They both drank from their beers. Sydney kept a stealth vigil on him.

"Perry MacDonald is a highly respected criminal attorney," he said somewhat pensively, holding the bottle loosely between his hands.

Sydney wondered why Mark had *really* come. "According to the news, the Assistant District Attorney who's prosecuting the case is also very good," she said for the sake of conversation, her trust in Perry unchanged.

"Yeah, I've heard," he said. Mark downed the remains of his beer, then set the bottle on the adjacent rail as he spoke. "I understand she's gone up against him twice before and lost both times. She's due for a win. But, like I said before"—he propped himself against the rail alongside her—"MacDonald is good."

Sydney nodded absently, recalling that Mark was a gambler. The muse took hold, and she began piecing together puzzling events: the money she had turned in to Mark had disappeared, nearly costing her her job; then, out of the blue, it had reappeared to earn her a high-priced pat-on-the-back lunch. She wondered whether Mark had gambled with Larry and lost the money, then killed him to get it back. She shuddered, suddenly frightened of Mark.

He faced her now, one of his pretty-boy smiles curling his mouth like a snake. Imperceptibly, she inched away from him just as he reached for her, too slowly. His fingers clasped her wrist. He was stronger than he looked, and her heart leaped into her throat. Franco was parked out front, in no position to help her. A scream froze in her throat.

The smile left his face to be replaced by a wry look. "Sydney, I . . ." he began gravely.

Instinctively she jerked her hand away, and unexpectedly Mark let it go. She rubbed her wrist where the imprint of his strength showed on her flesh.

". . . I owe you an apology," he said, as if he hadn't noticed her reaction. He turned away from her to lean over the rail.

As if not to disturb the quiet of the afternoon, Sydney quietly took in breaths until her pulse returned to normal.

"I guess you've already figured it out by now," Mark continued, rubbing his hands together. "My old man did." He chortled, then turned his head to flash her a rueful smile.

Sydney frowned. Too angry to be scared, she said accusingly, "You used that money to gamble with, then lost it." His gray eyes becoming dull, Mark dropped his head, embarrassed. "What else did you do?" she asked, backing cautiously from him. "Were you setting me up for murder? Did you kill Larry to get it back?"

"I swear to God I didn't," Mark denied imploringly. Raising his left hand, he repeated vehemently, "I did not kill him, and I didn't set you up." An expletive spewed from his lips; then he looked at her, regret in his face. "I was careless."

"Then how did you replace the money?"

"Hey, what's cooking over here?"

Sydney spun about quickly to see Jasmine climbing the

stairs onto the deck. She averted her head to face Mark. The moment of truth was over. Her answer was somewhere in the boyish smile that had found its way back onto his face.

Permission to treat Dr. Walter Webster as a hostile witness. Perry imagined himself saying that very phrase to the presiding judge. As uncomfortable as he felt now, he knew it would be worse with Sydney staring at his back in court. But he wasn't in court, and questions had to be asked, he reminded himself, forcing her from his thoughts.

He focused his attention on the man sitting across from him. The coffee table separated them, but their wary hostility seemed a tangible connection. Perry sensed that Walter Webster knew, or at the very least assumed, that he was sleeping with his youngest daughter. For a number of reasons—mostly that it would be the next natural step in their relationship—he wasn't about to elaborate on his intentions or attempt to soothe the jealous father's mind.

In his home on a Saturday evening, Walter Webster was casually dressed in a blue polo shirt, white walking shorts and deck shoes. He looked older, not as tough as he normally did, Perry noted, wondering if the weight of events was wearing Sydney's father down.

"Dr. Webster, you told the police you hadn't seen Representative Daniels at least two weeks prior to his death. Do you intend to stick to that story? And before you answer, Dr. Webster, you'd better remember that your daughter's life is on the line."

Walter Webster stared at Perry as if not sure of his response. He swallowed hard, then spoke reluctantly. "I talked with him that morning."

"Where was that, Dr. Webster?"

"He was in town."

"At his office?"

"No," Walter Webster replied succinctly. "His place."

"Why did you go to see him?"

Walter Webster took his time answering. In the silence, Perry made several guesses. He voiced the most likely. "He sold you out, didn't he?"

Calmly, Walter Webster pushed away from the couch to stand in front of the side window that provided a view of a blooming rosebush. He gazed out, his back to Perry.

"Dr. Webster, do I need to repeat the question?" Perry asked.

"No," Walter Webster said softly, shaking his head. "It's true." A breath escaped him as he faced Perry. "Larry had been the obstacle preventing the State Coordinating Board from closing the doors on Texas College. Several influential members are anxious to shut our doors for reasons other than saving money for the state. He swore that he would never let them close us down."

"Then he changed his mind, didn't he?"

"Yes."

"Do you know what caused him to do that?"

Walter Webster snorted, then suddenly smiled. "Plain, old unadulterated greed," he said with disdain.

"How?"

"Texas College was small potatoes," Webster replied, rubbing his face with one hand. "Larry was planning a move to the big time. In exchange for withdrawing his objection to closing down the college, he'd gotten a pledge of support for his bid for the US Congress in the next election."

Perry leaned forward in his chair, his hands clasped together under his chin. He stared at Walter Webster absently, a pensive tinge to his eyes. Sydney's father returned the look. "Dr. Webster," he said softly, "did you have anything to do with Sonni-Lauren's death?"

* * *

"That wasn't a very bright thing to do. What if he had other motives for just dropping in?"

"Well, he didn't." A remnant of anger remained in Sydney's voice. "I could kill him for putting me in the position he did. If his father hadn't figured out what happened to that money, I'd be in even more trouble." She twisted the top from another bottle of beer and took a long sip. "I still don't know how he replaced it, but I must admit, I feel stupid for thinking he'd come to kill me." She set the bottle on the table, her hands wrapped around the base.

"Why?" Jasmine asked, squinting from the sun coming down into her face.

"In the first place, it's a little hard trying to picture someone you know committing murder," she rasped sarcastically. "And in the second, Mark is not the type. He's too lazy."

Jasmine swiveled her bottle of beer around. "My husband made a mistake like that once, and it cost us everything."

Sydney's head flew up, and she stared, amazed, at her friend. There was no bitterness or hatred on Jasmine's face, as there had been none in her voice—just sad resignation.

"Oh, no," Sydney said, her voice full of empathy.

Jasmine averted her head to look sidelong out at the water glistening under the high hot sun. "Her name was Dianna Polk. She and Justin grew up together. She harbored a lot of expectations he didn't share. He took his degree in architecture; she studied interior design. When he started his company five years ago, she mapped out their future. But she didn't plan on me," she said with a rueful smile. "I met Justin at a home-design show in January. The attraction was instant. Three months after meeting, we were married and I was pregnant." She lifted the bottle to her lips and took a sip, then resettled it perfectly in the water spot. "I told him I was uncomfortable around her, but he didn't see it. He couldn't. After all, he'd known her all his life. To make a long story short"—she paused—"she canceled several supply orders, in my name, and Justin lost a major contract. By the time we'd sorted through the mess, he and I were not even on civil speaking terms."

"So that's why you left Houston to come here," Sydney guessed solemnly.

Jasmine nodded her head, then took another sip of beer. "Yeah. I needed a different environment to help clear my head, so I could figure out where Justin and I would go from there."

Sydney tried to put herself in Jasmine's situation, only to realize she couldn't progress beyond the sublime satisfaction of her relationship with Perry. She knew better than to say he would never take her feelings lightly, but she thought it. "And have you figured it out?"

Jasmine opened her mouth to reply, but no words came. Sydney stared curiously into her startled expression, then looked over her shoulder to where Jasmine was staring.

"Justin," Jasmine whispered, astonished.

Sydney watched, mesmerized, as a very tall, slender man of warm butterscotch complexion approached them with determined strides. He had classically handsome features, a long, narrow face and curly black hair.

"What are you doing here?" Jasmine asked softly as if the wind had been knocked out of her. "You . . . you promised me time."

"Time's up, Jasmine," he replied in a wonderfully clear voice. "I want you back where you belong—home with me," he added inarguably, a longing in his tone.

"Why did you lie about being at Larry's only hours before he was killed?"

Perry sat back patiently on the hard wooden chair placed alongside the hospital bed. Jessica was sitting up in the bed, pillows at her back, as she mulled her reply. Signs of the accident, a few scratches and bruise marks, showed on the right side of her face. Her left arm was in a cast, but she seemed as strong in character as she had in his initial meeting with her.

"Is that the question you're going to threaten to ask me on the witness stand?" Jessica said smartly, undaunted.

"I'm asking it now," Perry replied.

Leaving Walter Webster's, he'd caught up with Joanna Albritton at the university library. She had been upset enough for him to guess that Jessica had deliberately lied about the time she'd been on campus, using Joanna as her alibi.

"Yes, I was there."

"When Sydney arrived?" he replied, half stating, half questioning.

Jessica stared absently across the room and sighed wearily before she spoke. "Yes." She wet her lips. "She arrived as we were making up."

"Making up as after an argument?"

She nodded in the affirmative.

"Was it the first one you'd had?"

Jessica chortled softly. "No. I'd caught him in another lie. He'd been having an affair with Ursula." Her head lowered and she gazed at her hands folded atop the bed covering at her waist. Remembered pain defined her expression, and her eyes glazed with the threat of tears. "He admitted it. I forced him to, right after I told him I was pregnant."

"What happened?"

"Sydney showed up, full of righteous indignation," she said, laughing softly through her anguish. Then she shook her head, amazed. "My little sister. She lit into him like a mother hen. He just laughed; then she left."

"After throwing the rock at him," Perry said aloud. An unconscious smile stole over his mouth as he remembered Sydney's fiery essence. Recalling his wits, he said, "After Sydney left, what happened?"

"*She* came, complaining about Lloyd as usual," Jessica replied with bitterness in her voice.

"Ursula Andrews," Perry supplied. But Jessica showed no sign of having heard him.

"She wanted a divorce," she added before pausing to shake her head in bemusement. "They'd just gotten married last October. Lloyd wouldn't entertain the thought because—"

"Because?"

"Divorce to Lloyd is a sign of failure," she replied. "It's not in his nature to give up. Since she lacked the guts to leave him, knowing that way she wouldn't get a dime, she tried another route."

"She was sleeping with Larry to make Lloyd mad enough to give her a divorce?" Perry said, incredulous.

"Don't forget the money part of it," Jessica said sarcastically. "I left them together. Ursula and Larry. Comforting each other," she said snidely.

"Do you know where Ursula is now?"

"Don't know and don't care," Jessica replied.

The room was softly lit. Perry stood in the shadows near the bed, looking down at Sydney curled up in sleep. He noted the empty wine glass on the bedside table and wondered how long she had waited up for him. He didn't need to consult his watch to know it was late; his body's clock was winding down.

But not entirely, he mused. A smile crept onto his face. As his heart swelled with the most resolute of emotions, he felt the tumescence of awakening below his waist. Even in sleep, Sydney possessed the power to sway his senses. He suppressed a chuckle, amazed by her power over him and by his deep sense of satisfaction.

He rather liked the feeling. He had no intention of losing it, he thought, determined.

Then his mouth clenched in disgust. It had been a long

day of dead ends. He was no closer to knowing who had killed Larry Daniels than when he'd started.

Shadowed by this quandary, Perry walked quietly from Sydney's suite. Tired as he was, sleep was out.

He strolled across the upstairs landing and into the guest bedroom, his home away from home, and flipped on the ceiling light. Opening his briefcase on the bed, he laid out a myriad of folders. He decided to shower first, then review his notes.

The house seemed more quiet than before. Maybe because his mind cried out for information, Perry mused as he stepped from the shower. He left the bathroom, wearing a green bath towel around his waist. Purposefully, he dropped onto the bed and reassembled the file folders into four different stacks: primary and secondary suspects on one side, the two different sets of photographs on the other.

He sat with his back against the headboard and began rereading his interviews, updating them with the most recent material gathered.

He wished with all his heart that he could figure out who was telling the truth and who was lying, either outright or by omission. Then there was the question of how—or if— Beverly Lockhart was a piece in the puzzle. Adding to his confusion was the disturbing disappearance of Ursula Andrews.

Despite Jessica's staunch conviction that Daniels was having an affair with Lloyd Andrews's wife, he was ill at ease because Sydney couldn't conclusively identify Ursula as the woman she'd seen with Daniels days before he was to announce his engagement. And if Ursula Andrews wasn't the "other woman," who was? If she existed, which he was beginning to doubt, what did she know about Daniels's death?

Hours later, Perry was losing focus as exhaustion began to creep over his body. He dosed off, and his head hit the headboard. "Ouch," he exclaimed, rubbing the bruised spot.

It was time to call it a night, he decided, gathering the files to put them away. But his hands stilled on the sets of photographs. In the left were those given him by Sydney. Her face beamed up at him from the top one. He released the other photographs to study the picture of her.

His eyes softening to a murky glow and a smile turning up the corners of his mouth, he heard himself sigh as love coursed through him. He looked toward the door and his thoughts went to Sydney, asleep in the other room.

Without thought, he looked at the next picture and, before he realized it, had set another before his searching gaze. He stopped at that photo, the first that was not of Sydney. The camera lens had caught Jessica and Larry locked in an embrace and beaming like lovers.

Despite the pain Larry's philandering had caused her, Jessica seemed willing to overlook his shortcomings. There was no explanation for her becoming pregnant . . . except that she loved him.

There'd been a time when he'd have shaken his head, baffled by such behavior; he was amazed at how easily he accepted it now. He knew it was because of Sydney that he could. His thoughts veering, he imagined a bunch of little Sydney's controlling his life. Girls. Four, he decided with a soft chortle, relishing the image of being the object of all that adoring attention.

Love was inexplicable.

He started to put down the photos when a vague suspicion seized him. He stared hard at the photograph, cataloging every detail from the expressions of each person in it to their attire. The answer seemed right in his grasp, but he couldn't pinpoint it.

"What are you doing?"

Perry's head jerked up, but surprise didn't have a chance to register before want reigned as he devoured Sydney with his eyes. Wearing only a short pink, see-through gown, she stood, posing seductively in the doorway, her arms held high as if holding up the frame.

"Sitting here and thinking about you instead of working," he replied lazily, tossing the photos aside.

Her eyes fiery as burning coals, she sauntered into the room, deliberately swaying delectably. Enthralled, he rewarded her demure taunt with a gaze of approval and a swelling in his loins.

"Is there anything I can help you with?"

"Is that what you've come to do?"

"Uh-huh," she said softly, slowly bobbing her head up and down.

His hungry eyes fastened on her, Perry shoved his papers to the far side of the bed. "Then by all means . . ." His voice thick with his wanting of her.

Always the gentleman, he took her hand and helped her as she straddled his lap. She said nothing about the bulge pushing up against his bath wrap, though he knew she felt it. She merely traced his mouth with a finger. "I missed you," she said, a corroborating blush on her face.

"Did you now?" he asked, rubbing the length of her smooth, slender thigh and leg.

She sucked in a ragged breath. "Uh-huh." She kissed a muscled shoulder, then looked up at him from under long lashes as coquettish laughter turned up the corners of her mouth.

He took her face between his hands and placed a long, tender kiss on her mouth. It ended lingeringly, reluctantly, their lips parting only enough to draw in each other's breath as they gazed as if profoundly amazed by the depths of their emotions. Sydney's eyes shone with a drugged look that Perry knew was reflected in his.

"I love you, Sydney Lauren Webster. I never thought I would say that to any woman and *mean* it. In fact, I've never said it to anyone." To her startled reaction, he nodded as if embarrassed. "It's true. You're the first and only."

His hands grazing her silken flesh lovingly, he stared at her mesmerizingly. He felt possessed and possessing. Commitment consumed him.

"There will be no other man for you," he said with rough affection. "I plan to make damn sure you never want for love. From anyone," he emphasized. With a licentious grin, he added, "In or out of bed. So be sure you want to take this chance with me, my love." His hands stroked her shoulders and sides gently. "Be sure . . . For I'll never let you go," he declared, his hands stilling in a possessive grip at her waist.

She wrapped her arms around his neck tightly. "Perry, I never knew," she whispered, her breath fanning his ear. "But I'm sure. I'm not afraid. I've never been more certain of anything in my life. I want you . . . for always."

There being no further need for conversation or clarification, Perry pulled the gown over Sydney's head; then he leaned back to look his fill on her luxurious flesh. He noticed everything—the inveigling look on her face, the promise sparkling in her eyes, the shivers of anticipation that erupted through her and were transmitted into him.

He lowered his head and caught the tip of a warm brown breast between his firm lips, nursed it with his tongue. Sydney's cries of pleasure echoed sweetly in his ear. "Oh, Perry . . . Perry . . . Perry . . ."

"Perry what?" he said, delighting in her response. His sensual mouth and teeth and tongue troubled the other aroused nipple. When she cried out again, he merely increased the pressure of his loving ravishment. He licked her breasts as if they were melting ice cream cones, with long, slurping, savoring licks.

"Perry . . . please . . . !" Sydney let out a salacious moan.

"Please what?" he asked, lifting his head to look into her face. Voracious want blazed in her eyes. But he was in no

hurry to grant her wish. Not at this moment. He intended
to brand her his irrevocably.

Gently, he pushed her back onto the bed. Papers rustled
in the process, but he was singularly and intently focused.
He grasped a slender ankle in each hand to make room for
himself between the parting of her legs, and starting with
a big toe, licked his way up her body.

Reaching her face, he could tell she was eager—even
desperate—to have his mouth on hers, to have him buried
inside her. Taking perverse pleasure in heightening her anticipation, he stalled, trailing a path along the side of her
cheek with his tongue, then retreating to the pulse at the
hollow of her throat.

Cajoling him with carnal arsenal, she tempted him to
hurry, sending currents of desire shooting through him. Her
hands were everywhere, never still, leaving heat burns on
his body. Finally, he granted her desire as his lips met hers
in a hard, hot, wet kiss.

Demanding—needing—more than a kiss, she slid her
hand down his side to his manhood slapping temptingly
against her thigh. "Uh-uh," he grunted in denial. He then
pinned both her hands over her head as he tasted the smile
on her lips.

Erotically skilled in building desire, he worked his way
back down her body. His tongue was tepid in temperature,
yet firm in intent against her soft flesh. Attuned to her inflamed greed and his incited goal of arousing her, he dipped
it sharply into the sexual center of her hidden beneath the
curly dark hairs between her thighs.

He was aware of her writhing, frantically clutching the
sheets and whimpering his name over and over. Still, he
took his time, refusing stubbornly, despite his own needs
to be rushed. He imbibed her essence, savoring it with delight.

Her reaction served as a challenge to his control. Yet, the
more he feasted, the more he wanted. In due time, the savage

intensity of his want exceeded his control. He rose slightly to draw her legs together and turn her over onto her stomach. He molded the curves of her backside lovingly with his hands, then entered her. She gasped in ecstasy, closing around his manhood, like molten lava. With him buried in her softness, a ferocious shudder ran along their lengths. Her fingers stretched under her to cradle and caress his man-parts, and a moaning syllable of sexual assuagement escaped from him. His senses were never more alive, primitive and wild than when she returned his loving plunges with equal force and no desire to retreat.

They slipped into the flame then and rode the hot tide of passion. But all too soon, the turbulent ecstasy peaked and exploded, became sublime satisfaction. She lay limp beneath him, his arms around her, holding her. For a long time neither moved, then Perry shifted Sydney to stare down into her face.

This all-pervasive feeling inside him, this powerful emotion, could not be the result of indiscretion. He had committed none. He lowered his head and . . . kissed his love.

Eighteen

Sunday morning, just before the break of day, Sydney stretched her sore limbs. Her foot touched a muscular calf under the silk bedding, and a lovely lazy-cat smile filled with amorous memories came over her face.

" 'Bout time you woke up, sleepyhead," Perry said, his voice an erotic murmur.

Sydney purred in reply and rested an arm across his chest, the hairs there tickling her flesh. Setting an arm possessively about her waist, he pulled her against him.

"What have you been thinking about so early in the morning?" she asked, her hand sliding down his body, a teasing in her touch.

Perry sucked in a quick, hard grunt before he spoke. "That, too." He captured her erring hand and held it still on his chest. "But while you were snoring . . ."

She lifted her head indignantly. "I don't snore."

He chuckled, squeezed her affectionately, then kissed her on the nose. She settled back in his embrace, her head on his chest.

"While you were making those strange noises in your sleep," he amended, laughter in his voice, "I was busy planning our future."

"Oh?" she replied, a delightful tingle coursing through her.

"As soon as we wrap up the case, we'll get married. I figure no later than August."

"That soon?" she said with surprise. Although he was being his usual autocratic self, she had no objections or doubts.

"Yeah. We've probably already started on our family." He looked down at her significantly.

She nodded her head in concurrence, remembering they'd failed to take precautions.

"I figure four is a good number."

Her head shot up, and her brows arched in amazement. "Four children?"

"Um-hmm," he replied leisurely, smiling. "Girls, I think."

He seemed to have given the matter quite a bit of thought. "My, my, you are ambitious," she replied.

"What do you think?" he finally thought to ask.

"Wow," she said softly. "Four girls." She looked thoughtful.

"Well?" he pressed, a trace of anxiety in his expression.

"I think we'd better get started," she replied, sliding her body atop his.

Their future wasn't all he had thought about, Perry later recalled.

He was alone in the guest bedroom, organizing his notes in their folders. It was shortly after two in the afternoon. He and Sydney had vacated the bed finally. After a leisurely bath in her hot tub and another enticing romp, they had dressed, then had brunch on the patio.

In the middle of the night, the answer came to him while he was replaying his interview with Walter Webster. Webster had seemed resigned about having to face Sydney with the truth of her mother's death. Unbeknownst to the older man, Perry had wished to keep that secret. If Sydney ever found out he knew how her mother had died and had kept that information from her, there'd be hell to pay.

In denying he'd killed Sydney's mother, Dr. Webster had

added, "No matter what some people believe." The unsolicited comment had plagued Perry. He kept wondering why Webster felt it was needed. The answer that came to him was founded in the man's behavior toward Sydney; he treated her like a yo-yo. He wanted her near him; yet he always seemed to drive her away.

Why?

Perry had always believed it was because Webster was a parent who couldn't let go of his offspring. Yet, Sydney had gone off to college, and had even lived and worked in a different city for several years before moving to Dalston. No, he had to look at things differently, consider the evidence from another angle. It was as if Walter Webster sensed his daughter was in danger and behaved irrationally to protect her. Only one person could be a threat to her, Perry decided, and he now knew who had killed Larry Daniels.

It was really the shoes, he told himself, staring at the photograph that had caught his attention before Sydney had driven all thought from his mind. Ambivalence clouded his expression; he knew Sydney would not be pleased by his conclusion. He even suspected she had an inkling of it, though he knew she would never admit to or it accept it. Still, she had to have known who last wore those expensive shoes from Africa.

While packing on the day she'd left her father's home, she'd made a trip to an upstairs bedroom. He had assumed at the time that she was going to her own room until she'd led him out to the garage apartment shortly afterward to get the remainder of her possessions. If his guess was right, she'd gotten those shoes from Jessica's room, unaware that they could identify Daniels's murderer.

"Perry?"

As Sydney called from the hallway, he hurriedly stuffed the folders into his briefcase. Strolling to the door, he replied, "Up here."

She was already holding out the phone.

"For you," she said.

Sydney felt like a thief at sneaking into her father's home. Entering the quiet foyer, she closed the door softly behind her. She started to call out, then changed her mind. Instead, she checked the downstairs on tiptoe to make sure she was alone in the house.

She refused to spend another day like a dutiful little woman waiting around for her man to return. Shortly after Perry had left, she'd decided to go out. She hadn't forgotten his interest in the key. Since Javier discounted it as a match for the one taken from Larry's place, she assumed it opened something Jessica owned.

Satisfied that no one else was in the house, Sydney hurried up the stairs to the last room on the right and entered the bright colored, Victorian-style bedroom. She looked around, wondering where to start.

She eschewed looking under the bed, considering that too juvenile a place for Jessica to choose. The dresser was too obvious for a hiding spot, but the oak credenza looked like a good place to start.

Unsuccessful, she reverted to looking under the bed. Executing a slow pirouette, a puzzled frown on her face, she then scanned the room. She was facing the closed closet door, so she headed to it. A thin, silver chain dangled from the ceiling. She pulled it and the light came on. The modest-sized space was arranged in sections—professional wear, casual wear, and evening wear. A floor-to-ceiling rack of shoes stood against the back wall. Shoe boxes—nearly fifty of them—were neatly stacked on the two overhead shelves.

Disappointed, Sydney started to leave. Nothing stood out. Except, she couldn't figure out why Jessica kept all those shoe boxes when her shoes were on the rack. She retrieved the chair from the vanity table, then set it where she could reach the overhead shelf by standing on it. She picked up a shoe box. Its light weight declared it empty, she put it down, tried the next one.

Reaching the middle of the opposite shelf, Sydney shook a box that had some weight. She was excited at finding something and pulled off the lid. *In My Father's House, Volume 7* was etched in gold across the front of a blue leather-bound book the size of a small diary. She flipped through the box to find volumes six, five, and four.

Diaries were personal memoirs, not to be read by strangers, Sydney told herself as she carefully stepped down from the chair. Debating her next move, she sauntered into the bedroom, fingering the small books.

Some investigator she would make, she told herself disgruntled. She plopped onto the bed and stared absently across the room.

Just a little peek, she decided at last. Inserting the small key into the lock on the front of the diary, she turned it. It didn't work. She tried the key on the other books with the same result. Then she sighed, relieved that the matter had been taken out of her hands and she hadn't violated Jessica's privacy. She returned the box of books to the closet. When she shook the next box in line, it too was weighty. She opened it to discover volumes three, two, and one. Out of curiosity, she tried the key again and became almost cheerful at her lack of success.

But the key did unlock volume one.

The call he'd taken from Attorney Falon Hollister, the prosecutor handling the case, could only mean one thing, Perry thought. The meeting she'd invited him to attend must have been arranged by Jessica Webster herself.

Still, a confession was the last thing he expected as he strode through the electronically controlled doors of the hospital. Though it would mean Sydney's exoneration, he'd feel cheated. At least he had guessed correctly, he told himself as he stepped onto the elevator and pushed the button for the second floor.

He would have warned Sydney's sister about making a statement without benefit of counsel. Upon reminding Hollister of that, he'd been told Jessica Webster had insisted on having her way in the matter.

The elevator stopped and Perry disembarked, heading for Jessica's room. He entered it to a silent acknowledgment. In addition to Attorney Falon Hollister, the only woman in the DA's office who had retained her femininity, Detectives Melloncamp and Tomkins were present for the state. Jessica smiled weakly when she saw him. Lloyd Andrews barely acknowledged his presence.

"Okay, everyone is here," Attorney Hollister said. "Let's get started. Ms. Webster, it's your show."

Perry leaned against the wall, his arms folded across his chest. He couldn't help thinking about Sydney. Discovering a lie she'd lived with for most of her life was nothing compared to this. He could only hope his love would be enough to get her through the ordeal of learning how much her sister must have hated her all these years.

Some pages contained as many as four entries. Each was preceded by the day printed in capitalized, block letters. Sydney flipped through the book, scanning more pages than she actually read.

TUESDAY, February 11, 1968. *Today, I met Sonni-Lauren. She's pregnant! She was young and beautiful and very nice. I felt guilty for liking her.*
SUNDAY, February 16, 1968. *Daddy married Sonni-Lauren. I felt both happy and sad.*

FRIDAY, May 15, 1968. *Sydney Lauren Webster was born today at 10:15!*

MONDAY, May 18, 1968. *They brought Sydney home today from the hospital. She was cuddly, adorable. She looked at me as if she knew I was her big sister.*

Sydney moaned, with her guilt steadily growing, but she couldn't stop turning the pages, peeking into Jessica's girlish thoughts.

WEDNESDAY, September 14, 1970. *Daddy loves Sydney to distraction. If it were not for Sonni-Lauren making sure I was included, I believe he would forget he had another daughter.*

She didn't know what she hoped to find, Sydney chided herself. She was about to close the book. You've come this far, she told herself sarcastically, noticing only a few pages remained.

FRIDAY, April 19, 1972. *My life ended today. Sonni-Lauren is gone forever. Daddy made me promise never to tell Sydney that her mother was murdered. I think Daddy did it.*

Sydney's heart beat irregularly in her bosom. As soon as she wiped away the tears from her eyes, more took their place. She was angry, but the pain of betrayal was stronger.

She stole quietly into Jessica's hospital room. Despite the crowd of people assembled, there was no movement. The atmosphere was funereally quiet, as if someone had died. Sydney couldn't help but feel she was the one they had come to bury.

On the far side of the room, Detectives Melloncamp and

Tomkins stood, looking uncomfortable, near the air conditioning unit under the window. A brown-skinned woman of medium height, professionally garbed in a burgundy suit, her arms folded across her bosom, was standing near the left end of the hospital bed. Perry was leaning against the wall next to the bathroom. His back was to her, his appeal no less powerful for that, for his essence came to her immediately.

Sydney paused a moment to wonder if he had known. She squeezed back fresh tears as she held the door to soundlessly close it. Jessica's voice, barely audible, solemn, broke the awful quiet.

"Sydney didn't kill Larry; I did."

"That's a lie!"

"Sydney," Perry exclaimed, spinning to face her.

He looked at her with something akin to worry in his eyes. She returned the look, puzzled, then with wretched awareness. She remembered the diary; it had seemed like an extension of her arm she held it so tightly.

"Did you know about my mother?" she asked tightly, her ebony eyes searching his face anxiously. "How she really died?" she asked, swallowing a tearful gulp.

"Sydney."

Her name came weakly to his tongue, the expression on his face answering her question. A slashing pain ripped through her, and she stiffened, desolated. She dropped her gaze from his and made her way to the hospital bed. Reaching the end of it, she gripped the rail, looking at Jessica, both distress and disbelief on her face. She opened her mouth to speak, then noticed Lloyd Andrews standing by the bed like a guard and holding Jessica's free hand. Staring at the intimate picture they presented gave her a sense of déjà vu.

"That's a lie, Jessica, and you know it," Sydney charged.

"Sydney . . ." Perry reached out to her, a plea for understanding in his eyes.

The instant his warm hand covered her cold one, she steeled herself against the familiar sensation his touch wrought. She wondered if she would ever be whole again as she jerked her hand from his. She turned back to confront Jessica, needing more of an explanation than the rueful look on her sister's face. Though she now held evidence of a twenty-four-year-old lie in her hand, she refused to believe Jessica guilty of murder.

"Why?" she begged pitifully, unashamed of her anguish. She held up the diary. "Why, Jessica?"

"Since you've invaded my privacy and read my diary," Jessica replied, a hint of ire in her voice as she sniffed back tears, "then you know the answer." A crooked smile on her lips, she added, "I've been jealous of you a long time, baby sister."

"No!" Sydney declared, stomping her foot. She refused to believe it.

"Ms. Webster, if you can't be quiet, I'm going to have to ask you to leave."

Sydney spun about to glare curiously at the woman who had come forward, though she hadn't moved. Sympathy flashed across the strangers face, then vanished as if it had never appeared.

"I'm Attorney Falon Hollister, and I'm the producer of this show," she said in reply to Sydney's unspoken question.

"But she didn't do it," Sydney exhorted ardently.

Attorney Hollister raised a brow at Sydney, warning her to silence.

"After Sydney left," Jessica resumed, her recitation, quieting Sydney with her utter lack of emotion, "Larry admitted what I always knew to be true. I was his second choice."

"No!" Sydney shook her head fiercely. "No."

"Ms. Webster," Attorney Hollister warned, "one more interruption from you, and you'll be gone. Please continue, Jessica."

Jessica looked at Sydney maternally, apologetically. "He always wanted you. From the very beginning. Remember, Sydney?"

Sydney recalled that night well. She had many times since regretted inviting Jessica to the party and introducing her sister to Daniels. She hadn't known of his philandering then; she merely hadn't been interested in him.

"You dragged me to that party," Jessica continued. "Larry was a friend of your client, uh . . ."

"Randy," Sydney supplied. She cleared her throat. "Randy Collins."

"Yes, Randy. He'd opened a nightclub on the outskirts of town and was throwing a celebration. Larry tried to engage you in conversation all night long." She fell silent as if amused. "But you wouldn't give him a second glance. When I asked you about him, you merely said he wasn't your type. So, Larry invited me out to dinner the following night. He questioned me about you the whole time. He wanted to know why you wouldn't give him your number. He kept calling, but you were never in, so he settled for me. I was an easy conquest. I think I fell in love with him that first night. He seemed so attentive, gallant, you know the routine."

Another sliver of truth, Sydney thought, recalling that Larry had made a play for her, his intent so obvious she wasn't even flattered.

"What happened the evening you killed Representative Daniels, Ms. Webster?" Attorney Hollister asked, impatient with the personal details of the affair.

Jessica drew in a deep breath. "After Sydney left, Ursula showed up. Larry told her to just leave Lloyd and not come crying to him anymore. She went away and I came out of the bedroom. He was fussing about the mirror Sydney broke. But he wasn't really angry," she said, her eyes dazed with remembering. "He was . . . excited, aroused." She cleared her throat before continuing. "I told him I was pregnant. He laughed, said it was too bad. He told me to get rid of it." She swallowed, tearfully. "Everything inside me went still. I was shocked." She wet her lips with her tongue. "I ran out of the apartment. I thought I was going to die."

"Then what happened?"

"I took the stairs down. I was crying so hard, I almost fell. I got all the way to my car and remembered I had left everything in his apartment."

"Roger Simmons didn't park your car?" Perry asked.

"No," Jessica replied. "I parked it myself. I went back to the apartment. Larry was picking up the glass. He was still amused by Sydney. He told me I should be more like her. Fiery. Energetic. A man likes that kind of woman." She seemed to be speaking to herself now. "I didn't say anything. I went back to the bedroom and got my purse and keys from the dresser. He yelled for me to take all my belongings with me. I think I got mad then. I started going through the drawers to see if I had left anything. There wasn't much . . . a pair of stockings, a nightgown, gloves from the Christmas party we had attended together. I stuffed everything into my purse and walked out. The rock was on the floor behind where he was crouched down, still picking up the glass. I slipped the gloves on my hand and walked over there. He said he'd appreciate my help since my sister had created the mess." She sounded bitter. "I picked up the rock."

Sydney cried softly in denial, her hands pressed over her mouth as she shook her head from side to side. Jessica was doing what she had done all of Sydney's life.

"All I remember is swinging my arm back and bringing the rock down on his head. The first blow startled him. He looked up at me . . . Then I hit him again—and again."

"It's not true," Sydney mouthed to Perry, before she cast a pleading gaze on Attorney Hollister.

"Then I came," Lloyd said. He cleared his throat. "Jessica was in a state of shock. She was about to touch him when I grabbed her hand and told her to get out. She told me Sydney had been by. I knew it was her way of instructing me to fix things so that her sister would not be a suspect. Sydney didn't matter to me," he said solemnly. "I'm sorry, Jessica," he gestured to her. "The only thing I did was get rid of the gloves. I forgot about the shoes," he chortled, mocking himself. After a pause, he concluded, "And you know the rest."

"I'm sorry, Sydney," Jessica said. "Truly sorry."

"It's a lie. All of it," Sydney shouted.

"What shoes were you wearing that day?" Attorney Hollister directed to Jessica.

"A pair of Ozani's," Jessica replied in a more confident tone. "They were Sydney's. I'd borrowed them in February to wear to a party I attended in Houston with Larry."

"How did they get back in her closet if you had them?" Perry asked.

"They were in my closet at Father's house," Jessica replied. "I didn't know they were missing until after Sydney was arrested."

Sydney nodded solemnly, remembering taking them from Jessica's room.

"Why didn't you get rid of them?"

"Get rid of a pair of Ozani's?" Jessica quipped.

Perry sauntered to the side of the bed, a key tucked between two fingers. "Do you know what this unlocks?" he asked Lloyd.

Lloyd smiled to himself. *"The Book of Favors,"* he replied, chuckling lightly. "Larry kept a diary of political favors owed him."

"Blackmail?" Attorney Hollister asked, intrigued.

"Hardly, though some would call it that," Lloyd replied.

"Where is this diary?"

"I burned it," he replied.

"Then who was the woman with Larry at the hotel the day I went to finalize the engagement party?" Her actual motive for going to Larry's had never been sought by the police, so no one except Sydney and Perry had that information. If Jessica could answer this question, Sydney thought, she would have to accept the horrifying truth. If she couldn't, it merely proved what she already knew, that Jessica and Lloyd were lying.

She stared at her sister, demanding an answer. Her breath suspended, she watched a puzzled expression flit across Jessica's face. A tingle of satisfaction was beginning to swirl up her spine when Lloyd spoke up.

"Probably Ursula," he said sarcastically.

Feeling wrapped in the cruel arms of grief, Sydney didn't stay to hear more. She walked from the room to the elevator and went down and outside. Standing in front of the hospital, she hailed one of the cabs parked nearby. The driver responded promptly, and she got in.

"Where to, miss?" he asked.

"The Bandana Bar & Grill," she replied woodenly. She needed a drink—several in fact—to help numb the pain.

Perry was far from satisfied with the turn of events. Loose ends were still dangling out there, he thought pensively.

He was standing in front of the hospital. The evening sun struck his face, bringing beads of perspiration to his forehead and upper lip, but it wasn't the heat that bothered him. How Sydney had learned the truth didn't matter. The stark misery in her eyes did. It meant he faced a bigger problem than a fortuitous confession.

"Well, what do you think, Counselor?"

Coming out of his thoughts, Perry turned to see Attorney Hollister draw up to him.

"I don't know." Perry sighed heavily, stuck his hands in his pockets. "I felt certain this morning that I knew who killed Daniels. Jessica Webster." But during the confession, he'd had a sense of déjà vu. It was reminiscent of Sydney's initial visit to his office. He remembered then he'd believed

Sydney was lying to protect someone, and that someone had turned out to be Jessica. Though he didn't doubt Lloyd's involvement, he wondered who it was that Jessica would lie to protect.

"And now you're not sure?" Attorney Hollister laughed ironically. "It's your ego that won't let you accept a confession; you wanted to prove her guilty in court. There'll be another time for you and me to do battle before a judge. Don't take it so hard. Just be very grateful that I don't run you in for suppressing evidence."

Perry emitted a soft chuckle, fingering the key in his pocket. Most clients would be overjoyed to have a murder charge lifted from their heads. But Sydney was different. She was his lover, soon to be his wife and, quite possibly, the mother of his child.

"Where's Ursula Andrews?" he asked.

"Probably looking for a hawk like you to handle her divorce," Attorney Hollister replied, amused. "Lloyd Andrews is going to be too busy trying to save his own skin to worry about throwing his wife a few crumbs to make her go away."

"What about Jessica's mother, Beverly Lockhart?" Perry asked.

"If she bought that snake in Dalston, we haven't found any proof of it. Oh, and Dr. Webster has been cleared, as well," Hollister added. "He didn't kill his wife. There was an oversight when HPD transferred its records to computer. Some habitual thief confessed. He wasn't expecting anyone to be in the house. She was doing the decorating. He claimed it was an accident."

Perry nodded absently. For Sydney's sake, that was good, but the news gave him little satisfaction. He pulled the small key from his pocket and held it before his face. "You really bought Jessica's confession?" he asked absently.

"I'm heading for the office to do the paperwork right now. I'll see you in court tomorrow morning."

"Yeah," Perry sighed, running a tired hand across his

head. He looked across the parking lot as if undecided about what to do next. He knew he had to face Sydney about his indiscretion. The sooner he got it over with, the better, he told himself.

As he started for his car, he noticed Javier walking toward him.

"You're not going to believe what happened, Kemosabe," Perry said, a hint of amusement in his voice.

"I hope it's good. Ursula Andrews didn't get off that last flight," Javier replied.

The two men faced each other now, inches apart.

"The DA seems satisfied that the state got its killer," Perry replied. "Jessica Webster confessed. Can you believe that?"

"I can tell you don't," Javier retorted.

"I don't know what to believe," Perry blocked the sun as he looked absently around the parking lot. "Sydney found out about her mother."

"How did she take it?"

"Not well, I'm afraid," Perry replied, ruefully twisting his mouth.

"Oh-oh," Javier chided laughingly. "You're in trouble."

"Yes indeed. I was on my way to deal with that now. Where did she go?"

"I thought she was at the hospital with you," Javier replied.

For a fraction of time, everything went silent inside Perry. "No," he said warily, "she left a good forty-five minutes ago. Where's Franco?"

"Halfway home by now. He reported that Sydney went to her father's house, then came out crying and drove here. I told him to go on, that I'd take over."

A bad feeling in his gut, Perry bit off a curse. "Well, she's not here now," he snapped, bolting for his car.

* * *

"Looks like you lost your best friend—or maybe the best lay you ever had."

Carefully, Sydney turned her head, aware that any jarring motion might cause her to lose her balance and fall off the stool. A flicker of surprise crossed her face as she stared at Ursula Andrews. Holding a wine glass filled with a clear beverage in one hand and clutching a leather pocketbook in the other, Ursula slid gracefully onto the adjoining stool . . . uninvited. Sydney turned back to her double Scotch and fixed her tear-stained gaze on it.

She had been sitting quietly at the bar, drowning her despair in double Scotches. She certainly didn't need Ursula to pour salt in her wounds. "What do you want?" she asked, the words slightly slurred.

"Oh, it looks like I've got everything I need," Ursula replied.

Sydney looked at her, trying to clear her mind of the effects of the alcoholic drinks she had consumed. She felt a headache coming on.

"I guess you've heard by now," Ursula said. "Lloyd and Jessica owned up to killing Larry."

"It's a lie!" Sydney exclaimed.

"Yeah, well, don't knock it. I guess loyalty runs strong in the women in your family."

"I'm not in the mood for cryptic phrases," Sydney snapped.

"You're in a foul mood," Ursula taunted. "Jessica didn't tell us about your temper when she was regaling us with stories of your childhood antics."

Sydney eyed her suspiciously, but forbade herself from rising to the bait.

"Lloyd and Larry thought they were cute," Ursula continued, sneering at the memory.

"If you have anything to say to me, speak plainly and simply. What are you talking about?"

"Somebody's got to take the fall for Larry's murder," Ursula said.

"Do you know why Jessica is lying?"

"You mean you haven't figured it out yet?" Ursula asked, incredulous. "There's no statute of limitations on murder." At Sydney's dumbfounded look, she added, "Your father. The highly esteemed president of Texas College."

"Why would my father kill Larry?"

Honey, Larry was about to drop his support of Texas College. It's all right here," she said, opening her handbag, "in this little book." She pulled out a diary-sized book with a kente-cloth covering. When Sydney reached for it, she snatched it back. "Uh-uh, this is my insurance. Can't let it out of my hands for a second."

"I don't believe you," Sydney said stubbornly.

"And if your old man didn't go gracefully," Ursula continued, "Larry was prepared to clear up the mystery surrounding your mother's death."

Sydney shook her head in denial and was instantly reminded of the drinks she had downed. She massaged her temples. "What do you know about my mother's death?"

"Only what's here in Larry's little book," Ursula replied. "Once it was released, your father's career would have been flushed down the toilet like a . . . well, you get the picture."

"Down the toilet," Sydney chuckled sarcastically, thinking how aptly the phrase described her life.

She once had desires of becoming a doctor. She'd planned to discover the causes of aneurisms, so no one would suffer the death her mother had. But she'd been in over her head. After two years in the premed program at Xavier University in New Orleans, she'd changed her major to communications. As stupid and gullible as she had been in her youth, it was a wonder she'd made it through college at all. Not once had she checked to find out *how* her mother had died. She had just accepted her father's word. Supported by Jessica, it had to be true.

Only now she knew better. She lifted the glass for a sip. The alcohol burned her throat as it went down, and she shivered. Her entire life had been a stack of lies, piled on top of one another. Perry's deceit was the final disillusionment that toppled her.

Damn! Why did every lesson she learned hurt so bad?

"You know, Lloyd has yet to learn he can't hide anything from me," Ursula said, flipping through the pages of the diary.

Sydney ignored her, busy thinking she had chased Perry like a brazen hussy. She'd gotten what she deserved, she told herself philosophically. She didn't know why she'd thought he was different—or that she could matter enough to win his respect and love when she'd received these only in half measures from her family.

"Why did you marry Lloyd?" She didn't know why she queried Ursula; the question just popped out.

Ursula dropped her mask of sweetness. "I was fooled into believing he was a man," she said with venom; then the sugar was back in her voice. "You do know he's in love with your sister, don't you?"

Sydney hadn't, but her surprise was lost in the dull throbbing in her head. She couldn't think straight. She needed to clear her head, if for no other reason than to make sense of Ursula's unexpected appearance.

"How you doing, Sydney?" the bartender asked.

"Bring me an orange juice, please, Mike," she requested, slipping down from the barstool. "I'll be right back."

On her way to the ladies' room, she wondered if Ursula had been sent to cement the story Jessica and Lloyd had told the assistant district attorney. But she soon guessed the answer to Ursula's presence.

"Money," she snorted, pushing open the restroom door. Lloyd must have promised her plenty of it.

She bent over the sink, scooping handfuls of water into her face. When she heard the door open, she turned off the faucet. She was about to reach for the stack of hand towels when she came face to face with the barrel of a shiny steel gun pointed at her forehead. A chill shot along her spine.

"One word and you die here. Let's go."

Nineteen

Perry drove back to the Westwood subdivision like a madman. Frightful thoughts racing through his mind, he bore down on the gas pedal, pushing the car to its limits. Reaching Sydney's home, he ran to the door and rang the bell. When a response took longer than he expected, he hurried around the side of the house to the back door. He tried to peek in, but the curtains were drawn tight.

"She's not home."

Perry looked across the way and spotted a woman standing on her deck. He guessed it was Sydney's neighbor, Jasmine.

"I'm Perry MacDonald, her attorney."

"I know who you are, Mr. MacDonald." She sounded amused.

"You say she's not here?" Perry repeated. "Do you have any idea where she's gone?"

"No. When she left, she said she'd be right back. We were planning on going to a restaurant. She had counted on your return by then, as well."

Perry's fear intensified. "If she comes back, will you call me at 555-1213?"

"Is anything wrong?"

Walter Webster was his next try. Perry suspected Sydney would confront her father with what she had learned. "I hope not," he replied, taking off at a lope.

* * *

Assailed by asthmatic symptoms, Sydney tried to relax, to
control the rate of her breathing. Her head was pounding and
the wall of her chest was tightening. It was hard to focus, for
every time the car hit a pothole, she was tossed around in the
dark, stuffy trunk like a rag doll. Gagged, she was tied pretzel-
style, her arms and legs secured behind her back by a rope.

If Perry truly loved her as he claimed, he would have listened to her, she thought. Instead, he had treated her no better
than her father, discounting her opinions as if she were wit-
less. But being right was of little comfort to her now.

She didn't know what hurt worse, his betrayal or her family's. She did know that the possibility of finding out what
had occurred was being taken from her.

The car ascended a smooth path, then stopped. She was
grateful. Almost. She heard the long whine of a garage door
closing, then the car door opened and closed. She waited for
what would happen next, expecting the trunk to pop up. But it
didn't. Instead, the motor was running, and she was left in the
trunk.

She had no idea how long she could survive under the
circumstances. Chances were she would die of fear-induced
asthma before passing out from the carbon monoxide.
Struggling to free herself, she tried to force herself to think.
The trunk was sealed. She was probably safer than she'd be
outside the car. She stilled, straining to breathe through her
nostrils.

The car shook slightly as it idled. Fibers from the flooring
irritated her nose. The fumes from the exhaust pipe were
beginning to seep inside her holding pen. She closed her
eyes in the dark, but couldn't erase the picture of her doom
or the refrain in her head. She would die from carbon monoxide poisoning, if her asthma didn't kill her first. She
struggled to breathe around the constriction blocking her
air passage. The wheezing had begun.

* * *

On the way to Walter Webster's, Perry fretted over Jessica's confession. Though corroborated by Lloyd Andrews, her story was too pat for his peace of mind.

A good attorney could have gotten her a reduced sentence had she confessed to killing in the heat of passion. Instead, she'd told a tale of first-degree murder, thereby earning a death sentence. He believed it was a suicidal act.

Even Ursula Andrews could have seen through the holes that had been patched with lies, he thought. Knowing he was back at square one, he asked again who Jessica was protecting. Even more curious, why had Lloyd participated in the lie?

Perry sighed, frustrated, then a flash of memory crossed his mind. Sydney was unprotected. A buzzer went off inside his head—the kind that taunted a TV game-show player who'd made the wrong choice. He couldn't answer for Lloyd Andrews, but Jessica was as loyal as Sydney. How could he be so dense? He spun his car around, gunned the engine and sped off in the opposite direction.

Curse words and prayers for Sydney's safety spewed from his lips on the entire seven-minute trip. Mostly, he prayed that he was wrong. He reached a neighborhood whose residents were mostly retirees living on fixed incomes. His heart and mind racing, he slowed the car to check the curbside addresses painted in white. He spotted the house, but drove past it, parking three doors away and getting out. Walking back, he examined surroundings that were at odds with his inner feelings. It being Sunday afternoon, the neighborhood was largely quiet. He noted the few cars parked on the street, a group of young children playing catch with a beach ball in a yard several houses down; but nothing suspicious screamed out at him.

He skipped across the street to stand next to the black mailbox near the curb. A neatly clipped, velvet green yard with rows of flowers in bloom lining the sidewalk led to the pink door of a green and white bungalow.

Perry waited, tense as a coiled spring. He understood as

he had never before why lawyers were advised against representing themselves—especially in cases where their lives hung in the balance. He'd made that mistake by allowing his feelings for Sydney to affect his judgment. But his luck had to change. If it didn't, he was finished, for surely Sydney would die.

He walked up the driveway. As he neared the single-car garage, he heard a motor running. He paused, sniffed, and identified the odor of car fumes. His heart thump-thumping in his chest, he started hurriedly toward the front door of the house. He didn't have a plan in mind, but he knew he had to hurry. Time was running out.

"Psst."

At the familiar sound, Perry's steps faltered and he swung his head around.

"Psst."

Pinpointing the direction from which the bid for attention came, Perry cautiously walked to his right where a big oak fronted the parcel of land that separated the garage from the house next door. He was beckoned forward urgently by a flicked finger.

"What are you doing here?" he whispered to Walter Webster.

"My baby girl is in there," the older man replied belligerently but softly.

Perry eyed Sydney's father, an ugly suspicion consuming him. "Why didn't you call the police?" he demanded. The look that fell over Walter Webster's face was damning. "You wanted to play the hero with your daughter's life," he bit the words off contemptuously.

"We've got to do something right now," Walter Webster said urgently. "You're the attorney, think of something!"

Hurry! Hurry! echoing in his head, Perry raced back to his car. He opened the trunk and took out the tire jack. Jogging back, he saw Walter Webster disappear through the front door. This plan better work, he said to himself.

He used to be good at breaking in. He remembered doing it; and tried to keep panic at bay. Though he hadn't done it in years, he hoped, like riding a bike, the skill would come back to him.

Drenched in perspiration, he eyed the metal garage door, cursing sharply because it wasn't wood, in which case he could simply have knocked out a bottom panel. Though he was considerably bigger, he imagined he would still be able to squeeze through such an opening. But all that was moot now. In frustration, he noted that poisonous carbon monoxide was seeping under the door. His fear rose, and his pulse climbed with it.

He knuckle-rapped himself upside the head. Then, he sprinted off to check the side of the garage for a door. There was none. Swallowing a curse and the lump of terror in his throat, he continued to the back of the house. Voilà! He spotted a window. He peeked in and saw it was over the kitchen sink. Small, but passable. Now, if Walter Webster could keep her suitably entertained as planned. . . .

It was like riding a bike . . . again. Within seconds, Perry was crawling through the three-by-three sized window over the kitchen sink. With his hands splayed flat on the counter below him, he paused—not to revel in his success, but because of the voices wafting toward him from his right.

"You've never had faith in me, Walter," the maid said wistfully. "Never! You thought I was too stupid, or too drunk to know what I wanted."

Ask her, damn it; ask her what she wants! Perry admonished Walter Webster silently as he scanned the layout of the kitchen. He spotted two doors and promptly, discounted the one next to the refrigerator. Roughly twelve feet away, it seemed a long distance. He was confident he could make it. He had to: Sydney was on the other side of that door.

"All right, Corinda." The college president heeded Perry's silent urging. "Tell me. Tell me what you want," he said in a calm, patient tone.

"I want us to be a family again, the three of us . . . you, me and Jessica . . . like it used to be—"

The instant Corinda Webster, AKA Beverly Lockhart began to speak, Perry hoisted the rest of his body through the window, his arms bearing the bulk of his weight. Strain was evident in his face.

"I know you think I'm drunk," she continued, "but I'm not. I haven't had a drink since Jessica's car accident. I almost killed my baby," she lamented tearfully.

Perry grunted silently as he quietly swung his weight over the sink and his feet hit the tile floor. He flinched, fearing discovery and glanced warily in the direction of the voices. He could see the back of the maid, her right arm crooked as if she were holding something at waist level.

"Corinda, what are you saying?"

"Never mind!" she raged. "It's not important! I've done what I had to do. I'm a mother. I've got to protect my baby. When Jessica gets out of the hospital, we'll go somewhere . . . start a new life together. It would be nice if you would come with us," she said, her voice soft and hopeful.

Her mood swings were scary, Perry mused, tipping across the room, intent on reaching the prized door. *Promise her anything, just don't make her mad,* he warned Walter Webster in his head.

"What have you done to Sydney?"

"Why are you concerned about her?" she screamed. "She's not part of us. She's an outsider, a nuisance. She's no better than Larry Daniels. Neither one of them was good enough for my baby. I did you a favor; he was going to ruin you. Then when I heard him flirting with her . . . Sydney. I knew he wasn't right for our Jessica. I had to kill him."

Perry's sweaty palm reached the doorknob. He turned it.

"Oh God, Corinda, you're crazy!"

A shot was fired and Perry dove through the door into the garage where the smoky poison fogged the air.

* * *

As Sydney lay lifeless on the grass, Perry struggled to hold himself together. He suppressed the tears in his eyes and the urge to tear Beverly Lockhart limb from limb, breathing clear air from his lungs into Sydney's.

"Come on, baby, breathe; come on, baby," he pleaded between counts as he pressed upon her chest.

"Is she going to be okay?"

Perry couldn't respond to Walter Webster who had stumbled out to the front yard. He was trying to coax life from Sydney.

Curious children sidled cautiously to the house. Seeing the blood on Walter Webster's chest, several little girls screamed. A young boy started to question Perry, but the squeals of fear from the rest of the children scared him off. He joined the wild flight, running home screaming. "Mama, a man is choking a lady!"

Sydney was aware of a strange pressure as she struggled to climb from the depths of a black well. Something was pressing against her chest. Someone was calling her name over and over. With drugged slowness, she made out the voice. It was her father's, and he was upset with her again.

Her ball had rolled into his flower bed, and she'd gone to get it. He was going to be mad if she stepped on his flowers. *I'll be careful, Daddy.*

She didn't know whether she spoke the words or thought them. She was so tired, as if the life had been drained from her body. And there was that intermittent weight on her chest. Finally, her lids fluttered open and she took in blurry impressions.

"Sydney!"

She heard another voice. It was a man's, and loaded with relief. Her vision clearing, she stared into brown eyes full of an unquenchable warmth that caused a fluttering in her heart unrelated to pain.

"Perry," she slurred the word, no strength in her.

"Yes." His laughter contained residuals of uneasiness.

"Sydney . . . Sydney, are you all right?"

She turned her head slightly to look into her father's face engraved with worry. Then, aware of the noises that wrapped around them—sirens blaring, the high-pitched din of a crowd—it all came back to her. Her glassy eyes took in the two men she loved the most, and an awful ache squeezed her heart. A tired sadness overcoming her, she closed her eyes, whispering, "You lied to me."

There were no physical scars to remind Sydney of her ordeal, but they were present nonetheless, like parasites eating at her soul. She knuckle-rapped the dresser, then surveyed the hospital room that had been her residence for the past two days. She decided that she was leaving—not just the hospital but Dalston.

Plagued by a debilitating self-doubt, she had arrived here with only a vague sense that something was missing from her life, she recalled. As chance would have it, she'd stumbled onto Perry MacDonald. With that stroke of good luck, bad luck had stomped through.

The one thing she had believed was true—that one had to take chances in life—had nearly killed her. Now, not only was she leaving empty-handed, she didn't know what to believe anymore.

She sauntered to the bed and picked up a decorative bag. She stuffed her belongings in it after purchasing it at the hospital's gift shop. Misery slashed through her, sharp as a scalpel at the thought of leaving. She cursed Perry, but his name only added to her grief.

He had reached her in the nick of time, she recalled, scalding tears rolling down her cheeks. She had insisted on a room as far away from her father's as possible, for he, too, had been hospitalized for a gunshot wound in the shoul-

der. Neither she nor Perry had heard the second shot. Her
father had been wrestling with Beverly Lockhart for the
gun when it went off. The bullet had struck her in the chest,
killing her instantly.

If Perry had listened to her, she mused, sniffling, the cata-
strophic episode would never have happened. His refusal to
give credence to what she knew to be the truth was demean-
ing, a sign of disrespect. It proved that he was not someone
with whom she wanted to spend the rest of her life.

But as soon as he'd discovered his error, he'd come for
her: that should count for something, an inner voice told
her. Her father had known of Beverly's sick mind and had
come to her rescue, as well. Still, she derived no comfort
from the fact that, for once, he'd actually known what was
best for her. He'd also predicted that Perry wasn't.

To muffle a keening moan, Sydney stuffed her hands in her
mouth. She heard the door open and quickly dried her face
with her hands. Pasting a blank smile on her face she turned,
expecting the nurse with her release forms. Suddenly her expression congealed into a tight-lipped frown. She looked from
her sister to her father. Both were in robes. While Jessica
looked vacant and spent, Walter Webster seemed infinitely sor-
rowful as he rubbed the arm he had in a sling. Sydney sensed
their sadness and took a breath before she spoke.

"I don't think we have anything more to say to each other."

"On the contrary, we have plenty. Certainly you have lots
of questions."

"And the truth shall set you free," Sydney replied with
stage mockery, then gave them her back.

"One has to live truth to accept it," Jessica said quietly.
"Just because you don't like it, doesn't make it any less so."

Sydney nodded listlessly. She recalled that the local
newspapers had devoted extensive coverage to the events
that had unfolded. The only one that remained a secret was
Jessica's confession in the presence of the assistant district

attorney. It was this truth that mattered to Sydney as she turned to face her sister.

"I'd say that makes you twice a hypocrite. As for me, my life's been a lie for twenty-four years. Not exactly an honest start for living truth, I would say."

"Your life has not been a lie," Walter Webster insisted. "One has been told you, and I . . . I'm afraid I don't have a good explanation, except . . . except I thought it was best at the time."

"And later?" Sydney demanded, unable to suppress the sulky truculence that slipped into her voice.

"It never came up until. . . ." He began vehemently, then stopped cold, as if the truth stuck in his throat.

"Until Larry was murdered," Jessica concluded. "I'm sorry about Beverly."

Hearing the pain in Jessica's voice, Sydney realized with a start that she wasn't the only one suffering. Her sister had been as much a victim as she, she thought, expelling a disconsolate breath.

"I sensed the buildup of hatred in her, but . . ."—Jessica faltered—"but I never believed she was capable of hurting anyone. Especially you. She knew how I felt about you," she added, maternal pride and fondness coming through despite her distress. "She came to your house to visit me. Then Father called." Turning slightly to encompass Walter Webster in her gaze, she said, "Remember?"

He bobbed his head sadly. "I had just learned about the private investigator Mr. MacDonald hired. I knew he would find out about. . . ." His voice cracked and then stilled. He drew himself up. When he spoke again, his tone was matter-of-fact, his voice strong. "I called Jessica and asked her to come to the house. I wanted her input."

No doubt to discuss how to handle things when my attorney told me the truth, Sydney thought. Only, her lover-attorney hadn't, she frowned bitterly.

"When I took the call—" Jessica took up the explanation—"I left Beverly alone. I thought she stayed in the dining room. I suspect that's when she cut the brake line on your car. She apparently didn't know you and I had switched cars. I was returning from Father's when the accident happened."

"Don't blame Jessica for my foolishness," Walter Webster said. "All she did was carry out my wish to protect you."

"Protect me from what?" Sydney cried, fighting back tears. "What did you think was going to happen to me if I knew my mother was murdered?"

"Sydney, I was afraid," Walter Webster's eyes pleaded with her. "The whole situation surrounding your mother's death was so awful, the silent accusations that I'd killed her or hired someone to do it. . . . I just couldn't bear it if you believed them. Your mother and I were going through a difficult time. I said things to her that day . . ."—he swallowed hard—"things that I'll regret for the rest of my life."

The guilt and fear that haunted her father were easily detected in his voice, his manner. Another painful truth that could have been avoided, Sydney mused, thoughts of Perry inexorably slipping to the fore of her mind. She feared she'd never oust him from all the places he'd occupied in her being no matter what she did. He had turned her loneliness to joy, allowing her to grow with his strength. She had sincerely believed that the world was complete with just the two of them. Now she would have to learn to live without him. The blackness enshrouding her was a tangible thing.

"Why did Lloyd Andrews back up your lie?" Sydney asked, deliberately choosing the word. The instant she noticed Jessica flinch, she felt unkind and immature.

"Lloyd is a dear friend," Jessica replied.

Walter Webster intervened. "Sydney don't do this."

"No, Father." Jessica flashed him a pointed look. "Not this time. Lloyd fancies himself in love with me."

"Do you return his affection?"

Jessica shook her head ruefully as she replied, "No. Not like that."

"And the baby you were carrying?" Sydney asked, though she knew no relief because her trust in Jessica was justified. The same knife that twisted in Jessica, twisted in her, as well.

"It was Larry's baby. As I told you before," Jessica added, giving Sydney a significant look, "he was excited about our child."

Jasmine entered the room, followed by Justin. They froze, staring questioningly at the Websters. Sydney clutched the bag in her hand and forced herself to smile at them in greeting. They had made up and were returning to Houston together. Though their empathy for her was evident, she could sense the love between them. Riding with them was bound to be more torture than she could stand.

"Shall we come back?" Jasmine directed the question to Sydney.

"No, I'm ready," she replied.

"Sydney, let Jessica and me take you home," Walter Webster pleaded.

If he had been expecting a fanfare, he was in for a big disappointment. In saving Sydney's life, he'd saved his own as well, but Perry felt no sense of victory in him now.

He was sitting at the defense table, staring unseeingly at the courtroom clock over the bench. He wore a gloomy pensive mask on his face, an intense feeling of emptiness inside him. He'd gone to the hospital to coax Sydney to see him that morning, but she had left, checked out. At the risk of being late for court, he'd driven to her home. The place had been deserted, Jessica gone, as well.

All charges had been dropped against Sydney; yet, a finger of guilt was jabbing him in the heart. Going on three days now, he'd cursed himself a thousand times for his indiscretion. One simple omission had branded him a betrayer in Sydney's eyes. He'd broken a promise by withholding truth—something even he didn't abide in his practice. And now he was paying for it. He faced a lifelong sentence of loneliness if he couldn't convince Sydney to give him another chance.

"Mr. MacDonald . . . Mr. MacDonald?"

His sorrow so great, Perry could barely force himself to address the court. "Sorry, Your Honor," he replied lethargically.

The judge glowered at him expectantly. "Mr. MacDonald, do you have any questions for this witness?"

"Uh"—distracted, Perry pushed himself to his feet, fiddling with his notes—"yes, Your Honor."

As soon as the session ended, Perry raced off to resume his search for Sydney. The longer their separation, the greater his fear that he'd never see her again. As if infected by a deadly disease, he seemed to be dying without her.

"You've destroyed half of my family, Mr. MacDonald. And you have the audacity to come to me for help in completing the job?"

There was amazement in Walter Webster's tone, Perry noted. He had caught the doctor as Webster was leaving his office at Texas State College. Webster's left arm was no longer in a sling, but he looked tired, beaten. Perry felt no small measure of responsibility for that.

"You have a lot of nerve," Walter Webster said, mustering some animation.

He was right, Perry admitted to himself. But he didn't care if he had to beg; pride was something he could ill afford. "Look, Dr. Webster, I love your daughter."

"Love?" Walter Webster lifted an amused eyebrow. "You don't know the meaning of the word. I guess attorneys suffer from an oversupply of arrogance, to the point of disrespect."

Perry would have argued the former point if he'd thought it would change anything. The latter one . . . he was suffering because of that defect in his personality—had been since Sydney disappeared.

"I've never believed you were good enough for my daughter, and that hasn't changed. Even if I knew where she was, I wouldn't tell you. Good day, Mr. MacDonald."

Twenty

Tomorrow was the day. All cried out by then, she would be better tomorrow, Sydney told herself, when she would simply place her love for Perry in File 13.

She was staring absently out the window in the bedroom of her old house in Houston, the one left her by her grandmother. The sun shone, beaming with promise. She found she couldn't turn away, as if taking perverse delight in punishing herself, with hope that Perry would follow its light and come to her.

She'd done nothing but think. But not about her future. She had no future without Perry. Rather, she mulled over the recent past and Jessica's confession—that mixture of lies and truths spoken in the name of love.

The story Jessica had told her the night they'd spent together had been true: Larry was anxious to settle down, though partly because of the promise of a brighter future in politics. Jessica had not known he planned to renege on his support for Texas College.

As to the confession, it was true that Jessica had gone to Larry's and they argued, but not about Ursula: Larry and Ursula had broken up long before Lloyd married her. Rather, the argument had come about because Larry had bought a house without first consulting Jessica. She'd stormed out, forgetting her keys. Upon returning, she'd seen Beverly Lockhart, formerly Corinda Webster leaving his apartment to slip into another neighbor's place, supposedly to clean. But the door had been left unlocked, and she'd walked in to find Larry dead. Unthinking, she'd stepped in his blood, then Lloyd had arrived.

Knowing she was the last person to see him alive, Jessica had immediately known who killed him. She had been in a quandary. Who to sacrifice? Her mother, with whom she had recently been reunited, or Sydney, the baby sister she had raised? Unable to sacrifice either, she had confessed to the crime. Lloyd had promised Ursula he would grant the divorce she craved, as well as provide a tidy sum to back up their lie. She was already in the Bahamas enjoying the first installment paid her.

Hatred had built to uncontrollable proportions in Beverly Lockhart. She had seen Sonni-Lauren as Sydney, the obstacle to Jessica's happiness as well as the one who'd destroyed her own life. She had believed she should have been the wife of the president of Texas College.

Like many who are insane, Beverly Lockhart did not possess the capacity to love. Feeling as she did, a victim of loneliness, Sydney questioned whether love was a curse or a blessing. At least she had had a chance at happiness, she told herself. It was just her misfortune that she hadn't found it with someone who held it sacred.

Sydney turned her back to the window. "Tomorrow," she whispered. "Tomorrow."

Perry searched the city high and low for Sydney. Only two days had passed since she'd left the hospital, but driven by desperation, he wasn't going to waste another fruitless minute searching Dalston.

There had been no withdrawals from either her checking or savings account by her personally. Her house note was automatically debited from her account, and as far as he had been able to determine, there had been no use of her charge cards. She still hadn't returned to work, supporting his conclusion that she had left the city.

He could have hired Javier to go, but this was something only he could do. Instructing Ramona to postpone his court dates until further notice, he packed in preparation for expanding his search.

Locked tight in his memory was a paragraph from Jessica's confession, the one in which she'd admitted loving Daniels despite his indiscretions. It was only half true, for there had been none. The woman Sydney had seen with Daniels was a recent appointee to the Texas coordinating board, who, along with two other members, had met with him at the hotel to discuss the withdrawal of his support from Texas College.

But that was all academic now, and he could care less about the fate of the college. Snagging his suitcase from the baggage belt, he admitted silently that one person dominated his thoughts.

Sydney Lauren Webster was not going to get away from him. She was his, damn it! he told himself as he stepped out of Houston's Hobby Airport to hail a taxi.

Tomorrow kept moving out of Sydney's reach. She was tired, exhausted from lack of sleep and too much introspection. Another day found her sequestered in her bedroom. She hardly left it.

"Sydney . . ."

It was déjà vu. Not very long ago this ritual of caring had been performed in the reverse when Sydney had attended Jessica after Larry's death. Now, overwhelmed by despair, she needed the attention, and her sister had known exactly where to find her.

"Sydney, why don't you come eat? I fixed your favorite meal."

"I'm not hungry, thank you," she replied woodenly.

"You can't go on like this," Jessica chastised, a hint of frustration in her tone.

Sydney tried to manage a smile, but couldn't. She felt horrible about the death of Jessica's mother, after all, a bad one was better than none. But Jessica had put on a cavalier face and sworn on her crossed heart that she didn't hold Sydney responsible. "And you really must rid yourself of that tendency to play the sacrificial lamb," Sydney said, a fond look softening her words.

"I know," Jessica somberly as she sauntered into the room. Then she brightened. "And I will, as soon as I get you entrusted to competent hands. You need a keeper, Sydney Lauren," she added with amusement.

"You and Daddy have never given me enough credit, you know." There was no bitterness in Sydney's tone, only resignation.

"You spoiled us, that's why." Jessica stroked back a stray hair. "You were such an adorable child—affectionate, sweet. And you got into everything. We were always afraid you would hurt yourself, so we tried to protect you."

It was what Perry had done, Sydney thought. He'd claimed to admire her tenacious spirit, yet he'd never given her the chance to prove she could cope with the devastating truth about her mother's death. "But you can't do that," Sydney protested.

"We know—now. But what's done is done. And you're just going to have to accept us, shortcomings and all. That's what love is all about, baby sister."

The statement lingered in the air and burrowed into Sydney's mind. The more she thought about it, the more she realized that was exactly what she wanted from her family—to be accepted with all her virtues and vices. She was amazed at how she'd failed to recognize the value of reciprocating when it came to that very basic human need.

"Sydney . . ."

Sydney's head spun from her sister to the origin of the

smooth, self-possessed voice she'd heard nightly in her dreams. Her heart beat erratically, joy escorted astonishment and shone in her brilliant wide-eyed gaze, as she stared at the man standing in the doorway.

"Perry . . ." she whispered, awed. "What are you doing here?" Though love colored her view of him, she did note that he looked exhausted. Lines of strain crinkled the corners of eyes whose brown hue had dulled, eyes touched by an unfamiliar wariness. If he, too, had suffered, did she dare to hope? She cursed her weakness and glanced at Jessica, questions whizzing through her mind.

Perry must have noticed her unvoiced query, for he said, "I may be slow, I may stumble along the way, but eventually I reach my destination on my own."

This assertion caused a wild rush of emotions in Sydney. She tried to sever herself from the fine string of yearning tugging at her, but her resentment over the way he'd treated her now seemed elusive. She swallowed the lump in her throat and managed to return his intense stare with a haughty look.

"I have to go out," Jessica announced casually. "I'm meeting Lloyd for lunch."

With a sharp turn of her head, Sydney eyed Jessica, puzzled. "Andrews?" She wondered if there really was something to that intimate scene. "Why do you have to see Lloyd? I thought—"

A cheeky smile on her face, Jessica cast a sidelong glance at Perry as she cut her off, "You take care of your business; I'll handle mine." She flashed a wink at Sydney, then left.

"Did you think I was going to let you get away from me? I warned you in the beginning. I'm a possessive bastard, and you're mine."

Perry didn't wait for the tension between them to abate before he attacked. Sydney shivered at the ownership in his tone, but it temporarily squelched the mendicant desire in her. "I'm not a thing to be owned, Perry MacDonald," she said, pepper-sharp.

"Why not? You own me, lady. Lock, stock, and barrel, as the cliché goes."

"Perry, I don't want to argue with you." She spoke wearily, partly from fatigue, but mostly because of the sensual disturbance he had rekindled in her. She couldn't fight that and him when she needed to think. "I want you to leave."

"Only one thing will make me leave without you," he declared. "Tell me you don't love me."

"Perry, this is insane."

"What? That I've found someone who matters more to me than the law—or life itself. Or that you don't love me anymore?" There was a quiver in his voice, and his Adam's apple bobbed before he spoke again. "I admit this is new to me, loving someone. You'll have to teach me the rules."

Sydney twisted her mouth ruefully. "Apparently there are none." She chortled softly with fatalism in her voice.

"What about our child?" he demanded, his jaw tightening. He spread his feet slightly in an aggressive stance and shoved his hands into the pockets of his dark dress slacks, his coat open.

Sydney, struck by a wanton memory, stared at him, agony in her eyes. Oh, but he was not playing fair; he was pulling out all the stops. "What child?" she replied.

"We stopped using protection, remember? You're probably carrying our child now."

The odds were it was probable. If it was the case, she guessed their child could provide some measure of comfort to her. But without him in the picture, she was not elated. "If I'm carrying anything," she said, "I will let you know."

He started to argue, then changed his mind. She wondered what he would come up with next, noticing he was not as calm as he looked. His face was flushed with perspiration, and there was a kind of controlled desperation in him. She was tempted to take a chance on him even as a part of her argued against it, fearful of making a mistake.

With his customary animal assurance, Perry moved toward her. Instinctively, Sydney backed away.

"I made a commitment," he said fiercely. "Right here." He beat his chest over his heart. "And I don't run from commitments. I didn't believe you did, either."

"How can you commit to someone you believe is inferior to you?" she snapped back.

"I never thought you were," he retorted defensively.

"You withheld the truth from me about my mother."

"You withheld several facts yourself, I might remind you."

"We're not talking about shoes now; we're talking about my mother."

They bandied words back and forth each bringing the ugly pain out in the open.

"Sydney," he said, flustered, "I was only trying to protect you."

Though his voice softened, she could tell he was furious. He looked at her as if debating whether to curse her or plead with her.

"From what . . . my own stupidity?" she retorted.

"Damn it! You're not stupid!"

"Why? Because you can't admit what that would make you?"

"I love you, Sydney," he said emphatically.

She was already surrendering, if not just to the love in her heart, to the raw pain glittering in his eyes. "But not enough to trust me with the truth," she half stated, half asked. "You once told me you admired my perseverance, my ability to spring back from adversity. Yet, you never gave me a chance to handle the truth."

"Because I was afraid."

"You?" she replied astonished. "Afraid of what?"

"Afraid you would decide I was just a handy convenience to make up for the loss of your mother . . . that it wasn't me you wanted, after all." He finished on a tortured rasping tone of voice.

Watching his face crumble into a look of hurting and humility, his brown eyes uncannily bright as if he were on the verge of tears, Sydney reacted instantly. She preferred his dictatorial arrogance more. She covered the short distance between them, gathered him in her embrace and soothed his torment. His lips quivered beneath her touch as sweet tears, sublimely healing, formed in her eyes.

"Shhh, my darling," she whispered, hugging him to her tenderly. "How could you think such a thing?"

He wrapped his arms around her with crushing strength. "Sydney," he exclaimed in a husky whisper. "Please don't let me hope, if you're not coming back to me."

"But I am. Oh yes, Perry," she crooned against the wall of his chest.

"I know there are a lot of things I have to learn about being responsible for someone's heart. A lot of things I need to learn about love." His hands moved soothingly in her hair. "The first time I met your family, I felt a need to protect you from them because I didn't believe they cared for you as they should have. Slowly, my opinion changed," he said with self-mocking. "The more I fell for you, the more I was thinking and behaving like them, like your father. I knew it was wrong, but I couldn't help myself. You were so giving, so loving and free with your emotions and thoughts. I wanted it all—like a poor little boy who never had anything of his own. I'm sorry. Please . . . please forgive me."

"If you'll forgive me," she said, sniffing a little. With a smile of pure happiness on her face, she looked up at him, "We both have a lot to learn about love. Though I suspect, we've already got a good start."

He stared at her intently, searching her face anxiously. "Sydney, are you sure this time?" he asked emphatically.

"As sure as forever," she replied.

"When will you marry me so I can resume learning about love?" he asked, his animal assurance returning as a grin split his face.

Sydney chortled joyfully. Then her gaze shifted to the bed. "We can resume the lessons right now."

About the Author

Margie Walker has enjoyed writing since she was a little girl. After graduating Magna Cum Laude from Texas Southern University, she married her college sweetheart, then returned to school to earn a Teacher's Certificate and a Master's degree in Speech Communication. She worked in radio and as a journalist while raising her two sons. Margie Walker is in five year residence with Writers In The Schools, a program which places professional writers in the classroom. INDISCRETIONS is her fourth romance novel.

Look for these upcoming Arabesque titles:

August 1996
WHITE DIAMONDS by Shirley Hailstock
SEDUCTION by Felicia Mason
AT FIRST SIGHT by Cheryl Faye

September 1996
WHISPERED PROMISES by Brenda Jackson
AGAINST ALL ODDS by Gwynne Forster
ALL FOR LOVE by Raynetta Manees

October 1996
THE GRASS AIN'T GREENER by Monique Gilmore
IF ONLY YOU KNEW by Carla Fredd
SUNDANCE by Leslie Esdaile